Praise for the Titan's Forest series

"An engaging and beautifully wrought coming-of-age story."
) on *Echoes of Understorey*

"What a delight ı   ı the mainstream and so
beautifully realiz
—Juliet N   ward and the Alex Award

"Dyer's writing seamlessly melds a lush and layered canopy setting and a complex magical culture to form a unique fantasy world, filled with memorable characters in constant jeopardy."
—Glenda Larke, author of the Stormlord trilogy
and the Forsaken Lands trilogy

"A rich, brutal, fascinating world and an unforgettable heroine."
—Ilana C. Myer, author of *Fire Dance*

"Thoraiya Dyer is the writer I most want to infect people with."
—Anna Tambour, World Fantasy Award finalist

"Imaginative, original, inclusive—and pacy and exciting. Go get it and read it. Maybe twice."   —Pamela Freeman, author of the Castings trilogy

"A riveting novel."   —A. M. Dellamonica, author of *The Nature of a Pirate*

"Readers will be delighted by Dyer's polished prose and an exquisite new world of intricate mythology, rituals, and politics."
—*Publishers Weekly* (starred review)

"For her striking first novel, *Crossroads of Canopy,* Thoraiya Dyer reworks the stuff of epic fantasy in ways that seem organic, rooted in the natural world but just as true to human experience."   —*Locus*

"Recommended for readers who appreciate nuanced world building, as both *Canopy* and *Understorey* are strange, fleshed-out lands thrown into turmoil."
—*Booklist*

"A vividly beautiful fantasy about an epic quest where magic, mystery, and love are woven together."   —*RT Book Reviews* (4 stars)

BOOKS BY THORAIYA DYER

Crossroads of Canopy
Echoes of Understorey
Tides of the Titans

TIDES OF THE TITANS

THORAIYA DYER

A Tom Doherty Associates Book
NEW YORK

TIDES OF THE TITANS

Copyright © 2019 by Thoraiya Dyer

A Tor Book
Published by Tom Doherty Associates
175 Fifth Avenue
New York, NY 10010

www.tor-forge.com

Tor® is a registered trademark of Macmillan Publishing Group, LLC.

The Library of Congress Cataloging-in-Publication Data
is available upon request.

ISBN 978-0-7653-8598-7 (trade paperback)
ISBN 978-0-7653-8609-0 (ebook)

Our books may be purchased in bulk for promotional, educational, or business use.
Please contact your local bookseller or the Macmillan Corporate and Premium
Sales Department at 1-800-221-7945, extension 5442, or by email at
MacmillanSpecialMarkets@macmillan.com.

First Edition: January 2019

0 9 8 7 6 5 4 3 2 1

For Dad,
who gave me the gift and the curse of travel
and more than one place to belong

Acknowledgments

In addition to my formidable agent, editors, cover artist, layout and publicity people, publisher, reviewers, booksellers, readers, family, and friends, many thanks to the spec-fic community, to Australian and international fandom, and to my writer's groups in Sydney and K-town (folks who this solitary, stubborn scribbler was convinced she didn't need!). In the words of Sarah from *Labyrinth:* Every now and again in my life, for no reason at all, I need you. All of you! *cue "Magic Dance"*

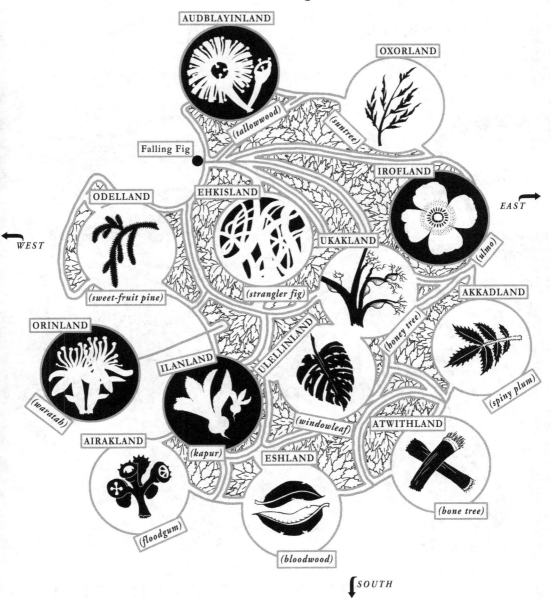

NORTH (to the ocean)

AUDBLAYINLAND
(tallowwood)

OXORLAND
(suntree)

Falling Fig

IROFLAND
(ulmo)

EAST

ODELLAND
(sweet-fruit pine)

WEST

EHKISLAND
(strangler fig)

UKAKLAND
(honey tree)

AKKADLAND
(spiny plum)

ORINLAND
(waratah)

ILANLAND
(kapur)

ULELLINLAND
(windowleaf)

AIRAKLAND
(floodgum)

ATWITHLAND
(bone tree)

ESHLAND
(bloodwood)

SOUTH

TEMPLE EMERGENTS OF CANOPY

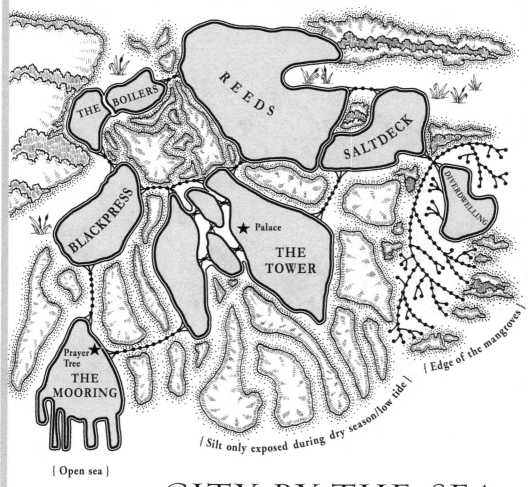

SOUTH

CANOPY

THE BOILERS

REEDS

SALTDECK

DIVERDWELLING

BLACKPRESS

★ Palace

THE TOWER

{ Edge of the mangroves }

Prayer Tree ★

THE MOORING

{ Silt only exposed during dry season/low tide }

{ Open sea }

CITY-BY-THE-SEA
(aka Wetwoodknee)

TIDES OF
THE TITANS

PROLOGUE

THE MONSOON threatens.

Leaper grins at the sky, gripping the rope with a gloved hand behind his harness to control his descent. He shouldn't be headed this way. In a past life, and in this one, he's vowed never to go down. Never to look back.

He shouldn't be headed anywhere. Yet it's his only chance to get his hands on Aurilon's sword.

The mossy, ridged bark of the hundred-pace-wide sweet-fruit pine is fish-scale grey. It breaks away in brittle flakes with every brush of Leaper's sandal soles.

Airak's teeth!

Dangerous to go down when it's raining. Dangerous to go down when it's dry. If the bark's not soggy and peeling, the pieces of it, falling through seven hundred human heights, are possibly giving him away to all sorts of people, high and low, when he'd much prefer the element of surprise, thank you very much.

When I climb back up, he thinks as he lets the rope out a little more, *I'll choose a different tree.* Perhaps the neighbouring spiny plum. Its brownish bark is hairy as tree bears but better than this one.

Faint raindrops fleck his bare arms and face as he drops faster. Faster again. There's no point looking down; there's no light down there to see by, only the captured lightning that Leaper brings himself.

It's more than a month since Odel's Bodyguard, Aurilon, fell from this tree. Deliberately. To her death. Leaper couldn't escape the scrutiny of his master, Airak the lightning god, until now. With sixteen monsoons behind him, he's reached his full growth; although the god has sent him on oc-casional political missions outside of Airakland, Airak's favourite furtive emissary has been harshly disciplined since a certain incident at Ulellin's Temple.

The rules have changed, and Leaper resents now having to ask permission to leave the emergent.

So, this time, he didn't bother to ask. Let them discipline him again.

He *needs* the sword. Aurilon's sword. The one she was holding—and possessed by—when she threw herself down. Orin, goddess of beasts and birds, had intended the weapon to drink deeply of innocent blood. Aurilon had foiled that purpose.

Leaper races the rain. He'll have to search for the body in the black soil below before the floodwaters wash it away. Since he's going all the way to Floor, he can't rely on his usual trick, once he's ready to return, of using a heavy, hacked-off, wooden counterweight to take him back up to the forest canopy in a hurry. A stolen pocket-clock, wound tight at daybreak, lies in the carrysack on his back, to help him keep track of time in the pitch-black sameness he expects to find.

He must keep track of time to make sure he doesn't lose the magical aura that allows him to pass freely through the gods-ordained and gods-maintained invisible barrier between Canopy and Understorey.

There's no magic barrier between Understorey and Floor. Floorian hostility, and the potential to be swept away by floods, are the only true barriers there.

Leaper's lantern lies in the sack, too, separated from the clock by chimera cloth to keep them from interfering with one another. Leaper made the magical, trapped-lightning lantern and its twin in secret. Yes, it gives light, they all give light, and some of them transport messages and some of them kill, but the pair made by Leaper transport all kinds of small, non-living objects from one to the other. Leaper has used them for all his best thefts.

Let the Servants of the lightning god search him upon his return. Let them suspect him. Let them shake out his bags. His grin widens just thinking about it.

Then the sky rumbles and the storm rolls in and although he can't sense his master's terrible power below the barrier, he stops grinning. The monsoon has arrived.

Just a few more hours. That's all he needs. *I hope that's all I need.*

Purple clouds turn to purple specks hidden by silhouetted black, thrashing leaves and branches. Purple specks turn to distant pinpricks of light. Leaper has reached Understorey. He has no fear of the infamously barbarous Understorian warriors. If he didn't already know they superstitiously avoided the emergents of goddesses and gods, he'd still feel safe; not only was he born an Understorian, but in Understorey, anyone but a fool hides safely away in their tree-trunk hollow at the first indication of the monsoon.

Leaper reaches a level a thousand paces down. His feet don't touch the ground. Odel's emergent is ludicrously tall. The rope's strong, and long enough. The knots tell him he's reached twelve hundred paces. Sweat beads on his body. There's no wind. Only oppressive heat.

Fourteen hundred paces.

He can't feel the raindrops anymore, but individual drops aren't the danger. Once the rain really gets started, the rivers running down the sides of the great trees will rage, turning a hundred winding ground-snakes of water nosing blindly towards the sea into a single, forest-wide flood.

The sword will be lost.

When he's at home in Airak's Temple, Leaper loathes being reminded of what he truly is. Not the high-class child of Canopy reflected by his carefully cultivated accent, but an Understorian abomination: king's blood mixed with slave's blood, and his magical talent watered down by it. In the earliest days of his apprenticeship, he failed often, but now he borrows the power of Old Gods' bones to make himself strong, and Floor is where the Old Gods' bones can be found.

His rump hits something hard. He swears, finds his feet, and rubs his bruised tailbone while rope coils tangle around his knees.

Floor.

Airak's teeth.

When he gets the lantern out of his sack and unshutters it, blue-white light bounces from the buttress-roots of the great tree, but shows little else. The neighbouring spiny plum, six hundred paces away, is a faint shape far to his left. Everything beneath his feet is black, feels sticky, and smells rotten. Leaper kicks at the mulch and jumps back at the horror of uncovered worms, white salamanders, and wriggling millipedes.

Pieces of fallen bark begin brushing his shoulders. He's the one whose descent disturbed them, yet he came down faster than they did. Now the pieces are catching up, making a mosaic of green and grey against the black. Raising the lantern, he watches them fall for a moment.

A pair of eyes gleam at the edge of the great tree trunk. No, it's only a flutter of falling bark. The sound of a footfall is his imagination. If Floorians had seen his light, they'd be putting spears through him at this very moment. They don't tolerate intruders, Leaper has heard, but they, too, must moor their floating villages in preparation for the monsoon.

Leaper unwraps the pocket-clock and checks it. The hand has only passed one of the twelve markers, but he knows it runs slightly faster in the first hours than it does in the later ones. He stows it away. Begins sweeping the area, lantern in hand.

There are footprints, but he can't read them. Areas of disturbed dirt and pine needles, but no body. No clothes.

No sword.

"Aurilon," he mutters angrily, "where are your gods-cursed bones?"

"They are not to be found," a woman's voice says behind him. "And you ought not to look for them, lest you lose your hair for transgressing. By that, of course, I mean lose your life."

Leaper whirls. Two paces away, a slender arm whips up to shield dark eyes from the blinding brightness of the lantern. The owner of the voice is shorter than anyone Leaper has ever met, with white streaks in her straight black hair. Her brown skin is speckled with mud and sap patterns, which are intricate and must have been time-consuming; her arms are smooth and left bare of the patterns but sag in the muscles, giving her age.

She seems to be alone. A woven string of dragonfly wings hangs, skirt-like but concealing nothing, from her hips. She wears no other clothes.

For a moment Leaper is speechless—and he's never speechless. In seven years spent navigating the great city of Canopy, he's used many sets of selves to camouflage himself within the classes of people that surround him, recalling images of branching trees to help him slip into their inhabitants' vocabulary and mannerisms, from the roots upward. A tallowwood represents, to him, the simple brusqueness of the hunter of Gannak, its branches ending in ritual rhymes where grunts won't suffice, while a floodgum is the formalised secrecy of the Temple. The firewheel tree helps him to assume the smooth obsequiousness of court.

He has no class association, no pattern of behaviour, to help him here. She doesn't look like any goddess, queen, farmer, or slave he's ever seen.

"I am called Leaper." He holds his empty hand out in surrender. "What are you called?"

"Ootesh," she says, motioning imperatively for him to lower the lantern. She carries a small carving of a crocodile.

Not a spear. A carving.

Leaper narrows the lantern shutter to a more tolerable width, looking to her face for approval.

"Men must not meet the eyes of women," she says, unsmiling. "Not even the eyes of a linker like me. No exceptions for ignorant outsiders. If they want to keep their hair."

Leaper stares at her bare feet, slathered in mud to the knees.

"Aurilon was my—" He begins boldly, hesitating over the lie that she was his mother; his skin is not dark enough for that, he remembers that much about her. "My friend. Why shouldn't I look for her? She deserves the proper ceremony."

In the corner of his eye, he sees Ootesh tilt her head in consideration.

"We will give her the proper ceremony. She was one of us. We will celebrate her soul in the winged-warded way. Our ceremony has nothing to do with her body: That is pollution now, and washed into the Crocodile Spine in any case."

"Pollution?" Leaper clamps his lips over the question: *What about the sword she carried? Is that pollution, too?*

"Certainly." The woman waves her carved crocodile in some general direction over her shoulder. "Strong pollution. Our boats now avoid the west bank of the Spine where it meets the Hanging Leaf. We already had need to avoid the east bank, since the speech splinters came to rest there at the end of the last monsoon and all bones of the Old Gods are to be avoided."

Leaper licks suddenly dry lips. He should have suspected the Floorians beneath Odelland would have different traditions to the Floorians beneath Airakland. The Floorians from Gui—who had freely traded Old Gods' bones with him yet threatened to kill him on sight if he ever came down to them—might have taken Aurilon's sword, if they had seen it.

These ones would not. They wouldn't come near it to touch it. Nor would they move human bodies. *If only I'd come to Floor right away, both sword and body would still be lying where they landed!*

Too late. The Crocodile Spine is the name of the main artery of Floor-flowing water. If Aurilon's body and weapons are in it, he'll never find them.

"This journey is wasted," he realises aloud. The journey for the sword is, anyway. What had she said about speech splinters? "Thank you for not kill-ing me."

"Wasted?" Ootesh answers with apparent surprise. "Did you not under-stand me? Aurilon lived with you in the trees for the greater part of her life. You should eat her flesh and speak for her at the boat-building."

"Eat her flesh? But you said—" Her eyes narrow at him, and he remem-bers to lower his gaze. And he'd thought the absence of a spear in the woman's hand was comforting. "You said her body was pollution, but you're going to eat it?" He should leave. She can't stop him from leaving. She's a woman alone without Understorian spines for climbing.

Ootesh sighs. She steps forward, holding out the crocodile carving.

"My words are not perfect," she says. "The flesh you will eat is the flesh of honey kiss fruit. We suspected that any who loved Aurilon would anticipate the preparations to release her soul and come to the cutting-place. Instead, you blundered about here. The Greatmother was wise to send me to wait for you as close to the pollution as I dared go." She shakes her head. "I was chosen late to be a linker. As I told you, we of the Crocodile-Rider clans do not use the speech splinters that the sorcerers and their slaves use. Our previous linker was killed. Unfortunately, I am proof that old women do not learn languages as easily as young men. But I try my best. " She wag-gles the carving. "Take this, for protection. Do not touch my hand. Do not touch any women or look into their eyes when we reach the village. Otherwise—"

"Otherwise I'll lose my hair. Understood."

Leaper takes the carving. He grips it tight. Ootesh the Crocodile-Rider turns to lead him into the dark. He should leave her and climb back into Canopy. The sword isn't here. But what about the so-called speech splinters? The thought of their potential tantalises him.

And he's being welcomed to a Floorian death ritual. What Canopian has ever had that chance? What else might he learn?

"Are there any other bones of the Old Gods along the way?" he asks, lengthening his stride to catch up with her, careful not to touch her, unty-ing the rope from his harness as he walks. "Strictly so that I can avoid them, of course."

In his head, the words of Orin's prophecy rattle and crash insistently against one another. They should be fresh in his mind, but already he's had an argument with his sister Imeris about exactly what was said.

I doom you—they agree on that part.

by my power—also agreed.

to wander far from home—Leaper remembers the wandering, but he doesn't remember the far-from-home part.

until your mate—surely it wasn't mate; surely that's a thing only animals have?

your true love

your heart's desire—yes, there was definitely specific mention of his heart's desire.

grows to love another more than you.

Only then will you be permitted to return.

But the wind goddess isn't the deity to whom Leaper owes his allegiance. His faith is in the lightning god. Besides, he has no true love. No heart's desire. He's never spoken to a woman he wanted to bed who didn't want to bed him, too, and he's never bedded anyone he wanted to bed twice.

Although he hasn't yet spoken to—no.

It is one thing to yearn for the heights of the forest. Another thing to reach too high. Even for perfection as described by a poet.

He straightens his shoulders as he walks.

"Listen to that song," Ootesh says, ignoring his question, and Leaper supposes it's the whisper of a nearby stream that she means. "It is the flow of one of the blossomcarriers. Hundreds of them course from the seat of your rain goddess into the Crocodile Spine." She shoots him an angry glance. "Once, the rains came all over. They were not concentrated all in one place, all in one season." Leaper can't help but roll his eyes. "We lived in the sun. There were no shadewomen and no demons. We did not battle the deep waters for our very lives."

"Your personal memories of those carefree days must be painful." Leaper has heard plenty of whining about the supposed good old days from grandmothers seven or ten generations removed from the founding of the forest. They still manage to make the fall of the Old Gods sound like a fresh grievance.

"I could keep you in a cage to learn your language better," Ootesh muses. "You fear pain more than the other one, I think. You would not cut out—"

"I'm sorry about the demons," Leaper interrupts. "But magic's the only thing that really works to keep them at bay, the chimeras in particular, and magic doesn't work down here. Well, my kind of magic doesn't work." He stumbles over a fallen branch, skinning his shins, and stops to unshutter the lantern again. He needs more light. The sound of the stream is closer. Unlike the rivers that run down the sides of trees, ground-rivers are known to be filthy, full of dirt and disease, and infested with snakes and piranhas. He hopes Ootesh doesn't intend for them to wade through one.

"Do not!" she instructs sharply, glaring at the lantern. "You will blind him with your cursed light! I left him behind at a distance when I saw it."

"Who will I blind with my cursed light?" Leaper asks, his shins smarting, but as he juggles the lantern, he sees it. A fat, spiny reptile with its heavy neck in some kind of wood-and-straw collar. Its front legs lie on dry leaves. Hind legs and scaly tail vanish into the fast-running stream. The animal is at least eight paces long.

Jagged, pale teeth stick out of the creases of its long snout even with its jaw closed.

We're going to ride on its back, he thinks with awe. *She's a Crocodile-Rider.*

"He's going to let you sit on his back?" he asks. "How, without magic?"

Ootesh ducks into a wood-and-straw hut that sits on the bank of the stream. When she comes out, she's holding a pole with a dangling string and something on the end that smells rancid.

"Your friend Aurilon," she says, "was one of many husbands to our Greatmother. A famous hunter, fighter, and crocodile tamer. Aurilon trained this crocodile. The men marked her as one of their own. But one day she went away."

"She went to serve a god, if that helps."

"It does not," Ootesh says, bending over the crocodile's collar, fastening ropes to either side. "If the men had known as much, they would have broken our law against climbing to bring her back, to cut her hair, and to burn her alive on her boat."

Yes, very peaceful, Leaper thinks. *Nothing like Gui.*

Leaper doesn't see the point in telling her about the barrier that would have blocked their way.

"In that case, no need for me to mention it to anyone else." *No need for me to mention the god I serve, either.*

"The men wished to treat Aurilon's desertion as a death, to cut down the honey kiss tree that was planted when she came to us, eat the fruit, and build Aurilon's soul-boat from the sap-wet wood. But the Greatmother somehow knew Aurilon was still alive. She felt it in her liver."

"Alive until last month, anyway," Leaper says, stepping lightly in a circle, avoiding the crocodile's head.

"I do not know months." Ootesh straightens. "Ants moved their nests into the trees a few sleeps past. We began moving the village away from the Crocodile Spine. We have no wish to be washed out to sea. That is when we found Aurilon's pollution. The man who found her is polluted forever and has gone to be a slave of the Rememberers. Come. Step onto the boat."

Leaper sees at last that the hut by the stream is a flat-bottomed boat. Two long poles with corresponding ropes harness the boat to the crocodile's collar. When Leaper's feet find the lashed beams half buried in mud, Ootesh flicks the rancid meat that dangles from her pole over the right side of the crocodile's head.

The beast turns in the direction of the meat. The boat shudders. Leaper leans against the upright beams of the hut, throwing his arms out for balance as the crocodile writhes towards the stream.

Then they're moving, in surges and lulls, along a watery path whose ripples glimmer in the feeble blue-white light escaping from Leaper's lantern; it occasionally glints off the crocodile's eye.

So, more than a few hours, Leaper thinks, refraining from checking his pocket-clock. *So what? I've still got plenty of time.*

ALONE AT last, the ceremony for Aurilon over, Leaper rakes through his carrysack in search of the pocket-clock.

Fighting to stay calm, he shines the unshuttered lantern on the clear glass face of it.

The pocket-clock has stopped.

Twelve hours gone.

Or more. He's got no way of knowing how long he's been down on the forest Floor.

The taste of honey kiss fruit still sweetens his tongue. In contrast, the sting of the sour, astringent rind lingers on his lips and under his fingernails. The ritual for Aurilon went on and on, and now he has no time to find what he's wanted to find since Ootesh said the words: *We already had need to avoid the east bank . . . the speech splinters came to rest there at the end of the last monsoon . . .*

He should climb as fast as he can. Right now. The monsoon has begun. His aura is fading. The barrier is closing to him.

Yet the monsoon flood is sure to shift those bone fragments from the east bank of the Crocodile Spine. He'll never have this chance again.

Ootesh has left him beside one of the small streams, a blossomcarrier. They all run into the Crocodile Spine, she said. Leaper holds the lantern to the surface of the water, to be sure which way it's flowing, and is forced back when a small crocodile lunges at him from the waterline.

Leaper's heart races. The animal's barely as long as his leg, but its teeth gleam blue-white. The level of the stream creeps up towards him as he watches. It's perceptibly rising.

He runs along the bank, downstream.

There's no undergrowth here. No light. The ground is the hardest and driest it can ever be, layered in leaves, waiting for the floodwaters to come. Or for one of the giant trees to fall and let in the sun. Leaper's relied on youth and natural fitness in his prior escapades. This is different. He needs to pace himself. He needs the easy lope of a long-range hunter.

He can't remember how. Wheezes like a choked flowerfowl. His feet hurt. His arm, holding the lantern out in front of him so that he can avoid the wall-like buttress roots of the great trees, aches.

Then he realises the roaring in his ears isn't the pounding of his blood; it's the Crocodile-Spine. He's standing on the east bank. The lights in front of his eyes aren't sparks of exhaustion but light admitted by the wide body of the river, where no great trees grow. The arms of the figs and flood-gums on either side almost meet in the middle, but not quite.

Leaper laughs with relief to see the sky, angry and lightning slashed as it is. The *night* sky, curtained by monsoon clouds, barely brighter than light-less Floor, even with the moon behind them.

Thick rushes and bamboos bar his way, here, but he finds the splinters of Old Gods' bones by swinging his lantern about. The lightning inside the lantern flares wildly with proximity to unshielded magic, acting as a bone detector.

Leaper sets the lantern on a grass tuft bent double by the driving rain. He blinks constantly and wipes his face with one hand to get the water out of his eyes. Calf-deep in mud, he digs a piece of chimera cloth out of his sack. He uses it like a potholder to break off a ladle-length splinter of what looks like a half-buried, empty-socketed jawbone the size of a house.

As I told you, Ootesh had explained, *we of the Crocodile-Rider clans do not use the speech splinters that the sorcerers and their slaves use.*

Meaning: *These bones are a shortcut to learning the languages of all the peoples of Floor. What an advantage to have!* Not just in service of the lightning god but of the kings and queens who can protect him and his life of luxury if any of his many misdemeanours ever come to light.

Noble families, and wealthy ones, who can protect him if he's ever expelled from the Temple, or demoted as his mentor, Aforis, was demoted.

Any and all advantages will do.

Opening the lantern pane, he thrusts the bone splinter inside. At first, it pushes back, seeming to resist, which tells him that the Old God who owned the jawbone is not the one who became the new god Airak. The magics are in opposition, not harmony.

Still, eventually it goes through. Disappears. In Leaper's room in the Temple, where the other lantern rests on his writing desk, the sliver of bone now waits for him.

He shutters the lantern triumphantly. Wraps it in chimera cloth and stows it in the sack. Runs ahead of the rising tide to the closest great tree, a suntree, all its brushy, burnished flowers turned to brown carpet underfoot. He flings himself at the grey, fissured bark, spines extended for climbing.

It's a long climb.

When he's halfway up the tree, at the level of Understorey, he longs to simply dig his spines deeply and sleep.

But there is no time.

His aura is fading. Maybe already gone. Maybe he'll have to find another way through the barrier. Beg a favour-owing god or goddess to open up the way. He is Canopian, after all. One of them. They'll help him.

Then again, Aforis might find Leaper's bed empty. Airak, who warned Leaper not to disobey his betters, will know Leaper went his own way again. Without asking.

I should have asked.

Airak's teeth!

Leaper puts his hand out into empty air. There's no blockage to see there. Nothing but a trickle of water, carrying dust and debris down the side of the tree. The leaves seem to shiver and sigh, like a titan finally taking a shower after a long journey.

Leaper's fingers bend back against the barrier.

It's completely solid to him. His aura has vanished as though it never was. The city of Canopy has abandoned him to the lower levels, their dangers and demons. He has no gliding wings, and his rope's far behind at Odel's emergent. To get to a different tree, to ask his favours, he'd have to risk crocodile-infested waters.

In desperation, Leaper unwraps his lantern. Wedges it into a bark-crevice in the side of the tree. He licks his lips. Looks at it.

He's never tried to put anything alive through it before. He doesn't know if it can work. Whether a breathing creature would still be breathing on the other side. Even if it would, could a soul pass through?

Leaper grits his teeth. The chance of dying seems less important than getting to his room before Aforis does, at this moment. *You are rash,* Unar the Godfinder told him once. *One poor decision stacked up on top of another, until the whole tower falls. That is your life, Leaper.*

Like she can talk.

Leaper opens the glass pane and forces his hand into the lightning. It doesn't hurt. It feels like nothing. It goes in to the wrist, stops, and he thinks, *It won't work. This is as far as I can go.* But then he realises his fingers aren't touching the glass pane on the opposite side of the lantern. They're touching the polished wooden surface of his writing desk.

He pushes harder, and abruptly he's in the lantern up to his shoulder, which is wider than the open pane should be able to accommodate. The world tilts. His hand feels heavy, like his arm's hanging down from a tree. The rest of his body aches to follow.

Leaper falls through the lantern.

He lands, sideways and sprawling, on his desk, overbalances and crashes to the floor. When he untangles himself, his torn, strained muscles feel on fire and his collarbone is bruised. The light's blinding. At the same time, the rush of his returning powers fills him, helping him to forget the physical pain: his mind is linked momentarily to the sheet lightning dancing from cloud to cloud over Canopy. He's bashed his head against a pair of boots that he had left in the middle of the floor.

No.

They are Aforis's boots.

Aforis stands in the middle of the floor, looming and frowning in that frightening way only a craggy old Skywatcher with one white-irised eye can loom and frown.

"What have you done?" he asks in the deep, authoritative teacher's tone that makes lesser men wet themselves.

"Testing," Leaper says faintly, trying to get a grip on the room, the solid feeling of the tree that forms the floor. It's carved floodgum over his head, not the glorious raiment of the sky; he is not the storm. He's a man sworn to a god, sitting on his arse after squeezing himself through a magic lantern. "Just testing a thing I made."

"Two things?" Aforis arches an eyebrow. "Two linked lanterns? They are for—"

"They are for the Shining One to make, I know," Leaper gasps. He shivers, soaked to the skin. If he weren't still dizzy, he'd gloat. The Shining One has never made anything like Leaper's linked lanterns before! "Has the Holy One sent for me, Aforis? Is that why you're here? How long have you been here?"

Aforis holds up a splinter of bone, and the lantern on the writing desk flares. It's the splinter that Leaper stole from the bank of the Crocodile-Spine.

"Long enough. To whom does this belong?"

"To—to Aurilon's people! To nobody in Canopy, Aforis, I swear to you! Can I have it back?"

"You can have it back," Aforis says sternly, "on the condition that you immediately return the pocket-clock you stole to its rightful owner, the queen of Airakland."

The queen of Airakland. The one too high for Leaper to set his sights on.

Leaper shivers again, not from the cold.

PART I

The Rememberers

ONE

LEAPER PRESSED himself flat to the wall inside the queen's wardrobe.

He was going to ask her. He'd waited long enough. He'd waited ten years, since he'd returned her pocket-clock. That was more than one third of his life. First he'd waited because he'd been too much in awe of her. Next, when he'd seen how they treated her, he'd kept silent because he didn't want to complicate her life. Finally, once he'd witnessed her astounding capacity for forgiveness, he'd understood that complications were a thing they would just have to put behind them.

Together. Later.

I am going to ask her.

Not right at that moment, though. It was a bad moment.

Soon.

Cloth lengths hung from four paces above the floor, on brittle obsidian rails over Leaper's head. Metal and stone embellishments to the silk garments tinkled as he straightened them behind him. The smell of hollowed floodgum was almost physical, as though if he wished to escape, he'd have to swim through oil of eucalyptus.

Beneath were *her* smells.

The ones Leaper still found intoxicating after ten years of obsession.

Ozone and sulphur, her royal right. Purest whale oil from seas so distant they might as well be imagined; marine behemoths so unlikely that it was easier to believe the oil some dead demon's distillation instead. Snow cherry and mountain cedar, which were almost as mythical as whales.

He was going to ask her to run away with him, if she came into the room alone.

A slave's child doesn't ask a queen to elope.

A slave's child shouldn't have asked a queen to bed him, either, but he had, after ten years of longing, and she had, and now, only a few weeks after their consummation, he was more obsessed than ever.

She didn't come into the room alone.

Sentries, clanging hilts against breastplate buckles, chorusing *Your Highnesses* from outside the doorway, signalled the majestic couple's return to the bedroom together. Leaper couldn't see them, but he scowled, imagining them still resplendent in their evening feast clothes. Queen Ilik said something muffled to King Icacis, and he responded with a rough guffaw.

Leaper risked a peek through one of the tree-shaped airing holes in the hinged calamander-wood doors. The queen preferred the cold blue light of the lamps, but her king insisted she have whale oil, insisted she burn it, both as a statement of wealth and because the warm, smokeless flame flattered her black skin.

It's useful for maintaining the clocks, she'd told Leaper last monsoon, and yet today her favourite clock was broken, whale oil or no.

King Icacis's turned back blocked Leaper's view. The king, wrapped in silver-embroidered crimson, fancied shaving his greying head, followed by a charcoal-powdering of the stubble; skin rolls at the back of his thick neck made Leaper think of a shaved tapir.

"Aren't we getting too old for toys?" Icacis rumbled.

And yet she loves him, Leaper thought.

"Give it back, please, Icacis." Her measured voice made Leaper's heart jerk like a leashed gibbon, but the king was already raising his voice, speaking over her.

"Don't pull on it, woman. Let me look at it. If it means so much to you, let me fix it. Look, that spring is broken in half. A simple matter!" There came a clatter as he set it down on the side table. "In the meantime, I'll have the slaves wind the clock twice a day instead of once. You see? You've been crying over nothing."

Leaper clapped both hands over his mouth to keep the ugly laughter inside. Ilik's voice came again, sounding tired and patient.

"I wish you hadn't asked the slaves to wind it in the first place. Overwinding broke the spring."

The king's remorse was immediate.

"It seemed like a way to free you of a chore. I wanted to make things easier for you. That's all I ever want."

"I know." She sounded helpless in the face of his solicitude, which made Leaper furious with both of them. She wasn't helpless. Why pretend?

Leaper fumed some more while Icacis rained kisses on his wife.

Get on with it! Off you go!

As usual, he waited for a slow count of one hundred after the king had departed. Then, a deep breath, another peek to make sure the queen wasn't in danger of being caught by the swinging doors, and he pushed hard against them.

"Twice a day!" he exclaimed, unable to contain his disdain.

He spoke to her in the language of the Crocodile-Riders. It was their secret language. He'd taught it to her, a few words at a time, beginning with their first meeting a decade ago when, partway through returning her pocket-clock, he'd been seized by the aftereffects of the translation bone he'd swallowed. It had tasted like dirt, that sliver of stolen bone from Floor. A dozen different tongues had come bursting into his throat, and Leaper had needed to share them with somebody or choke. It had made for a memorable visit.

Ilik turned reluctantly from the clock. She was short and plump with a perfect bottom and pert breasts. When she smiled, one endearingly crooked tooth parted the pronounced bow of her lips before the others did. His heart jerked again. She was self-conscious about that smile and rarely shared it; certainly he'd never seen it in the early days when he was Aforis's pupil and she was a distant, jewelled thunderhead gazing serenely over a green, glass-floored royal audience chamber.

Older than Leaper, she was not as old as the king. Her grey hairs went unnoticed in the magnificent tower of her royal coiffure. Grey stormbird feathers and strings of silver and diamond alternated with her long thin braids to form a glittering, open-throated flower shape, flowing up and back from the crown of her head.

She kissed him. Gave him a warning look, which he ignored. He went straight to the clock, turning it over, cradling it along his forearm. A tree shape of green soapstone fronted the case. Slippery-smooth branches disguised the wooden cage where the mechanism was mounted.

Inside, the spring was broken. Not in half, though. It had snapped near the attachment at one end. The position of the key showed that the clock had been freshly wound when it happened.

"That's it, then," she said, also in the language of the Crocodile-Riders, sighing, sagging a little against him.

"No," Leaper said. "Why? I'll fetch a replacement."

"The maker of this clock died during the Hunt. Before you and I met. She was from Eshland. The only one who used springs and"—Ilik touched the two places, at root and crown of the soapstone tree, where slivers of bone were inset—"two bones, one to balance the other, to slow the clock in the first few hours after winding." They were slivers of Old God's bone. Here in Leaper's home niche, where his relatively weak magic was strongest, the hairs on the back of his hands lifted at the clock's proximity, and he could smell tallowwood and bone tree bark.

"Somebody must have taught her," he said. "This clockmaker from Eshland. She couldn't have been the only one."

"Whoever taught her is long dead. My clockmaker, already ancient when we met, was away for years herself. She learned on her travels, failing to specify *where* she travelled. Some of her neighbours refuse to believe she's dead. They think she's on another of her journeys."

Leaper made an irritated grumbling noise.

"How can it be, that of the hundreds of thousands of people in this city, only one was capable of work like this?" *For you, I would travel along the dead clockmaker's trail, if not for the prophecy.* "Could there be a comparable clockmaker in Understorey or Floor?"

"It is the law of specialisation, my brave climber," she said, tucking a lock of his fringe, half black, half white, back behind one ear. "In a place of many people, the work of survival is accomplished quickly. For the upper classes, there may not even be any work to be done. A woman may dedicate her life to one area of specialised accomplishment. Where there are few people . . ." She shrugged and turned away. "Where there are few people, as in Understorey, each one must carry the rough knowledge of all, for survival. If a woman of Understorey dreamed of greatness, even if her labour could be spared, is it likely she'd find a teacher expert in whatever it was she wished to learn?"

"My sister learned," Leaper pointed out darkly. "She was Understorian."

"She learned in Canopy. After she'd learned as much as possible from those in Understorey who specialised—from a desire to destroy Canopy."

"For survival!"

"Yes," Ilik agreed soberly. "For survival. That was before Imeris made peace between Loftfol and Ehkisland."

"Why do you say the clockmaker from Eshland died during the Hunt?" Mention of Imeris stirred some vague memory of a clockmaker dying ten years ago, when his mortal sister had been set against the goddess of beasts. He lowered the broken clock carefully back down to the table. "Do you mean Orin's monster killed her?"

"Yes. Leaving neither apprentice nor descendants."

"But some of her neighbours think she's travelling."

"Some do. Others have had her workshop boarded up. Stuck spirits were said to haunt it even while she lived there. She worked with bones. It's not known if her body fell or is still in there, sealed away with all her raw materials like an Understorian."

Leaper still often exercised his impulse to break into buildings and steal shiny things, and he managed somehow both to perk up at the news the old workshop was boarded up with treasures intact and to turn sour a second time.

"Haunted by her stuck spirit," he repeated scornfully, uneasily recalling the instances of Nirrin's and Igish's souls still being in the ether when the birth goddess Audblayin called them back to their old bodies. The word for "spirit" in the language of the Crocodile-Riders was sharper and deeper, making it sound a menacing, ill-omened force instead of something harmless and insubstantial. "There's no real reason other people couldn't have moved in there. No reason a complete stranger couldn't have taken over her work."

But Ilik, unimpressed by his reaction, snapped sharply back into the royal syntax and the Canopian tongue.

"Do you think one who walks in the grace of Airak hasn't considered it?"

Leaper stared at her.

"Considered what?" he asked in the same language.

"Sneaking off in disguise to be a clockmaker in Eshland." She waved one hand. It was spiderwebbed with silver chains. "Do you think one who walks in the grace of Airak doesn't know that the haunting is a foolish tale? That all the woman's tools, her scrolls, her materials, must still be there? I could have pretended to be her long-lost niece and spent my life doing what I love, solving clockwork puzzles, deciphering hard-won secrets."

"You hadn't met me then," Leaper said winningly. "It's like you just said. When the clockmaker died ten years ago, we were still strangers." *So why would a queen have plotted to run away? That wasn't the time. The time is now. Ask her, Leaper.* But the words wouldn't take shape in his mouth.

"Do you think," Ilik continued quietly, "one who walks in the grace of Airak knows nothing of the hidden nest you've been building for ten years, Leaper, in the guaiacum tree on the southern edge of Eshland? The southern edge, where the sun shines all the time? Where our Airakland king holds no sway? Do you think I haven't noticed that the goods stolen by the so-called Adept Sneak Thief have all been luxury goods of the varieties I favour?"

Leaper felt five years old again, standing before Oldest-Father with stolen saltbread on his breath.

Ashamed. Inept.

"Have you been laughing at me all this time?"

"No." She took his face between her hands. The chains chimed softly. "Never that. But I cannot betray him."

"You've already betrayed him."

"Only recently." She lowered her lashes. Now they were both ashamed. "Is a man who doesn't know he is betrayed betrayed? For that matter, is a god?"

Leaper jerked his face out of her hands. He didn't want to talk about his oath to Airak: to serve faithfully. To serve until death. To leave all other bonds and affections behind, and not to love.

As though that were something a person chose.

Admittedly, Leaper had chosen to flit above and below the barrier, as well as across the borders of various kingdoms, so that the magical bindings that helped enforce his oaths were weaker than they should have been. He'd been cautioned by the Godfinder, Unar, who'd been his guardian for a time, but he'd ignored her advice and done it anyway.

Certainly, in contrast to his fellow Servants of the lightning god, he'd had no trouble engaging in acts of physical love.

"One who walks in the grace of Airak," he said, "will go to Eshland for a replacement clock spring. For now, that will satisfy me. To see your favourite piece functioning again."

"I love you," Ilik whispered, and Leaper felt fleetingly nauseous. How could he know that she meant those words, since she spoke the exact same words to Icacis as well? "I love you more than I love him, more than any-one, but he needs me more than you do."

"I'm yours to command," Leaper whispered back, and that was also something he'd told Airak many times, forming the words with his lips but never feeling the binding nature of them in his bones.

She gazed at him in silence.

They should have taken to the king's bed then, and sweated passionately in unison, but Leaper turned away, love and resentment tangled with a sud-den claustrophobia. Without a word of farewell, he went to the wardrobe, and slid a carved panel in the back to one side. He heard fricative fabric and the feathery *whoomp* of her sitting on the bed, but didn't look back.

If she'd called his name, if she'd commanded him, he would have gone to her.

She said nothing. Had never been the type to forcibly contain man or beast. Ilik never begrudged him his freedom, his secret roaming about the palace, even though she herself was not free. Who else in his life had loved him without restricting his movements? Not his mothers. Not his fathers.

Who else had loved him without telling him what to do? Not the God-finder. Not Aforis.

Not the lightning god, Airak.

The hidden tunnel was revealed. Whale oil greased the edges of the panel; fish smell mingled with the fresh flower scent of the queen's perfumed water on Leaper's skin. He didn't have to slither on his belly through the dark-ness, but could manage a sort of crouching shuffle.

He had to turn to slide the panel back into place behind him. Ilik watched him, bright-eyed, still silent, from her perch on the edge of the bed. Her hair ornaments glittered in the glow of the whale oil lamps. Water ran through a dozen clocks behind her.

Closing the panel cut off Leaper's last source of light, but it didn't matter. The tunnel brought him to what he knew from long experience was the smooth back of a relief map of Airakland.

I was going to ask her, he fumed. *Instead, she laughed at me. I'll ask some-body else! I don't need her.*

There he paused, listening, to make sure the other room was empty. Then he pressed on the corners of his exit.

The map popped out of its frame onto a thick carpet strewn with loung-ing cushions. The trunks of the represented trees were inlaid carvings from the actual wood of their real counterparts. Leaper pushed the map back into position and gratefully straightened his knees and back. *Calm, now. A job to be done. Think about Ilik later.*

He was in the king's study, a place he'd been visiting far longer than the queen's bedroom. If Airakland's guardian deity didn't take a covert hand in running the kingdom, who would care for the citizens whose tributes and belief gave the lightning god his power? King Icacis was completely incompetent, and for all the things that Leaper loved about Ilik, she thrived in an inner world of poetry and clockwork puzzle solving. She was no saviour of the stricken or the slaves.

Leaper padded over the carpet to the other side of the study. He drew a sheet of square-cut paperbark from a pigeonhole set above the writing desk, selected a stick of charcoal, and composed the missive in his head.

> Royal salutations from One Who Upholds the Glorious Law of Airak, Lightning Lord, to One Who Upholds the Glorious Law of Akkad, She of Fruitful Bounty.
>
> If One may remark on the light rainfall provided by the minimal, most recent monsoon;
>
> and if One may remark on the inclination of the current young incarnation of the rain goddess Ehkis to rebel against what she considers "the suffering and indignity of being born host and hostage to an immortal";
>
> and if One may remark on the deep desire of the citizens of Airakland for fresh fruit to supplement a currently inadequate diet in the face of the failure of forest floor flooding and resulting minimal prey;
>
> and if One may remark on the spectacular height of Your Majesty's palace, which is almost the equal of a Temple emergent, garlanded by metals, dried out by the lack of rain, and highly susceptible to strike by lightning;
>
> One might be tempted to offer the following solution to our mutual problem: that One Who Upholds the Glorious Law of Akkad send a secret caravan of fresh fruit to the palace of One Who Upholds the Glorious Law of Airak.
>
> One would clandestinely make a generous gift in Your name to the Lightning Lord, protecting Your palace without drawing

the ire of Your patron goddess. Meanwhile the excess fruit not given in tribute would bring relief to the hungry innocents of Our kingdom.

Leaper paused, charcoal in hand, the paperbark page still blank.

Pain and anger at the queen's rejection threatened to overwhelm him, but after a moment or so he was able to set his feelings aside and return to the task assigned to him. He drew a deep breath and tried to release his additional irritation that the letter composed in his head, the letter a true king might write, would need to go unwritten and unseen, since Icacis, the actual king, had bananas for brains and an unpractised scrawl in place of a scholar's calligraphy.

Leaper pressed the charcoal to the paperbark. First too heavily. Then too lightly. He brought to mind, not the proud fierceness of the regal firewheel tree, but the weird, crooked shoots that sprang from rootstock after the main trunk of the tree was lightning-split and killed. He made some words larger than others. Inserted random capital letters.

What emerged was a tragically accurate imitation of King Icacis's hand.

RoYal SALUTaTiONS to ONE WHO UPWHOLES the glorbouS law of Akkad, Fruitful LadY.

One haS been unable to ignore Not Much RAIN in the LAST YEAR'S MONSOON due to the rebellion of the raiN goddess EhkiS against her adViSers. One has been warned of the vulnerabilitY of YoUr pAlace to lightening caused bY drY winter thunderstorms; meanwhile MY PEOPLE are without efficient freSh fruit thanks to the Shortage of water. In the service of Your palace and MY PEOPLE, one who upwholes the glorious laW of Airak begs You to send me a secret caraVan of assorted fresh fruit. One will enSHURE that Airak's protection is eXtended to Your High hOme, and that the hungry children of this niche are fed. REGARDS. ICACIS OF AIRAKLAND.

Leaper folded the missive, dripped its lips with beeswax, opened a drawer lined with chimera skin, and hefted the hand-span-wide, carved-bone royal seal. The seal left the impression of a burned tree but also imbued the skin-smooth bark with magic. Once the message was read, the paper would catch fire and turn rapidly to ash.

There would be no evidence that the king of Airakland had ever suggested such a thing as a secret trade with the king of Akkadland in defiance of the rain goddess.

Nor would there be evidence that Leaper, an infiltrator from the Temple, had forged a message from his king.

Now there was time for tears.

Now there was a place for his hurt to take hold of him, to rattle the hot rain loose from his eyes.

I do need her. There is nobody like her.

Airak's teeth.

TWO

WHEN LEAPER left the palace, it was after midnight.

Possums hurled shredded bark and screeched insults at one another. Bats dropped honey kiss fruit with only one or two bites missing. Leaper left the forged message, hidden inside cheaper, commoner wrappings, in the box at the courier station with a silver coin. Then he dodged a few sleeping slaves and went on his way.

Eshland was his destination.

The realm of the wood god.

The kingdom next door.

In Airak's Temple, in a few hours, when the sun came up, Aforis would miss Leaper, as the old man had missed him so many times before, oblivious to Leaper's other duties, and accuse him of shirking. Aforis was not privy to the added tasks that Leaper carried out on Airak's behalf—or on his own behalf, dreaming of a future with the queen. As always, Leaper would earn Aforis's forgiveness with ready excuses and by making good on his debt of labour to the other Servants.

You aren't an infant, Leapael, Aforis had thundered last month when Leaper had sneaked off to investigate the sumptuous tree-crown dwelling of some arrogant nobleman. *You have twenty-six summers. You are a man and a Servant of the lightning god. I'm fading, I have sixty-two summers, I'll expire presently, and then who'll make excuses for you?*

Aforis wasn't old. Not really. He could live another ten years, maybe twenty, so long as he didn't fall. He wasn't going to fall, was he? Old people's bones were wobbly and their eyes were weak, but not Aforis. Though he did have a triangle-shaped scar on his cheek from walking into a sharp branch recently. Having one white eye wasn't supposed to diminish an adept's vision, but Leaper had made a joke about it anyway.

Leaper shimmied down a ladder. The low roads might be speckled with excrement, but Airak's lanterns punctuated the high roads; down here, nobody would see him clearly enough to recognise him, especially since he'd wrapped his half-white hair in a black cloth and swapped his Servant's robes for a merchant's blue shirt and short, split skirt-wrap.

Nor would there be any adepts around to recognise the cold, sweet smell of the magic-imbued potion Leaper now swigged that would let him sprint faster than any ordinary runner.

He'd had to steal glassware, clear goblets and silver-backed mirrors, from his own Temple to trade for the potion, but what of it? The Servants had all his remaining days to exact their price, all his muscle and magic gifts, free of charge, as they had done since the Godfinder had brought him to the Temple at a mere twelve years old.

They owed him.

They owned him.

Only the trust extended to him by the god himself mattered to Leaper, and how much did it really matter, since he was risking it every moment he spent with Ilik?

He wasn't going to think about that now. He was going to run to Eshland.

And maybe that great tapir-headed lump of a king would actually notice that somebody had fixed his wife's favourite clock. Would he himself investigate? Or would he set his dolt of a vizier to the task of unmasking the queen's secret lover? Leaper had never previously allowed himself to deliberately slip, but Ilik had agreed to his mission to replace the clock spring.

Of course. She could simply claim credit for the repair herself. She was so clever when it came to clocks. She was so clever, but not clever enough to free herself from—

Why was he still thinking about her? The decade-old fantasy was over.

I love you more than I love him, more than anyone, but he needs me more than you do, she'd said so earnestly of King Icacis. How could she love someone so stupid? Leaper couldn't bring himself to pity the king in his dim-witted struggles to understand the workings of the world. What must the brute be like to bed?

Ultimately unsatisfying, Leaper guessed savagely, *as in every endeavour of his unremarkable reign.*

The potion reached his belly and magic electrified his limbs. His gut felt cold and his muscles hot. He'd never tried the potion of the winds as a precursor to bedding; maybe that would convince her to leave the palace and become his.

Do you think one who walks in the grace of Airak knows nothing of the hidden nest you've been building for ten years in the guaiacum tree on the southern edge of Eshland?

Leaper ran towards Eshland, away from the casual agony of having his deepest hopes and dreams exposed to wither and die like a snail pulled out of its shell. He raced over the rough, kinked low roads in the dim glow of Airak's blue-white lanterns and under the mocking leer of the moon, as if he could outrace the memory of his proposal, the proposal he had not yet dared to present, already discarded.

"We will want that pretty silver," a low, guttural voice said. A muscular arm that ended in an iron hook caught Leaper by the back of his collar and swung him.

He dangled dangerously off the end of the low road. A fatal plunge to Floor lay below.

His silk shirt began to rip along the seam.

Leaper squinted, left eye closed, along the white, hairy arm into a jowly face with pale Understorian eyes, a gummy mouth, and no teeth. Further back along the branch road, two accomplices lurked. Lanterns blued the left sides of their black faces. The moon silvered the right sides, as though they, too, were Servants of Airak.

He could have struck them dead by magic. Weak as his abilities were, he'd honed them since first joining Airak's Temple. Leaper gathered power to his mind with a heady rush of enhanced scent. His flared nostrils filled. There was the oily palm smell of fresh bark clothing. The copper of clotted blood. The sweet rot of an open wound beneath twine-tied wrappings, breath made sour by slow starvation, and sweat, newly sprung of exertion and desperation. Beneath it all floated the perfume of moth-pollinated blossoms springing open in the night.

With a flick of his focused will, he could have connected the cloudless sky to his attacker's thick skull with a finger-thin bolt of lightning.

He chose not to.

After calling lightning to slay Orin's beast, Leaper had sworn an oath never to do deadly violence again, by magic or by hand. Instead, he imagined himself to be the man's kin. Rooted in the same place the man was rooted. Buffeted by the same winds. He imagined himself a thin passionfruit vine, tenuous and clinging, its origins the darkness below the city, at the mercy of the stronger trees it leaned on.

"The master knows!" he gasped in his clumsiest Understorian accent. He kept his left eye, the eye turned silver in the lightning god's Temple, tightly closed. "Someone seen you. Someone told that you were still alive!"

Frowning, the toothless man jerked back, drawing Leaper and his ripped collar to safety. Airakland was not Odelland; despite Imeris's triumph of diplomacy, slaves were neither routinely freed nor allowed to buy their freedom here. If this once-captured warrior was roaming the low roads at night, he might be on a sanctioned mission, passing the spoils of robbery on to his master, but if that was so, why was he starving?

More likely, Leaper thought, he was a runaway, unable to drop below the barrier because of his branded tongue, and starved due to staying out of sight. Fellow slaves could be bribed to tell a master that a man had fallen to his death.

And currency among slaves trading favours was sometimes knocked-out teeth.

"Who are you?" the man demanded, shaking the hook so hard that the silk collar tore completely free. Leaper sprawled sideways onto the branch road.

When he looked up, miming terror, left eye still closed, he could see the other's suspicious expression smoothing out, presumably as he realised that Leaper, too, was lighter-skinned than an ordinary Canopian, that his nose was too narrow and his lips too thin.

"Came to warn you," Leaper said, crawling to the man's knees, pressing elbows against shins, looking up, wide-eyed in appeal. "Soldiers coming."

The toothless man panted heavily. He shifted his weight from foot to foot indecisively. Then he snatched at Leaper's necklace of silver links, breaking the clasp, bruising the back of Leaper's neck. For a moment it seemed like he might tear at the earrings and finger rings as well.

But then he stuffed the broken chain into a pocket and fled. The two accomplices were silent shadows at his heels.

Leaper waited until they were long gone before he got to his feet and brushed down his ruined clothing. He shouldn't have let himself get so distracted. In Canopy, growing too deeply distracted was a good way to die.

At least he'd resisted the instinct to use Airak's magic.

I don't need to hurt, maim, or murder. I'm not Imeris, to reach for a sword, and I'm not my goddess-sister, Audblayin, to reach for ultimate power. I'm smarter than they are. Quicker than they are. I don't leave bodies behind. I'm not the Godfinder, to topple trees, and though I am the soul of the Godfinder's dead sister, I'm not a cold killer like Frog was. Not now. Not ever again.

Besides, the god always sensed where and when his borrowed power was used. Leaper rubbed at the marks on his neck. Slaves, runners, and low-ranking citizens whispered to one another and pointed at him. He tried not to glare at them; none had offered to help him. They might have aided a Servant of Airak; it might have been profitable to have a Servant owe them a favour. But he'd disguised himself, hadn't he?

Leaper partially unfolded and pulled his cloth head wrap down so that it covered his white eye. Pointing himself east, towards Eshland, he ran, once more, like the wind.

THREE

LEAPER MADE good time.

He arrived at the clockmaker's tree shortly after dawn.

Since crossing the border from Airakland into Eshland, he'd found the great trees growing thicker and closer together, their limbs broader. His magic felt far behind him, always out of the corner of his eye, and he knew, even as he reached experimentally for it, that it would not be there.

The attempt left him feeling like a dead tree, hollow, with a faint, swirling whiff of semen and menstrual blood; those were the dark default tributes given in Eshland.

The clockmaker's tree was a grey-barked ebony slathered generously with moss and carved forebodingly with death symbols. Single and paired pinkish fallen flowers on the path showed the ebony to be a female tree.

It wasn't boarded up with planks and pegs as an abandoned Airakland tree might be; instead the tree was sealed by the power of the wood god, Esh, as though there had never been an entrance. Leaper walked along the old road from the neighbouring tree. The path now penetrated the ebony tree near the foot of the filled-in doorway. He put his hands against the place where the opening had been.

Then, pulling an axe from a belt loop, he tapped with the back of the steel head against the trunk.

It was solid. The echoes, if they were there, were deep. Scowling, Leaper chiselled off a section of bark and found what he'd half expected; the grain had grown inward from all directions, forming an intermeshed knot of axe-wrecking stubbornness in exactly the place where he wished to enter.

As if ebony weren't already an irritatingly hard wood.

But he wasn't without resources. Like Audblayin and Imeris, he'd been raised by three hunters of Understorey, and he had the climbing spines to prove it. Kneeling, he chipped experimentally at the spiny plum branch road that supported him. It wasn't a true branch at all, but a modified leaf stem. Esh-hardened, like all the roads, to keep travellers safe. It was nonetheless much softer than the ebony.

Leaper rolled up his sleeves. He rolled down his boot tops. Dropping from the path to hang by left forearm spines and left shin spines from the bark of the ebony tree, he began chopping at the spiny plum path with the axe in his right hand.

The sound of chopping drew a few curious children. In the path's shadow, in the low light, he knew they'd have trouble making out much more than the dark blob of his shape. Wood was not usually taken by force in Eshland. Instead, it was a gift of the god in response to tribute. But Leaper had no time for that, and he wasn't supposed to give tributes to any goddesses or gods besides his own, in any case. By the time Esh was drawn by the tree's pain to punish the offender, Leaper planned to be long gone. Anyway, what was one more deity's doom-filled pronouncement compared to the curse of the wind goddess he was already under?

To be banished from Canopy until my heart's desire grows to love another more than she loves me. Or was it to wander far from home until she loves another? Who could remember the exact wording of prophecies? It was ten years ago. Besides, Leaper had been distracted by the imminent prospect of death at the time. *Maybe it was to be banished from my true love's home. Which would make more sense, since her home is not mine. I don't have a home.*

He'd lived in the home of his three mothers and three fathers as a child. He'd lived in the Godfinder's flowerfowl farm for a few years after that. Then it was the Temple of Airak. None of them sanctuaries. All of them rigid with other people's rules.

Long, pale splinters flew. The children melted away as the road trembled. Leaper cut all the way through the half-pace thickness of it, wishing he had something like the toothless man's hook to help pull out the severed plug. Instead, he stuck it diagonally with his spines, set aside the axe in favour of a bore-knife, and twisted the tapering tip of the road until old, dried-out fibres gave way.

Leaper sheathed his spines quickly as the road ending tumbled away, but he wasn't quick enough to save his bore-knife and swore as the handle jerked out of his hand.

Never mind that. Greater wealth waits inside. The opening was only just wide enough for him to wriggle his shoulders and hips through.

The air was stale. It took a full body length of squirming and cursing before Leaper was able to stand up in the passageway behind the sealed entrance. Sneezing in a cloud of dust from the crumbled path remnants, his head cloth pulled loose by the edge of the tunnel, he wished he'd brought his precious transport-lantern for easy recovery of whatever loot lay deeper inside the tree, but he hadn't thought, until that moment, of taking anything more than the clock spring needed by the queen.

Still distracted. Still a fool! Pain flared up in him again at the memory of her retreat into formality, and he shook his head. Tousling bark, flowers, and splinters out of his hair with one hand, he used the other to unfasten one silver earring, reverse it, and snap it closed again. Thus manipulated, it formed the miniature cage shape of a thumbnail-sized lantern, flaring to life like a captured star.

Leaper held it up to light his way.

The passage was spiral-shaped. It began in wide, high-ceilinged corridors through the creamy sapwood. Then it curved in on itself, entering dense, skin-smooth, night-black heartwood.

He couldn't help but put his empty palm to the ebony. It seemed Ilik had spoken the truth and that nobody really had walked here since the clockmaker was killed by Orin's beast. No animal droppings were evident. No footprints disturbed the faint trace of dust on the formerly shining floor.

As he moved deeper, empty spaces where cylinders and cog shapes had been appeared in the walls at shoulder height. It was as though the clockmaker had invoked Esh and the pieces had come free at her bidding, of a piece and perfectly formed.

Then the walls fell away and Leaper raised the meagre light source to reveal what he could of a wide central room. It was round and low-ceilinged, with sharp, square, identical repeating alcoves around the rim. *A cog,* he realised belatedly, *or rather, an internal gear.* Each alcove contained a fire-resistant surface of honey-tree wood. Most were cluttered with works in progress.

His magical senses twitched, despite the distance from his niche. The tiny lantern buzzed like a trapped fly, flickering. There had to be fragments of Old Gods' bones in the room. Leaper stumbled over the edge of a shallow iron bowl embedded in a honey-tree slab—a fire pit—and realised he'd walked towards the strongest source of the pull without knowing.

Standing heedlessly in the cold ashes of the pit, he turned from one alcove to the next like the shaft of the gear, holding out the lantern to get the flickering reaction from it that betrayed the priceless nature of the hoard.

BIRTH AND DEATH, read an inscription running over the tops of the alcoves, MUST BE SEPARATED BY TIME.

There were hundreds of bone fragments. Thousands. None were shielded by chimera skin, or if there were any shielded pieces, they were in addition to the ones making his tiny lantern flicker.

Why had the wood god, on his visit to seal the tree, left these relics undisturbed? What was going on—or had gone on—here? If the clockmaker was an adept, how had she been so easily dispatched by Orin's beast? Leaper took another step forward, out of the fire pit, and stopped.

No ordinary thief, without a magic lantern, or magic of his own, could have revealed the room's riches. For a moment, he felt the impulse to laugh. *Might as well be standing on a mountain of gold on a tribute tray in a Temple.*

Yet wealth had always been, for him, a means to an end. Stealing had been for a single purpose. Now that he knew the desired end would never come to pass, now that he knew there was no purpose, what did he care about the scarcity of old power-imbued bones?

"I don't want any of it," he whispered to the empty, gloomy room. "Keep your mouldy dust and secrets. All I want is to repair Ilik's favourite clock."

She will never come away with me.

He went to the closest table and searched it for springs. The pocket-clock that was there, disassembled, a seashell of bronze cupping the moving parts, was too small for its components to be a match for the broken spring. He moved to the next table, and when that was similarly unhelpful, to the next, ignoring precious gems and bone slivers, knocking aside gold filigree and all-but-legendary mother-of-pearl.

At last, he found the replacement spring he was looking for. He pocketed it. Then he rummaged in a cupboard for a rusty bore-knife, which he sharpened with oil and stone from the clockmaker's kitchen. There, too, he slaked his thirst from an old, stale barrel.

In case Esh was waiting to destroy him by the front door, he departed by the toilet hole, which contained a wooden board on a hinge that acted as a one-way valve.

Leaper climbed carefully down on his spines to a place where a paper-bark branch road brushed by the bark of the ebony tree. The dappled early light was blinding after the tomblike darkness inside the tree.

Instead of returning immediately to Airakland, he turned south. Three hours later, he reached the hidden home he had been building for ten years in the guaiacum tree on the southern edge of Eshland.

It was now hot, and the unscreened sun had begun to burn the back of his bruised neck. Below Eshland, the unparalleled splendour of the southern grasslands spread. It looked like an emerald leaf threaded with the bright blue veins of rivers. Their sources sprang from the distant plateau Leaper could never explore, not just because of duties owed to the Temple, but because of the curse laid on him by Ulellin.

He sat on the broken-branch platform outside the secret, orchid-screened entrance to the place he'd longed to bring Ilik, and resisted the urge to bawl like a baby once more. It wasn't really over yet. He hadn't really tried to persuade her, and he was practically the most persuasive person in the whole of Canopy. Part of what he had hoped for was that she'd make the suggestion to elope by herself; clearly that wasn't going to be the way of it, so he would bring all his charisma to bear.

I convinced the Godfinder to take me to Canopy. I convinced Airak to accept me, even after failing the Temple's tests, even though I was born and raised a birth-magic adept in a bole beneath Audblayinland. I've convinced Aforis to forgive a hundred transgressions, and I've convinced the mighty god of lightning himself to forgive a thousand more.

I can convince my lover to leave the dimwit she calls king.

He crawled, yawning, under the orchids and entered the dwelling. Removed the silver earrings and finger rings that had almost lost him his life in Airakland and set them on a sideboard.

After I've had a full night's sleep.

The paired thieves' lanterns he'd used to stock the house with stolen luxuries shone brightly on the cloak hooks in the entry hall.

Maybe two nights. Airak will expect that I've carried his letter personally to the fruit Temple. No need to disabuse him of that notion.

Leaper woke a long time later in the floating, feather-mattressed bed. Guaiacum fragrance surrounded him. Its layered swirls of orange-brown and darker greenish-brown were soothing. The bedroom walls were lumpy, but he'd hollowed and polished them with his own hands.

He drew the clock spring out of his pocket and stared at it for a while.

Maybe I shouldn't take it to her. Maybe I should stay away until she pines for me.

Until she comes to me.

No. Acting like a petulant child would not help. Leaper didn't want to remind her of the ten years' age difference between them. In terms of athleticism, he compared favourably against her husband, but in terms of maturity, he was afraid he did not.

She doesn't think I need her.

Of course he did. He simply hadn't revealed the extent of his need to her. He would face his fears, if weakness was what would win her over. He would cry in her presence and beg with all the desperation he possessed. He'd give her one of his thieves' lanterns and send her scrolls of tearstained poetry.

That'll make a nice contrast to a king who can barely spell his own name.

Leaper put the clock spring back into his pocket, feeling drunk with hope and despair. He picked up one of the paired lanterns, wrapped it, and fixed it to his belt. There was enough potion of the winds left to see him swiftly to Airakland.

As he ran, he reconsidered the tears and poetry plan. Perhaps there was something else she needed, in order to choose him over King Icacis.

She thought the king needed her love and loyalty. Why was that important? For his sake, or because love and loyalty would allow King Icacis to do his best for the people of Airakland? Perhaps she suspected that Leaper's interference in palace matters was in aid of those same people, but she didn't know. Not for sure. Instead of acting in front of her, instead of trying to manipulate her, maybe all he really had to do was tell the truth about what he'd been doing all this time.

Maybe actual truth was the answer.

When he reached the palace, however, it was to discover King Icacis in crimson mourning robes and the hallways bristling with spears. Through a red glaze of terror, he managed to elicit the cause.

While Leaper was sleeping in his secret love nest, Queen Ilik had been murdered.

FOUR

IN SHOCK, Leaper stood alone among the gossips of the court in the hall of mirrors, holding the now-useless clock spring loosely in one hand.

Scalped by a barbarian in her own palace, one of the old women had whispered. *Blood all over her bedchamber, still fresh!* She'd been unable to tell him much more. Only that the king was carrying chunks of the queen's hair around in his hands, and it wasn't right, it wasn't natural, and why hadn't that barbarian taken the hair with him, it being all bound up in precious metal and stones like that?

Leaper understood much, much more.

He understood that the queen had been killed because of him.

They are not to be found, Ootesh had warned him all those years ago. *And you ought not to look for them, lest you lose your hair for transgressing. By that, of course, I mean lose your life.*

Leaper had ignored the warning. He'd stolen the Old God's bone and used it. It had amused him to share a secret language with the queen, but somehow, somebody had overheard her speak it. Somehow, news had reached the Crocodile-Riders of Floor, and they'd sent an assassin, an executioner, to take her hair.

To take her life.

That was why the killer hadn't cared about the diamonds.

Ilik loved them.

Ilik had loved them.

"The king will see you now," a palace servant said, opening the doors to the royal audience chamber. Leaper hadn't asked to see the king. Confused, he wandered into the cavernous hollow; it was hung with silver lanterns and still smelled, after generations, of sinus-clearing eucalyptus.

The green dais stood empty. Icacis, king of Airakland, slumped in a corner with his back to the wall, holding something in his huge hands that looked like a dead animal in a silver net.

Leaper wanted to retch on the rich, green carpet when he realised what it was. He pulled the cloth wrapping from his head, hesitating to approach the hunch-shouldered shape of the king, some part of his mind reminding him that he was supposed to stand lower than Icacis at all times.

"Come here," the king rumbled, lifting a tearstained face. His eyes were bloodshot. "Ever has the Lord of Lightning speedily answered my prayers. He's sent you to find and punish the queen's killer."

The truth that Leaper had arrived by coincidence and had no instructions from the Temple in this matter was on the tip of his tongue. Leaper swallowed it.

"Yes, Your Highness," he said, squeezing the clock spring tightly.

"What's your name? I've seen you before."

"One who walks in the grace of Airak is known as Servant Leaper, Your Highness." The words came woodenly. "If the queen's killer is to be brought to justice, I must know everything that you know." If anyone had heard Leaper speaking the language of the Crocodile-Riders, if he was to be rightly blamed for this disaster, it would be best to know at once. "Where's your vizier? Has he spoken to the servants?"

"Nobody saw anything. Nobody knows anything." Icacis raised his hair-filled fist. "All that was left behind was my wife's hair. Her blood. A knife made from the jawbone of a crocodile, with the teeth still in and covered in more blood." Leaper suppressed a shudder at the mention of the word "crocodile." "My vizier, may Airak have mercy on me for my weakness, has taken tribute to the Temple of Ilan."

"I see." If the goddess of justice was to act, no doubt Leaper would soon feel an irresistible urge to confess.

Nothing.

He would not confess.

If Leaper was guilty of bringing vengeful Floorians to the palace of Airakland, this dumb beast, the king, was guilty of keeping her caged here in ignorance and boredom for the better part of her too-short life. Anger flared in Leaper's chest. It must have shown on his face.

"Airak have mercy on me," Icacis said again, desperately, attributing Leaper's anger to the jealousy of a rival god. "Speak to the servants. Speak to anyone you wish. Take as many of my soldiers as you need."

"Indeed," Leaper said icily, "this insult must be answered. Without your wife to produce heirs, who will inherit the kingdom?"

"No. That is furthest from my thoughts. No!" The king shook his head deliriously. "I've known for years that Ilik and I would have no children. My mother sent to Ulellin to find out the fates of my brother and me, to discover what would become of our line. The wind goddess prophesied that when I died without direct descendants, blood of a slave would take my throne." He shook his head and lowered his fist in a moment of regretful clarity. "You must not repeat what I have just said, except at the request of our god, Servant Leaper."

"My lips are sealed, Your Highness," Leaper said by rote, thinking, *Blood of a slave! My mother was a slave. It should have been my children, mine and Ilik's!* "But I don't believe Ulellin's prophecies can be trusted absolutely." *How is my heart's desire supposed to leave me for another now? She's dead.* "Perhaps we think we remember them correctly, when actually we've muddled them, reversed them, or heard them wrong."

"One who walks in the grace of Ulellin," a steely woman's voice interrupted sternly, "will not tolerate the airing of such blasphemies in her presence. Not even, and especially, from the lips of one who serves He of Black and Silver."

Leaper bowed to a diminutive woman with blackbean-lustrous skin. She was crowned in polished green glass and clad in fresh, new, spring leaves sewn together with sky-blue silk. Her feet were bare beneath her leaf-gown, but a slave had strewn white ulmo petals in the doorway for her to walk upon.

"Apologies, Highness," Leaper said to Queen Ukillin of Ulellinland. "I didn't realise I was in your presence."

He'd never officially met the royal widow of the wind goddess's realm before, but he had seen her.

Ilik's mother.

Leaper hadn't heard of the goddesses and gods being called by their designated colours before, but noted the old queen's declarative fashion choice.

"Ulellin *told* one who walks in her grace the name of her youngest daughter's destined husband, mere moments after that youngest daughter's birth," Ukillin went on, crushing petals underfoot as she made her way stiffly towards Icacis and his grisly trophy. "All six of my daughters were matched in like fashion. None of the husbands named by the goddess refused the matches. Ulellin's prophecies always come true, and that is how I know my youngest daughter is alive."

Leaper gasped at the assertion, but the old queen had eyes only for her son-in-law.

"My heart leaps to believe you, mother-of-my-wife," King Icacis said, knuckles white around the jewelled coif, "but tell me plainly what it is the wind goddess has prophesied."

"Ilik will build palaces," Ukillin intoned, raising eyes and palms to the ceiling, "with her own two hands."

"Were those words also spoken by the side of the birthing bed?" Leaper asked sceptically, thinking, *So many years ago, your prophecy is older than mine, and stinks worse!*

But the king and queen ignored him, and Icacis laughed hollowly and led the queen to a side wall of the chamber. Still holding Ilik's hair in his left hand, he used his right to tear down a painted paperbark hanging; there was a sealed doorway behind it. Leaper stiffened. He should have known it was there.

"What is this?" Ukillin demanded.

"I'll show you," Icacis answered. "Have your slave help me to open it."

"Better yet. Have your pet Servant open it by magic."

Leaper glared at her. He stepped up to the blocked door and traced it with his fingertips in an eerie echo of the way he'd contemplated the blocked clockmaker's workshop in Eshland. This was no magical regrowing, but a poor imitation of boards, pegs, and dowels. Sap set into the cracks had hardened decades ago, but a focused application of Airak's power could soften it.

The aged cement sizzled away under his hand, and the king helped Leaper pull the wooden plug out of place.

Inside was a child's playroom. Musty and windowless, it was filled with candle hollows and bright-painted chests. Shelves held colourful, illustrated scrolls, clay blocks wrapped in waxed paper, ground-up paint pigments, clamps, glue pots, and woodcarving tools. Sketches of tree-cradled castles remained, including one of the old Temple of Airak. Leaper had come to Canopy after that Temple was destroyed, but he recognised it from its model, delicately made and jewel-encrusted, which the god Airak kept in his treasure room.

"You knew from the morning of her birth who she would marry," King

Icacis said dully, "so you sent her here when she was still a child. Eight monsoons, she'd seen, and she worshipped Ulellin."

"That's why I sent her," Ukillin said. "She needed to learn to worship Airak. To feel at home in this wretched place."

"She built palaces in this room. My mother discovered them. She had a fondness for gambling, my mother, and had lost a small fortune on the Games in Orinland. Ilik's beautiful miniatures were exactly what she needed to buy back Airak's favour."

Leaper was horrified to realise that the model in Airak's treasure room had been made by Ilik. *And she never told me.*

"Indeed," Ukillin said, nostrils flared, arms folded.

"Ilik was distraught. She withdrew into herself. She didn't speak for many months. My mother, when she couldn't encourage the child to resume her work, had the room sealed. Ilik showed no further interest in creation while my mother lived. Some years ago, when she started her clock collection, I thought it a sign she had forgiven me at last for my dead mother's failings. It was most encouraging to see her tinker with them. But you see, mother-of-my-wife, she has already built palaces with her own two hands. Some remain at the Temple, if you'd care to look upon them."

Leaper couldn't stay in the same room with them—Ilik's playroom—a moment longer.

He left the bereft king still gripping Ilik's sawn-off hair, eyeing the flustered face of the widowed queen in denial, and went to witness whatever there was to witness in the bedchamber.

Steeling himself, he stepped through the main front entrance to her rooms, an entrance he'd never used openly before.

For once, the gossips were right. There was blood. Great streaks and clots of it, culminating in the stained sill of the wide, lightning-bolt-shaped window that faced Airak's charred Temple.

Leaper leaned over the edge, jaw clenched, to see if anything below could have broken her fall.

Nothing.

Back at the side table, he found the gore-splattered crocodile-toothed weapon beside the broken soapstone clock.

The desire to smash the clock against the floor was powerful.

I should have been here. To protect her.

But how, without using my magic to kill? If I had been here and tried to stop the assassin with physical force alone, it'd be me with my windpipe sawn open by a crocodile jawbone. Me thrown out the window.

At least she would've had a chance to run.

She was innocent. I was the one who stole that speaking-bone.

Leaper set the replacement spring down on the table.

She hadn't been innocent, he realised. Neither had he. She'd gone to her grave without being found out by one who should have ruled her heart.

It was time for Leaper to face Airak, god of lightning, who should have ruled his.

FIVE

THERE WAS no sign of Aforis at the Temple.

Midday sun in a clear sky blazed over the scorched emergent. Leaper greeted the sentry Skywatchers at the glass gate. They pulled the smooth, silent obsidian mirror back on its green hinges to allow Leaper through.

They murmured things to him, but he didn't hear. Whatever expressions they wore for Leaper to read, to learn what punishment to expect after a three-day absence, he didn't see. Would he have been this excoriated by the death of the god he served?

No. I wouldn't. Which means my service is a lie. I don't deserve the gifts Airak has given me. I've always been faking. My whole life in Canopy is a lie.

His body made automatic turnings in the blue-lit halls. His feet left heavy prints in the black sand underfoot.

I'm going to leave him. If there is a way to leave his service. Maybe death's the only way out. Either way, I'm going to go back into darkness where I belong, the darkness where I stole from Floorians and sentenced the queen to death. Anger warred with self-recrimination. *And then I'll make them pay, lawful sentence or not, for moving against a Servant of the lightning god.*

A queue of slaves and citizens waited at the entrance to the god's open-roofed tribute hall. The hall was where Airak met with mortals and made pronouncements over the future of people's vulnerable homes, livestock, and crops. Their hands were heaped with goods to gift. Some of the slaves looked bone-weary, as if they'd trudged along for a week or more. Not everyone had access to the potion of the winds. Not everyone could afford to take lodgings.

Leaper strode past them to the head of the line. More Skywatchers waited there. Their job was to admit worshippers one by one. He expected them to stop him. He expected anything—a sarcastic rebuke, an order to wait in his room for Aforis, a banishment from the Temple—except for what he got, which was the opening of the door and an immediate indication that he should proceed.

Inside, blinding light. A crackling assault on his ears. An ordinary citizen would have scrambled for the exit. Leaper's stride never faltered.

Airak stood alone, arms raised, in the centre of the room. A tall, hairy, broad-shouldered man, he was wrapped from chest to knees in black silk. He was barefoot. The left half of his body was black-skinned. The right half was unnaturally white. His outstretched fingers reached marginally higher than the branching silver headdress that he wore.

A continuous stream of lightning connected his palms to a clear glass globe. It was as wide as his arm-span and hovered three body lengths above his head.

It was a work in progress. Magic speared through Leaper's awareness; he smelled the sinter, sweat, and salt seeped into the fragrant wood floor, sensed the charge flickering over the silk and metal of the headdress, over the god's curly, fireproof locks.

"Holy One," Leaper said.

Heat radiated from the glass globe. It compressed and revolved, warped and changed form, until it was shaped like a round shield, or a mango stone, thicker in the middle and dangerously thin at the edges.

Leaper knelt at Airak's back. He lowered his head in deference, but he could still see the god's feet, one white and one black.

The feet turned. Leaper sensed the hovering glass object turning, too.

"Eyes up, Servant Leaper," Airak said. "Arms up."

Leaper obeyed. The glass object floated down towards him. It landed, flattened side down, across his outstretched forearms, burning his skin with a horrible hiss and, a moment later, searing agony.

"My arms, Holy One," Leaper gasped.

"Oh, can you feel them?" Airak asked, his power still bearing most of the weight of the transparent shield. "Do they trouble you?"

"Yes!"

"Is the pain of the body greater than the pain of your loss?"

Leaper wanted to laugh and cry at once. So Airak had known. Of course he had known.

"Mercy, Holy One. Please."

He was trapped, kneeling. All he could do was continue to slowly smoulder and stare upwards, confused, into Airak's face.

"The spark is in you," Airak said, and Leaper thought he meant the lightning; then he realised his master meant the spark of life. "You move and speak. Sing and steal. Prepare yourself to abandon me for the arms of Queen Ilik." Leaper opened his mouth to explain himself, but no words came out. "I knew. Aforis knew. And now you want to live."

"Where is Aforis?" The thought, and the words, formed with difficulty around the distraction of the searing surface of the glass sticking to his charred skin. Leaper would have liked to say farewell to his mentor. Instead, he was going to be melted down into glue while his god interrogated him.

"Not here. Looking for you."

"Looking for me?" The sensation of hot nails was fading. Maybe the damage was too severe for him to feel anymore. He didn't dare look away from Airak. "Where?"

"In Audblayinland." The god loomed like a harrier over a trapped snake. "Perhaps he thought you'd seek confirmation of Ilik's rebirth. Perhaps he thought you'd seek your fathers. They're greater hunters and trackers than you are. They could help with the search for the queen's killer. Aforis knew of your obsession with her. He would have forced you to desist. It was I who forbade him from doing so. I allowed it to continue."

"But why?"

"Lightning blazes bright and is gone." Airak's dark eye flashed. "Blackness is left behind. All my best Servants have lost the thing they loved most. It gives them greater mastery."

Leaper gaped, suddenly suspicious and angry.

"How could you know that I'd lose her? Did you . . . ? Was it you who killed her?"

"No." Airak lifted his chin. "I'll help you find her killer if you choose to live. If you choose to die, I'll help you with that, too. So, I'll ask you again, is the pain of the body greater than the pain of your loss? Do you still care for your mortal form, with its scars, with its memories, or would you rather death by the will of Atwith and rebirth from your sister Audblayin this day?"

Leaper's despairing thoughts about wanting to die evaporated. His arms *really* hurt. The idea of being reborn was not remotely tempting, not when he considered the full implications: All of Ilik's secrets, all the things he knew about her that nobody else knew, would be erased if both were to be reborn in the same day. She would be twice as dead.

"I care," Leaper said. "I don't want to die."

SIX

AIRAK CALLED his Shining One into the chamber.

Leaper waited, trembling under the weight of the glass, in pain.

Ousos entered by a smaller, rear door; the door Leaper used when returning from his more secretive forays into Canopy.

She was middle-aged. Stocky. Muscular beneath the fat. Her knotty, un-kempt hair covered her shoulders, half white, half black. She carried two lanterns and half a dozen axes on her person at all times, and she slowly, idly chewed nothing with her greenish teeth when she wasn't speaking. In the course of their lessons with her, during their Skywatcher days, the odd habit had driven Leaper and the other students to distraction.

She ducked her head in deference to the god.

"Yes, Holy One?" Ousos spoke with one side of her mouth, as if keeping her imaginary cud in the closed half. As always, she was difficult to understand without paying close attention. Leaper had once remarked to Ousos that she had not been chosen for the Hunt in which his sister, Imeris, had been chosen; the bruise Ousos had given him on the jaw with her axe handle had been easy enough to understand.

"Carry the lens, Ousos, if you would." Airak took a step back from Leaper, to give his Shining One room to remove the glass burden from Leaper's arms. Leaper cried out sharply as Ousos pulled it away from his ruined flesh; her hands were gloved in dayhunter leather, and she seemed not to feel the heat. "Come along, Leaper."

Airak led them both out the rear door. The tunnel there ran down and around, coming out onto a nondescript, little-used branch road Leaper hadn't really paid attention to before. It was half hidden in the shadow of a wider, parallel branch road running directly above it.

While the higher road was a branch originating from the Temple, the smaller, lower road was a yellowrain branch. It connected, even further down, to the trunk of a tree too narrow to be used for any real purpose; at least, that was what Leaper assumed. It was barely six or seven paces across. Any attempt to build in the little yellowrain sapling would surely end in disaster come the wind and rain of the monsoon.

Confused, his forearms throbbing, cracking and stiffening—*I agreed to live, aren't you going to let me go and get this seen to by a healer?*—Leaper followed Airak and Ousos into the tree. He should have been warned by the fierce glow emanating from the open doorway.

Inside, the little yellowrain tree had been hollowed into a perfect cone, widest at the top and narrowest at a round opening within arm's reach above Leaper's head. He had to squint to look at it. Lightning flowed continuously through the hollow trunk. No, it wasn't lightning. There was no smell of ozone. No sense of magic.

It was sunlight, magnified by a transparent glass shield shape high above them.

"Put the lens in place," Airak instructed his Shining One. Ousos pushed the glass shield into a groove that ran around the rim of the aperture.

At once, the beam of light narrowed. It focused onto a place on the floor that, Leaper was now able to see, was set with green-veined marble.

"Holy One?" he asked tentatively, baffled as to what he was meant to see. All he could think of was that Airak, having scorched him with hot glass, now intended to set fire to him using this light-focusing torture mechanism.

"This is my seeing tree, Leaper," Airak answered, putting his hand out to keep Leaper back from the dangerous beam of light. "Canopians are complacent. They buy my favour, but they forget to watch the sky. Danger comes from all directions. My seeing tree can't be used in daylight, because of the sun. At night, however"—he jerked his chin to indicate the marble— "this stone opens. I go below, to the observing room. There, I can keep watch on my enemies, who stole my lanterns and fled with them into the sky."

Ousos spat into the beam, showing what she thought of her master's enemies. Her spit landed on the marble in the full glare of the sun and turned to steam within seconds.

"I don't have prescient dreams." Airak lowered his arm. "I can't make prophecies. All I can do is watch, and when I can't watch, set a watch on people and places of great importance."

"Do you mean important people like Queen Ilik, Holy One?" Leaper struggled to ignore the pain, to think.

"Do you suppose nobody besides yourself was watching her?" Airak answered.

"Of course," Leaper said. He shook his head. "She was watched. We both were." Anger stirred in him again, that his master had watched his betrayal and said nothing. Had it been convenient, to have Leaper tied even more tightly to the palace? What had Airak planned to do if Ilik and Leaper eloped to Eshland?

But then his anger was diverted by the thrust of the god's question.

Do you suppose nobody besides yourself was watching her?

Leaper's seared arms demanded attention. He tried to focus.

"So?" Airak said expectantly. "My people guarded her. You guarded her. The king guarded her. How did she come to harm?"

"From below!" Leaper exclaimed. Once again, he found words trying to form in his mouth: a confession about the Crocodile-Riders he'd slighted, about the speaking-bone he'd stolen and the secret language he used with the queen. Once again, no words came out.

Airak inclined his head slightly, the silver prongs of his headdress lowering like the horns of an animal offering challenge.

"From below," he agreed. "A strong barrier makes us complacent. Danger comes from all directions. Go to the healer. Have those burns salved and wrapped. Then meet me on the high platform of the Temple."

Leaper quickly left his master and the little yellowrain tree behind.

Habit. Obedience. Pain. Indecision.

The healer took one look at Leaper's burns and pursed her lips.

"I think that's a little beyond salving," she said. "If I don't use the magic of another niche, it's beyond saving. He wants you to remember the pain, but he doesn't want the inconvenience of injury. The real question is, rejuvenation or justice?"

"I don't understand what you're asking," Leaper admitted.

She loomed and looked down at him, piercingly.

"I have one medicine here," she said, "from the realms of the birth goddess. I have another medicine from the realm of the goddess of justice. The former will heal you completely. But you could lose those climbing spines from Understorey that you treasure. Viper's fangs, aren't they? They'd be ejected in the healing process. The latter medicine will bring you justice.

That is to say, if your wounds are more severe than you deserve, they will be reduced accordingly. If not, nothing will happen. Or they could be made worse."

Leaper swallowed.

"Our master trained me to lie," he said. "He made me lie. Not just to kings and queens but to goddesses and gods. I lied to him. Is he so different?"

"Lies? Is that all?" The healer raised an eyebrow.

"I . . . I was going to leave him. As I once left Audblayin, under whose auspices I was born." *No reason to leave him now. No danger that I'll reoffend. He said he'd help me find Ilik's killer.* "He never stopped me. For ten years, he watched and waited, to test my loyalty. To teach me a lesson. I'll take that medicine from the realm of justice."

It was bitter, and only the deepest pain faded, but Leaper's spines stayed fixed in the bones of his forearms. The healer assured him the salve would take care of the rest.

With time.

Leaper dragged himself up the final flight of winding stairs, supplied with salve and wattle leaves for washing, to the high platform of the Temple, to keep his appointment with the lightning god.

Airak waited there in full sun. His robes billowed, and his shadow fell over the polished floodgum like the gnomon of a sundial. Ousos flanked him, as did his tall, slender Bodyguard, Eliligras. The high platform, built around the jagged, blackened end of the tallest branch of the tallest tree in Canopy, swayed in the slightest breeze.

Leaper fought the desire to empty his already-empty stomach. His arms were numbed by the unguents of the healer, beneath bandages that reminded him of the assailant with the hook. If his wounds became infected, as that man's had, he, too, could lose one hand, or both. Would that be justice?

"Holy One," he said, kneeling on the edge of the marble bowl that was set into the floor of this platform. As with most platforms, they were crucibles for placing black sand or other raw materials to be transformed by lightning.

"Stand," Airak said, and Leaper obeyed.

Around them, all of the forest and the lands beyond were visible. Past all of Canopy, over the northern horizon, lay the sea. To the south lay grasslands and the distant plateau. Leaper had avoided the high platform as much as possible during his service. Ulellin's curse on him, he had believed, would prevent him from ever seeing those other lands. It was no use gazing at them and wondering. Better to gaze into the endless depths of Ilik's eyes.

Now Ilik's eyes were closed forever. Leaper looked into Airak's mismatched ones. There was no curse that concerned him anymore. He was free.

Free to do exactly what he was ordered to do.

"King Icacis," Airak said, "sent a messenger to the Temple as soon as his wife's murder was discovered."

"Yes, Holy One." Leaper said stupidly. *I pretended to be your response.*

"He asked for a Servant to help hunt down her killer."

"Yes."

"I sent Eliligras." Leaper's eyes focused on the Bodyguard at that piece of information. Her hair was cut close to her head, half white and half black as usual but divided by a thin section dyed red. The shafts of the paired javelins shackled by her bony hand were stained red as well. "Eliligras arrived at the palace only moments after you left."

"One who walks in the grace of Airak had no intention, Holy One, of—"

"Eliligras," Airak interrupted sharply. "Place the thing you carry into the bowl at my feet."

The thing that Eliligras unwrapped from her belt pouch and placed in the marble bowl was the crocodile mandible that had been used to cut Ilik's throat.

Leaper swayed.

Or perhaps the platform swayed.

Or perhaps the whole world.

"Lightning," Airak said, "doesn't strike just anywhere. Lightning has an origin and a destination. Watch the skies, Leaper. Watch the land. For you, for the sake of what you've lost, I'll connect this weapon with the place where it was last purchased. The place where it last changed hands. I will send you, as you wish, on a quest for revenge."

"Yes, Holy One." Anticipation made his legs tremble.

Or perhaps the platform did.

"In payment," Airak said, relentless, "if you return, when you return, you, or another with gifts equal to yours, will serve me with your whole heart. You, or that other, will swear your oaths a second time and be more deeply and tightly bound by them than any of my Servants has ever been bound before."

"Yes, Holy One."

"Take a step back. Watch the skies. Watch the land."

Leaper did as he was commanded. Heart in his mouth, certainty in his mind, he turned a fraction towards the north.

North is where the Crocodile-Riders live. Airak will strike the heart of the forest, marking the guilty ones, fixing them like a grub under a bore-knife.

North.

Lightning sprang up from the bloody jawbone, which turned to ash in an instant.

It fountained upward, splitting the sky. It curved. It crackled. Stray filaments escaped, but there was no mistaking where the bulk of the deadly shaft descended.

Directly to the west. Far from the edge of the forest.

West.

Leaper was wrong about the Crocodile-Riders. He was wrong about everything.

"Gui," Ousos remarked, and spat. "That filthy squeezing trader town."

"Gui," Airak agreed. "Leaper, you'll use the storeroom lantern. Send a message to our factor in Gui, demanding not a delivery, but an escort. I don't care how they feel about Canopians trespassing on their soil. If they'd rather we attacked Gui from here with more lightning strikes like that one, let them refuse."

"Yes, Holy One."

"Pack lightly for your journey. Arrange to meet your guide at the roots of this tree. And, Leaper. In addition to finding satisfaction for King Icacis, there is another task, from me. None of us felt any breach in the barrier that a Floorian killer could have used. Find out how it was done."

"As you wish, Holy One."

"You'll go with him, Ousos," Airak added. The Shining One's eyes went wide with surprise before they narrowed at Leaper in apparent hatred.

"Yes, Holy One," she said.

"Won't you need her to make lanterns, Holy One?" Leaper blurted out, equally surprised.

"Maybe she'll make better lanterns," Airak said lightly, turning to go, "after a few moons in the Sneak Thief's company. She has no divided loyalties, Leaper. Have a care that you do not betray me again."

SEVEN

LEAPER STAYED, staring at the place where the lightning had landed, long after Airak and Eiligras had left.

The sun sank towards the west.

West.

Not north.

The weapon that killed her came from the west.

"Jump," Ousos suggested, bumping roughly up beside him. Her shoulder was at the level of his elbow. "Quickest way to get down there."

"We buy sand from Gui," Leaper said, ignoring her spite. If the Crocodile-Riders were innocent, he had to work out a new connection between himself, the merchants of Gui, and the queen of Airakland.

Some motive that made sense. Some explanation whereby he would still be to blame, because he was always to blame, wasn't he? The Temple wasn't the only customer of the affable-seeming agents of Gui. Icacis's palace did business with them, and no doubt there were other glass guilds or independent manufacturers, too. Leaper had used the Temple contact, Slehah, to bring him Tyran's Talon, the bone that enhanced his lightning powers. Who else had bribed Slehah to break forest laws; where else did she owe her loyalty? Was it as simple, as coincidental, as a trade negotiation gone wrong?

"Sure are a quick one," Ousos said, spitting.

He turned to face her. Loathing still distorted her nose and mouth.

"Why don't you want to go?" he asked sarcastically. "Might be a good opportunity to knock me on the head with one of those axes."

"I had a sister," she said, greenish teeth showing as her lip curled. "She had bad dreams. When we were both little ones. Dreams so bad, she'd wake up choking. Imaginary hands at her throat. Odel couldn't help. Ulellin couldn't help. None of our immortal lords or ladies have the power to control dreams. 'Try this dreamer's ti from Gui, one of the market slaves says. Oh, it's wonderful for dreams.'"

Leaper looked into her flinty eyes and didn't dare say what he knew was coming.

"Killed her, didn't it?" Ousos barked. "Not right away. Bit by bit. She needed more and more. More than what we could get in the market. Had to buy it direct, passed through the barrier, and they wanted a danger tax, didn't they, those squeezing dick-fleas from Gui? Said they'd be killed by Rememberers, or Understorians, if they got caught in the trees or on the Floor."

"I'm sorry," Leaper said, though he didn't feel sorry. She wasn't real to him in that moment; less than a leaf shadow, with a shadow axe. *Was Ilik trading something illegal through the barrier?*

Ousos took a step back from him and dusted her hands off dramatically.

"I don't buy from them of Gui. Won't talk to them, even. M'Lord Airak knows that. He makes sure Eliligras or Aforis is always between them and me. Guess he knows some of them'll need to die, this time." She fondled her axes.

Leaper said nothing.

"Guess he knows you're too much of a dick-flea to do any killing," Ousos added.

Leaper tried to recall if he'd ever spoken of his secret oath against violence to the lightning god.

It was after he'd summoned lightning to slay Orin's monster during the great Hunt with Imeris. Only, the monster wasn't born a monster. It was an amalgamation of Orin's Servants, whom the goddess believed had betrayed her. As Leaper's power had run over them and through them, Leaper had smelled their fear; not of death but of leaving loved ones behind forever. Of mouths sealed by boar bristles and blood that would never say things that needed to be said. He had smelled the scalps of newborns they would never bear and tasted the kisses of their dreams, and as the life had leached away from them, as the rot washed over their yearnings, he had known regret so deep and unbearable that his own next breath had come as a surprise to him.

Soon enough, the goddess Ulellin had come to lay a curse on him, temporarily distracting him from the horror of his deed. Yet it haunted him.

"I guess," Ousos said, turning him forcibly around and giving him a little push towards the ladder, "we ought to get started. Send that message to the sand seller. Get your things together."

"I guess we ought," Leaper agreed, wrapping his elbows clumsily around the ladder edges, stopping and grimacing at the pain. He didn't want to climb down. He wanted to catch his breath. The world was moving on, but Ilik had stopped as surely as her clock. Ousos was behind him, and he had to talk to her, but words deserted him until he called on his catalogue of identities and pictured the bold brilliance of the suntree, letting courtliness take over his tongue. "Shining One, I confess to weakness. You're going to have to help one who walks in the grace of Airak to get down. Not only from the Temple, but from Canopy. Far be it for one who walks in Airak's grace to question him, but I fail to understand why our Holy One hobbled me this way, when he intended all along that I should seek the queen's murderer."

Did the god intend all along that Leaper should fall in love with the queen? That his own inclination to break into the palace undetected would position him to be a superior spy?

You can have it back, Aforis had said ten years ago, *on the condition that you immediately return the pocket-clock you stole to its rightful owner, the queen of Airakland.*

When he'd returned the clock, Leaper had spied on its rightful owner, or at least her bouncing bottom and the dimples in the backs of her thighs as she scrabbled, half-naked, under the bed for a dropped sash. Once she was dressed, he'd been delighted by the sounds she'd made on discovering the lost pocket-clock, and struck by how she'd opened, checked, disassembled, and reassembled it, hypnotic in her earnest concern and proficiency. He wished he'd hidden something interesting inside for her to find.

A puzzle for her to solve.

I will find your killer, Ilik.

"He did it to make you grateful," Ousos sneered as she seized Leaper by the harness, half turning, half lowering him onto the rungs, "when you get the use of them bone-stabbers back. Besides, you won't need them when we get to Floor. A man needs legs when he finds dirt. A woman, too."

"A man needs legs and also needs a woman?"

She slapped him on the back of the neck where he was bruised and burned.

"You know what I squeezing meant. Besides, this way you can't climb back up without me. Won't be no giving up and going home until I say it's time to give up and go home. Holy One knows you're a coward."

HOURS LATER, Ousos seized his harness again.

She grunted as she lowered him, fastened him, lowered him, and fastened him again. She had to work twice as hard with rope and pulley, but they were rarely on a level, and after a while, in the dark, with her lanterns above him no brighter than a break in the foliage to sky, he could forget that she was there. He could examine his own confusion. Take a moment to catch his breath.

He gave himself permission to cry again, but when tears didn't come, he forced himself to wallow in the memory of Ilik's smell, in the sound of her laugh, to try to bring them back. He couldn't possibly be done with tears already, could he?

How can it have been true love, if that's it? Ilik's husband had seemed completely incapacitated by the loss. No doubt King Icacis was still clutching the diamond-woven hair in his audience chamber. Something had to be fundamentally lacking in Leaper's lowborn slave's mind and body, after all. Maybe that was the jest of the wind goddess's prophecy. Maybe he'd never been capable of a heart's desire, because he was actually heartless.

Ousos bumped into him, scraping him against the bark. Wheezing, she unfastened him from the steel wedge she'd driven into the tree. Lowered him deeper into the black. He jerked when he reached the end of the rope.

He waited for her to remove the wedge and climb down to him. Without spines, because she was Canopian. They did not climb with spines, they climbed with ropes and knots and rings and bends and wedges of metal. That was how upright, gods-fearing, civilised citizens climbed, when they climbed at all.

If I find Ilik's mangled corpse, Leaper wondered as they descended, no closer to untangling his emotions, *will that make me cry? If I go from the roots of the tree, not to Gui, but to the roots of the king's palace, will Ousos put her axe in me?*

Maybe the Rememberers, like the Crocodile-Riders, considered dead flesh to be pollution and avoided it at all costs. Maybe they would be the ones to kill him if he approached the place where Ilik's body had been flung.

Maybe they buried their dead or boarded them up inside trees; maybe they ate them.

Airak doesn't care who is down here. Nor does Ousos.

Nor do I.

Airakland and Odelland were separated by a vast, round grassland that bit into the side of the forest. At the level of Floor, Crocodile-Riders could be found on the northern edge of that grassland, while Rememberers could be found on the southern edge of it. Leaper knew very little about the Rememberers, who might or might not stand between him and his destination, Gui. Slehah had answered his request for a guide with the pointed reminder that it was only safe for her and her people to approach Airakland in the two weeks before the monsoon. That was when the Rememberers evacuated their ground dwellings and took to their floating boat-houses. That fortnight was when deliveries to Airak's emergent were customarily arranged.

Cannot approach due to Rememberer presence, Slehah had written curtly. *March west ten thousand steps, and I will meet you at the edge of the trees. You will be safe enough if you move in lantern light. Rememberers will not slay Servants of the lightning god.*

No doubt, when he stood face-to-face with them, Rememberer language would come tumbling out of his mouth, but for now, Leaper knew essentially nothing of them besides the name, and he was not even curious about that. What did they remember, and why? Who cared? All he cared to know, if he even encountered any at all, was why they had let Ilik's murderer pass through their territory and what they had done with her body, if they had done anything to it at all. If demons hadn't ripped it apart. If bone women hadn't taken her for a trophy.

None of his grim imaginings were enough.

Leaper looked up, dry-eyed.

Ousos's lantern light, with the woman a ragged half-white, half-black shape within it, came slowly and steadily towards him. Soon they'd be level, and she'd lower him further down again.

His thoughts darted all over the place, like a blowfly unable to settle on just one pile of dung; he wondered who would cry the most if the Crocodile-Riders cut his throat with a jagged jawbone, too.

Oldest-Mother, who had crushed tallowwood leaves into a poultice for his chest when his nose was runny, who was his mother but also his grandmother, with her frightening white hair and terrifying tales of the slave keepers of Canopy? He could picture her face if she discovered he mourned a queen. Queens were all wicked, in her opinion. How could she have helped raise the kind of boy who would fall in love with a queen?

Yet she had fallen in love with Youngest-Mother, who was not far from being a queen. Daughter of a vizier. Beautiful enough to inspire a war. Complicit in slave-keeping. Vibrant with magic and music. Oh, the songs Youngest-Mother had sung over Leaper's cradle. She would sing over the void if he fell, over his death chamber or grave or ashes. She had a soft heart. Surely she would cry the most.

But what of Middle-Mother, who was Leaper's birth mother? She swam with him in the tree hollow, told him he had been a frog in a former life. He had loved that thought, until he found out that Frog was a girl's name. Together they'd made up the names of all his future children: Tadpole, Snake Egg, Millipede, and Fishy.

Middle-Mother had kissed him far too often. He could clearly recall the slobber her loving lips left behind. Yes, she would miss him the most, despite all the messages over the years saying that if he didn't have children soon, his testicles were going to shrivel up and fall off. She would cry, and she would blame Imeris and Middle-Father for encouraging him to go to Canopy in the first place.

How she would punish them, for a decision she'd made herself. Middle-Father would have to join Imeris in her travels. Imeris and Anahah had lived happily in Floor for eight years, before leaving to search for their disappeared daughter, but if anyone could find them, Middle-Father could.

They'd all have to hide from Middle-Mother for years. Decades, even.

Leaper chuckled.

If he died, the Godfinder would cry for him, too, in the secretive, tears-denying, blustery way that she had. *Don't call me Unar! I'm the Godfinder now, and that's what you'll call me, sprout.* She'd been an impatient teacher. Quick to crow at his childish errors. As passionate in her dismay over his failings as she had been bursting with pride when Aforis accepted him, first as a student and secondly, into the Temple.

Aforis.

Aforis would not cry. Aforis had not cried since the murder of his lover some thirty years ago. *I am fading,* he had raged, *I have sixty-two summers, I'll expire presently, and then who will make excuses for you?*

The murder of his lover. Why hadn't Leaper gone to Aforis? Aforis would have understood, could have told him what to do next, how to feel, how to make things right. How to fix them.

Look, that spring is broken in half. A simple matter!

Except that they couldn't be fixed.

I'll have the slaves wind the clock twice a day instead of once. You see? You've been crying over nothing.

EIGHT

Ousos's lantern light fell on one old stranger and one young one.

It was past sunset at this point. Leaper and the Shining One had slept a handful of hours in a bark fold at the base of the tree before taking the dangerous step of actually setting their feet to the soil.

He hadn't slept deeply enough to dream. The pain in his forearms had lessened, though he still had difficulty forming a grip, and he'd needed help uncorking his water gourd and getting undressed when it came to necessary bodily functions.

Ousos allowed him to first search, not for Slehah and the forest's edge, but for the base of the palace floodgum.

They had walked around the tree. In a slow, expanding circle, they'd searched the ground for Ilik's body. One hundred paces from the trunk. Three hundred paces. At six hundred paces, they started finding the trunks of other trees, and Leaper knew they wouldn't find her. Her body had been concealed or moved. Either taken as a grisly trophy or hidden in the emergent.

Afterward, he'd watched in silence as Ousos had gathered up coils of rope and stowed their harnesses. Leaper had made no move to unpack either of his own lanterns from the carrysack strapped to his back, instead staying in the bright, blue-white circle provided by his Temple superior.

You will be safe enough if you move in lantern light. Rememberers will not slay Servants of the lightning god.

Ousos's first magic lantern contained Airak's cold fire; it was suitable for sending messages back to the Temple and for lighting the way. Her second would send out a spark when unshuttered, useful for starting cooking fires but not for keeping back demons. Leaper, in the emotion-filled muddle of his quarters, using his neck and shoulders as much as his elbows and hands to manipulate his belongings, had chosen a chimera-skin-wrapped death-lantern and his thieves' lantern, connected invisibly to the one he'd left in his hidden house in Eshland, as the best tools for facing the threats of Floor.

But it was the blue-white light that had drawn the two men.

They were wide-shouldered and brown-skinned. Both stood solemn and unsmiling, dwarfed by the buttress of a gap-axe tree, barefooted and barechested, wearing identical short leather skirts. The young man's waist-long, straight black hair was caught over his left shoulder in a braided leather cord. The old man, bald but for a white fringe over his ears, held a bark cloak, beautifully patterned, in his wrinkled arms. They were beardless, square-jawed.

Something in their stern serenity made Leaper feel a lump in his throat.

"Good evening to you," Leaper said in no tongue he'd heard spoken before, and the lump vanished like a bird freed from the cage of his larynx. "We are only passing through."

Ousos, wide-legged at his side, left hand holding the cold lantern and right hand lingering near an axe loop, fixed Leaper with a flabbergasted stare.

The man with the bark cloak shook it out gently and settled it over his shoulders.

"I am Wennel, with the Weight of the Westwood behind me," he said in gravelly tones. "Who are you and how have you learned our language?"

The younger man lifted brown, empty, callused hands, to pull his black hair free of the constraining cord. He shook it out, loose, down his back, without his long-lashed, dark eyes ever leaving Ousos and her axe.

"I am Leaper," Leaper answered, once again feeling the lump in his gullet, the lifelong-lingering translation magic he'd stolen from the Crocodile-Riders flowing over him, a river in flood, and, he'd thought when the queen was murdered, not without price. Yet it now seemed Ilik hadn't paid that price with her life, after all.

"What are you saying?" Ousos hissed at him. The language of Canopy grated against Leaper's ears, too trilling and birdlike for this calmer, quieter place of dangerous echoes. Did she want to draw demons to them?

"I am Leaper," Leaper said again, ignoring her, "with the Weight of Airak behind me. I have some words of your language. My sister Imeris and her husband, Anahah, made their home in Floor."

That was true enough, but deliberately misleading.

Imeris, Daggad, and Anahah were the gods knew where, two years into a self-appointed Hunt provoked by eight-monsoon-old Igish, who had transformed into a panther and, without explanation, absconded into the bamboo thickets of the Bright Plain.

"What are you telling him?" Ousos tried again.

A third stranger padded quietly through the soggy leaf litter into the circle of light from Ousos's lanterns. She was taller than the two men. Her black hair was as long as the young man's, braided over her left shoulder. In addition to the short leather skirt, she was covered by a pair of gourds; her breasts had been squeezed into them, and they seemed to stay against her chest of their own accord.

When she saw Leaper and Ousos, she nodded at the old man, then began to unbraid her hair.

"Does your sister dwell among the Rememberers?" Wennel asked.

"No," Leaper admitted. "Gui is our destination. Will you show us the path?"

Wennel and his companions turned their backs on Leaper to confer quietly. It was only then that Leaper saw the glowing symbol burned into the skin between the woman's shoulder blades.

No, not burned. Embedded. Slivers of bone, pressed into the skin like a work of fine marquetry, formed a stylised tree bear.

"Airak's bones," Ousos swore, and that was exactly what was causing the blue glow on the woman's back.

When the stranger finished loosening the braid and threw her hair back, the glow was extinguished, just as it was on the backs of the men.

A signal, to summon others without sound. Or are they all bone men and women, with the god's powers at their command? Leaper shifted uneasily. Perhaps he shouldn't have told them that he served Airak, despite what Slehah had advised.

The Rememberers turned once again towards the intruders. Leaper realised there were two new arrivals. One was a tall, long-necked yet square-headed young woman. She had acne scars on her cheeks, short hair that stuck out in all directions, a suspicious squint, and a weapons belt loaded with one short horn bow and two long, trapezoidal grass-cutting knives.

Her fellow new arrival shared her square head, but there the resemblance ended. A short, pointed beard and sparse moustaches framed a thick-lipped, laughing mouth. His ample bare gut overflowed the ties of his loincloth, and the cloak in his arms looked as though it had been fought over by rival piranha schools. He was the only one shod, in flat-soled sandals with straps that crossed at the calves and tied at the knee.

A leather sash hung over the big man's shoulder. It had seven or ten laced pockets sewn into it; Leaper couldn't be sure if all were pockets; some of them could have been patches, for the sash was as tattered as the cloak. *Thank goodness the loincloth isn't full of holes,* Leaper thought. Unless the pockets were full of tiny throwing knives, the man was unarmed.

"There is one path you may take to Gui," Wennel said. "Estehass and Ellin, brother and sister with the Weight of the Eastwood behind them, will show you the way."

"Many thanks," Leaper said, nodding to the square-headed pair, "for providing us with guides. We are not well acquainted with the customs of Floor, nor its natural dangers."

"What's going on?" Ousos all but shouted, hands on hips, her axe drawn.

"What's wrong with you?" Leaper shouted back, exploding with rage he hadn't realised was simmering inside him. She would not stop talking. Canopian discourse was offensive and unsafe. Translating for her was a waste of time. She didn't need to know what Leaper was saying. She was only there in case the exchange with the enemy came to blows, despite what Slehah had said about Rememberers being reluctant to slay Servants of the lightning god.

"What's wrong with *y*—"

Leaper bent and drove his shoulder into her midriff. All the breath went out of Ousos. He saw her axe blade gleaming by his eye. She could have used it on him.

He wanted her to use it on him.

No, he didn't want her to use it on him. He had to live. To find Ilik's killer.

A knee in his face jarred his eyeballs in their sockets. Blood filled his nose and mouth. Hands held his arms spread-eagled. Pulling him back. Restraining him.

Rememberers.

The enemy had him.

Why wasn't Ousos helping him? He saw her shocked, green-toothed grimace in the lantern light.

"You're not my sister," he bawled, falling to his knees, feeling tears track through the thicker smears of blood on his cheeks. *Here they are, but why now?* "You're not Imeris, and you never will be. Too stupid and slow to be a Hunter. You can't even find animal prey, forget about human. I wish she was here now. She's worth a hundred of you!"

"That's as may be," Ousos said huskily, staring at him, "but your squeezing sister isn't here, so you'd best get used to it. What did them dick-flea dirt-swimmers say to you, to make you crazy all of a sudden?"

Leaper slumped in defeat. His injured arms burned from being stretched. When he met the eyes of Estehass and Ellin in turn, the siblings reluctantly released him.

He scrubbed his wet cheek against one shrugged shoulder and swallowed his sweet-salty blood.

"These two are taking us to Gui," he mumbled contritely. "Try not to do anything in front of them that would reflect poorly on Airak's dignity."

NINE

"So," Ousos said to Leaper as they thrust through a thicket.

Unlike the branch-paths of Canopy or the bridges of Understorey, the trail along the wet dirt of Floor was a mere suggestion of compression. The freedom to step in any direction, the inability to fall, was uncomfortable. Unnatural.

And every direction seemed the same.

The bamboo turned Ousos's lantern light to splayed bars of bluish white, striping Ellin's brown limbs and bared back. Leaper had seen bamboo before, but only as single clumped specimens in cultivated gardens, not erupting like mushrooms from every bare bit of earth.

"So?" he repeated. .

"So they don't squeezing look like Floorians. Why aren't they white? Ask them."

Leaper asked them. The scarred woman, Ellin, only glared back at him from her position in the lead, but behind Leaper, Estehass laughed and answered.

"He says the white-skinned people, the ones that ride birds and eat figs, were brought to the Titan's Forest by the brown-skinned human servants of the immortals," Leaper translated. "The Bird-Riders and Fig-Eaters were refugees fleeing the ruined mountain city, taken captive. He says Crocodile-Riders invaded the roots of the trees from their villages in the Bright Plain, when the rains stopped coming everywhere and only came to the Titan's Forest. There was no choice but for them all to share, he says, but only his people are true forest people. When his ancestors' forest was crushed by the titans, this one sprang up in its place. He says it's theirs to protect now."

Ousos guffawed. Parted a fern frond with her axe. Batted aside a bitter melon vine heavy with long, lumpy, gently curving fruit.

"If all they want is naked dirt and darkness, they're welcome to it."

It wasn't all naked dirt, not anymore. The bare, soggy ground had long since given way to a wet, clinging, relentless undergrowth, which only parted slightly to either side of the so-called path. Leaper, in his grief and exhaustion, had lost track of time. He thought the sun had risen and set while they'd walked in the dark, deep part of the forest and now that it was night again, they were nearer to the edge. His sense of direction was confused. Yet at some point in daylight hours, he suggested to his guide, direct sun must fall on the bamboo, ferns, and wrist-thick creepers that surrounded them.

"Yes," Estehass agreed, "sunlight reaches here." But he would say nothing more. He trod amazingly lightly for such a big man. Bringing up the rear, he practically floated over the deep footprints left by the Canopians. Leaper couldn't at that moment see the glowing sigil in Estehass's back, a snake eating its tail around a five-pointed star, but Ellin's leaping fish was plain.

"What does the symbol on your skin say?" Leaper asked her. Ellin ignored him. "What's the difference between the Eastwood and the Westwood?" She ignored him again. "If you're brother and sister, why are your sigils different?" No answer. "How much longer until we reach Gui?" He didn't mention that he expected to meet Slehah on the way, nor that he hoped to meet the buyer of the crocodile jaw, whom he would make pay.

"What are you asking them?" Ousos asked, and this time Leaper didn't react by assaulting her.

"I'm asking whether we're there yet. Does it seem to you that we should have come out into the open by now?"

"It seems to me that we haven't stopped all day, and my water gourd's almost squeezing empty," Ousos grumbled. "Wonder if the fat man's got snacks in those pockets of his, or if the woman's on heat with a husband at home and that's why we can't take a bit of time to hunt and eat."

Ellin stopped short and turned to face them, her face furious.

"If you did not have the hair, half white and half black," she said in heavily accented Canopian, "I would never believe you were first among a god's slaves."

"We're not slaves," Leaper said calmly, thinking, *Ellin's been able to understand us this entire time. Did I say anything I shouldn't have? Did Ousos?* "But perhaps you were."

Ellin lifted her chin haughtily.

"I have traded emeralds and freshwater pearls for canoe paddles and pulley blocks with the House of Amborab in Eshland. Pretty rocks are yours to own. For the most part, in our territory, there is no light, and what matter how a thing shines where there is no light? We of the Eastwood are not pretty rocks. We are not yours to own. We have never been yours to own. And our wild brothers and sisters are not yours to slay. You will eat in Gui. They understand you there. They discard their dead underneath or on top of the dirt, as you do, instead of lighting fires to bring embracers and send them back into the cycle."

Ousos's fists pressed into the flesh of her hips.

"I'll squeezing eat what and when I squeezing please," she said balefully, "and the when of it is now, or I'm not taking another step. What time do you call this? The boy needs some squeezing sleep."

"Squeezing," Estehass repeated faintly, chortling.

"I'm no boy," Leaper objected as Ellin and Estehass stepped aside from the trail to confer among themselves.

"Does the brother speak our language, too?" Ousos asked Leaper. "Because I can't see him climbing a tree to trade with Eshlanders. Just look at the size of him. Like one of the great trees, isn't he? Solid, real solid. Take a dozen guards to shift him against his will." She winced, as though aware of the weirdness of what she'd said, tugging at her collar and ducking her head.

"No," Ellin said, turning to glare at Ousos. "He does not speak your language. He does not trade."

"What's in the pouches?" Ousos's chin was level again, her eyes full of fire.

"Bones. He is a bone man."

"What the squeeze is a gods-kissing bone man?"

"Why do you say the word 'squeezing' so often?"

Ousos reached for a bitter melon growing beside her and yanked it off the vine. Leaper expected her to hurl it childishly at the other woman. Instead, she bit off and spat out the pointed end. Then she took a wide-legged stance, stuck the fruit under her silver Servant's skirt, and wriggled her buttocks until it had vanished between her legs.

"God's bones," Leaper gasped in Canopian. "Didn't I say nothing that would reflect poorly on—"

After a moment of fierce concentration, Ousos pulled the bitter melon out again. It was crushed into halves. Pulpy in the middle. Barely hanging together by the skin. Leaper was speechless.

"Squeezing," Ousos declared. "It's a skill. Mess with me, and I'll send you back into the cycle."

This time she did fling the fruit, at Ellin's feet.

"Here is not a safe place to stop," Ellin said stonily. "We must go a little further."

"No tricks." Ousos seemed disappointed not to have gotten a better re-action.

"No tricks." Ellin remained grimly focused on their destination. As though she couldn't wait to part company with the Canopians. "We shall camp close by until morning." Ellin turned her back, leading on.

"Squeezing," Estehass said again, this time with awe.

The place Ellin selected was some way to the left of the narrow, over-grown path. A dense stand of bamboo completely encircled a cluster of ten tree ferns. The woody green bamboo stems were twice as tall as the black trunks of the tree ferns, which were themselves twice Leaper's height.

Ellin set about slashing the bamboo at waist height, each stem cut at a sharp diagonal, so that they became a razor ring of upright spears in the ground. She instructed Estehass to find and purify enough water for them all; when he took Ousos's hand and whispered the word "squeezing" invit-ingly in her ear, she let him lead her into the undergrowth, unresisting, leaving both lanterns behind with Ellin and Leaper.

Leaper watched Ellin work, warily. He did not collect bamboo shoots for boiling. Nor did he fold palm fronds or cut bamboo segments into makeshift containers. His arms were ugly, the skin streaked with black, yel-low, and green, bloody in the crevices. Pain shot from wrist and elbow to armpit and shoulder, even at rest. Leaper remembered again the infected wound of the man with the hook and could only hope that the potion of justice had some lingering effect.

He did nothing to help while Ellin cut a fork into the end of a fresh length of bamboo. She used it to trap the head of a black snake, coiled and sleeping in the heart of a tree fern top. Then she decapitated the reptile with the heavy-bladed knife in her other hand.

After she'd skinned and gutted it, she sliced the snake flesh thinly and offered it to him raw. Despite what she'd said about Leaper and Ousos not being permitted to hunt her wild brothers and sisters.

"That lantern," he told her reluctantly, not reaching to take the cold pink flesh, "will start a cooking fire. Even wet wood will burn."

"No fire," Ellin said curtly. "You forget, there are demons. The lights on our skins can be seen by human eyes only, but open flame carries no such protection. We eat raw food. We sleep in the tree fern hearts."

Leaper glanced up at the spreading fronds.

"In the tree ferns?"

"Yes, in them. Where the snake was sleeping. Snakes know as well as people do that needleteeth find the tree fern difficult to climb. The bark is like burned moss. It crumbles." She put her hand to it, to demonstrate. "Even if the spotted swarm smells us, they'll move on. Dayhunters hunt in the day. Obviously. Fiveways prefer the Westwood to the Eastwood." She tapped a spear of bamboo with her knife. "Embracers don't like to crawl over cut bamboo, but they will, if they smell smoke from a fire. You and your friend brought light and heat, which are useless here, but no food." She offered him the snake a second time, tight-lipped. "You need sustenance if you are to go on."

We didn't bring food, Leaper thought, frowning, *because we're supposed to be in Gui by now.* He supposed that, injured, he was moving more slowly, and perhaps Estehass and Ellin were showing them the easier, yet more circuitous way.

"There's one type of demon you left out." Leaper accepted the morsel, resigned to the pain of movement. "You didn't say anything about making us safe from chimeras."

"We just have to take our chances with chimeras."

The meat was almost tasteless, the sample sinewy and peppered with small, sharp bones. Leaper made himself eat some more. It waked his gut, until he was forced to ask Ellin to dig a hole for him to squat over.

By the time Ousos and Estehass returned, bearing bamboo segments brimming with clear water, Ellin had tried and failed to drag Leaper up a leaf-lashed bamboo ladder into one of the tree ferns. It was decided, much to a flushed Estehass's disappointment, that Ousos and Leaper would share one tree fern nest, while the Rememberer siblings shared another.

Estehass crouched down obligingly. Ousos helped Leaper onto the bulky man's shoulders. Then Estehass straightened slowly while Leaper clung painfully to down-hanging tree fern fronds and tried to keep his balance. Ousos scrambled ahead of Leaper, up the bamboo ladder into the black snake's nest, where new, hairy fern fronds remained tightly curled. With Ousos pulling him by the climbing harness and Estehass shoving him by the calves, Leaper was able to tumble awkwardly into his sleeping spot.

Ellin tossed a few bamboo-leaf-wrapped packets up to Ousos, who showed no signs of dismay at the raw snake contents.

"I'll take first watch," the Shining One called down to Ellin, jaw working tenaciously at the rubbery tendons. "Leaper, tell them I'll take first watch."

Leaper told them.

"No," floated Ellin's reply from the ground, where she squatted over the same hole she'd dug for Leaper. "Servants of the lightning god don't know what to watch for. We will watch. I will watch first. Estehass will watch second. You will put out those lights."

Taking a moment to spit with displeasure, Ousos packed her lanterns into her carrysack. She then arranged it for a hard, no doubt uncomfortable pillow. Her curled body took up most of the soft, hairy heart of the top of the tree fern, leaving Leaper to try and find a comfortable position on the unevenly splayed slats of the fronds.

Without the lanterns, the only light came from the glowing sigils on the backs of the siblings in the neighbouring tree fern. When Leaper lifted his head, he saw, turned towards him, Estehass's five-pointed star in its snake circle. Apparently the man was capable of sleeping in a sitting position, fleshy arms wrapped around his knees, back of his black-haired head drooping between them.

Ousos slapped loudly at a mosquito, and it was only then that Leaper realised they were whining all around him. He looked at Estehass a second time, but there was no sign of the insect cloud around the top of the other tree fern. In fact, the bluish glow seemed to banish the bugs.

Their sigils, he thought, unpacking a second silk robe, half black and half white, with its hood and long sleeves, *for human eyes only, aren't just for signalling.* He swapped robes awkwardly, using the shorter one to cover his face below the eyes. *And Ellin won't let us have a fire for its insect-repelling smoke.* Finally, he stuck his bare shins inside his carrysack in an attempt to protect them from bites. Water collected in fallen, broken bamboo. If not for the threat of embracers, it would have been a poor choice of campsite.

"Enjoyably diverted by Estehass, were you?" he whispered to Ousos as she slapped herself again. "I thought you called him a dick-flea dirt-swimmer."

He expected to receive a slap, a curse, or a dismissive snort, but she rolled over so that their faces were half a pace apart, revealing googly, startled eyes.

"I squeezed that gods-kissed bone man," she said. "First squeeze since I made my vows. I promised old Airak no squeezing, and now look what I've done."

He wanted to laugh. What she had done. It was nothing compared to what he had done.

"You're below the barrier." The robe covering his mouth muffled his words, but he knew what he was talking about. The Godfinder had warned him, and he'd found the truth of it himself. "Bonds are weakened. Broken. He'll forgive you."

"Will he? For sure?" She glanced at the silk over Leaper's forearms, where fluid from his burns was beginning to weep through. "Like that? I've seen you shaved before, seen your power drained before, but I've not seen that. That's your forgiveness for squeezing the queen?"

Leaper didn't want to talk about the queen.

"I hope your big bone man was worth it. As nimble off his feet as on them, is he?"

Ousos grimaced.

"Pretty squeezing disappointing, actually. Rather quick. Though he seemed to enjoy himself."

"Did he say so?"

"He said plenty, but I couldn't understand him." She gave Leaper a cool, appraising look. "How'd you learn their language? Aforis did say he was your teacher before you came to the Temple, and what that old bastard doesn't know could fit on a bee's dick. Aforis taught you? You never learned a word from that runaway Hunter, your sister, I know."

"It's a long story."

Her hand flew distractedly to the back of her neck; the whites of her eyes were blue in the light of Estehass's sigil as she glanced across the gap between tree ferns at his slumped shape.

"We lay down in a kind of mud wallow. I think a boar had it for a nest. I've got ticks crawling all over me. I didn't see any on him."

Leaper wriggled imperceptibly, subtly putting more distance between them.

"I think their magic protects them," he said. "Ours doesn't work below the barrier, but theirs does. All we have is our lanterns, and she's asked us to put them away."

"We don't get to the edge of the forest tomorrow, I'll put her away."

Leaper smiled under the silk where she couldn't see.

Long after Ousos had stopped slapping herself and digging at ticks, he lay wide-eyed in the dark, looking in the opposite direction to Estehass's glow, imagining where Ilik's killer was, what he or she might be doing that very moment. When Leaper himself had killed Orin's Servants to save Imeris, he'd felt irrevocably soiled. Leaving the scene hadn't been enough; faking nonchalance in the face of Ulellin's curse hadn't been enough. Avoiding Ulellinland was futile, as was dodging around the subject of the beast's demise whenever Imeris or the Godfinder tried to bring it up.

Only telling himself that he'd learned, that he'd changed, that he'd never do it again, helped the memory to subside.

Despite the evidence of Gui, it was still possible that Ilik's killer had been nominated by their society to carry out the deed. It was possible that person felt as sullied now as Leaper had felt ten years ago. Was that why the killer had left silver and diamonds behind? A hurried escape, guilt-racked, the crocodile jawbone abandoned accidentally on the floor?

No. The night's darkness seeped into him, so that he no longer knew whether his eyes were open or closed. *Whoever killed her isn't human. Whoever killed her is going to die slowly, after telling me how the barrier was breached. And it won't be Ousos who does the killing. It'll be me.*

It's not breaking my oath to put down a demon.

So what if I haven't learned.

So what if I haven't changed.

I was born with the soul chosen by my sister Audblayin, goddess of new life. She was the one who put the soul of Frog inside of me; Frog, who would have destroyed the Godfinder, the loved and loathed older sister whose power she coveted, if the Godfinder hadn't destroyed her first.

TEN

Light pierced Leaper's lids.

It was daybreak. He, Ousos, and the two Rememberers really *were* close to the forest's edge. Morning cicadas pulsed. Horizontal sunbeams pierced the undergrowth, butterfly shadows made bigger than bats by the sharp angle of the dawn. The heavy smell of Floor was like snorted water from a mulch-filled lake in all of Leaper's sinuses.

He spent a moment lying very still, taking stock of his battered back and sore, stiff, insect-bitten limbs before he realised what was bothering him.

The sun was rising from the wrong direction. It was rising from the direction in which Ellin and Estehass had been leading them.

They have been leading us east, not west.

He closed his eyes and took a slow, deep breath, trying to attack the discovery from all directions. He could easily have become turned around since leaving the trail. It was the Rememberers who knew the forest floor, not Leaper. Leaper was a climbing creature, and flat earth made little sense to him. Yet only by travelling east could they have stayed within the forest, and they were within the forest, despite the siblings' promise to guide him to Gui.

The four of them were within the forest, and the sun was rising in the east.

Perhaps there was some waterway they had to go around. Impossible; he knew from Slehah that there were no obstacles between Airak's emergent and Gui aside from the barrier between Canopy and Understorey. Aside from the Rememberers themselves.

Estehass and Ellin, brother and sister with the Weight of the Eastwood behind them.

The Weight of the Eastwood.

Rememberers from the east, to take us east, but why? If they mean to murder us, why take us east first?

Slow breath in. Slow breath out. *Think, Leaper.* Cicadas increased their tempo, in time with the increased beat of his heart.

Airak will feel our deaths if we die within the forest boundary. They don't want him to feel it. They don't want to anger him, but they are plotting something in the west that they don't want his Servants to witness.

Leaper flicked through his mental images of trees, the ones that represented all the castes of Canopy. He needed to act, now, as he'd never acted before, but which role would suit? Which performance would save them? He wasn't fit to defend himself with weapons, and his magic, even if it somehow miraculously functioned, would be unlikely to overpower the superior local magic of the Floorian bone man, Estehass.

He had to defend himself with words. A flash of inspiration saw the jumbled caste templates in his mind abandoned. He didn't need them. All he needed to do was recall his jealousy while he'd hidden in the wardrobe the last time he'd seen Ilik alive.

Leaper sat up, blinking. He struggled free of his carrysack and long silk sleeves. Estehass, also sitting up on the crown of the neighbouring tree fern, covered a yawn with his hand. Ellin slept in a sitting position beside him, sunlight licking yellow over her brown back, drowning out the glow of her sigil.

Ousos snored, supine, at Leaper's feet.

He kicked her awake.

"Pleased with yourself, are you?" he yelled.

"Eh?" Ousos slurred, overbalancing as she rolled, catching at fronds to keep from falling out of the tree. "What's that, now?"

"I said you must be pleased with yourself. Look how soppily that dirt-swimmer's looking at you." He pointed accusingly at Estehass. "Did you break your oaths with him?"

Ousos, gaping, tried to focus bloodshot eyes on his face. "Got spiders in your fruit-hole overnight, you squeezing imbecile? Of course I—"

"I don't care if you did. Do it again, right now, for all I care. Do it enough times so you don't ever need to do it again after today, because we're leaving them behind when we reach Gui, and you'll never see him again." Leaper had never spat in disgust before, but he borrowed her habit, even though his mouth was dry. Pathetically thin spittle flecked her cheek. "If you try to abandon our master, I'll kill you." He raised his voice even louder, hoping to wake Ellin, the one who could understand him when he spoke Canopian. "The lightning god will feel you die, but I won't wait till we're beyond the forest, I'll do it anyway. Go on! Right now. Get all your disgusting urges finished with. Go purify some water with your lover, or whatever you want to pretend you're up to!"

Ousos's eyes narrowed. One moment of hesitation was all he needed, to know that she had understood him. They glanced together across the open air between tree ferns.

Estehass smirked. Ellin's eyes were open, thinly lidded.

"Get your big behind out of that tree," Ousos called, beckoning to Estehass, "and bring me the squeezing ladder." She stabbed a finger at it, her meaning clear despite the language barrier. "We need more water." Then she smirked as well. Estehass looked questioningly to his sister, who nodded her assent before adding her own smirk to the general circle of mocking mirth. She lifted a bamboo container to her lips and drank, as if to remind Leaper that they had plenty of purified water.

Leaper didn't smirk. He put all the envy and contempt he'd ever felt for the king of Airakland into the looks he gave all three of them. Estehass dropped down from his tree, landing with his habitual lightness. He picked up the ladder that Ousos had pointed at, propping it against Leaper's tree.

Ousos climbed down without hesitation. She took Estehass's hand. Led him into the forest. Leaper stared after them for as long as he could will himself to stay still and silent. He kept his back turned to Ellin, even though a rapid descent by her would ruin his plan.

He kept his back to her, despite the fact his life depended on reaching the ground before she did.

At last, he turned.

His hand went to the ladder.

The carrysack was heavy on his back.

He crossed his legs and jiggled ostentatiously like a little boy needing to pee. Cursed. Put one foot on the first bamboo rung.

Climbing down the two-pace ladder was the slowest descent of his life. At the foot of it, he shuffled to the toilet-hole, uncovered the lid of loosely woven leaves, and emptied his bladder over all the rest. Retying his loincloth was an awkward affair, and all the time his ears were pricked for sounds of Ellin moving. Leaper crouched at the base of Ellin's tree, grabbing handfuls of soil to scatter over the waste in the hole.

He pretended to drop his carrysack. It slipped over his shoulders. He cursed again, louder, letting himself feel every split and jolt in his forearms.

He imagined Ellin's bird's-eye gaze between his shoulder blades as he bent over his carrysack. When he straightened and slung the sack over his shoulders again, he left a squat, cloth-covered shape behind.

One of Airak's lanterns, shrouded in black.

Leaper took five long, swift strides away from the base of Ellin's tree, hunting for the forked stick she'd used to trap the snake, cursing himself for his overeagerness after all, wishing he'd thought to locate it from his place in the tree before coming down.

"What are you looking for?" Ellin asked lazily. "The water is up here with me."

"Cut bamboo," Leaper answered, hands closing around a reassuringly solid length of it. Five paces long.

"Fool. I told you, no fires!"

Agony shot through his injured arms as he made a spearing motion with the cut bamboo, snagging the cloth over the lantern, flicking the black fabric high above his own head.

Except that the cloth was no longer black. It took on the green-and-gold slashed with brown of the bamboo thicket against the shadows of great trees.

A blue-white circle of light sprang into being at the base of the tree fern's trunk, brushing the underside of the leaves where Ellin knelt. The chimera-skin cloth drifted down, landing at Leaper's feet. He threw the bamboo length like a spear in the direction of Ellin's tree. Where it touched the circle of light, it exploded, struck by lightning that blazed from the heart of the death-lantern.

"Do not move!" he commanded Ellin.

She froze. Her nostrils flared with clench-jawed fury. Burnt bamboo shards fell in a light rain around her, but she obeyed.

"What have you done?"

"Stay in your tree. Don't try to come down." Leaper picked up the chimera cloth and brandished it at her, a trophy of war. "I don't know what my fellow Servant and I have done to break your laws and earn a death sentence, but I'm going to Gui. You have enough water to last three days. If Estehass agrees to take us on the true path, I'll give this cloth to him, so that he can return here and free you."

Ellin said nothing, but she sat back down in the tree fern heart, eyes blazing.

ELEVEN

ESTEHASS HAD no choice but to lead them west.

He ran, light-footed, through the forest.

Leaper and Ousos ran after him, less gracefully but both keeping pace. Neither openly carried a lantern. Nor did Leaper wear a shirt. Estehass had grudgingly explained that only by falsifying Ellin's sigil on Leaper's bare skin could the party pass safely through the Westwood. The siblings had permission to move freely. Without a sigil, Ousos would be invisible to the watchers. And so Leaper had allowed himself to be marked, passing his carrysack to Ousos, ignoring the shivers creeping up his spine at the possibility the bone man would put some other, more deadly spell on him. Estehass had asked for a sliver of bone from one of his leather pockets and consumed it with a fierce grinding of teeth while tracing the pattern between Leaper's shoulder blades.

That was yesterday. Today they had passed the foot of Airak's emergent, near where they had first met the Rememberers, and continued west in deeper daytime darkness. The glow of Leaper's and Estehass's sigils revealed a carpet of pink and white petals fallen from springtime Canopy. Butterfly corpses, too, made trails of brilliant blue.

There was no visible path at all in this part of Floor. No thickets to pass through. From behind, Leaper could see Estehass veering close to the intermittent buttress roots of the great trees, fondling projections that turned out to be wood carvings smoothed by many generations of human hands.

Leaper touched them, too, with wonder. They were a sharper, deeper, more violent-cornered style to the wood carvings found in Canopy, which made them easier to decipher even in pitch-blackness. Some might have been simple markers. The triple bamboo stem became the double bamboo stem, and then became a single stem before vanishing completely, an obvious-seeming indication that they were moving away from the East-wood. Less obvious were two-headed embracers swallowing rafts of villa-gers, or spotted swarms turning titans into skeletons who, in a subsequent sequence, clothed their bones in the bodies of human women and men. These could have been warnings, or stories. Sometimes the carvings went on in a string thirty paces long or more.

"Don't," Estehass snarled at Leaper when he noticed him touching the trees. "These aren't for your hands. I agreed to show you the way west."

"You agreed that once before," Leaper pointed out calmly, but he stopped touching the carvings, content to follow. They paused at around the time of the evening meal to eat snake meat and dried fruit from one of Estehass's pockets, and to drink water from the stoppered bamboo that Ousos carried. She had no smiles for Estehass now, and would have bound his hands if he hadn't said he needed them to find his way. His leather sash with its pouches of food and magical accessories, she'd examined with a grunt before adding to her already oversized burdens. Then she'd tossed his cloak, loincloth, and sandals into the bamboo and told him to run naked.

As they ate, the sun crept below the level of Canopy, illuminating the mighty foundations of the great trees from one side like they were only half there. Pollen hung and danced in the light's path, and the air was cooler and not so close.

West. The sun is west. He is keeping his word, taking us west.

A strange silhouette blocked the sun directly before them. Leaper squinted, trying to decide if it was the torn-out roots of a fallen tree, a branching human-built structure, or something else altogether.

"What is that?" he asked Estehass around a mouthful of pointy snake bones. When he moved into the shade, he could make out a long, curving boat shape at the base of a maze of branches.

"Dusksight" was the Rememberer's reluctant reply. "Jewel of the West-wood and throne of the Westerman. Just as Dawnsight is the Jewel of the Eastwood and throne of the Easterman."

"It doesn't look much like a throne. More like an enormous, ancient, and broken-down version of the village houses that your people build on top of your canoes."

The trio had skirted several such villages. All the season, Rememberer boat-houses had been empty and uninhabited, many tilted on their keeled sides. The Rememberers would not begin filling them with food until a month before the monsoon, and the monsoon was still some two or three months away.

Estehass gnawed a slice of dried mango that Ousos had given him from his own rations and said nothing.

"Are we going around that thing?" Ousos asked, waving an axe in Dusksight's direction. She looked keenly at Leaper. "Is he telling you how many soldiers are inside it, or is he pretending it's abandoned so they can swarm out like hornets when we get closer?"

"I think it might be like a Temple," Leaper said. "Give me my carrysack to cover my fake sigil. I'm going to sneak inside it and see what's there. Don't let Estehass escape."

Ousos rolled her eyes and spat, but she gave Leaper his carrysack.

"Is the throne of the Easterman grander than that?" Leaper asked Estehass. "Or are your kings only truly happy when wallowing in mud? Did we turn west too early to appreciate its mosquito-infested majesty?"

He didn't expect the taunt to work; Estehass had displayed remarkable equanimity thus far. But the big man said, after a long silence, "In the dry days, Dawnsight customarily rests to the east, as far from Dusksight as it can travel. But I think today it is close by. East and West are here in numbers. Rouse them at your peril. Dead men have no need of guides to lead them to Gui."

Leaper took the length of chimera-skin cloth from around his waist and held it in his fist in front of Estehass's face.

"Is there anything I need to know," he asked, "before I go to take a closer look at your ugly throne?"

Tyran's Talon had been kept in a temple-like clay structure before Leaper had paid for it to be stolen. The chances of finding Old God's bones in this one seemed promising. Leaper's magic wasn't working for him below the barrier, but if there was some sort of weapon that the Rememberers didn't want the lightning god's Servants to see, he owed it to Airak to investigate.

Estehass sighed.

"There is a bubble of poison air around Dusksight, contained by bone woman magic. Do not travel straight towards it. Find a sandpaper fig by the feel of its fallen leaves. Dawnsight must always be moored by a calamander tree, and Dusksight must always be moored by a sandpaper fig. The entrance will be shielded by its roots, an arch with an eye carved over it. You have until the sun is completely down. After that, the acolytes return from their ceremony to farewell the last light of the day."

"Acolytes?" Leaper asked. "Are they apprentices to the bone women? Male or female? Are they fighters or fisherfolk? Do they wield magic?"

"They are from every gender and every rank, except for slave rank," Estehass answered dourly. "Avoid them. You cannot survive an encounter with them, and if you die, Ellin dies as well."

Leaper ducked his head.

The tunnel to the Rememberer temple hugged his shoulders with uncomfortably close earthen arms. The roots of the fig tree poked through the dirt like whiskers, larger sections forcing the tunnel to contort around them. In a way, the closeness of the air and the smell of smoke reminded him of the hollow-tree home he'd grown up in.

When he uncovered his thieves' lantern to keep from stumbling over roots, he discovered Rememberer children had scrawled untidy messages on some of those roots, most likely illicit. When the acolytes came through the tunnel, they probably made their way in darkness, as Estehass had made his way, quite comfortably, using the carvings on the trees.

> Love. Peace. Trees. River.
> Clams with pickle sauce.
> Amilta wrote this. No I did not.
> Orjor is a huge dimwit. He only has one nut.

Leaper grinned, reliving the moment when he, Imeris, and Ylly had engraved their names on the ceiling of Middle-Mother's swimming hole. Then he realised he was reading not the alphabet of Canopy but glyphs of trees, animals, and human figures that he'd never seen before.

A lump rose in his throat. He squeezed his eyes shut. *It was only my voice. The speaking-bone only affected my tongue, my ability with spoken language!* But when he opened them again, the pictographs were still there and he could still understand them, as he had not been able to understand the more sculpture-like markers his guide had fondled. Were those markers too much like art, too little like formalised ideograms?

It didn't matter. This language must be for the initiated only. Yet here

Leaper was, violating another Floorian people with his very presence. Had he learned nothing? Who would he manage to get killed this time? Ousos?

I'm here now. I might as well see what is hidden inside. It's not like Orjor's single nut is of sacred significance, and besides, Estehass didn't seem too worried about my breaking or taking anything.

The tunnel turned steep. In the final twenty paces, it was more like climbing a jagged chimney of roots and compressed earth than walking along a path. Leaper emerged into a rectangular wooden room with only one opening, and that opening covered by reed hangings at the distant end. He supposed that was the way to the poison gas. A water clock made of some green stone dripped ominously at the base of a calamander calendar covered in notches.

At the close end of the room, Leaper's lantern showed a broken ring of bleached white bone. When whole, it would have been five paces in diameter. At least one third of the bone ring was missing, eroded away somehow, but it obviously once had been perfectly round, a completed puzzle of overlapping, scale-like sections. The two remaining pieces rested on a black glass plinth, under a wooden arc engraved with the rays of the dying sun.

No wonder he wasn't worried. Even the broken pieces look too heavy for me to lift, and too awkward to get out the door, much less carry off down the confines of the tunnel.

When he got closer, Leaper noted its resemblance to the sclerotic ring bones of leaf-tailed geckoes and peregrine falcons. These were the bones actually buried inside the tough white lining of the eyeballs. If this one was proportional, the Old God it had belonged to must have had a lizard- or birdlike head at least twenty paces across.

Two eyes. Two bones like these, and this is one. Maybe they're connected. Maybe this is a doorway. If the bone rings could transport people between Dusksight and Dawnsight, though, the same way that Leaper's lanterns had once transported him, why wouldn't this one be mounted in an approximation of its original shape? *Or maybe it has some other, complex, specific purpose. Maybe bringing the broken pieces into alignment permits healing, or unleashes destruction.*

Leaper shivered, thinking of Orin's beast and its ability to come apart and heal back together again. He'd slain that beast, trapped and wounded by the Hunt, with a forbidden wielding of Airak's power in Ulellin's niche.

He set the lantern on the wooden floor. The closest bone section was smooth under his fingertips. It felt like normal, nonmagical animal remains. Leaper sensed none of the gods' power through it, nothing like what he'd felt when he was above the barrier holding Tyran's Talon. There were no intense smells or temperature swings. No feelings of movement or dissolution of self.

Nothing.

Then his fingers found a rough spot on the lower rim of the arc. Leaper bent over, bringing his lantern to that side, raising it to sit on the plinth, and saw a place where bits of the bone had been subtly scraped away, presumably with a blade. The lantern crackled and spat, two magical objects in too-close proximity, but the lantern's glass panes contained the errant lightning. Trace amounts of white bone powder showed up against the black glass of the plinth.

Leaper pictured Estehass crunching down on the bone hidden in his leather pouches. He remembered the ashy taste of the so-called speaking-bone in his mouth.

They can't do magic here without eating the stuff of the Old Gods. Leaper swiped one forefinger through the dust on the plinth.

He raised it to his mouth. Touched it to his tongue.

The wooden room, door, clock, bone, and lantern vanished in a blaze of colour. Leaper's mind came loose from his body. The last thing he felt was the back of his wide-flung hand knocking the lantern from the plinth. Visions seized him like raptor talons sinking into his skull. There were no smells. There were no sounds.

Only light.

Searing, blazing light.

He saw a dark-skinned man and woman, on foot, made tiny by distance. They followed a goat trail to a vast stone bowl sunk by weather and time into the heart of a snowcapped mountain range. Inside the bowl was a ruined stone city. On the rock wall that shadowed the city, a relief carving gleamed, as tall as Airak's emergent, and as wide.

The carving unmistakeably depicted Leaper's lost queen. *Ilik.* Her hair-crown was woven with diamonds. Miniature lanterns hung from her carved robes. *Ilik, I will find your killer.*

The scene shifted. Leaper saw a crimson fruit falling in slow motion from a child's hand. Shiny red against the green. Rolling under the shade of a tree, at the edge of the Titan's Forest, and as it rolled, tree roots erupted behind it, flinging black, worm-filled earth like rain.

The forest shrank into view, so that Leaper could see it all at once. He recognised the yellow-flowering northern edge of Oxorland, where it gave way to the Bright Plain. The charred, lightning-struck emergents of Airakland to the southwest. Those blackened arms bordered the bite of grasslands between the domains of Airak and Odel where Rememberers and Crocodile-Riders dwelled.

White animal bones, bigger than the emergents, erupted between the trees. Connected into monstrous shapes. Some looked more than half human. Others were more like two-legged lizards. Colours rippled across their new-formed scaly skins, as though their rejuvenated bodies would turn invisible. *Like gigantic chimeras.* The ripples camouflaged them against the greens and browns of the forest.

But the forest was dying. Great trees toppled like grass stalks under the onslaught of heavy rain. A final skull was rising, wet and filthy, from the ruins of Airakland. One side of the jaw was elongated and bristling with python-like teeth. The other was twisted and shortened, with flat, ape-like molars. On that second side, the eye socket was human, with no sclerotic ring. On the first side, the ring was a thick tunnel of bone ten times the size of the one in the Temple.

Leaper had never seen it before, but he knew whose skull it was.

Tyran's skull.

Tyran's Talon, the bone Leaper had been using to augment his power, was nothing. Not even visible. A deformed punctuation point at the end of a disproportionately tiny forelimb. Vertebrae flew upward to connect with the skull, forcing it higher and higher, making room for massive hind limbs and swinging tail beneath. The wood of the great trees shattered into jagged splinters that clothed the bones and turned to living flesh.

Leaper gagged and found himself back in the single-lantern safety of the wooden room, on all fours, vomit between his hands. The lantern hit the floor. All he'd witnessed he'd seen in the time it had taken for the lantern to fall.

It was history, he thought. *They call themselves the Rememberers.*

He'd seen the carving of the queen; it had to have been Ilik's ancestor. Her ancestors must have lived in that mountain city.

Yet she was brown, and Estehass had said that the mountain people were pale. Besides, the destruction of the forest was not in the past. It was in the future. *Not possible.* The face on the mountainside couldn't be one of Ilik's descendants. She was dead.

Leaper heaved again. Sparks danced before his eyes.

Dusksight. It isn't named for the last glimpse of the day, but for the last glimpse of our civilisation. Kirrik's soul is trapped in the bottom of the rain goddess's lake, but she, or somebody like her, will find a way to strike down all of the new gods at once. The Old Gods will rise again. It will be the end of Understorey and Floor.

It will be the end of Canopy. I must tell Ilik.

Leaper crawled to the wall. He used it to get to his feet.

No, she's gone. His grief tasted like dry dirt from the uprooted trees of the vision. *She's gone, and I can't tell her.*

Rubbing his eyes, shaking his head, he turned slowly to look at the sclerotic ring bones. At the thieves' lantern still sizzling and spitting on its side in response to it.

People of power must see this vision. Make sure it can't happen. Kings and queens; queens other than Ilik. Unar. Imeris. Goddesses and gods.

Leaper crossed the floor. Picked up the lantern. Opened one of the glass panes in the side of it. Lightning bolts immediately escaped, curling wildly around the sclerotic ring bone, which began to glow a pale blue. Cringing back from the bolts, so near to the recent burns that still caused him so much pain, Leaper thrust the bronze casing of the lantern closer to one section of bone, trying to force the end inside the rectangular opening.

At first, the lantern resisted, as it had when Leaper himself had travelled through it. Yet after a few strenuous moments of straining and cursing, the bone began to elongate before his eyes. The wide broken edge became the thin end of a wedge. Leaper used all his weight to force the lantern down over his prize, the Rememberers' sacred object. When one piece was mostly through, he started on the other.

I'm not really stealing anything vital. They're not food. They're not medicine. Just memories. Or visions—visions are only future memories anyway. They're still intangible. Like Ilik, the day she was killed. The day she was turned into a memory by an assassin.

He wasn't stealing it so that he could see her face again, carved into that mountainside, whenever he wanted. That was not the reason. It was in the service of his master. It was for the good of Canopy.

The Rememberers would have killed me. I don't owe them anything.

The blue-white light in the heart of the lantern raged. The last of the broken ring of bone disappeared, and Leaper closed the pane behind it. Far overhead in Eshland, it would rest now, on a fine carpet in the hidden home he'd made for himself and for his lost queen.

Ellin would have killed me, and I'd be a memory, too.

TWELVE

THE OLD Temple of Airak had been destroyed before Leaper was born.
Yet here it is.

When the sorceress Kirrik cut down the tree, the cut had been at the level of lower Understorey, still four hundred paces from the ground. The Rememberers were making use of what was left. Glowing blue symbols moved in the shadows, teams of women and men carrying full baskets, wielding adzes, or pulling saws.

They've cut it again, Leaper thought, parting the ferns to better see. *Twenty paces from the ground, this time.*

They had used the four-hundred-pace length of great tree, it seemed, to build the greatest canoe Floor had ever seen, or was likely to see. The log looked naturally hollow at its widest end, heartwood striated many shades of brown, insect-eaten and untouched by fire. The narrow end appeared human carved. Burnt out to finish the rough canoe shape and then made more symmetrical by sharpened steel.

"Are your people going somewhere?" Leaper whispered to a sullen, naked Estehass.

"Not my people," Estehass murmured, and that was all he would say. He scratched his arse idly. The three of them were squatting behind the fern clump.

"Let me go see what they're doing," Ousos said with one side of her mouth, chewing furiously at her teeth.

Leaper had returned quickly to Ousos and Estehass with his thieves' lantern safely stowed. They hadn't gone more than a thousand paces before stumbling on the hive of Rememberer activity. In the last light of day, the cut buttress roots of the old emergent formed an elliptical caged arena some fifty paces across. Sunbeams travelled upward along crumbling wood spears streaked with livid green moss.

Leaf litter of quandong and satinash foliage was a poor match for the white sapwood and grey bark of the ancient floodgum, which had not produced its own leaves since that moment of Kirrik's victory. The main focus of Rememberer commotion seemed to be within that caged arena.

"What are they doing in there?" Leaper asked Estehass, who grunted and shrugged.

"Don't you leave me with him again," Ousos warned Leaper in Canopian. "It's my turn to go do a bit of ~~squeezing~~ exploring. True, I haven't got as pretty a disguise as you two, but once the sun's completely gone, I can find my way without making a noise in the dark."

"Once the sun's completely gone," Leaper said, "we've got demons to worry about."

"My people will soon go to their boat-houses and lock the doors," Estehass said. "The bone women will expand the bubble of poisoned air to cover the whole village, so that embracers cannot come. We should leave. Keep moving west. It's what you wanted."

"I want to know what's going on," Leaper said, hands on hips, glowering at Estehass. "Or I'm sending Ousos to find out."

"Sending her to die."

"If she dies—"

"If she dies, Ellin dies. I know, boy, I know." Estehass scratched his arse again and sighed. "They're digging for bones of the Old Gods."

"Something big?" Leaper guessed. "Dusksight was the size of a house, and it held a bone the size of a man. That canoe could fit twenty houses. Which bone are you—" His jaw clicked shut as he realised which bone they were digging for. *Tyran's skull.*

And Tyran is the Old God who became my master, Airak.

Estehass must have seen the awareness in Leaper's eyes, because sudden rage contorted his face.

"How dare you," the Rememberer growled. "You tasted it, did you? How dare you partake of the holy—"

"What are you going to do with the skull once you have it on that boat? Worship it? Eat it? What will it do for you? Why is it worth this considerable effort?" His mind raced. *They don't like it when we have their bones,* Imeris had told him once. The Rememberers had their reasons. Reasons for not

wanting Airak's Servants to see what they were doing. Reasons worth killing for, to avoid rousing the lightning god's wrath. He stared at Estehass.
"You're moving it. You're taking it away. Why?"

"You saw why," Estehass said, glowering, leaping to his feet. Ousos
reached around him from behind and put her axe to his throat, forcing him
back down onto his haunches. "Only taking the skull to the other side of
the sea can save us all from the fate you saw."

"What's he saying, Leaper?" Ousos asked urgently.

"They're Rememberers—they remember," Leaper told her bitterly. "But
it's not the glory of the Old Gods they remember. It's the terror and destruction. They have a vision of the Old Gods rising again, crushing the
forest to dust, and they want to prevent it. By taking Airak's bones away.
They're going to put his skull on that raft and let the monsoon carry it out
to sea."

"But the bones make his trees grow," Ousos said, her jaw dropping. "The
bones give him the power to maintain the barrier. Without them, without
the great trees, the worship of the people would mean nothing. We have
to stop them." The wrist of the hand holding the axe twitched. "How
long have they been digging? How much longer before they bring up the
skull?"

"I'll ask him."

But Estehass's anger had cooled, and he would not reveal anything more.

"Kill me if you must," he said, "and Ellin, too. I promised to take you
west. No more and no less. The trail is that way." He indicated with a lifted
chin. "The workers grow quiet."

Leaper peered through the fern clump. It was true. Fewer basket-bearing,
glyph-lit bodies were emerging from the digging site. They trailed away into
the gloom like dispersing fireflies.

"We're going to get poisoned if we stay here," Leaper told Ousos.

"Poison gas might be able to protect them from demons," Ousos said,
spitting. "Poison gas might be able to protect them from Canopian warriors
or the Servants of Airak. It can't protect them from the monsoon."

"What do you mean?"

"I mean your squeezing sister won revenge for the rain goddess by captur-
ing that sorceress, Kirrik. Ehkis owes you a favour, and the last monsoon
we had was pathetic. Must be a lot of water waiting around up there in the
clouds. Go and see Ehkis. Convince her to bring the monsoon early, right

now, flood this part of Floor, and those squeezing dirt grubbers will drown like pinkie possums in a hole."

"I'm going to Gui to find Ilik's killer."

"Look, I hate those Gui traders as much as you do. I can't wait to open up their fruit-holes through their bloody throats, but this is more important! If you wait till these Rememberers have got the skull onto that squeezing canoe—"

"We've got time to go to Gui first," Leaper argued. He blinked, and the stone image of Ilik seemed to swim before his eyes. "The monsoon isn't for two months, and think about what you're suggesting. These people are not prepared. It's not just the workers you'd drown, but families. Children. Even if they manage to get to their boats, they won't have food to last them. Not to mention all the other Floorian societies, which have nothing to do with the Rememberers but rely on animal signs to know when the rains are coming. Besides all that, any clues in the grasslands will be washed away if—"

"Those squeezing Rememberers could get the skull out tomorrow! All you know is it's not there right now. You don't know how close they are to getting it out, and he's not about to squeezing tell you!" She was waving her axe in Leaper's direction now, ignoring Estehass. "The monsoon coming in two months is what they're counting on, to wash that canoe all the way through the forest and into that northern sea, under the tree-killing salt, where lightning can't follow."

Memories of the monsoon flood chasing him through the grasslands of the Crocodile-Riders. Himself stealing the speaking-bone. Being trapped below the barrier.

"My aura's faded," Leaper said, knowing full well he could force himself through his thieves' lantern if he had to. Ousos didn't care how many Floorians died. Did she think they were animals? Was that how she'd justified sleeping with Estehass to herself, that she wasn't really breaking her oaths because he wasn't really human? "I can't go through the barrier."

"Eliligras can meet you at the barrier," Ousos said at once. "She'll ask the master to let you through. Remind Ehkis that it was the king of Airakland who called the Hunt that saved her people from Orin's monster. Promise her a fortune in lanterns and glass. Tell her whatever you have to tell her to bring the monsoon now, right now."

"We have to move," Estehass interrupted in the Rememberer's tongue. "We have to go."

"Show us the trail," Leaper told him. He switched languages. "Let him lead the way, Ousos." The trick of focusing on which person he needed to communicate with became easier each time. "We can decide what to do when we're away from the poison gas."

"The decision's made already! I'll cut this traitor's throat, and we'll start climbing the closest tree!"

No throat cutting. I am not a killer. I am not Frog.

Leaper wordlessly held out his arms.

Scar tissue was beginning to form in the fissures that crisscrossed his skin. It looked like pale rivers running through a mudflat, as seen from the high platform of an emergent. Purple ridges lined the seams where his snake-tooth spines should have slid easily out and in. Instead, the swelling and weeping meant that if he tried to extrude them, he'd slice his own flesh.

"We were supposed to climb back up with these. They're not healed. I'm not healed."

Ousos touched the bone man's leather pouches, which hung from her harness.

"Let him heal you," she said. "I bet he can."

"I bet if he tries, my spines will fall out."

"Eliligras can let down a rope for us."

"No more talking!" Estehass cried softly. It was abruptly too dark to see his expression. When Leaper looked towards the diggings, he couldn't see a single glowing sigil. He couldn't see anything, including his scarred forearms.

"Let him lead the way," he told Ousos again. He saw the flash of her axe blade as she removed it from proximity to Estehass; she was standing behind the big man, the light from his sigil falling on her face, the only thing he could still see.

"Quickly," Estehass urged, turning his back to Leaper. "Run!"

They followed his snake and star through the eerily quiet blackness. It was like running with his eyes closed, a thing no Canopian could do. Leaper's feet tried to stick in the muck. He almost slipped once, twice, three times. Heavy breathing echoed in his head like the rhythmic thrashing of treetops in a storm.

All he could see was Estehass's blue glow. All he could hear was panting and pounding footsteps.

Then, above Estehass's false star, he saw true stars.

They were out of the forest. Grass to his shoulders. Starlight on a thin stream.

"Stop," Leaper gasped.

When Estehass pulled up short and turned, obedient, Leaper put his hands on his knees and sucked at the cooler air like a drowning man finding a lake's surface. Ousos, beside him, did likewise.

"Go back," Ousos wheezed, careless now of the volume of her voice. "We have to go back."

"We can rest here," Leaper contended. "Shelter in the grasses. Formulate a plan in the morning." He didn't say what had been on his mind since seeing the digging and piecing together the Rememberers' plan: that the ruin of the forest had been horrific to behold. That perhaps they were right to want to take Tyran's skull far away. Perhaps Airakland's size and influence would be reduced, but wasn't that a fair price to pay?

In payment, Airak had said, *if you return, when you return, you, or another with gifts equal to yours, will serve me with your whole heart. You, or that other, will swear your oaths a second time and be more deeply and tightly bound by them than any of my Servants has ever been bound before.* Had he known that Leaper would be tempted to betray him? *I don't have prescient dreams. I can't make prophecies. All I can do is watch, and when I can't watch, set a watch on people and places of great importance.*

"Formulate a plan in the morning," Ousos repeated stonily. "Very well. I'll take the first watch."

She took ropes from her harness. Trussed Estehass like a tapir for slaughter. He was still naked and horribly exposed, though his sigil protected him from insects. Leaper's false sigil protected him likewise. He made a nest of sorts from the grasses. Closed his eyes, trusting Ousos to wake him at the zenith that marked the middle hours of the night.

Instead, the sun woke him. It strained at the southern edge of Canopy through ominously gathering clouds. Leaper, clawing free of dreams about a giant, mobile stone Ilik tearing her own palace out by the roots, splashed his face with water from the little stream. Estehass remained tied beside it, throat uncut.

But Ousos was gone. Along with her equipment and the bone man's supplies.

Leaper looked again, aghast, at the sky.

A single raindrop slashed his cheek.

THIRTEEN

"Take this," Leaper told Estehass.

He held out the chimera-skin cloth despairingly.

It was happening again. *What, the monsoon or the betrayal?* Purple storm clouds massed. Lightning streaked between them, and grey sheets touched the towering, sky-blotting silhouette of Canopy, indicating that the flooding rains had already begun over Ehkisland. The thin stream at his feet grew perceptibly deeper even as he watched. How had she done it? How had she betrayed him?

Her lanterns. They were not death-lanterns. They were not thieves' lanterns. Yet they were perfectly capable of sending messages back and forth. *How did I forget that? How did I forget that my reluctant companion was the Shining One of the lightning god?*

And now the monsoon had arrived. Two months early, as Ousos had vengefully suggested.

Meet Eliligras at the barrier, she had said, and also, *Eliligras can let down a rope for us,* not thinking she'd need to remind Leaper of the fact that they could send messages with the lantern.

Estehass frowned. He looked up.

"Is this a trap? Is the other Servant—"

"This is the monsoon." Leaper gestured impatiently around them. Wind tugged at his clothing, flattening the long grass into temporary tunnels and paths. Only the bamboo clacked together and didn't lie down. The surface of the little stream reflected the silver sky and the black, monolithic-seeming forest, the patter of early raindrops shattering that surface into a thousand mirror shards. "Take the cloth for covering the death-lantern. Go and save Ellin before she drowns."

Estehass took the cloth.

"My plants and powders," he said, looking around again for Ousos. "My pieces of bone."

"She's taken them, imbecile! I don't know where she is! Go!"

Estehass hesitated a moment longer. Then he vanished into the grass with the whisper a mouse might make, instead of the lumbering rustle of a hulking naked man holding a trailing length of cloth.

Leaper felt the faint wet spit of the storm turn to a more insistent, cool drumming on his upturned face and shoulders. He held out his forearms, so that the rain could be a balm to his aching arms. The monsoon was normally warm, but it wasn't yet summer.

What should I do?

His choices were two.

Try to find his guide, Slehah, before the water rose too high. Take shelter in Gui. Seek Ilik's murderer there. She could forgive anything, but Leaper could not forgive this. If the destruction of somebody so blameless could be without consequences, the entire notion of Canopians making their homes above demons, of being better than dark-dwelling animals, was meaningless. Leaper's climb into sunlight was meaningless. As was his search for somebody who could see his true self without turning away.

His other choice was to run home. Force his broken body through the thieves' lantern for the last time, because leaving it here on the floodplain would mean never finding it again.

And what waited for him in Airakland? Ousos, to name him traitor. King Icacis, to ask why he had failed. Aforis, to list all the ways in which he was inadequate. Ilik was not there.

Ilik will never be there.

Leaper made his way through the long grass to the closest stand of bamboo. There were a few different clumps of it there. One type had thin yellow-streaked canes. Another was a thick emerald green type with nodes close together. A third one was thick and greenish-black with nodes far apart.

A skinning knife was the closest thing that he had to a proper cleaver, and he hacked at the emerald green bamboo for a few minutes without making much of an impression on it. All around him, birds sounded alarm calls, trying to find one another, trying to flock to safety, but there would be no safety. The birds hadn't woven their floating monsoon nests any more than the Rememberers had provisioned their boat-houses. Insects hadn't waterproofed their hives. Tree bears hadn't fattened themselves. More than just a village or a whole society of people was going to be obliterated, and it wasn't only Ousos who didn't care. Ehkis didn't care. Airak didn't care.

Leaper switched angrily to the greenish-black bamboo, and chips flew from his very first swing. The stalks were still as tall as five Floorians on one another's shoulders, but their woody walls were, it seemed, quite a bit thinner.

Hairlike prickles began itching his palms, and he realised he'd been chopping an immature stem. Cursing, scraping his palms against his robe, he paused to run to the stream, kneel, and drink with his hands behind his back.

Then he started again, this time choosing mature stems with blooms of powdery mould over their smooth, greenish-black skin. He cut four long legs to drive into the marshy ground, each one with a v-shaped cleft in its upper end, to hold the horizontal poles that would form the four sides of the structure. Smaller notches in the four uprights of Leaper's bamboo tower held rungs of the thinner, yellow-streaked bamboo, for him to climb up on. There wasn't time to lash the poles into place, and he didn't know which of the grasses were suitable for lashings, anyway.

He topped his tower with a bed of split bamboo to sit on. Used his bore-knife and a dozen pins of split bamboo to reinforce the main supports.

By then, the storm had completely obscured the blurry circle of the sun. The stream, liberated from its bed, swirled around his ankles.

Leaper took one final stem of the yellow-streaked bamboo, to make a kind of fishing pole from which to suspend his lantern. Then he climbed to the top of his tower. Able to see over the top of the long grass at last, he hoped that his guide, somewhere between the forest's edge and the rain-obscured western horizon, would similarly be able to see him. Or at least his lantern.

The rain turned from droplets to heavy curtains. Water pattering on grass and bamboo became indistinguishable from water on water. In the eastern sky, by the black wall of trees, curling whips of dark grey clouds collided, connecting to Canopy with lightning-filled columns of rainwater.

Although, Leaper noticed, the lightning was nowhere near as frequent as it should have been. It was bizarre to see it but not feel it.

Leaper shivered.

No humans emerged from the trees. Neither at the high levels of the forest, nor the level of Floor. Whatever the Rememberers were doing amongst the great trees, escaping to the grasslands was not it. No matter how he squinted, Leaper couldn't see any movement of magical sigils.

He heard only one scream. A woman's scream. And then he wondered if it had been a demon. Or a tapir. The innocent stream he'd stepped over an hour ago frothed brown and white. One minute it surged towards the forest; the next minute it rushed away.

Within another hour, the water had eaten half the height of Leaper's tower. His hands, gripping the fishing pole with his thieves' lantern dangling at the end, were numb and bloodless. There was no reason for him to keep holding it up. Slehah hadn't seen it. Slehah hadn't come. It was past time to squeeze himself inside the bronze frame.

Yet even as he stared at the baleful blue-white light inside it, the lantern flickered and went out. Cutting off his retreat to Canopy.

Leaper drew the lantern down to the top of the platform, hand over hand on the bamboo pole, arms shaking. What was happening? Had an enemy, Ousos perhaps, found the sister lantern in Leaper's lair and smashed it? Or had he, Leaper, simply taken it too far from the city? Had Airak's deal with Ehkis weakened the lightning god? Had tribute intended for Airak been paid to Ehkis instead?

You fools, he thought, his lips as numb as his hands; he was going to drown here; he was going to die without ever speaking to another human. *You were so desperate to keep the Rememberers from sapping Airak's power that you went ahead and did it for them. Is the barrier open in Airakland? Have you murdered all those people for nothing?*

He would not drown. He would abandon the lantern and swim back to the forest, if he had to. Middle-Mother was a strong swimmer. Leaper was, too.

The lantern flared back to life. Glass panes protected the interior from wind and rain, but the light dulled almost immediately, as though it was a naked candle in the monsoon. Leaper rattled it helplessly. It brightened for a count of ten. Died again.

By its fading light, Leaper glimpsed an irregularly lumpy ridge in the rising water, not two paces below the split-bamboo bed where he sat.

There was the swish of a spiny tail. Two reptilian eyes, facing away from one another, blinked barely above the swirling brown. The current was strong enough that the creature had to exert a reasonable amount of energy just to stay by Leaper's side.

A crocodile.

The last time he'd seen one, he'd been sixteen years old and trying to find Aurilon's sword in Crocodile-Rider territory.

He curbed the urge to fling his lantern at it. Wondered, if he was quick, if the transporting light flared up again, whether he might reach over the edge of the platform and jam the open lantern over the crocodile's toothy snout, sending it, claws and all, to a luxuriously appointed room in Eshland where it would either starve to death or fall terminally from the hidden door.

That would be a wasted opportunity. I'll be ready. The next time it lights up, I'll dive straight into it myself.

Holding the lantern in his numb hands, he gazed at it, willing it to come alive again.

Nothing.

Leaper's teeth chattered, and the lantern stayed resolutely dark and cold. When he looked over the edge of the platform, he could see the crocodile waiting, wedged against the bamboo supports to save energy.

"You think I don't have the strength left to stick my bore-knife between your eyes?" he snarled.

A moment's notice was all he had. Behind the crocodile, a black, bulky shape loomed through the screens of rain. It was a generously proportioned log canoe. A thatched house squatted in the belly of it, and wide-eyed Floorians lined the gunwales, bark cloaks streaming from their shoulders.

Glossy, oval calamander leaves and tiny white flowers littered the deck. *Dawnsight.*

"Catch me," Leaper cried in the language of the Rememberers, sticking his bamboo pole into the swirling water and vaulting towards the startled priestly passengers. The lantern blazed in the moment where he hung over the water, its blue-white light reddening the eyes of half a dozen crocodiles below.

Leaping over them felt like leaping over Ilik's sightless, bloody corpse. Her body would be washed away. Her murderer's trail, washed away.

Gui, and everyone in it, washed away. Or would some of them manage to survive, as these few desperate Rememberers had survived, by clinging to anything they could find that would float? What was he going to do now? What was the point of anything, now?

Leaper, leaping into the dark. Lord of Lightning trying to drown me instead of showing the way.

Then he was over the canoe's rim, dumped on his behind in ankle-deep water that sloshed up his lower back as his weight, and the weight of those who ran to inspect him, tilted the craft. A woman lost her footing; she lost her bundle. It disappeared over the side, out of the circle of light, and her devastated eyes made white circles over the black circle of her mouth in the brown circle of her face.

His lantern went out.

"Throw him back," shouted an angry voice in the uncertain light and shadow of Leaper's eyes readjusting. "This flood is Canopy's doing."

"He's injured," a young woman's voice replied. "Struck by lightning. His god has cast him out for stealing the lantern. The enemy of our enemy—"

"Our enemies are the Old Gods, not the new—"

Leaper stared past them at the fast-approaching great trees. Their trunks were spaced widely. It didn't seem that the floating temple would strike any of them. Especially since the craft was now slowing.

A strange, strong wind whipped up at ground level out of nowhere, blasting the boat back towards the grasslands even as the ferocious flow of the floodwaters tried to drag it into the forest.

"They battle one another," a new voice said with awe. "Wind against water." Bright afterimages had faded enough from Leaper's rapidly blinking eyes that he actually could see this speaker; it was a bark-wrapped man crouched behind him, gripping the wooden wall and peering over the side. The wind strengthened and the boat tilted alarmingly. Everybody who was standing staggered. A door to the thatched building flew open.

"Inside," bellowed a grey-haired man, gripping the frame with swollen-knuckled fingers as the wind threw calamander leaves and twigs in his face. "We can reconsecrate the interior if we survive!"

Everybody rushed to obey, lurching across the deck. The crouching man lifted Leaper by an elbow and helped shove him through the opening into a rectangular room remarkably similar to the room Leaper had visited in Dusksight. Except that this water clock was overturned and emptied, and Leaper could catch no glimpse of any giant sclerotic bone between the twenty or thirty sweating bodies present, some retching with the increasing spin of the canoe.

Another unexpected tilt sent Leaper sprawling. His outflung right arm found the sharp edge of a fallen glass plinth. The lantern came to life, and Rememberers cringed away from it.

Leaper lifted his forearm to shield his own eyes from the blinding light—*is Airak fighting for his life? Is he dying? Is the lantern lighting when the water spins us closer to the forest and fading whenever the wind pushes us further away?*—and saw a white powder dusting it. A residue from the plinth.

Bone powder. *There's another Old God's bone in here, somewhere.*

Impulsively, Leaper put the powder to his mouth.

FOURTEEN

LEAPER ENJOYED a high, clear view. As if from Airak's emergent.

He was seeing, in silence, down from a mountaintop. A wide, crystalline river frothed from a cave opening in a cliff. It meandered across a rocky plateau, fell down to a grassy plain, and headed for a northern coastline.

A forest lay between plains and coast. It was a small forest. These trees were a mere four times a man's height. The folk of an alarmed, brown-skinned tribe peered from rickety watchtowers. These trees were only ankle deep to thirteen monsters approaching the edge of the forest.

The brutes slithered or walked on paired hind legs. Spiny whip-tails trailed from those that resembled upright iguanas. Some were laterally compressed. Others had forward-facing eyes. Some were spring green, some were charcoal black and some were covered in colour-changing scales—*like chimeras*—that made them invisible but for the shadows they cast over the frightened people.

The monsters fought amongst themselves. No, they weren't fighting. It was how they spoke to one another. Leaper could understand them, even in the absence of sound. The pictograms of the children's graffiti at Dusksight were reproduced in the ribbon-flick of a tail or the carve of a claw. Their language was violence, whisked wind and wounds torn in scaly flesh. As they spoke, their signatures were stamped in every sentence.

Leaper saw their true names, but his mind translated them into the language of Canopy, into the names by which they were known in the present.

To the sea, next and nearest, Ehkis demanded, drawing blood from her neighbour, whose wounds healed quickly but not so quickly that Leaper couldn't read the words. *The sea!* The rain goddess flickered a hundred different blues in her eagerness. *Oh, to be beneath it!*

I crave the cold creatures it holds, Orin agreed.

There are no woodlands beneath the sea, Esh argued. *I will not go.*

Fall behind and die, then, as our fourteenth part did, Orin said scathingly. Esh didn't bleed where she'd bitten him, but splintered instead. The splinters re-formed into unbroken wood beneath bronze-coloured, bark-textured scales.

I will go to the sea, Audblayin said. *We shall all go. There is new life in the sea.* Oxor's blow turned Audblayin's green head on its swanlike neck.

The sun is weak beneath the water.

There is no wind beneath the water, Ulellin put in. *We should go to the mountain.*

Audblayin was swift to reply. *We gave that mountain away to the winged.*

We can take it back, Ulellin countered. *The winged aren't our equals. They're thieves. They steal my winds, and they steal my leaves. We should not have left even one alive to challenge us.*

Ehkis twisted gracefully, conciliatory even as she clawed her companion. *The movement of the waves is like the wind, Ulellin.*

It is not the wind! Ulellin snapped.

And what of those creatures, Audblayin, Oxor asked, *who inhabit our tread? You care for them also, Odel. How will they live under the water? How will they breathe? How will they eat?*

Leaper's gaze followed Oxor's along the path that the monsters had followed, and in following, it seemed he saw into the past. Though their shapes were ever-changing, the monsters wended their way, by foot or by sliding scale, over vast grasslands. When they fought and killed one another, or aged and died after decades of rage, their essences—what Canopians might have called their souls—sank into the soil.

There, those essences were watered by rain and worshippers' tears before becoming corporeal and growing up to clothe their bones in flesh again. The Old Gods walked on, leaving fertile patches of fruit and grain crops behind for the humans to harvest, but these patches never lasted more than a few years. Starving human populations trailed in the titans' wakes again, foraging desperately in hostile lands until their gods died to provide for them.

They must wait, Orin said carelessly. *We will come again onto the land.*

As the Old Gods, the titans, stood arguing at the edge of the puny forest, the humans who worshipped them lagged far behind. It would take the people a year, Leaper estimated, or two, to reach the edge of the sea.

The worshippers carried colourful silk tents and bright pennants. They were black- or dark-brown-skinned, their bodies crowned and jewelled.

How long will you stay in the sea? Leaper wondered. *I don't actually think they can wait that long.*

The forest people's watchtowers were nowhere near the height of the great trees Leaper had been born into. These folk, alarmed by the arrival of the monsters, couldn't see the titan-worshipping peoples coming.

Nor could the golden-skinned guardians of the plains, who surged into view as Oxor considered them. Finally, Oxor considered the pink-skinned sentries squatting in boulder-built fortresses in the foothills. These people used leather tubes and glass lenses to observe the invading titans in turn, and Leaper wondered if he saw what the sun goddess saw because the eye bone in the boat was Oxor's eye.

Dawnsight, he thought. *Oxor. The sun.*

They must wait, Orin repeated with greater emphasis, cutting deeper into Ehkis's skin. *They will wait. They will do what they always do when they cannot find us. Sing songs. Write histories. Fashion our likenesses and make prophecies of our return.*

What say you, Atwith? Ulellin cried. *Will these things die without our leavings to feast on?*

Tell us yourself, Orin said spitefully, her teeth bloody. *Read the wind while you can, for the deep sea must be our next destination.*

The beastlings will die, Ulellin said, *many of them today, because you will not listen. I will not go to the sea. Atwith is silent, he will be fattened by slaughter and well pleased, but what of you, Airak? Say something.* Ulellin appealed to the largest and most hideous of their company, who flared his nostrils and was silent. There was no need for him to say there was no lightning in the deep sea.

The water on the mountain is frozen, Ehkis said petulantly. *I will not go there.*

Lend me your power, Oxor urged, *and I will melt the snow.*

I will not serve you! The superficial wounds of Ehkis's speech turned abruptly into something deadlier. A clear intent to kill. *Let my teeth serve you!*

Oxor—and Leaper, living through her—met the threat with her own teeth bared. The bone-bordered orange frill around her neck sprang open, skin folds turning to fans of open flame. Ehkis shied away from seizing

Oxor by the neck, instead balancing on her tail and kicking at Oxor's rib cage with webbed hind feet.

Leaper instinctively tried to grab his chest, to hold the wound closed, but he had no hands while trapped in the vision, only eyes.

Ehkis's claws seemed to rake his own beating heart.

Red blood fountained over the forest.

Behind Oxor and Ehkis, Airak—*Tyran*—transformed into a shape more nebulous. His eyes shone silver. Forks of lightning lashed, tongue-like, from between his jaws as Orin, transformed into a flattened, wedge-headed serpent feathered with a thousand razor-sharp blades, coiled and struck.

Odel battled Atwith. Audblayin fought Esh. Not one stood aside from the battle. Teeth gnashed. Titans raged, silently singing their hatred through throatfuls of blood.

Oxor, choking, dying, fell heavily into the ankle-deep forest. The humans scattered, their towers destroyed, the course of the river changed forever. Oxor's flames had been quenched by the liquefied body of Ehkis—of the aspect of Oxor's own self that was aligned to the rains. Leaper understood for the first time that all thirteen of them were somehow separate, and yet whole. *Thirteen titans, but also one titan.*

The vision shuddered as Oxor trembled. It calmed as her body lay still.

Leaper knew she was dead, and yet he remained able to see through her wide, lifeless eyes. Events continued to unfold before her corpse. Audblayin and Ulellin were the last titans left standing. One had pursued the other across plains and plateau.

The blows they drove at one another turned the mountains around them to rubble. Audblayin, shrinking like ice melting in the sun, dangling entrails, missing an arm, made as if to wedge her mangled body inside the cave where the river ran. Wooden watchtowers fell there, too, and pink-skinned sentries crashed to their deaths in the froth at the bottom of the waterfall. One of the claws on Audblayin's remaining forelimb snagged the edge of the cave, but broke off under her great weight as she tried to pull herself to safety, and she fell on top of the broken watchtowers.

Ulellin, equally injured, sides heaving and streaming with blood, seized one of her opponent's hind legs in her jaws. She dragged Audblayin back towards the forest where the other aspects had fallen.

No, her furious footsteps read. *You will not die alone on the mountain. You will die with the rest of us, that we all may rise!*

Clutching one another, one monster with smooth, humanlike arms, the other with bird wings ending in strange curved hooks, Ulellin and Audblayin collapsed into the carnage along with all the others.

Night fell, and a small dark green conifer grew out of Audblayin's mouth. Tiny white blossoms covered it, taking on the lustre of the moon.

The night-yew, Leaper thought.

The moon also showed the advanced decay of the flesh and exposure of the white bones of the titans. Slowly but surely, the separated sections of torn-apart skeletons moved through the trees into patterns of alignment.

Before the sun rose, however, an advanced party of worshippers from the dark-skinned peoples arrived. They rode on the backs of some kind of tame, striped plains creature that Leaper had never seen before. Two women and two men came to stand directly before the empty bone circle of what had been Oxor's eye.

"Your dream was a true dream," one woman murmured to the other. They were regal-postured. Richly robed. Leaper read her blue-painted lips, still unable to discern sounds.

"Your steeds carried us faithfully," the other woman replied respectfully. "As you promised that they would. I concede your aptitude with animals is equal to my ability to whisper with the wind."

"Chimera souls," a third woman whispered. "The souls of the winged. They are candles to this bonfire. We have our chance, at last. Our long journey is ended."

Leaper realised there were thirteen of them gathered now, each standing in a muted silvery glow of human power. It was puny compared to that of the titans, yet visible as they delved into the bones of their dead idols with tendrils of timid strength. It was possible they said more to one another, but in the tightening circle, Leaper couldn't see their mouths.

He could see forest people, wounded, terrified, peering at the magicians from interrupted hunting trails and the ruins of their story-paths. The newcomers erected a tent of peeled Godskin and bone, concealing their rites from the baleful eye of the moon, while in the forest, messages spread from palm to palm, in silence.

At length, one brown-faced, blue-lipped man emerged from the Godskin tent. Purple cloths were wrapped around his brow, and his belt-pouches brimmed with shiny black seeds. He walked to one of the striped steeds that had lingered, dozing, in the moon shadow of the night-yew.

The Great One is slain, he carved into the steed's hide with a dagger in his right hand. With his left hand, he brushed a faint blue light over the wound. It stopped the bleeding, and must have somehow numbed the pain, for the creature continued to graze contentedly. *We, the Speakers, will keep the Great One's soul quiet inside our human bodies. It will serve us, as we have served. It will abide by our laws for an age, as we have submitted to its chaos, and let the young never know the hardships endured by the old. Let them forget.*

At the same time, Leaper glimpsed warnings being traced between Rememberer shoulder blades or on the backs of Rememberer hands.

We have never seen such destruction before. Our people must Remember.

The blue-lipped man slapped the grazing creature on the hindquarters, and it startled into a swift gait that carried it out of sight, into the west. Those small trees left standing were pushed up and out by the roots by something bigger growing out of the earth beneath them.

The great trees.

Leaper felt himself losing the vision, even as the night-yew erupted skyward, clinging to the terminal shoot of the biggest tallowwood tree the world had ever seen.

FIFTEEN

Sounds shattered the silence around Leaper.

Vomiting acolytes. Wind screaming around the old man wedged in the open doorway, still bellowing at the top of his lungs. Leaper tried to understand him. Audible words were strange after the script-speech and lipreading of the vision. He shook his head, lantern still in one hand, the stone plinth at his back. His other hand, he lowered from his mouth, feeling his rib cage still intact. He was not Oxor. His beating heart had not been sliced open.

"Brace yourselves!" Yes, that was what the old man was shouting over his shoulder. "Hold on to one another!"

Beyond him, Leaper glimpsed a sharpened, patterned prow like none he'd seen before. No, wait. He had seen it. It was the vast canoe the Rememberers had carved from the remnants of Airak's old Temple. Surging from between the trees like a swung axe.

The wind spun the craft where Leaper sprawled. Bodies tumbled away from him. A complete ring of bone, bigger and thicker than the shards from the other Temple, bounced off the wall and broke his nose. He brought both arms up to protect his face, but luckily the boat tilted again, the bone fell away at the last second, and his skull wasn't crushed. The thieves' lantern came to life.

Airak is going to save me after all, he thought wildly. *My god is giving me one last chance.*

Leaper fumbled to open the pane of the lantern just as the bigger boat smashed through the side of the cabin. *Dawnsight* flew apart. In the buzzing blue-white light, Leaper saw the whites of eyes and the crescents of teeth in howling mouths. Then he lost his grip on the lantern.

It fell, open, onto the curved edge of Oxor's bone and swallowed it whole, as though forcing pieces through it at Dusksight had given the thieves' lantern an appetite for Old God's remains. Leaper snatched it up again before it could tumble further, wondering if it would swallow the whole monsoon, transporting it to Eshland in an endless loop; a fountain that would never stop flowing.

The two halves of the torn craft spun apart into the dark. Water entered everywhere. Leaper didn't know if it was floodwater or rain. He rolled down the sharply tilted floor of the wreck and was caught by his harness on a carving of ravens.

One. Last. Chance.

He tried to force the hand not holding the lantern inside the open pane, but blasts of wind erupted impossibly from the heart of it.

Leaves came with the wind, too.

Windowleaves. Where no windowleaf trees grow.

At last, Leaper realised why he couldn't squeeze himself through the lantern this time.

Ulellin's curse. It's her wind blowing, keeping me away from Canopy.

Still stuck on the carving, he rolled underwater as the canoe-section rolled. Surfaced as it surfaced. Choked and spluttered. He should have let go of the lantern, to use both hands to untie his harness, but as long as he held it, somebody might see him.

Somebody might save me!

The lantern went out.

A hand seized Leaper's wrist where he held the upraised lantern in the dark. Somebody smaller than he was hauled him up and onto something ridged that felt like a bamboo raft.

"Ellin?" he gasped. "Ousos?" But no, that was wrong, they were bigger than this person. His oxygen-starved mind seized on impossibilities. "Youngest-Father? Anahah?"

And then the whirlpool carried them, spinning sickeningly, out of the forest again. In a dim grey gloom, through battering rain, a lightning strike showed him the bare back of his rescuer, someone golden-skinned with black hair in a tight, fist-sized bun.

There was no glowing Rememberer's sigil between the little man's shoulder blades. Instead, raised scars like firewheel tree bark covered him from neck to heels.

Not like bark. Like a crocodile's ridged spine.

A Crocodile-Rider. A Crocodile-Rider has rescued me.

Water washed over the raft and tugged at Leaper's torso. He wedged his fingers between the uneven poles of the raft, in the gaps where green lashings held it all together. Death seemed certain. If not by drowning, then by execution, when this man realised who he was.

He closed his eyes against the nauseating twisting of the raft and remembered how he had once told his oldest-father that he wished Airak were his father.

Airak is powerful, he'd shouted. *Airak is never afraid!*

Yet Oldest-Father had never drowned children. Leaper remembered the woman losing her bundle over the side of the boat only minutes ago. Had it been nut cakes and fruit, and her horror the horror of a woman staring into the future at her own starvation? Or had it been a baby? Had the death in her eyes been her own, or another's?

Oldest-Father wasn't perfect. He killed in self-defence. He killed Kirrik's men. Airak is doing the same. Airak is doing this to defend himself. But Leaper couldn't convince himself that it was equivalent. He couldn't stop seeing the expression on the woman's face, imagining it multiplied a thousand times.

I can't serve you again, Airak. If I survive this, you'll have to find another, of equivalent gifts, or whatever it was that you said, because I can never serve you again.

The raft shuddered and slowed. Leaper opened his eyes again. His end of the raft had struck something. Something heavy lay over the edge of it, stabilising it against the flow.

He had moments to realise that it was a crocodile. Huge head as long as Leaper was tall. Legs pressed to its sinuous sides. Jaws wide. Its gape was a pace from tip to tip. One more wriggle of that powerful tail, and the teeth would snap shut on Leaper's head and shoulders.

And then the little man with the scars, giving a hoot of wild glee, dived with outstretched arms for the crocodile's gullet, as though the back of the reptile's obscene yellow throat, akin to Leaper's lantern, was a magical doorway to light and a long life.

PART II

The Bright Plain

SIXTEEN

LEAPER WOKE, sprawled on his back, to the sound of cheerful humming rising over the pattering rain.

Above him, the afternoon sky was empty. No branches. No leaves. Just clouds. Droplets aiming themselves at his eyes. Empty. Leaper turned his head. He'd imagined the sea to himself sometimes, but the frightening blankness of the flooded plain was nothing like what he'd imagined.

He'd imagined waves. The woodcarvers always depicted white wave crests so crowded with boats and masts they might as well have been a forest in miniature. This was nothingness.

He shivered.

"They keep me awake," Yran confided from the far end of the raft when he spotted that his dazed companion was awake. "My little songs do. You know what happens if I can't stay awake."

"No," Leaper said stiffly in the language of the Crocodile-Riders, sounding nasal to himself, sitting up and gingerly probing his broken nose. "Tell me."

The little man who had saved him from the floodwaters that morning had already proven himself an inveterate liar by introducing himself as Yran of Gui. When Leaper answered that he recognised the raised ritual markings of the Crocodile-Riders, Yran said nonchalantly that he'd been sent as a spy from Gui to live among Crocodile-Riders in disguise.

What about the language we're speaking? Leaper had asked sluggishly, rolling to regurgitate river water over the edge of the bamboo raft.

I learned it by studying, the same as you, Yran called back brightly.

What about the crocodile you wrestled, force-fed, and tied to our raft with flimsy little ropes? That crocodile right there?

The flat-headed, ten-pace-long menace floated, quiescent, on what Leaper considered an ineffectually puny tether. Eyes half lidded, scales speckled olive-green, yellow, and grey, it flicked its body every now and then for a course correction or to tug the raft on a jerky detour around trapped logs or protruding greenery.

Besides the bamboo, the whole world, then as now, had been a grey nothing. Grey waters covered the plain. They reflected the grey sky. Only a black smudge on the horizon hinted at the presence of the Titan's Forest well to the east of them.

Yran hadn't answered, at that time.

"The crocodile will go wild again when I fall asleep," he said now. "And she'll be angry that we made her help us. Really angry. She's got eggs inside her, but this way is not where she wanted to build a nest for them. Now the monsoon's here, she can't lay them at all, so it's either waste them into the water or they'll get stuck inside her and she'll die."

"How exactly did we make her help us?"

"We asked nicely."

"What?" Leaper shifted carefully so that he was facing Yran. "What are you talking about? How do you know all that, about the eggs?"

"We prayed to the crocodile god." Yran made an odd gesture, palms pressed together, eyes closed, chin tilted upwards.

"We did not." Leaper fumbled for grip on the bamboo as the raft kicked over a rill. "I did not. There is no crocodile god."

"We made her help us," Yran confessed, sighing, "with magic. The magic wears off when I fall asleep, though."

Yran punctuated this pronouncement with a flash of perfect, straight teeth. The grin was visible through a slit in his hat that he angled towards Leaper when he was speaking.

Then he turned away and went back to humming his bizarre tune.

Leaper's carrysack, lumpy with such useless items as his no-longer-functional thieves' lantern and an assortment of adzes with no trees within reach, had not provided the most comfortable of pillows. More painful were the dreams he'd endured while the hostile winds of Ulellin's curse had driven the bamboo raft in a wide circle that skirted the circumference of Canopy.

Ilik, throat gaping, blood running over the land like the waters of the monsoon. Ousos and Airak, laughing as lightning struck the plain, knowing Leaper was being tossed on a raft in the relentless rain.

Despite the water bubbling up between the bamboo poles at his feet, Yran kept relatively dry beneath an umbrella-like hat he'd made that morning. At the first protruding bamboo clump they'd passed, Yran had somehow signalled the crocodile to keep them still while he cut himself enough canes to poke through the black bun on top of his head. Then, using long leaves from the first clump of rushes they'd passed, he'd woven it watertight, leaving only the wedge-shaped gap at the front for peering through. It covered him from crown to heels where he crouched, humming, with the reins of the crocodile's harness in his fist.

Yran's only luggage was a long bundle wrapped in cloth of indeterminate origin and tied with the same lashings that held the raft together.

"What's in your bundle there?" Leaper asked. "Food? Water?"

Yran bonked himself on top of his bun with one fist, which Leaper was learning to interpret as a sign that the Crocodile-Rider thought Leaper was crazy.

"Water? In this rain? We can catch some at any time!"

As if to emphasise that they couldn't, they drifted too far to the west and the rain stopped.

"Rain comes from the goddess," Leaper said tightly, "and she's tied to the forest."

"The current will carry us back, closer."

"And when it does, the wind goddess will drive us away again!"

"You must have made your wind goddess very, very angry. Please tell me the story."

"The monsoon must have caught you unawares," Leaper said, changing the subject. "You did well to get the raft finished so quickly. Or did you use magic for that, too?"

Magic to tame crocodiles. That isn't how it's done. Or is it? He struggled to remember what the woman he'd met so many years ago had said about magic among Crocodile-Riders. She hadn't wanted him to look for Aurilon's bones because they were pollution, he remembered that much. The Old Gods' bones, too. All pollution. They *didn't* use magic. Was he recalling the exchange erroneously? Or was Yran lying to him again, trying to discourage him from any thoughts of rebelliously taking over the raft and hoarding Yran's presumed bundle of supplies to himself?

Rebellion would serve no purpose. There was only one way the raft was going, despite the current's best efforts to carry it towards Canopy, and that was at an angle to the forest, deflected by winds that emanated from amongst the trees but could only be most effective in close proximity to it. The crocodile kept them from disastrous collisions but was helpless to dictate their overall direction.

"I can tie knots faster than anyone alive," Yran boasted.

"What—" Leaper started to say, but in a flash the wiry man was behind him, tightening a noose around his neck. Leaper slid a hand in between the rope and his neck, and before he could recall that he was injured, the spines in his forearms extruded.

Pain brought an involuntary cry to his lips. The lashings sliced and fell away, freeing him. Yran balanced, wide-legged, on the raft to one side of him, looking down in amazement through the crack in his hat.

"Got some good tricks, yourself," he sputtered.

Leaper held his forearm out in front of him, staring at the throbbing, blood-smeared spines. His tight burn scars had burst at the seams like swollen fruit. It was a mess. With conscious thought, he withdrew the spines into his long bones.

"Those scars," Yran guessed, squatting abruptly, his umbrella hat covering his knees. "Are they from years of putting those arm-teeth out and in? Killed a hundred warriors with them, have you?"

"No," Leaper said, watching the blood run into the water, feeling suddenly light-headed and wondering if it would attract more crocodiles. "I took an oath against killing."

"Oh, me too. No killing. Not me. That rope around your neck was a joke! But you didn't laugh."

"Do you have any way to purify water?"

"No." Yran shrugged. "Bad water might make us vomit or bleed when we squat, I know. My nasty mother used to strain water through a clay bowl first, or through cups of dried fungi. In dry season, we'd cut watervine and hang it over bamboo pots in the evening, so we could drink clean water from the pot the next morning."

"Will you stop listing things we don't actually have? What *do* we have?"

Yran held his belly while he threw back his head and laughed, the back edge of the woven, waterproof hat tapping at his heels.

"Crocodile tears, Canopian," he hooted. "We'll eat crocodile eggs and drink crocodile tears until we get to the sea. It is safe for her to drink from the flood, and she will make the water safe for us."

Leaper assumed his odd companion was joking again. So he was surprised when Yran got to his feet, wrapped the reins around one bamboo pole of the raft, and used both hands to unravel his hat. He opened one corner of the long bundle, and stowed the hat components inside. Leaper glimpsed staves and stoppered bamboo containers of various widths and lengths, and a shimmer that might have been chimera skin sliding over the browns and golden-striped greens.

When he tied his bundle tightly again, Yran came up holding a bamboo cup.

"Watch this!" he cried, and ran out along the crocodile's back. He dropped down onto its neck, dangling both his legs in the swirling brown water, and held the cup to one of its eyes. "Cry! Drink now, and cry!"

The crocodile's jaws opened and closed, working up white froth in the water. Tears ran over the glassy surface of its eyeball and into Yran's cup. Leaper itched to rub his own eyes, hesitating in anticipation of pain, but wondering how this could be happening.

Yran danced back to him on the raft. Pressed the cup to his lips. Leaper sipped the crocodile's tears, finding sweetness where he expected salt, and saying so.

"Only when we get to the sea," Yran said. "Now she must conserve salt. Later she must shed it. Hold the cup."

Leaper gripped it loosely in the hand that wasn't covered in blood. He watched, wordlessly, as Yran assaulted the swimming reptile once again, lying facedown along its length, his head at the crocodile's tail end, and groping around underneath it with one hand.

He came up with a crocodile egg. It was dirty white, oval shaped, and leathery shelled. Yran bit into it, tearing a small hole, and squeezed the contents into the bamboo cup, which Leaper still held. The yolk was blood-spotted and air bubbles were trapped in the surrounding slime. In Airak-land, eggs were always cooked. Not so in Understorey.

"Drink half," Yran exhorted, and Leaper did as he was told, reaching futilely with magical senses that had deserted him, wishing he could sense what Yran was doing. The Crocodile-Rider drank down the other half of the raw egg, smacking his lips with satisfaction. "She can catch fish for us, too, later. It is not the rope that binds her, after all, but the magic."

"Oh, good," Leaper said.

And then Yran began to yawn and stretch.

"I'm tired," he murmured, as if in confidence. As if he hadn't been travelling through the night when the monsoon caught him in the open, built his raft in the early hours of the morning, and then stayed awake all day while Leaper dozed. "We're both tired, my crocodile and me. I'll tell her to sleep, and I'll sleep while she sleeps. That will be safe, but you mustn't sleep. That's very important. You'll wake me before the crocodile wakes."

"How will I know if she wakes?" Leaper asked, indicating the darkening sky. "It'll be night." His cold, dead lantern remained packed in his carrysack.

"Sleep," Yran commanded the crocodile, ignoring Leaper, and the crocodile closed one eye. Yran hooted. "You see how she tries to fool me? Sleeping with one eye open. It's how she sleeps, usually, but it's not how I need her to sleep now. Sleep, I say!"

The crocodile closed her other eye, and her tail movements stopped.

"Is she sleeping?" Leaper asked.

"Lie there," Yran instructed. "Put your hand on the tip of her tail. You should just be able to reach it. If it twitches, you'll feel it. When you feel it, wake me." He left Leaper at the front of the canoe and fetched the hat makings from his bundle.

This time, he made the hat disconnected from the hair on his head, so that he could partially curl up beneath it, his thin bare legs poking out, his head resting on the bundle. "Oh, and one more thing," he called drowsily from beneath the woven dome. "The water is rushing east towards the forest, while the wind is blowing us back. You can see the little white wave at the western edge of our raft. It's possible something large, like a log or a Rememberer canoe, could be blown towards us by those winds, from the direction of the forest. But it will be against the current, just like our raft. It will make a white wave, the same as us. Only, bigger. And it will sound like this." He made a hissing noise. "Listen for that. Wake me if you hear something like that."

IN THE darkest part of the night, Leaper heard something that sounded like the hissing noise Yran had demonstrated.

He lifted his cheek from the bamboo. Despite the monotony, he hadn't fallen asleep.

The right half of his body was numb with cold. Water surging through the poles kept him continually wet, and the wind was on that side. His left arm, extended to touch the crocodile's tail, tingled too, from the strange pressure of holding the position for so long.

Was it his imagination, or was the wind stronger? He thought the current had increased in speed and brought them closer to the forest. Could the louder sound be simply because Ulellin's curse was pushing harder against them, due to their proximity?

Light flared momentarily at the seams of his carrysack.

The thieves' lantern.

Leaper withdrew his arm and rolled onto his side, ignoring screaming muscles and feeling coming back into flesh made lumpy by the ridges of the bamboo. With numb fingers, he unlaced the sack, only to find his lantern dead again.

No, not quite dead after all. Something like the fitful flicker of a star lived inside the clear panes of glass. His first instinct was to stick his arm into it, but then he remembered the windowleaves and wind that had kept him out of it the last time. Ulellin's curse.

Stop staring into it, Leaper. Lift it. Use it to scout the way. Not to ruin whatever night vision you might have had!

Leaper lifted the lantern in the direction they were drifting. The crocodile floated, inert as a corpse, in its traces. The hissing noise grew louder, and it started to rain.

They had to have drifted closer to Canopy. Ulellin's wind, Ehkis's rain, and Airak's lantern were all growing in strength. Increasingly dense falling droplets reminded Leaper again of the diamonds in Ilik's hair. He wondered what he was doing, where he was going, reminding himself again that her killer's trail was covered in monsoon floodwaters, that finding her murderer was no longer an option, and neither was returning to Canopy.

And then he spotted the whirlpool.

Some one hundred paces ahead.

The white ring of the whirlpool's rim wasn't especially wide; it was barely wider than the raft. Yet Leaper could clearly see the flotsam ahead of them tilting at the edge of it, like a spectator hesitating to stick his head through the bone ring of Oxor's eye. After that moment of hesitation, the flotsam sped straight down. Floating dirt clods, reed bundles like bird nests, and the heavy fronds of distant trees were all sucked sharply under.

They did not reappear.

Leaper danced awkwardly across the raft.

"Yran," he said, crouching, shaking the legs that stuck out from underneath the hat. "There's a whirlpool. Wake up." He lifted the bell-shaped hat off his unresponsive host.

Yran's groggy, gummy-eyed face looked like an overboiled bulrush root in the feeble light of the lantern. He raised his arm to shield his face from the rain.

"What?" he croaked in Canopian. "Who are you?"

Leaper was silent for a startled moment, tongue-tied by his desire to answer in the same language even as his mouth formed the words in the language of the Crocodile-Riders.

"One who walks in the grace of Airak is called Leaper," he managed at last. "And our raft is heading straight for a whirlpool, Yran. It's time to wake that crocodile, if you can."

Yran stared at Leaper a second longer before tapping himself on the temple.

"Good thinking," he said. "Waking me."

He rolled into a crouch beside his bundle, while Leaper held the hat in one hand, the lantern in the other, and helplessly watched the whirlpool grow closer. Before he realised what Yran was doing, the smaller man had whipped a rope out of the bundle and lashed Leaper's lantern hand, along with the lantern handle, to the raft.

"What are you—"

"For safety!" Yran cried, pulling the knots tight.

The next thing he pulled out of his bundle was an unsheathed sword carved from a single piece of ivory. Along the hilt and forming the curved quillons were some variety of rosette-spotted cats. Jaguars, fishing cats, or ocelots. Maybe leopards. Leaper wasn't great with animals. His fathers had been hunters, but the trade had become his sister Imeris's legacy, not his own.

He recognised the weapon, though, and was dumbfounded.

Aurilon's sword.

It was what he'd been looking for, ten years ago. Had Yran found it then, or now? Why was he scraping at it with an axe?

"Hold this," Yran said, sticking the sword, hilt first, into Leaper's climbing harness. He held two tiny slivers of bone from the sword, and immediately swallowed one of them. Nothing happened that Leaper could sense or see.

Yran took a valuable few seconds to tie his bundle tightly back to the raft.

"What are you—" Leaper started to ask again. The whirlpool was practically upon them. Yran took a short run, jumped, and landed on the crocodile's head with both feet.

She came awake at once. One terrible eye caught the light. She twisted and lunged, openmouthed, at man and raft. Yran tipped into the water. He came up with both arms wrapped around the crocodile's lower jaw, snagged on her crooked, stained teeth. Those jaws snapped shut, blood ran, and as the crocodile began tilting, headfirst, towards the whirlpool, Leaper fought the urge to close his eyes against the drowning death the three of them were rushing to meet.

But then the crocodile rose out of the water, propelled by her powerful tail.

God's bones.

She seemed to hang vertically over the whirlpool. Her scales glistened. Half the sky was blocked by the sight of her. Leaper hung by one wrist from the bamboo raft, which dangled in turn below the slowly twisting column of her bulk. It was all he could do to hold onto Yran's hat. Yran himself hung from both arms beneath the crocodile's head.

They landed in air, then dirt, then water.

Leaper held his breath for so long that a branching red pattern showed behind his eyelids. When he opened his mouth, he wasn't sure if he would suck in life or death; he only knew that he had to suck in something, that his lungs were the deep river and his lips the white circle of the whirlpool on the surface.

He breathed Ulellin's winds, with a smattering of cold rain that made him wheeze. After a minute or two, he realised he was kneeling on the raft, that the crocodile was quiescent, and their journey down the river had resumed.

Yran's hat was gone.

The Crocodile-Rider untied Leaper's trapped wrist with a hoot of laughter. He recovered sword from harness in a gleeful, bloodied grip and shook it under Leaper's averted gaze.

"We've both eaten from Orin's body. The crocodile and me. It makes us one. We think each other's thoughts. Until we go to sleep again, but it's your turn to sleep, friend. Might I hold your lantern while you take your turn? I judge it an hour before dawn still."

"No," Leaper said. "The sword goes in your bundle. The lantern goes in my carrysack." He put it away slowly. Carefully. Tying the laces methodically. "Where did you get that sword, by the way?" *Strong pollution*, the woman had said. What had her name been? Leaper wasn't old, but he felt old, thinking of the human faces that had passed in and out of his life, and no way to know who they had truly been or where they were now.

"Got any food in there?" Yran asked, ignoring his question.

Leaper's stomach growled.

"No." He tried not to show his anger at Yran's dissembling.

"Hungry?" Yran laughed. "Not yet. One hundred eggs. One hundred days until we reach the sea. We must be sure that we do not exhaust her before then."

Exhaust her? I'm exhausted. Forget starvation and infected wounds. Forget lack of sleep. Being alone on a raft with this man is exhausting.

"What's at sea," Leaper asked bitterly, "that you're so keen to arrive there?"

"The City, of course. Wetwoodknee, the City-by-the-Sea. Don't you know of it?"

"No."

"Good for trade. Almost as good as Gui. And my nasty mother will never find me there, I know it in my liver. She'll never be able to make me marry!"

Leaper didn't ask the obvious questions. He refused to be led down the trail Yran had shown him. Just as Yran had refused to be led.

"What's at the City-by-the-Sea," he repeated, "for me? Why share the crocodile's eggs with somebody unknown? Why did you tie me to the raft instead of letting the whirlpool take me? You'd have been able to steer whichever way you wanted, once you'd gotten rid of me."

"One," Yran said, "I need somebody to wake me when my crocodile wakes. Too risky, otherwise."

"And two?"

"Two! You'd be good for trading. A most excellent slave. You could be a translator, since you've stolen and eaten a splinter of the throat bone of the Old God now called Odel. I've eaten it, too, but you knew that, future slave. Agile slave. Cunning slave." Yran grinned. "You could be a fighter, with those razors you hide, but the best thing to do with you would be to trade you back to Canopy for a fallen tree. Wood's precious at the City-by-the-Sea, and the last time they tried to take some without asking, your god sent a few lightning bolts to burn them to the ground."

"I see," Leaper said mildly, wondering whether to cut Yran's throat immediately, or to wait for the next time the Crocodile-Rider went to sleep.

"You're thinking you won't be a slave." Yran waggled one finger. "You're thinking you can use bone magic the same as me. But you weren't born in a crocodile's nest. You weren't taught to separate her thoughts from yours. You try to take her from me, and you'll get stuck in her body forever. Your human self will stop eating or drinking, waste away and die. And then you'll die, Canopian, because your soul can't survive in a crocodile's body. Besides, you don't know the way to Wetwoodknee. Once you reached the salt, you'd die at sea. So you'd best be taking care of me."

SEVENTEEN

NINETY-EIGHT DAYS went by on the waterlogged plain.

Leaper mulled over the visions he'd seen of the forest's creation and destruction. He thought about how the beings he'd known as goddesses and gods were simply adepts who'd had the presence of mind to scoop up the titans' essence and weld it to their souls at the opportune moment, giving immortality not only to their spirits but to their memories.

If I'd been there, if I'd been one of them, would I have become, post-godhood, as callous and selfish as they are now? Would he have drowned thousands of people for the sake of maintaining his own power?

He didn't think so. But then, his sister Ylly had been raised in Understorey, and showed no sign of distress at the fact that Understorian villages were regularly decimated by demons. Could one deity stand up to the twelve others, declaring the barrier open, or would they cast her out, as they had seemed to cast out the mysterious fourteenth member of their company? The fourteenth aspect of their single self? *You never know what you will do, or won't do, until the choice is yours.*

Rain came and went. The great crocodile sailed on alone, or with an escort of smaller reptiles hoping for the scraps from her meals. Leaper's clothing was rarely completely dry, but he'd discovered that sleeping on the lee side of Yran's long bundle, protected from the wind, kept him from losing too much body heat.

Passing days were marked by Yran's collection and their shared consumption of crocodile eggs. Yran induced their steed to catch fish for them at every opportunity. These they ate raw. Since the night of the whirlpool, every time that Leaper checked his lantern, it gave no light, and he contemplated lighting a fire for cooking fish in the sturdy lantern frame, but decided against it in the end. The forest stayed in the distance, shrinking to a grey blur on the horizon to the south as time went on but, except through the deepest fog, always visible.

Always tantalisingly out of reach.

Every day, at dawn, after Leaper had woken Yran but before Leaper went to sleep, Yran told a different story about why he had left the safety and comfort of his own society. Leaper blatantly avoided explanations of why he'd left his.

"I was born to a couple with very low status," Yran related, his profile made lumpy by leech and fly bites. "It wouldn't have been possible for me to marry, ever. Not a clean wife, anyhow. The best I could've expected, if I tamed an exceptional crocodile and built a paragon of houses, would've been a wife who'd been soiled by touching bones or finding her first husband dead by her side. Our people are a closed-in people. Nobody enters, and nobody leaves. I would have been lonely all my life. Would you have stayed, if it was you, Leaper, never to marry?"

Leaper's glowing sigil, given by the bone man, Estehass, had faded, taking his protection against insects with it. His skin was similarly spotted and itching, though his bites were from enormous striped mosquitoes in the night rather than the black biting flies of the day.

Occasionally he considered hiding from the swarm by floating behind the raft, mostly submerged as the crocodile was, yet a single glimpse of a highly venomous snake swimming along beside them had induced him to abandon the idea, and he had started to dream pleasantly of being dry again, of holding his hands out to the hearth flames of the home where he was raised.

Occasionally, the dreams seemed more real than the raft, and he started to wonder if slow starvation on the meagre fish and egg diet was better than being bitten by a venomous snake.

"I thought you were running away from your nasty mother, who wanted you to marry."

Yran's grin split his face.

"Oh, yes! Of course. That is the true story."

Leaper had heard so many so-called true stories that he spent half his time with his hands pressed to his ears, feeling the rain run over them and wishing to dissolve like salt. Apart from the snake, they'd passed other sad and sodden-looking animals, stranded on the fixed tops of bamboo clumps or crowded onto uprooted cattails, pythons and parrots sharing islands no more than a pace across, predator and prey too tired to even look at each other.

"You had to run, hypocrite," he told Yran. "You're the one who's soiled, according to your customs. You told me yourself that you ate the speaking-bone. They'd punish you with death if you went back to them. Taking your hair, they call it, right?" He shook his head, trying to clear the image of the king gripping Ilik's diamond-woven tresses. *She refused to come away with me. Would I have stayed, never to marry?*

"There's a bundle," Yran cried, pointing at a package floating past. "Leather wrapped. Grab hold of it. It could be food!"

Leaper sighed and slipped a bamboo rod from Yran's trussed bundle. It could be food, or it could be another pregnant pig drowned in her burrow, with her hide all loose and horrible.

The bamboo rod was chopped into a hook at one end. Leaper used it to snag the man-sized bundle, gagging when it turned out to be a body. Cloak and hood came free, showing a skull with shreds of worm-eaten flesh still covering one cheek. Leaper shoved it angrily away with the rod. It was the tenth or twelfth body they'd seen, and he wanted it gone before Yran insisted on searching it, as he'd exhaustively searched drowned Remember-ers he'd found while Leaper was sleeping.

"What are you doing? There could have been valuables in the pockets!"

"Was he buried with valuables in his pockets? Because this one was under the ground! Whoever buried him didn't dig deep enough!"

"He was from Gui." Yran waved dismissively. "They don't usually bury their dead in the month before the monsoon. They preserve them with spirits until the water goes down, a waste of spirits if you ask me. This time, thanks to your gods, nobody knew it was the month before the monsoon. Or do I owe *you* my thanks for this flood?" He hooted abruptly, showing his perfect teeth. "The rain covers human tracks. No better chance to get away from my nasty mother! Well? Tell me! Was it you?"

His head was tilted slyly, and his eyes sparkled with good humour, but Leaper sensed that Yran cared as much about the question as Leaper cared about where Yran had gotten Aurilon's sword.

"Somebody killed the queen of Airakland," he began carefully, but Yran leaped ahead to excited conclusions.

"The monsoon is vengeance!"

"The monsoon is not vengeance! The monsoon has nothing to do with her, or with me. I didn't want the rains to come early. It covers human tracks, like you said. Now her killer can't be found. My mission is over. I never even saw her body."

Yran shrugged.

"Why should you see it? Is that what Canopians do with their dead? See them?"

They don't usually bury their dead in the month before the monsoon.

"We don't see them," Leaper said slowly. "We let them fall."

Yran's people aren't supposed to touch the dead. The Rememberers said they lit fires to call demons to their dead. If Ilik wasn't there to be found, does that mean she might have been buried? By somebody from Gui? But Slehah said it wasn't safe for anyone from Gui to come between the trees.

"Have you heard the story of Grandfather Gollorag?" Yran asked cheerfully. "He was killed by a falling cone from a false palm. Those cones are as big as your head, and spiky. The nuts make good eating, though, and that was why Grandfather Gollorag's clan built their boats beneath the tree. In the wake of his death, it became clear that Gollorag had made a poor choice, so his son Ollorag moved the clan to the roots of a spinach tree. Ollorag had no way of knowing that the tree-dwellers kept tapirs in spinach trees for the healthful, tapir-fattening foliage, which our people enjoy eating very much when birds and animals break the branches loose. What the tree-dwellers, perhaps, should have considered before taking their livestock into the trees is that tapirs do not fly. As Ollorag discovered when one fell on his head, killing him."

Leaper couldn't think while Yran was telling his stupid stories. *Is it obvious what happened to Ilik? Can I not see it plainly because of my grief?*

"Is that the end of the story?" *Please, let it be the end.*

"Ollorag's son Orag dutifully moved the clan again," Yran went on, waggling his feet in the air with mirth, "to the roots of a floodgum tree. Nothing useful ever falls from a floodgum tree, the saying went, but at least the clan's people would be safe, according to Orag's calculations. Unfortunately, Orag had no idea how often Canopians enjoy killing their gods. So he, in turn, was slain by the falling corpse of Airak."

"That's funny. Very funny. What a great story. Is it over?"

"That was the end of Grandfather Gollorag's line. The women consulted amongst themselves, deciding what to do. It was they who appointed the first of the Greatmothers, who have been ruining men's lives ever since.

Including my father's. He's one of the Greatmother's royal husbands, did you know? I am actually a prince. Yet not even my exulted position could keep me beneath the trees. I've always felt the urge to live in the light."

Leaper hardly heard him. Words buried in his memory came back to him like a blow: *Burned alive on a boat. That's what the woman I met ten years ago said they would do to Aurilon. Cut her hair and then burn her alive on a boat.*

The dead are only pollution after they're dead.

"I have to go back," he said, shocked by his conclusion. He reached for Canopy with both hands as though he could seize its shadow and drag the raft towards it despite Ulellin's winds. "She could be there, in Crocodile-Rider territory, waiting to be burned alive!"

"Never," Yran said, rolling onto his back and holding his new hat over his face with his feet. "Burning is for clan members only. Clan members who treacherously worship Canopian deities. Besides, no Canopian queen could be brought into Crocodile-Rider lands. She would pollute our pure women by her presence. We don't mingle with outsiders."

"Don't you?" Leaper shouted, losing his temper suddenly as he had with Ousos. "You don't mingle with people like me? Just like you don't grab corpses with a bamboo hook, in case they died with valuables in their pockets? Just like you obey your mothers, or your Greatmothers, or whoever's in charge of you? Just like you don't touch the bones of the Old Gods?" He grabbed Yran's cloth bundle and would have thrown it overboard, if the little man hadn't kicked his hat out of the way, flown at Leaper, and latched onto the bundle with hands, feet, and perfect teeth.

"Mine!" he growled through a mouthful of cloth. "You want the crocodile to turn on us before we get to Wetwoodknee?"

"Where did you get the sword?" Leaper tried and failed to keep holding the bundle. When he let go, Yran dropped, bottom first, back onto the raft, opening his mouth and looking mildly stunned. "It's Aurilon's sword. Did you get it from her dead body? What else did you take from her?" He heard the outrage in his voice, the hypocrisy.

We are as bad as one another. We deserve one another.

"Don't give up, poor boy," Yran entreated. "Angry boy. Cursed boy. Don't kill us both!"

"Why shouldn't I?"

"If you're dwelling on what I said about slaves, of course I didn't mean it. I wouldn't sell you to the women of Wetwoodknee. They don't keep slaves, don't you know that? And they can't be enslaved themselves. Too bad, since they're so pretty. You're pretty, broken nose and all, but I still wouldn't sell you. Not even to the Master of Cast."

"Not even to who?" Leaper snapped. He'd never heard of the Master of Cast.

"You saved my life! You woke me when you saw the whirlpool. We share the same liver. I've never had a friend before. Calm yourself and let's eat a crocodile egg together. Egg number ninety-nine. Our journey is almost over." And Yran began shedding great blubbering tears, unmistakeable even in the rain. "Not one friend! That's why I left home and never looked back. I could have endured every indignity the Greatmother heaped on me if only I'd had just one true friend to talk to."

Leaper's anger drained away.

EIGHTEEN

"Look," Yran said at dusk when he shook Leaper awake.

Leaper uncurled, stretched, and looked. It was difficult to concentrate. He was so hungry. The bones of his hips and spine were painful against the corrugations of the raft.

"What is it?"

"Our destination. You can see. The palace at the heart of Wetwoodknee."

The monsoon was over. The skies were clear. The winds had fallen away. Yran's crocodile towed them under its own power across a mirrorlike surface showing lemon yellow sky faded overhead to a deep, soft blue littered with stars.

Ripples from her passage spread ahead and to the sides of her, sending waterfowl honking into the skies. Leaper peered past the crocodile to the route ahead. With the exception of the solitary-seeming structure Yran had named a palace, the City-by-the-Sea was concealed by a mangrove forest that touched the eastern and western horizons.

Leaper supposed the spread of semisubmerged trees was a forest, though the greyish, shrubby mangroves were stunted in comparison to the great trees of Canopy. Those spindly mangrove branches would surely hardly bear the weight of a full-grown human, much less the weight of a great palace.

The protruding part of the so-called palace was a tall, grey, round tower, built from what appeared to be driftwood. Arched windows and shaded semicircular balconies spiralled around the upper half of it, while the conical roof was covered in a kind of leathery white weed. A pair of elegant, pale grey birds of prey perched on a twig nest at the very top.

"Should we . . . I don't know . . . should we moor here at the edge of the trees and approach in the morning? What if the raft becomes trapped by some narrow passage or we lose sight of the tower in the dark?"

"No! They will light lamps in the tower soon, you'll see. If the raft is trapped, we'll set the crocodile free and climb the rest of the way. We've nothing to eat but more raw fish, and Queen Erta is famous for her hospitality. She'll feast us for a song. She's very fond of music. Do you know any songs, Canopian?"

It was true enough about the food; their crocodile had stopped giving eggs six or seven days ago. Leaper stared at the lanterns coming to life in the arched windows of the wood-and-white-weed tower. They were feeble things. Not like Airak's lanterns.

Airak the white with his forked swords of light
stole the gleam from the Old One's eye
while the winged and the furred, the beast and the bird
come when summoned by Orin, or die.

Oldest-Father had taught him the Understorian version of the godsong. Later, Youngest-Mother, laughing, had sneaked him into her workroom and taught him the mnemonic her mother had taught her for remembering the names of all the Canopian deities. *Every Imbecile Agrees: One Angry Orange Ant Is Under An Ugly Old Entrance.*

"There's one song I know fairly well," Leaper sighed. "I can't sing it. I don't have a good voice. Not like my youngest-father. They called him the Nightingale."

"The birds that sing at night here," Yran said, "are curlews. Nicknamed screaming womanbirds. When you hear one, you'll understand why."

They entered the close margin of the mangrove forest. Leaper had seen the round-leafed, short-trunked trees with their dense, arching, stilt-like roots carved on the Gates of the Garden; that was how he knew what they were called. In the depiction, the mangroves' roots formed labyrinthine sanctuaries for pearl-producing oysters and giant crabs, their branches providing perches for egrets and sea eagles.

Yet whatever edibles were to be found clinging to the roots, they were well hidden by the floodwater covering the river delta, which reached the level of the lowest leaves.

"Yran. Once you've traded your sword, along with whatever other valuables you've got in that bundle, where will you go?"

He expected a boast about wives, mothers, or queens.

"I don't know," Yran said instead, sounding somewhat desolate. "Where should we go?"

Before Leaper could even try to answer that question, four extremely tall, thin, warriors, all men, dropped, shrieking, from the trees. Their short bows were drawn, their stances wide and steady on the tilting raft.

So much for the trees not being able to bear a person's weight.

Leaper, kneeling, held his empty hands in front of him, thinly lidding his left eye, trying to read the men's expressions. His hair and beard had grown out during his more than a hundred days on the raft. Yet the distance from Airak and his magic meant that the spell that usually turned Leaper's hair half white was as faded as the lantern. Would these strangers know what one white iris meant? Would they see the seams where his forearm spines were, or only the burn scars? Leaper's skin was a lighter brown than theirs. Would that make them more or less likely to misidentify him? And in which language should he address them?

"We are peaceful traders," he called confidently to them in words which he knew magically were in the language of the Bright Plain, answering his own silent question, though he'd never seen anyone wearing clothes like theirs before. They had knee-length trousers and sleeveless blouses, striped vertically with white or green strings of dried seeds. Woolly brown wraps were around their hips, and red-beaded caps covered their hair.

The arrows they'd nocked bore crescent-shaped steel heads with the cutting edge on the internal curve. Their bare feet were muddy to the knees.

"You are a Servant of Airak," the foremost of the men replied, "and must die."

Leaper opened his eye and threw himself into a desperate roll. Arrows flew, missing him. Yran seized Leaper by the back of his climbing harness and threw him; he was strong for a little man. Leaper landed in the water sideways. It wasn't deep. His fingertips brushed the muddy bottom.

"Go with her!" Yran's voice sounded strange in the one ear above water. Leaper couldn't be sure he'd heard him properly at all.

He had time to suck in a breath before his carrysack hit him in the face and pushed his head under. Muddy water filled his nostrils. His arms reflexively circled the carrysack.

Crocodile jaws closed over his legs.

Go with her.

Leaper didn't kick. He didn't fight. Instead of completely closing her jaws and breaking his bones or going into a death roll, the enormous crocodile gently pulled him through the water. Feet first in the dark. Holding his breath. He could hardly believe that Yran was helping him.

You'd be good for trading. A most excellent slave, Yran had said, but also, *We share the same liver.*

The crocodile deftly changed direction. Leaper's face broke the surface. He gasped for breath and glimpsed Yran dangling from a mangrove tree while the bamboo raft fell apart in the water below. The little man had loosened the lashings just as he'd loosed the crocodile.

"The crocodile has broken free," Yran yelled at the seed-striped warriors sinking through the separating rods of the raft. It was their own language; he'd taken Leaper's lead. "The monster wants revenge!" There was no sign of Yran's precious bundle. Yran didn't look behind him in the direction he'd sent the beast; didn't give any sign that he knew his companion was escaping.

With a surge in speed, the crocodile dragged Leaper under and away once more.

How far away, Leaper wondered, *do we have to get before Yran loses his ability to control the beast?*

And then: *What good is it to be away from those warriors if I drown for want of a breath?*

Before he could drown, the crocodile hauled herself and Leaper onto a floating, woven mat. It was half a pace thick. Ten paces long, like the crocodile. The mat sagged under the great weight of her front half, but didn't submerge.

The mat was oval-shaped with a raised rim like a lily pad. It connected by a long, snaking path of smaller, floating mats to a thicket of wooden stilts with woven ladders hanging down.

Leaper realised he was seeing the underside of the floors of human houses. It was the outskirts of the City-by-the-Sea. Faint glows of candles or lamps made flickering patterns in the water.

He lifted his legs gingerly out of the crocodile's gape. There were puncture holes. He was bleeding. Not heavily. Estuarine waters dribbled from his nose and mouth. *There's the salty taste of crocodile tears that I was expecting.*

The crocodile looked at him with one unblinking eye. He looked back. She was utterly still. Presumably Yran still had command of her.

"What am I supposed to do now?" he whispered.

Get away from her, some part of him answered, *before she really does get free and seek revenge. We ate every single one of her eggs. We made her drag us all the way to the sea.*

He tottered along the floating mat. Hopped lightly across the gap onto the next one. When he reached the closest wooden stilt, he leaned against it for a while, trying to gather his thoughts. A ladder dangled in front of his face, but he couldn't use it yet. The strangers had recognised him. He couldn't go amongst them looking the way that he looked at that moment.

Opening his carrysack, he pulled a pane of glass from the frame of his thieves' lantern, which seemed unlikely to come to life again, and broke it over a bronze corner. With the resulting sharp edge, and using a lather of wattle leaves he'd been given in Airak's Temple, he shaved his head and his face. Then he wrapped the glass in chimera skin and restowed it. It might still be valuable, or come in useful a second time. He bent over the water to rinse his naked skin completely clean.

Next, he broke some shellfish away from the wooden stilt of the closest house. When he smashed them open with the heel of his hand, he could feel slime and muscle amongst the broken shells.

I shouldn't put it in my eye. It might make me blind, for all I know.

Leaper used the slime to glue the lids of his Airak-given white eye together. He smeared a bit more of the dead animal on his cheek, to make it look like an infection was keeping that eye closed.

Sounds of splashing water and crocodile jaws snapping together made him glance back towards his steed. She was in the water. Circling towards him.

Leaper flew up the ladder to the closest stilt-house.

There, he sat cross-legged on the platform for a while, looking down at the hungry, circling shape. The crusting of shellfish gave the impression that the wooden stilts were more solid than they truly were. If the crocodile had known that her formidable strength could have knocked down both stilts and house, that her jaws could shear through the wood and deliver Leaper to her, she might have struck.

But without Yran's intelligence animating her, she was left stupid and small-minded; calculating structural strengths was beyond her.

With the night deepening around them, she gave in and floated away.

Have they killed you, Yran?

Is that why she's free? Or are you curled up somewhere, sleeping? A guest of the green-and-white striped men? He didn't know how to feel about the Crocodile-Rider who had saved him, threatened him, and then gone ahead and saved him again.

A clothes-drying line was strung behind the house where Leaper had climbed. He crept along the platform, trying not to make any of the boards creak, and took a semidry garment from the line. At least, he hoped it was a garment. It was rectangular, with a hole for the head, and seemed of a suitable size to fit a man. A belt seemed to have been incorporated into the sheet of beaten, twisted reed fibre, at waist level. Shoulder line and belt were trimmed with hanging shells.

Surely a carpet or a wall hanging wouldn't have coincidentally human proportions?

Leaper untied his climbing harness, stowing it with his robes in the carrysack and putting the strange garment on over his loincloth. It made his silhouette a rectangular one, covering him from shoulders to knees, open at the sides and only slightly gathered at the waist by the belt.

He felt naked beneath it, so long had he worn his harness. For a moment he felt too afraid to move. What if he fell?

Then he wanted to laugh. If he fell, he'd fall into the water. Hopefully there would be no crocodiles. More important was finding food. Without encountering any more tall, thin, seed-trousered archers.

Leaper looked back at the clothesline, wondering why there were no seed-trousers hanging there.

He'd hardly crept by a dozen houses before a woman backing out of a doorway, wide wooden platter in her arms, collided with him, bottom first. She straightened immediately, blocking his path, her expression startled but not afraid.

Light from the open doorway showed she had only one eye. Its iris was streaked blue and brown. Leaper had never seen an iris that colour before. Skin had grown over the other, empty socket, its depths crisscrossed with scars. Scars aside, her brown face was young and lovely. Two black braids hung over her breasts; the rectangular garment didn't show much of their shape.

He looked from her blue-and-brown eye to the platter. It held a pyramid of pointy-ended yellow fruit, slathered in honey and sprinkled with smaller, red, translucent fruit.

His first thought was *Thank Airak, she's wearing the same hairy costume as me. It is clothing, after all.*

His second thought: *I haven't had honey for a hundred days.*

"Can I have some of those?" he asked pathetically in the language of the Bright Plain.

The woman with one eye laughed. Out of the corner of his eye, Leaper saw children curiously peering at him from the doorway.

"They're a gift for the queen," the woman said. "But you can have one. Just one, to match your one eye."

NINETEEN

THE ONE-EYED woman's name was Mitimiti.

Taking pity on Leaper, she allowed him more than one honey-covered fruit. Most of them, in fact. Then she led him back to the house where he'd stolen the garment, and gave the owners something from her purse as payment for the thing.

A windturner. That was what the hairy garment was called.

"In the night," Mitimiti explained, "when it's cold, you stand front on, facing the wind, so the tight weave blocks it and you can stay warm. In daylight, when it's hot, you stand side on, like this, so that the breeze enters under the arms and passes through, keeping you cool."

She demonstrated and Leaper imitated her, thinking, *I wonder how much standing around these people do.*

"Why are you helping me?" he asked.

"We've each lost an eye. That makes us siblings-under-the-sky."

First a liver. Then an eye. Will I still be her sibling once she sees I've still got mine?

"Won't the queen be angry about her plate of honeyed fruit?"

Mitimiti's laugh tinkled in the dark.

"Come with me, and we'll ask her."

She spun like a leaf flipped over by the breeze, and he had no choice but to follow her hairy block-shape past the little square stilt houses, along a raised boarded path over the wavy tops of bulrushes. They came to an arrangement of long, rectangular stages lined with what Leaper thought were canoes. When they came closer, he realised they were troughs half filled with brine, white with salt and dirt- flecked at the waterline.

"Where we were," Mitimiti said, pausing and turning back to face him. "That precinct is called Reeds. This precinct is Saltdeck. When the tide is in, we fill these wooden ponds, bring them up, and set them in the sun for the first stage. Second stage means washing the slurry to get the mud out. Third stage is roasting the salt fourteen times in bamboo to produce our truest treasure. We call it two-week salt, but perhaps you know it by another name. Outsiders, including the men of Cast, call it Coin-of-the-Sea."

"Why are you telling me this?"

"Did you come to find coins? Because no matter how you fill your pockets with Coin-of-the-Sea, when you jump in the water and swim away, your coins will vanish as if you never had them."

Even siblings-under-the-sky need to be watched. Leaper shivered at the thought of jumping back into the sea. He remembered how Middle-Mother had made a special cake for Ylly to celebrate the occasion of her first bleed, and how he had eaten it and blamed ants. *Airak's bones, it was the most delicious thing I ever tasted. But I certainly haven't come here to steal from my sisters, new or old.*

"The early monsoon caught me," he said. "It brought me here while I was seeking my lover's killer. I've never heard of Coin-of-the-Sea."

Mitimiti squinted at him with her single eye.

"You're telling the truth," she said. "I can always tell when someone is lying. Do you mean any harm to my queen or her people?"

"No." The strong salt smell was making him thirsty. "Do you mean any harm to me? It doesn't seem that we're taking a direct route to that tower, which my travelling companion told me was the palace."

"It would be best if you didn't meet the Master of Cast. His city, broken up by the flood, is trapped by trees near the Mooring. We of the City-by-the-Sea offer succour to all who require it, no matter where they have come from, but though you nourish them both alike, it is folly to keep the injured osprey caged with the injured fowl. Do you have a name?"

"Leaper."

He thought a flutter of wary recognition passed over her face, but she said only, "The monsoon marks a new beginning, and so it is with you. While you stay here, you will answer to Lee, which is the sheltered side of a craft, and our queen will shelter you from harm."

"Do you mean the kind of harm," Leaper asked, licking his lips, "that wears green and white seeds sewn into its clothing? That kind of harm?"

"The men of Cast are confined to their own city, and to the Mooring, by our laws. Did you see them in Reeds? Did they set foot upon our boards?"

"There was no foot-setting," Leaper conceded. *Have they taken Yran to their broken-up, flood-swept city? Is he a slave? He told me translation was a useful slave skill.*

"All is well, then. Do you have any more questions before we go to the palace?"

To the palace.

To see the queen.

How could he make himself useful to her? What adapted persona, what bargaining or flattery, would earn him a position of security so far from all the power structures he knew?

He had a hundred questions.

A thousand.

"What does it mean, 'when the tide is in'?"

She laughed again.

"Stay with us a season or three, and you will see."

"A season or three?" Leaper shook his head in bewilderment. "Is this something like monsoon-right, where all are offered safety in a time of danger, or do you really intend to clothe, feed, and house me without knowing anything about the kind of man I am, my history, or what possible contribution I might make to your society?"

"I know there are those in Canopy who want you dead, Lee," Mitimiti said soberly, shocking him, "but I intend to defy them. Canopians, like our guests of Cast, require obedience as requisite for life. If Cast had caught you on your way to us, you would have been enslaved by them, or oathbound to serve their Master. I will defy the men of Cast, too, but I will not defy them with violence. I will not defy them with rage. I will defy them with my love and my protection. That is what Wetwoodknee is. What it means. To our queen, and to me."

"You're not real," Leaper said with wonder. "I'm still on the raft with Yran. I'm dreaming."

"I am real," Mitimiti said, "and like I told you, I always know when someone is lying. If a mother eats a certain type of mangrove killifish while pregnant, her child can always tell the difference between falsehood and truth. If not pregnant, well. She will start spouting truths herself, for as long as the effect lasts."

"Are you the goddess of this city?"

"I am no goddess." She prodded him with one finger between the eyes.

"And that rubbish about the raft is the first falsehood you've uttered since we met."

VOICES APPROACHING down the otherwise empty spiral stair seemed to give Mitimiti pause.

She'd thrown off her windturner at the back door to the palace kitchens. Beneath, she wore a finer, sheerer, clingier version of the single-piece garment in purple, trimmed with strings of pearls. From a pocket in the windturner, she extracted a pearl and lace cap, pulling it snugly over the crown of her head.

One larger, pinker pearl dangled down from the cap on a silver chain, positioned over the sunken, scarred socket where her other eye should have been.

Leaper and Mitimiti had passed by larders, boilers, and briquette-fuelled ovens in a wide, windowless yet airy maze of grey coral chunks. Coral formed a sturdy artificial island on which the rest of the palace was built. The kitchens, storerooms, and clay-sealed freshwater cisterns, in turn, formed a platform for the tower. A discrete servant's entrance hung with iridescent seashells had opened into the tower's main spiral stair.

Mitimiti had hardly taken two steps before the voices reached them. Her head gave a little jerk; she held up one hand and turned to Leaper.

"We shouldn't be seen," she murmured. "Go back."

Leaper hardly heard her. Passing through the seashells had transported him back to the palace in Airakland. He floundered amongst the memories.

Sneaking through sumptuous corridors. Mirrors and music. Silks and pearls. Slaves and courtiers in their immiscible clusters.

A lone queen at the heart of the palace. Secluded and surrounded, a pearl smothered by the meat of its mother. Leaper, the grandson of a king, nonetheless too lowly to be seen walking openly. Whispering. Hiding. Slinking. And what if he had brazenly strolled where he wished? Used his gods-given powers to strike King Icacis dead as he'd struck Orin's beast? Would she have forgiven him, in the hours they would have had before Airak destroyed him?

"Ilik," Leaper whispered, staring at nothing.

He saw her as he'd first seen her, bottom in the air as she stretched her arms under the bed in search of her sash. Heard again the pleased sound she made when she seized on the returned pocket-clock. The babbling he'd made when all those languages had burst out of his throat. He'd been mortified. Then shy. Then grateful to have escaped with his life.

The second time, months later, when he'd snuck back in to see her again, he'd found her weeping with frustration, sprawled across her bed, her chain-and-lantern trappings scattered on the floor, overdue at dinner but too tired of the courtiers' connivances and ambitions to face them and their pregnant wives.

She'd given him that elucidation later on. Explained how her life's path had been laid out by Ulellin at birth. How her mother had learned her future husband's name. That Ilik's life had been aimed entirely at giving children to Icacis, but that no children were coming. The king had gone, ostensibly to see his mother-in-law, but actually to see Ulellin again.

What King Icacis had discovered on this second visit to Ulellin, not learned by Leaper until after Ilik's death, was that Icacis would die without any direct descendants.

Middle-Mother sometimes cried the way that Ilik had cried on that royal bed, but there was often something calculated about Middle-Mother's timing. What Leaper had seen in Ilik was genuine distress, at a time when Airakland was still celebrating the success of the Hunt, Imeris's peace with Understorey, and the eradication of the sorceress Kirrik. Leaper had been sixteen years old. Brash. Made belligerent by his disgrace at the Temple. Utterly incapable of understanding.

A queen's life must be truly terrible, he'd remarked scathingly.

Ilik had sat up swiftly, snatched a screwturner to hand and raised it threateningly against him.

Get out, she'd seethed. *There will be no language lessons today, Understorian!*

I'm not Understorian, he'd answered angrily.

"Lee," Mitimiti hissed on the stair, bringing him back to the present. "Move!"

When Leaper met this queen, the queen of Wetwoodknee, he would say the opposite. He would say, *I am Understorian.* No, he couldn't say that. Mitimiti would know it wasn't true. He would tell this queen the truth. That he had been a Servant of Airak, but that he must find a new home outside the forest now. That a Canopian queen, his lover, had been killed because Leaper hadn't followed the rules.

The rules were that Canopians should not go to Understorey. Understorians should not go to Canopy. Leaper himself, specifically, should never go to Floor. Unless his master told him to go to Floor. Deities should be respected and paid tribute, even when they disagreed.

Even though they are imposters. Mere men and women with the looted spirits of selfish, deformed lizards.

Oldest-Father had served them. Had served Audblayin, unknowing, by refusing to join a raid on Canopy. All his life, he'd protected the tree where he lived, but it was also where the birth goddess had her Temple, and so he had protected her.

Oldest-Mother had spent most of her life a slave in that same Temple. Serving.

Middle-Father had served as Bodyguard to Audblayin. He'd taken hundreds of lives in her service, even though he was Understorian.

Middle-Mother had suckled the future incarnation of the goddess with her own teats.

Youngest-Mother had wielded Audblayin's magic as Servant.

Youngest-Father had pursued Kirrik for the better part of his life. Kirrik, whose crime was to desire the new gods be cast down, and the future shown by Dusksight be made manifest.

"Lee! What is wrong with you?" Mitimiti demanded. Musical notes fluttered up the spiral stair. Voices floated down. But Leaper couldn't move. He had to follow his train of thought to its logical conclusion.

Casting the new gods down is the wrong way to go about it. Kirrik was wrong. Resurrecting the Old Gods only leads to more death and suffering.

It wasn't just Understorey that served the Canopian gods against its own self-interest. Folk of Airakland took food from their children's mouths to bring to the lightning god. Leaper had served Airak's Temple. Imeris had given a whole chimera skin to Odel. Unar, once obsessed with serving the Garden, was now the Godfinder, in service to them all, despite everything they had done, or failed to do for her.

The Rememberers' way is the wrong way, too. Making a direct strike against Airak was bound to draw his attention, even if only at the last moment. It has to be something less noticeable. Something slow and steady like a water clock dripping.

Aforis had served with every fibre of his being. Skywatcher. Servant.

Skywatcher again. Nothing was good enough for the lightning god. Nobody was exempt from retribution.

I have to bring the adepts out of Canopy.

Leaper saw the scars on his forearms. Heard himself promise to prostitute himself to the god who had scarred him.

Not by force, as Kirrik did, to use as puppets in a futile war. By convincing them. By finding another way.

Mitimiti had vowed, mere moments ago, to defy Canopy, and Cast, not with violence or rage, but with love and protection.

I have to show them how people can live outside the forest.

Leaper's nostrils opened to drink the air of the City-by-the-Sea; it was salty, mangrove-sour, and permeated with the hot stone smell of a storm's aftermath in a wealthy, glass-roofed district of Airakland.

I'll have the slaves wind them twice a day, King Icacis had said indulgently.

What say you, Atwith? Ulellin had cried. *Will these things die without our leavings to feast on?*

Mitimiti grasped Leaper's arm, her pincer grip painfully tight, trying to turn him by force. He looked into her eye, at the blue and brown stripes radiating out from the dilated pupil. There had to be some way to break the curse on him and return to Canopy. He had to show everyone in the forest, from root to leaf tip, what he had come to know.

If only my eyes had bones in them. If only I were a god. I could die and leave them my magic bones and show them everything, from my beginning to my ending.

I could show them this one-eyed woman. This kind, happy, godless city. I'd give them my earbones. The splinters of my broken nose. They could listen to the music and smell the briny sea.

If ordinary Canopians saw what Leaper had seen, they'd see Orin's Servants, suffering, melded into a single grotesque shape, through no fault of their own. They'd see the flood that Airak brought to Floor and the woman's face, the one who lost her bundle, who haunted Leaper as much as memories of Ilik. They could see how little their deities cared.

He doesn't care, but without his people, without worshippers, Airak will fade away, the same way that Tyran faded on the battlefield of the Old Gods.

"We can help you, Master," a woman's voice said from around the curve of the stair, and Leaper thought he must still be lost in a dream of past

disasters. The voice was Ellin's, speaking the language of the Rememberers. "The Wetwoodknee woman says they're too poorly provisioned themselves, but she's lying. She says all their boats are gone, but it's an excuse
not to help us. Let me find their hiding places. Lend me sails and an out-
rigger to fetch back my temple from the open sea, and in exchange I'll root
out the best—"

A dozen people came into view, descending the stair. Mitimiti stopped
trying to pull Leaper away. She pulled down at his elbow instead, growling
at him to kneel, to bow his head. Shocked by the sight of Ellin and Estehass, Leaper dropped obediently, straight into Mitimiti's shadow on the step
below her, where the pallor of his skin would be less apparent. He had to
hope his emaciation and his silence would help hide him.

Mitimiti didn't bow.

"I see why they say the sun rises over Cast both from the east and the
west," she called drolly in the language of the Bright Plain.

She folded her arms and stood wide-legged on the stair. Leaper glanced
briefly upwards and saw an amused smile playing about Mitimiti's lips. Ellin
broke off midsentence. Her pockmarked cheeks flushed, and her grip tightened on the short horn bow in her hand. The man she addressed, the man
at the head of the party, wore trousers, shirt, and sash similar to those of
the attackers in Leaper's earlier encounter; in fact two such men flanked
him, seed-beaded, as towering and lean as their predecessors.

The leading man's beads were green and white polished stones. His broad
shoulders and great girth bore them without strain. More beads hung from
his black, braided beard and shoulder-length hair. They were even strung
between his fingers and toes, making him useless to run or to fight.

"You're slow returning, Cast's Master," Mitimiti accused. "Sunset's well
in yesterday's window."

"Her illustrious majesty invited us to stay late, Queen's Maid," the big
man answered, smiling.

Mitimiti shook her head, amusement deepening.

She knows when people are lying, Leaper thought.

"The music enchanted me," the Master of Cast said. "I was incapable of
moving."

Mitimiti silently refuted him a second time.

"It was to save a life," whined a different voice, one that Leaper recognised with mixed hope and despair. "My new, great, and most generous

Master was bringing me before the queen's physician. My journey has been long and terrible."

Yran. He wore a pair of green-and-white seed-strung trousers and held a red-and-white cap in his hands, but his gleaming white teeth and tight black bun were unmistakeable.

Mitimiti pursed her lips.

"You saw the physician," she conceded. "And your journey *was* long. I wish you all pleasant dreams in the sanctum of Mooring. Even you, forest dwellers, who keep our cousins of Gui as slaves in the dark and now have had darkness visited upon you."

Estehass and Ellin stared so hard at Mitimiti as they passed that they didn't seem to see Leaper at all.

She sighed when the Master's party was safely gone.

"Stand up," she muttered. "Her illustrious majesty will be displeased that I needed to insult them to keep their attention on me. That Crocodile-Rider. He was your travelling companion?"

"Yes," Leaper replied soberly. "His name is Yran. He and his crocodile saved my life. But he tells a lot of lies."

"I'm surprised he was able to steer his animal into the mangroves," Mitimiti mused. "Crocodiles don't normally come near the city. The prop roots are pointy on the crocodiles' soft underbellies, and the larger roots can trap them and kill them. This Yran must be a very skilled trainer."

Leaper said nothing to that. He followed Mitimiti up the spiral stair. Intermittently, it gave way to lavishly appointed circular rooms with cushions, balconies, and cooling breezes, before resuming its inexorable rise.

When they reached the apartments beneath the eaves of the conical roof, Mitimiti used a hanging block of hollowed wood to tap against the frame of the closed door in a musical combination.

"Enter, saltling," called a muffled voice, and Mitimiti pulled on a carved fish with seashell eyes, opening the door into the stairwell and stepping lightly inside.

A raised bed draped with insect netting dominated the room. Two wide women sat on the balcony with their backs to the door, legs dangling through the balcony railings. Silver bells hanging from the arched opening, alternating with the lanterns, tinkled in the wind.

The women reluctantly clambered to their feet, helping one another, coming to face the new arrivals. One was middle-aged with inviting lips, deep creases of amusement fanning from the corners of her blue-and-brown streaked, deep-set eyes. Her thin neck was unbent by the dozen strings of pearls that encircled it, all but burying the front of a windturner stitched from cured crocodile hide.

Silver strands escaped the long braid of the second, older woman. Black paste coated the inside of a mostly empty bamboo cup in her wrinkled hands. Her windturner was sheer and dyed purple, as Mitimiti's was, but without the pearls, her saggy, bare breasts were visible beneath. Her eyes were black, and her small mouth solemn.

"My Guiding Tide of Wetwoodknee," Mitimiti said, grinning and bowing briefly to the woman with the pearls. "I went to bring you a sweet platter and found this fish head instead, washed up in the Reeds."

Leaper wasn't sure if he should bow to the queen; he managed a wobbly half bend, knees shaking from climbing the tower stairs. *Lips or no lips, she isn't as beautiful as Ilik.*

"Should I thank you, saltling, or send you away in disgrace?" the queen answered wearily. She dusted her hands together, and salt from the balcony floated away. "A Bird-Rider or an Understorian? He's very pale."

"He said he was seeking his lover's killer. Sorrow soaks the colour from an already well-washed waif. I had a thought to put him to work in Blackpress. Let charcoal and sweat disguise him."

"Disguise him?" The queen shared a glance with the old woman. "From whom?"

"His name was Leaper," Mitimiti said meaningfully, looking ruefully at him over her shoulder. "I've given him a new name. Lee."

The queen thoughtfully licked a black smudge from the corner of her mouth.

"He still isn't tall enough to be a charcoal burner," she said.

"The men of Cast can't see past a windturner. Look how skinny and starved he is, and bitten by crocodiles besides. Did you tend to one called Yran, Physician Unsho?"

The old woman raised her eyebrows.

"I did," she said. "Yran's otherwise very pretty teeth are loose from eating poorly, but a month of mangrove fruit and red banana will cure him."

"We can't call the court of acceptance," the queen interrupted. "Not while Cast is crushed up against our eastern edge. Too many of them would want to stay, without realising what becoming a pact-keeper of Wetwood-knee would mean."

"You could make the pact with Lee right now," Mitimiti said quickly. The queen looked at her keenly.

"I should have bought you a parrot for a pet. From that half-a-moustache sailor."

"You know he wanted to trade them all for me." Mitimiti grimaced. "Even with a full knowledge of what happens to slaves taken from the City-by-the-Sea."

"What happens?" Leaper interrupted, sick of being ignored. He took another step forward from the doorway, not caring if he was violating taboo. If the City-by-the-Sea had no slaves, why was he being ignored and discussed as though he wasn't in the room?

"You speak the language of the Bright Plain," the queen observed. "I am Erta, seventh monarch of that name. Please forgive our poor manners. We're all caught unawares by this monsoon. Many matters require my attention, and I am tired."

"We don't keep slaves," Mitimiti told him, "nor can slaves be taken from our peoples. Removed from the City-by-the-Sea, those who've given their heart and mind to it go to sleep and never wake. They dream of floating into the sky and returning home." Mitimiti shared a glance with Erta. "Men of Cast keep their Bird-Rider slaves in the dark. They say it reminds the Bird-Riders of the forest floor and keeps them calm, but there's no calming the enslaved of Wetwoodknee. Their souls fly back to the sea."

"I understand," Leaper said. *I know a suicide pact when I see it.*

"It will happen to you, too, if you make the pact."

"I don't want to make any pact. I want to go back to Canopy, but there's a curse on me. The wind goddess put it there." He met Erta's gaze. "Please help me."

The queen tilted her head to one side.

"How do you propose we do that?"

"And why should we?" added the queen's physician. "Why, when your goddesses are so generous?" She set the bamboo cup onto the floor beside the bed and pulled a large, brass-bound wooden chest from under it. Unsho threw open the lid to reveal thick, beautiful tree-kangaroo hides and rolls of bear leather. Leaper's heart sank. There was only one place those could have come from. "Look what the one called Orin sent us, in the hopes we might reciprocate with your head. Or the heads of the ones called Imeris and Anahah. And the contents of this chest are but a taste of the promised reward. We have no great trees here, at the edge of the sea, and yet great trees we must have to replace our lost ships. Sending dead heads to your deities may be the only way we can get wood without inviting their wrath."

Erta tsked.

"Put the chest away, Unsho."

Leaper stared at the edge of the bed where the chest had been restowed by the physician. *Ulellin's curse keeps me from Canopy, but Orin's memory is just as long, and she wants me dead, too.*

"I'd prefer that my head and body return to Canopy together," he said lightly. "The one way I know to break the curse is impossible, so I have to find a different way." *I'll beat them both. I'll live, defeat Ulellin and her winds, and steal every adept in Orin's niche. If I can't make the people see what I see with magic, I'll do it with words, poor substitute that they are.*

"Queen's kisses are good for breaking curses," Mitimiti said impishly, puckering in a manner that made Leaper suspect she'd tasted Erta's mouth before.

"Enough, Mitimiti." Erta frowned at Leaper, in almost the same way Ilik had once frowned at him, and he suddenly found himself tearing up. "Let him live here for a time, rather than bind him before he knows his mind. Find him a place to sleep in the kitchens. In the morning, put him to work with the charcoal burners, as you wanted, and tell the others to keep him behind them whenever the Master passes. Cast was surely bought with a fortune in furs and feathers, too, and they need wood from the forest as much as we do. But we of Wetwoodknee do not use lives as currency. Are you thirsty, Lee? Will you take a drink of water before you go? It is meaningful to us, the sharing of fresh water."

Leaper accepted a bamboo cup of water from the queen's hand. It tasted strangely sweet. Then salty. He realised he was crying after all.

"If my head really can buy something so valuable to you," he asked, "why haven't you simply called your warriors and had me killed?"

"As we have already explained to you," Erta replied kindly, "that isn't our way."

It was a question Leaper had asked Ilik, at their first meeting. Why hadn't she called her guards? Weren't they right outside her bedroom door?

I'm not used to being threatened, Ilik had admitted. *I suppose I don't know enough to be afraid. I hardly ever meet anyone new, and my teachers never prepared me for assassins. Besides, what would be the benefit in killing me? Killing a goddess to get her soul for your child—that I understand. The gods wield the real power around here. But me?* She'd laughed in self-deprecation. *My blood is no help to anyone.*

TWENTY

LEAPER COULDN'T see Canopy—it was too far away—but he gazed south anyway, hesitating with bunches of bulrush stems in his scratched, stinging hands.

In the daylight, the variety of plants growing in and around the City-by-the-Sea became apparent. It wasn't all mangroves and bulrushes. Red banana trees and black-stemmed bamboo stood up from the water, and every house on the side of Blackpress that faced the palace showed fruit and fragrant flowers being cultivated on flat, woven-seaweed roofs. Herons and egrets perched on eaves as easily as they did on mangrove branches. Black-and-white-flecked geese and purple-eyed pelicans sailed about in flotillas, and flowerfowl pecked at bamboo seeds in bamboo pens stacked on top of one another. The birds of prey from the palace, which Leaper had learned were ospreys, circled hopefully over the Mooring, which remained empty of the fishing fleet.

A riot of life, in the absence of immortals.

The goddesses and gods of Canopy should fade away. I'll make them fade away. We don't need them.

Ulellin's powers didn't reach this far from the forest, but were Leaper to attempt a return, it seemed a foregone conclusion that the stiff winds would pick up again. The curse. If only he could remember exactly how it went.

I doom you.

By my power.

To wander.

Your heart's desire.

Loves another.

"Heart winged to her already?" the senior blackpresser asked him, breaking Leaper's reverie, and it occurred to him that by gazing south, he was gazing at the palace where the queen likely still slept, even as the squat, shortening shadows of the mangroves slid off the platforms and into the water that swirled around their submerged roots.

"Excuse me?"

"Or maybe to her maid, Mitimiti? It's no use, lad. They've been paired ten floods or more, those two."

He took the bulrushes from Leaper and stuffed them through a fuse-hole in the bottom of the kiln. A boy with a kind of small, web-footed pig for a pet ran forward with a taper to light the fuse. They all stepped back, and a girl with a necklace of tiny turtle shells brought a bamboo ladle of fresh water to each worker.

"My heart's content to stay in my chest. But thanks." Leaper smeared his charcoal-dusted forehead with the sweaty back of his hand.

The blackpresser unconsciously altered his stance so that the flat, protective face of his windturner faced the heat-radiating row of clay kilns. Dried reeds and the broken branches of mangroves had been smouldering down to charcoal in their airless prisons since sunrise.

"She's watching, you know. Our queen. She has a collection of mountain eyes. Those long tubes with the glass in them? Look too long, and she'll wonder if you're planning to climb the tower and try to kiss her."

Last night, in her presence, he had wanted to kiss her. What was it about queens?

It's not trusting myself, Leaper concluded glumly. *It's trusting another man's judgement, or another society's standards, more than I trust my own judgement, my own standards.*

"I could fall in love with her," he confessed. "If, as you say, her fondness for Mitimiti wasn't so apparent." He'd come a long way in his observations of human interaction since playing with ants in the isolated tree hollow of the three hunters' home. And his paired mothers had never been reluctant to express their affection. "Who, if I may ask, is the queen's heir?"

The senior blackpresser grunted.

"Well, that's the maid Mitimiti also. The queen's consort's firstborn."

"The queen has a consort?"

"Had. His name was Eturis. Getting his bright and beautiful blood for her heirs was the main reason she married him. Saw how pretty his grown daughter was, but couldn't get heirs from the daughter, now, could she?" The blackpresser paused in his explanation to pick up a made-for-purpose timber, turning the hinged, circular plate on top of the kiln so that it was completely sealed but for the vents at the bottom. "Eturis was a diver. Everyone thought the job would kill him, as it killed the mother of his children, so many years ago. He and his first wife competed on the water, pushing each other to greater depths. She went first, tragically, making way for him to become queen's consort, but who could have guessed that this early monsoon would sweep him and his safebucket out to sea, along with most of the other divers and half the fishing fleet?"

"I'm sorry," Leaper started to say, but it appeared the time for action had come. The blackpresser beckoned him past the active kilns to a second platform, where another row of kilns seemed to have been left to cool overnight. Women brought buckets of bulrush-root porridge, but not for consumption. Leaper was given the least skilled job, that of breaking the flaky black charcoal up with his hands and mixing it with the porridge. The slurry was poured into moulds, compressed with plates and hammers, and then ratcheted free to join the great piles of cubic, turd-looking fuel for the cooking fires of the city, not to mention the royal water distillery. He hadn't seen briquettes before.

Wood is more precious than magic here, and yet they were barely tempted to trade me.

He needed to find out who wielded magic in the City-by-the-Sea. Only magic could defeat Ulellin's curse. Was it the physician, Unsho? Or the queen herself? Mitimiti had spoken of a way to bind a person to the city. Could the agreement he'd thought was a suicide pact actually be magic? Or was it simple conditioning and suggestibility that caused those taken away against their will to die in their sleep?

He'd need to get closer to Erta in order to find out. If the blackpressers thought he was in love with her, so be it.

Leaper wiped his face again, forgetting the charcoal slurry, and wondered if the queen truly was watching him at that moment. If she was, he was hardly at his most attractive. He knew Ilik hadn't found him attractive, at first, and that she'd dismissed him as a child. Her clock collection, as it grew, bound them tighter and tighter.

Until it ended. Until their bond snapped like an overwound spring.

"I'm to take the new 'presser," the kid with the web-footed pig was saying to the senior blackpresser. "Queen's maid asked for him. Is his name

Lee, or what? They need four buckets of briquettes to the kitchens, and then he's to wait there for her."

"But we're almost done. He'll miss worship."

"Miti says she'll take him to worship after."

Leaper tried not to show his interest. *Worship? Is there more than magic here? Are there gods after all?*

The senior blackpresser curled his fingers into a makeshift spyglass, peered through it at Leaper for a moment, then gave him an *I-told-you-so* grin.

"Off you go, Lee," he said. "Lad, show him where the dried briquettes are. Get him some buckets and a long handle from the storm cupboard."

The palace kitchens were packed with bustling bodies and brushing windturner fringes. Leaper put the buckets where the boy told him. Somebody seized on the buckets at once, taking them to the ovens. Leaper waited by a cold fireplace for Mitimiti to appear. When she did, she wore not a windturner, but a kind of skintight, abrasive, grey leather suit that went from wrists to knees; its dried seaweed collar and cuffs seemed to have been sewn shut onto her body, along the seams. Only her face, bare lower legs, and hands were unenclosed.

"Stingray skin," she said. "Greased with whale oil to keep me warm. It's strong enough that small sharks and crocodiles can't bite through it, and rough enough that big ones don't like the feel of it in their mouths." She held out a second suit of the skin, folded over the crook of her arm. "If you're feeling shy, I can string up a curtain for you. Otherwise, there's whale oil in that tin can there for filling the lanterns. Get your clothes off and slather it on nice and thick. You're too skinny to stay warm without it."

Leaper swallowed his questions about worship and bent obediently to open the lid of the can.

The powerful fishy smell washed over him, transporting him back to Ilik's wardrobe.

It's useful for maintaining the clocks, she'd said.

He realised he was on his knees, insensible in his distress. That Mitimiti's gentle hand lay on his shoulder, under the edge of the windturner, warm and smooth against his skin.

"What is it, Lee?" she asked.

"Why are you taking me fishing?" he mumbled.

"To teach you about tides. To hide you, while the Master of Cast takes a tour of Blackpress. To discover all I can about your feud with the goddess. How you were able to strike at her, and whether sheltering you without first forcing you to make the pact places my queen in danger."

"It might." *All mortals are in danger from the deities of Canopy. Everyone, from the ones who grovel at their feet to the ones who toil at great distances.* "Do you have gods here? Do you have magic with which to defend yourselves?"

"Our gods were driven out long before living memory," Mitimiti murmured, and Leaper's heart sank. "We have no magic but that which washes out to sea. The scraps from Canopy's table. How is it you were able to harm Orin?"

Leaper laughed hopelessly.

"By using Airak's power."

Mitimiti's eye lingered on him a long time, her lips pressed tightly together.

"There was almost no lightning," she said at last, "with that early monsoon. Did you notice? In regular years, most monsoon nights, your god would whiten the skies, brighter than day. I'd see the purple lines up and down my eye, long after it was over, and smell that lightning smell. We'd get it, even here. But not this year."

Leaper put his hand into the whale oil, staining it with charcoal, letting it run over his fingers. Each viscous drop hitting the surface made a crater, but no ripples. *Who cares if she knows? What can she do? What can any of us do?*

"It's almost as though he paid for that flood with his own power, isn't it?" Leaper said. "I hope his part of the barrier is too weak to keep the demons out. To Floor with the agreement between Canopy and Loftfol. I hope Understorey is tempted to raid. I hope it rises up and its people slit the king's throat while he's sleeping."

She ruffled the stubble on his head, a consoling motion.

"We need to get you a better razor, Lee," she said quietly. "Also, a patch for that eye. Now that I know what to look for, I can see you're squinting with the white one. Come on. Let's get you out of those clothes."

THE FISHING grounds, Leaper guessed, were beyond the edge of the mangroves.

Mitimiti didn't lead him from the palace to the Mooring; that precinct was too close to Cast. Instead, they crossed Saltdeck and entered the precinct of Diverdwelling. There, the houses had garden beds built from shells below every shuttered window, and the network of floating mats was so extensive that each mangrove was encircled; every open stretch of water was webbed with strings of the pale, bobbing pads.

Many of the divers had already returned from their day's work, their floating wooden buckets full of plate-sized white shellfish, things like enormous leeches, or many-legged things like the hand-sized crayfish of Canopy that here were each big enough to fill a bucket. Mitimiti laughed when she saw Leaper staring. She named the fruits of the divers' labour in turn.

"Sea oysters," she said, "much bigger than their cousins that stick to the mangroves. Those black ones are sea cucumbers. We dry them over fires and eat them during the monsoon, when it isn't safe to dive." She paused. "This season, we have no choice but to be unsafe. There isn't enough food stored, and our fishermen haven't returned with holds full of the salted deep shoals. May never return. You need to know the dangers, and to know our ways, if you are to become one of us. Those giant lobsters we call bluebloods, but the men of Cast call them 'bites-back,' because of the power in their claws. They don't actually have teeth. Well, they do, but down in their stomachs, not their mouths."

"Are we . . . are we going to catch those?" Leaper looked askance as Mitimiti tied a rope around his waist, over the tight leather suit she'd sewn him into. A wide wooden bucket was knotted by the handle to the other end of the rope.

"No," she said. "We're catching killifish. This is as low as the tide will go, with the river still running. I promised to explain the tide to you."

"You did."

"One day, the goddess Orin came to this shore in the shape of a giant crocodile. The waters were sweet in those days, and the great and glorious winged would come to perch on the red banana trees to sip from the edge of the clear, pure sea."

Leaper didn't say what he now knew of Orin, that she, or her predecessor, was only one part of the many-faced being first considered to be a titan and that he suspected she couldn't survive except in close proximity to her other parts. He didn't ask about the winged, which he had seen the smaller, fragmented titans mention as thieves banished by their betters. He didn't tell Mitimiti that the mortals who had come upon the souls of the titans had called the souls of winged and chimeras "candles" in comparison.

"Orin wished to eat the largest and most beautiful of the winged," Mitimiti went on, "whose name was Wept. Wept was always crying because her children had left her to become the stars, and because she cried, she was always thirsty. Orin lurked in the mangroves, a voice out of sight, urging Wept to drink more of the wondrous water, drink more! Orin knew that eventually, Wept would grow too heavy to fly, with all that water in her belly. Then Orin could catch and kill her without difficulty."

Mitimiti climbed down a rope ladder onto one of the floating platforms, beckoning Leaper to do the same. She made it look easy, but Leaper swung about on the ladder, one-handed, clutching his bucket in the other hand, wishing he weren't in a tight leather suit so that he could extend his forearm spines and catch the wooden piling to steady himself.

"Drop the bucket into the water," she called, and when he did so, she went on with the story. "Wept drank until the water level went down and down, exposing the roots of the trees, leaving the killifish to flop about on dry sands. Orin thought her time had come and tried to spring at the winged from behind the trees, but the roots of the mangroves pierced her belly, and she bled to death beside the flopping fish."

She never did think very far ahead, Leaper thought, stepping onto the floating mat. *But then again, neither did I.*

"Wept tried to fly, but when her wings wouldn't lift her weight, she gazed up at the stars and started to cry again. Her tears turned the ocean to salt and gave us the livelihood we have today. Eventually she grew light enough to leave us again for the sky, but ever since that day, the ocean has risen and fallen in a steady rhythm, to remind us that the goddesses and gods of the great forest are never to be trusted."

If only Unar had told me this twenty years ago. She and Aforis, who should have known. They would have saved me a great deal of heartache.

TWENTY-ONE

"DON'T TAKE the ones with brown spots," Mitimiti warned.

Leaper poked distastefully at the fish packed tightly inside the rotten mangrove branch. He'd broken it where the queen's maid had suggested, and been startled by the prominent, globular fish eyes staring at him from the soggy cavity.

"How do they get inside the tree branches?"

"The river practically disappears during the dry season." Mitimiti's nimble fingers expertly flicked the killifish into her bucket. The fish had pale brown bodies as long as Leaper's forearm, muscular pectoral fins and cockleshell-shaped tails. Some were spangled with blue spots, some with brown. "You'd never guess at how these fish battle for territory during the wet, the way they cuddle up and hibernate together inside old worm burrows when the estuary starts getting too salty for them."

Leaper got a grip on one behind its tiny, rubbery lips and bulbous eyeballs. He'd only gotten it halfway to the bucket before it gave a powerful twitch and escaped him into the water.

"That one had brown spots anyway," he said hastily, recalling too late that Mitimiti magically sensed when he lied and trying to change the subject. "What's wrong with the brown-spotted ones?"

"Those are the ones that went into hibernation too early." Mitimiti grinned at him. "They eat the brown algae that grows inside the branches and turn toxic after a while. Eating their flesh will make you dizzy. Your mouth will go numb. You'll feel hot and cold. In a day, or a week, you'll die. Cooking the fish makes no difference, and there's no antidote to the poison."

"Right," he said, pulling another fish out with a pincer grip and juggling it into his bucket. "I understand. Blue spots only."

"You found one with blue spots?" Mitimiti gasped, grasping his bucket to check inside.

Leaper grabbed her bucket in turn, and found himself squinting down at two dozen killifish with red-spotted tails.

"Let me guess," he said wryly. "The blue ones kill you if you touch them, and I've only got hours to live." He let her bucket float away on its rope tether and joined her at the edge of his own bucket again, thinking that the blue spots were glowing a little in the dim bucket-bottom. Like his thieves' lantern had at the outskirts of the forest.

"On the contrary," Mitimiti said with barely controlled glee. "Look how dark their bodies are. All the better to keep camouflaged in the deep lakes of Canopy."

"Canopy? What are you talking about?"

"Most of these fish breed in our mangroves, but some that come from Canopy migrate back to Ilanland, where they were born. That's where their tail spots begin to glow blue. This matter has been investigated by our physicians. Unsho has even been to Canopy, which is why she mistrusts you, yet I have heard mostly truth from your mouth, and now you know how my knowledge is possible."

"The blue-spotted killifish." Leaper relaxed as he realised why she was so excited. *This is one of the special fish she was telling me about, the kind that pregnant women eat to make their babes turn out like her. Gifted, as she is. Able to tell truth reliably from lies.*

A valuable gift in a city of traders. A city surrounded by enemies.

"Canopian citizens might catch and eat them in Ilanland and find themselves behaving strangely, spouting truths against their better judgement for an hour or two. Pregnant women might be lucky enough to find one in the market. Only a very few of these fish are washed back into the river by the following year's monsoon, for us to find and to use. You're extremely lucky, Lee. You're my new good luck charm." She splashed him abruptly with her free hand. "Who said you could stop? Find me more!"

"Mitimiti," he said with such seriousness that her grin faded.

"Yes, Lee?"

"Tell me more about the Master and the city of Cast."

She shrugged.

"What is there to know? Cast is the home of the marsh people of the Bright Plain. They are wealthier in wood and metals than we are, for they plunder trees from the edge of Canopy, remaining mobile so that your gods can't strike in retribution. They take pacifist, moon-white Bird-Riders for their slaves and set them to rowing and tree-felling until they die."

"So why save Cast from the sea, why let them tie up here?"

"Our customs of hospitality make us who we are, Lee. Did we turn you away?"

"In the queen's palace, I heard Ellin speaking with the man you called the Master in her language. She told him you were hiding food from them. She told him she could find it."

"We're hiding nothing," Mitimiti answered fiercely. "We have nothing."

"Aren't you frightened they'll discover your fishermen aren't returning after all, that the men of Cast outnumber you and can take anything they want by force? Aren't you frightened of starving after they've rowed away with your precious Coin-of-the-Sea? What's the queen planning to do to defend her people?"

Mitimiti picked the blue-spotted fish out of the bucket, planted a kiss on its rubbery little lips, and returned it carefully to the bottom of the bucket.

"The queen," she said, unperturbed, "is planning a banquet. Now, hurry, or we'll miss the afternoon worship, too."

MITIMITI PULLED down a green bamboo pipe from its groove in the corner post of a house.

Freshwater streamed from the open end of it.

"From the distillery," she told Leaper in between taking thirsty gulps directly from the flow. "It runs everywhere in the city except for the palace tower. I draw the buckets up to the queen's rooms myself. At least"—she paused to grin at Leaper—"I used to. Before you came. I'd say you have four-bucket shoulders."

She stripped off her diving suit under the partial cover of a windturner and rinsed the mud from her hands and feet. Her white soles were wrinkled from the seawater, contrasting against her brown knees as she balanced on one leg at a time.

Leaper followed suit, rinsing himself before popping his face through the head hole in the windturner, ripping the seams of his suit, and reaching for the bell-covered belt.

"Shouldn't we wear something fancier, for a banquet?"

"Not yet. First we have to go to the Mooring for worship. Quickly!" She replaced the pipe, stopping the flow, and bounded ahead of him so quickly he could barely keep up. They passed Saltdeck, the palace precinct, and the beehive-covered edge of Blackpress before a sudden abundance of bead-covered warriors with woolly sashes and red-beaded caps warned him that they'd reached the Mooring, the precinct where the men of Cast were confined.

There was no sign of any women of Cast. Leaper felt safely invisible in his windturner, but kept his head down anyway. Through the corner of his eye, he saw tall masts tipping back and forth beyond a long series of warehouses. They could have been the masts of what remained of Wetwoodknee's fishing fleet. Or else the mobile swamp city of Cast had sails.

Mitimiti slowed to navigate a crowded wooden walkway. Leaper bent over her closest ear and asked her about the masts.

"That's Cast," she whispered back, distracted. "You can examine it from the tower at your leisure, later on. Their women, children, and slaves stay there while the men wander. The queen's been invited to Cast to inspect the damage, but she's no desire to see it up close, nor to smell the desperation of prisoners chained in the dark."

On the other side of the walkway, a broad platform encircled the trunk of a wide tree; at least, it was wide by Wetwoodknee standards. Even the biggest trees here looked too small to Leaper, like they were thousands of paces away.

Its buttress roots were submerged in the river waters. Leafless branches spread wide, and a thick trunk was covered in savage, thumb-sized thorns. A wooden carving of some sort of spiny animal, with steps and a small single-person-sized dais in front, had been built against the south face of the thorny trunk.

The queen stood on the dais in her pearl-weighted windturner, head held high, facing the crowd.

"The kapok loses its leaves in the dry," Mitimiti told Leaper with ten or more rows of windturners still between them and the dais despite her best efforts to squeeze past. "It's still confused by the weather and hasn't budded yet. We pin the dead leaves to the carving of the winged."

Leaper squinted at the carving. The leaves made its outline difficult to distinguish, but it definitely had wings folded along its back, a long neck, a tail, and two muscular legs tipped with long talons.

Then he turned his attention back to the queen. Her eyes seemed glazed, and there was a black smudge on her lower lip. Unsho stood at the foot of the stairs, empty bamboo cup in her hands.

"What's that in the cup?" he whispered to Mitimiti.

"Nothing," Mitimiti answered, scowling. "And if it was something, it would be no less than the queen deserves to calm her, considering the loss of her consort, her younger brothers, and their children. Her grief is more terrible than you can imagine. You don't know what it means, to be unable to lay your consort's bones in the hollow beneath the statue of the winged."

"You speak as if you didn't also lose a father."

"She is everything to me," came the curt reply. "I refuse to lose *her*."

As the queen raised fists full of silver bells and called on Wept's soul to open her ears to the salt winds that passed through Wetwoodknee, Mitimiti slipped past a few more rows of people. Leaper followed.

"I really don't know what you meant about putting bones underneath the statue. Can't you explain?"

"Before the great forest grew, our ancestors worshipped the winged and their cousins the chimeras. The souls of our dead always came back to us within a few days of their dying, as falling stars. Now they return infrequently, seemingly unrelated to the time that has passed since they departed. Unsho interprets whose soul has returned from the home of the winged, so that the relevant bones can be burned, but the queen doesn't have my father's bones to burn, even should his star fall."

"That doesn't make any sense to me." *Souls falling from the sky, returning from the home of the winged? That's not right. Souls drift in the ether, seeking rebirth.*

"As I knew it would not! Come, we must get closer, it's my duty to fill the clock as the tide turns." She escaped past the flap of somebody's wind-turner. The next rotund body she squeezed past was that of some sweaty, shirtless onlooker with long black hair.

Leaper stared and made no move to follow her. The long-haired, shirtless onlooker was Estehass. He'd come, with his sister, to try to recover their so-called temple washed out to sea. Ellin could have meant Dawnsight, when she'd begged the Master of Cast to help her fetch it back, but equally she could have meant the enormous canoe the Rememberers had built to try to get rid of Tyran's skull. Without ships, the queen of Wetwoodknee was a waste of time to her, and so she'd allied herself with the Master, who commanded those masts at the edge of the mangroves.

Salt winds, which the queen hoped would carry her words to the winged, carried instead the words of Yran the Crocodile-Rider to Leaper's ears.

"I am uncomfortable," Yran was saying in the language of the Rememberers, clearly unafraid of being overheard, "and so should you be. This is bad. I know it in my liver."

"Why should I be?" Estehass inquired complacently.

"Crocodile-Riders say that if you dream of the winged, something bad is coming. Like a sickness, or a war. This is more than a dream. The creature is their god."

On the dais, the queen turned, a little unsteadily, to the statue.

"Forgive our ancestors," she implored. "Release them from the sky!"

She laid wreaths of bells over the statue's snouted head, letting them hang from its elegant, sinuous throat and sing in the wind.

Estehass bent his head towards his smaller companion. Leaper saw the Rememberer's furrowed brow in profile. The bone man shouted his reply over the sudden exultation of the crowd, loud enough for Leaper to hear clearly.

"Yran. Tamer of crocodiles. That so-called god is a wooden carving. The Master of Cast is your god now, and we are his servants. Take hold of your liver, will you? We *are* the bad thing. *We* are the war that is coming."

TWENTY-TWO

THE QUEEN'S banquet table, spread under the open air at the base of her fabulous tower, branched and billowed around the plush sitting cushions. It was reminiscent of the way Wetwoodknee's floating mats surrounded the mangroves, albeit this network was carved from hard, pale wood, each table section sturdy on three stumpy legs.

Seventy-seven dishes graced the sprawling table. Eleven dishes for each of the city's seven precincts. Mangrove fruits and honey from Blackpress. Crabs and killifish from Diverdwelling. Spicy eels from the Boilers, and periwinkles in coconut milk from the palace precinct itself. Rock cods, coral trout, and flat-headed fish from the Mooring. Bulrush roots baked in red banana leaves from Reeds, and from Saltdeck, whole swans stuffed with berries and crusted in Coin-of-the-Sea.

Leaper had every opportunity to count and salivate over the dishes; he'd been clothed in a finer, thinner kind of windturner and put on food-serving duty by Mitimiti. The maid herself was doing plenty of running between the banquet and the kitchens—however, in the altogether more enviable position of tasting the queen's food for poisons.

"Don't eat any fish tonight," she'd whispered to Leaper as they passed one another in the coral convolutions of the lower palace. Crisped, blue-spotted skin had been carefully carved and discarded, but the baked flesh of the killifish, he assumed, remained potent.

"No need to tell me twice," he replied wryly, the leaf-covered wooden serving platter heavy on his scarred forearms. His broken nose didn't seem to have dented his sense of smell.

"What I find odd about you," the Master of Cast was expounding to a hunch-shouldered Yran, "is that you not only touch bones"—Yran dropped the swan leg bone back onto his woven plate immediately—"but you've eaten fish and snake. I had heard that among Crocodile-Riders, eating scaled animals and touching bones was forbidden."

"It was, Great Master," Yran babbled, taking a swig of fermented mangrove fruit. "It is. Of course it is. I pledged my life to your men on our very first encounter, yet it was only last night, when you accepted my oath of personal loyalty, in exchange for the sword-of-the-wild, that I completely became your man and left my old customs behind."

His new overlord ignored him, single plump forefinger upraised with authority.

"Don't mistake me, I'm pleased to find you so contrary to expectations. Everybody in Cast knows Crocodile-Riders are dirty, smelly, and stupid. Yet you—what is your name again?—are courageous, generous, and wise."

Poor, stupid, swindled Yran. The Master of Cast had paid for Aurilon's priceless sword with what? Words? Mutual loyalty? A sense of belonging?

I pity him, yet here I am, serving Wetwoodknee in exchange for that same sense of belonging.

"My name is Yran, Great Master."

"Yran." The Master laughed as he heaped an opened oyster with bamboo salt. "It sounds a little like 'I ran,' does it not? And that's exactly what you did when the flood came early, didn't you? I shan't forget your name again. Tell us more of the prowess of this bony blade."

"It makes animals obey, Master. That is how I reached the legendary city of Canopy. You see, I hid myself in the belly of an embracer. It slithered through a hole in the Canopian barrier." The Master laughed harder, waving one hand disbelievingly in a gesture of derision, but Yran only spoke louder and more insistently in the language of the Bright Plain, which all but Ellin and Estehass, seated six table segments distant, understood. "The demon vomited me up into a magical palace, the likes of which you've never imagined, Great Master!"

Leaper could imagine it.

"Leave such imaginings for my minstrel. He's performing later." The Master of Cast belched, pushing a bowl of empty shells away from him, and Leaper moved like a man in a dream, silently scooping up the leavings, making room to set down the platter of killifish that he held in his other hand.

Yran's lying. Again. He's never been to Canopy.

Queen Erta sat across the table from the Master. Her eyelids didn't so much as flicker at the appearance of the main course.

"Let me taste that for you, My Guiding Tide," Mitimiti murmured, mincing a bit of white fish flesh from the edge of it with two fingers and pretending to put it into her mouth. Instead, while she chewed ostentatiously, she dropped the morsel into Leaper's low-held load of oyster shells. "It is safe for eating, my queen."

The Master of Cast eyed the platter.

"Wind's teeth, I'm not sure I can fit much more in."

"But you must sample this dish," Erta said gently. "It's a seasonal specialty, ordinarily reserved for royalty."

At the mention of royalty, the Master's countenance brightened, and he helped himself to half the fish. As soon as he'd taken a bite, the queen spoke again, still very gently.

"I wonder how long you intend to stay with us, Cast's Master."

"Forever, I think," the Master boasted carelessly, intent on finishing his fish. "We'll wait long enough to be certain that your drowned men aren't returning, and then this rich city is ours for the plundering. I've loaded one of my twenty-pace seagoing ships with water and provisions that I've stolen from you. It's hidden in mangroves off the southern end of Reeds."

"Indeed?" Erta's manner indicated neither surprise nor distaste, while Yran gaped, horrified, at the man he now owed his allegiance. Amidst the general hubbub, no others loyal to the Master were close enough to overhear him.

"Tonight," the Master went on, "I'm sending the Rememberers out to recover a rather large temple-ship they lost in the flood. The bone man can find it with magic, he says. Something about using lightning to connect an artefact with its origin. The Rememberers think they're keeping that temple-ship, but actually I'm taking it for my new palace, since it won't have as many awful stairs as your tower. Floorian magic workers are slightly more difficult to kill than Canopian adepts, but it can still be done, once they are separated from their hoards of bone. Canopian adepts, in contrast, are completely helpless below their barrier. Sometimes they try to flee their deities. I've killed hundreds of the filthy creatures, myself."

Yran's astonished stare went from his Master to Leaper, whose blood ran cold.

Yran isn't fooled.

He knows who I am.

Leaper wanted to take the oyster shells to the kitchens but felt unable to move; unwilling to draw any more attention to himself.

Has he told anyone?

"But if you stay in one place," the queen prompted, "Cast will surely be found by those same vengeful deities."

"Wetwoodknee has a good distance from the forest." The Master shrugged. "The City-by-the-Sea has always been far enough away to keep you comparatively safe. We never took it before because your fishing fleet was faster and more manoeuvrable. None of our spies were able to steal your shipbuilding secrets. But now your sailors are safely disposed of by the new gods of Canopy, our enemies, in a stroke of good fortune." He licked his lips. "You know, I never liked the taste of fish. I like the taste of this one, though."

"Lee," Erta said, making Leaper jump, "please make sure our guests Ellin and Estehass also have an opportunity to try the killifish."

"Yes, My Guiding Tide," Leaper said, forcing his legs to take the first step, followed by the second, until he was all the way to the kitchens with the bowl of oyster shells in his shaking hands.

He's killed hundreds of adepts? That can't be true. He's a liar, just like Yran. They're made for one another.

But the killifish makes them tell the truth.

Leaper closed his eyes and rubbed at his temple, leaning heavily against the lumpy coral wall.

I can't bring adepts here. It isn't safe. Without their powers, they'd be helpless. Just as helpless as I am. He remembered the chest full of furs and leathers. Bribes and treasures, sent from Canopy to Cast and Wetwood-knee, the most obvious places for runaways to go. His brother-in-law, Ana-hah, was no fool. He'd hidden in Understorey to escape Orin's wrath years ago. The Master's logic explained why Anahah had stayed in proximity to goddesses and gods despite the danger from Orin's beast; the danger of being powerless was even greater.

Leaper opened his eyes. His hands had stopped shaking.

How is the queen going to stop the Master from taking the city?

He tipped the oyster shells into the lime bucket. Picked up another platter of killifish and headed to Ellin and Estehass's table. The royal physician, Unsho, sat across from them, smiling blithely at the small mountain of bones in front of Estehass.

By the time Leaper had unobtrusively delivered the platter to them and returned to lurk in Mitimiti's shadow, the Master had moved from the subject of his invasion to the tale of how he'd gained the scars on his chest; said scars were revealed by the parting of his black, beaded beard-braids.

"So you see," he boomed, "I narrowly escaped that she-Bodyguard by the turning of blade on rib. I vowed never to plunder trees from the edge of Airakland again. Then again, if my old retainers hadn't been slaughtered by Eliligras, there'd be no room for you, little man, would there? What's your name again?"

"Yran," Yran said drunkenly. "I'm not afraid of Airak. I've killed a queen of Airakland with my own two hands."

Leaper swayed like a bell cracked by the strike of its own clapper.

"You haven't," he said, despite himself.

"Oh, yes, Great Master," Yran said fawningly, as if it had been his own superior who questioned him, "I killed her, not long before the monsoon. An embracer carried me to her palace, as I said before, and I cut her throat with a crocodile jawbone, just so I could have the diamonds in her hair!"

"Where are these diamonds?" the Master asked sharply. "You said you had given me everything of value that you owned."

"Yes, Great Master, but I had to deliver those diamonds to the king of Airakland as proof of what I'd done. He'd discovered that she loved another, you see, and ordered me to do the deed. His wife had come to him from Ulellinland, a place of prophecy, so he couldn't have done it himself. Her family might have peeped into the future and seen him with blood on his hands."

TWENTY-THREE

THE WATER glimmered darkly, and the tide was high.

Leaper struggled to break the mangrove branches beneath the water. To grip the freed killifish before they could escape. Each one that he brought up to the feeble light of the city lanterns resolved fuzzily into red-spotted, or even blue-spotted rarities, but those weren't the ones he sought; he needed the brown-spotted kind.

The deadly kind.

Cooking the fish makes no difference, Mitimiti had said, *and there's no antidote to the poison.*

Finally, one of the slimy, thrashing shapes proved to be the kind of killifish that Leaper wanted. He'd gone into the mucky water naked, to keep his serving clothes clean. Sounds of the feast were far-off, but he'd be back there soon. He killed the fish with his shin spines, not wanting the blood of broken scar tissue showing on his arms.

He rinsed his body with fresh water from the bamboo pipe, got dressed, and headed to the coral kitchens with his prize.

It was King Icacis who gave the order to have Ilik killed.

He knew about us. Yran was his tool. I'll bring his palace down. I'll find my way back to the forest somehow, gather Old Gods' bones until my natural power is augmented enough to bring down one of the mightiest emergents. Unar did it! I can do it, too.

Cooks and serving folk filled the kitchens. Any could have questioned him, but all were intent on their own tasks. Leaper kept a wary eye out for Mitimiti but ignored the others, using his windturner to block all line of sight. Double-wrapping the fish in scalded red banana leaves for roasting as he'd seen the cooks do, he waited till they evacuated on a mead delivery run before finding a coal-filled oven not packed with metal trays of fruit pies and honeyed pastries.

Kirrik's side was always the right side, Leaper thought, *but I believed my fathers when they spoke ill of her. I believed my mothers when they said Kirrik was my enemy. I believed everyone who said that I, in my former life, had been brainwashed and led to my death by her.*

He slipped his leaf-package in the cinders.

I should have gone to her, before Imeris took away that chance. I should have helped her to evict Audblayin's parasitic soul from my other sister's body. Exchanged Kirrik's vows to leave my family unharmed for the tools to destroy Airakland.

Serving folk, returning, called for the final sweet courses and kettles of tea. Leaper slipped under a preparation bench to hide while the cooks emptied the ovens, laughing and tasting and burning their mouths.

How could Icacis have deceived me, though? He was too stupid to formulate a single cunning thought in that wooden head. How could he possibly have deceived Ilik? She would have seen any dimming of his adoring sun in an instant.

He was still crouching under the bench, making sure everyone was gone, when he heard Mitimiti's voice, coming closer.

"If you empty the Bag of the Winds," she argued to some unknown companion, "our sailors will have no way to counteract the wild winter southerly. How do you expect them to come home from the Far Island fishing grounds?"

"I expect that if we don't use the bone powder in the Bag to blow Cast back to where it belongs," came Unsho's calm reply, "there won't be any more journeys to the fishing grounds. You heard the man. He intends to take the city. If the effects weren't instantaneous, I'd put the Bag's contents in their tea tonight."

So Erta does have a plan. A way to send Cast scudding back south. That explains why the Master hasn't already been murdered.

Mitimiti was silent a moment. Her footsteps stopped, not far from Leaper's hiding place.

"They must take it while aboard their own buildings," she surmised eventually.

"Good girl," Unsho said. "Yes. We should've accepted their hospitality from the first. You must begin hinting that Wetwoodknee custom dictates the men of Cast return the favour and hold a banquet for us within a few days. The Master won't remember the truths he's revealed to us under the influence of this meal, but our people have heard, and whispers will spread. We can't afford for the Blackpressers to take matters into their own hands."

The Bag of the Winds. That sure sounds like magic.

Magic in the fish to find truth. Magic to fill sails. They do have magic, and they're hypocrites to heap scorn on Canopy's adepts.

The physician's voice grew fainter; she was leading Mitimiti away.

When Leaper was certain they were gone, he sprang out from under the bench and took to the open oven with a charred wooden paddle, hoping against hope that the single serving of killifish wasn't burned beyond edibility.

The outside banana leaf was blackened, but its contents were still good. Leaper emptied them, steaming, onto a smaller platter and swooped back out to the banquet table, avoiding the urge to lick his fingers.

Killing with poison wouldn't be anything like bringing lightning down on Orin's beast. *In a day or a week, you'll die,* Mitimiti had said. Leaper wouldn't have to watch the poison at work. He wouldn't have to hear the screams or smell flesh burning. He'd vowed not to kill—he'd thought to return the murderer to Canopy for justice—but now he knew only death could answer for Ilik's death, and Yran's death was only the first; Icacis must come second.

It'll be like setting a trap for a rat. Not like sensing lost loves and silent sorrows, like feeling flesh crisp and curl away. Nothing like that.

Leaper felt more like himself than he had since Ilik's loss.

He found Ellin and Estehass now seated with the Master of Cast. All three seemed absorbed by the chanting and strumming of a white-bearded man holding a seven-stringed, turtle-shell lyre.

The minstrel was garlanded with even more green stone beads than his chief, these ones slightly larger and carved with tiny faces of varying expressions.

> *O Oniwak,* he sang. *O Oniwak*
> *of lightning blood and bow arm black!*

Leaper recognised *that* name.

As stars began to fill the clear skies above the tower, not only the queen's party but more and more men of Cast huddled closer in the lantern light, straining to hear and see the performer pacing back and forth before them, plucking in time to his poetry.

> *O Oniwak of Airakland,*
> *the crossbow steady in his hand,*
> *prepared to battle, all alone,*
> *while cornered in Ulellin's home,*
> *a beast of naked blood and bone;*
> *a beast of murdered Servants sown!*
> *The Hunt had called him, all alone*
> *to battle in Ulellin's home!*

Hunched beside and behind the Master of Cast, Leaper froze with his arm outstretched, his intent to slide the killifish in front of Yran momentarily forgotten.

All alone? Is this a mockery? A jest?

"Is that for me?" Yran slurred eagerly, twisting in his seat, taking the fish from Leaper's hand. "Everyone else is eating sweets, but the Master ate all of that fit-for-royalty fish you brought before. I didn't even get a taste."

Leaper hardly heard him. The singer strummed and carolled on.

> *The fateful arrow struck it so*
> *yet Oniwak endured a blow*
> *designed to bring him to the fold;*
> *designed to set him in the mould*
> *of mindless terror! Beast-fur grew*
> *but one pure purpose kept him true;*
> *New Gods' power, he saw through,*
> *that greatest of the chosen few!*

Greatest of the chosen few?

Leaper's fists clenched. *I was there when Orin's beast was destroyed, and Imeris, too. One pure purpose? Airak's teeth!*

"It's not just that the women owned all the crocodiles and boats," Yran complained to his empty cups in a whining counterpoint. "After my tenth monsoon, when I became a man, I wasn't even allowed to speak to my mother. Or my sister. Can you imagine? I loved them, but they wouldn't teach me women's words, so I had to go and find the speaking-bones, even though it wasn't allowed. How else could I understand them? And also—"

> *O Oniwak, O Oniwak*
> *of lightning blood and bow arm black!*
> *Despite the corpse's soulless slack,*
> *the demon's claws were in his back . . .*

Leaper didn't mean to hoot so loudly and derisively, but the laughter leaped to his lips.

"—I never wanted to lie down with a woman. Don't you sometimes not want to? Lie down with a woman, I mean?"

"What is this song?" Leaper hissed in Mitimiti's ear. "I thought you hated Canopy, why are you all listening to this?"

"I was not very good with the crocodiles, either," Yran said sadly to his cups. "Which woman would choose me to steer her boat? Without that sword I found, I'm no crocodile rider."

Mitimiti leaned back, answered Leaper's question wryly.

"Any tale of enmity to Orin finds a happy home here." Her expression became abruptly concerned. "Lee? Are you feeling well?"

> *The demon claws were in his back!*
> *No lightning blood, no bow arm black*
> *Could bring it back, could bring it back*
> *The soul that served the god Airak*
> *The demon claws deep in his back,*
> *Despite the courage others lack . . .*

Leaper felt his face flush. Energy surged through him. It wasn't magic. He couldn't smell anything over the stink of fish, alcohol, and honey.

It was his ability to feel, his ability to care, coming back to him in full force. Along with the mental picture of Imeris on the day she'd set out to hunt tree bears with Oldest-Father. *They have sharp claws,* Ylly had whispered. *I would be afraid.* Imeris had laughed. *Tree bears should be afraid of me,* she'd declared, tossing her head.

Men like Oniwak were always taking women's glory.

Men like Yran and Icacis are always taking women's lives.

If only he had enough of the medicine of justice to force it down every throat.

"O Oniwak," he shouted frenetically instead, springing up onto the banquet table in front of the queen, "perhaps your soldier's robes are black, but there's nothing in your small ball sack!"

"Lee!" Mitimiti exclaimed imperatively, but Leaper was too furious to listen to her. The minstrel's arms, bearing pick and lyre, fell to his side, and he gaped at Leaper. The queen leaned back from the table, but otherwise remained still, her expression stony.

"O Oniwak," Leaper crowed, "your small ball sack! Though Imeris formulated each attack, you scorned her, and you hung well back! When Orin killed you, Hunters mourned, but when the news reached old Airak, he shrugged his shoulders, ate a snack, and sent us to take your trophies back!"

"Master of Cast," Ellin barked, jolting to her feet, her heavy, trapezoid knives in her hands. "Have a care for your safety! I recognise this man, a Servant of Airak!"

Everything happened at once. The Master bellowed in wordless outrage, hurling his cup of mead. Blackpressers smeared with charcoal and smelling of salt appeared from nowhere to surround the queen. Ellin lunged towards Leaper, but somehow Mitimiti stood behind Ellin, twisting Ellin's arms into knots, restraining her. Beaded men produced strung bows and began fitting arrows to the strings.

He'd been a fool to reveal himself, but at such a memorable banquet, at least he'd made his sister's name heard. At least he'd shouted it over the heads of the leaders of Cast and Wetwoodknee.

Anyway, I couldn't have stayed. Not after poisoning Yran. I couldn't have made the pact. Not when I have a king still to kill!

I couldn't have become one of them.

And Leaper found himself running and diving, diving from the banquet table's rim towards the edge of the platform, into the arms of the mangroves. It was too dark to see through the water. He didn't know if he'd crack his head on the riverbed or swim to relative safety.

A provisioned ship, hidden off the southern edge of Reeds, he remembered, right before his hands touched the surface. *I'll steal it!*

He slid into the silty, briny embrace of the river.

Immediately, his windturner became a suffocating blanket, dragging him down, tangling him in submerged reeds. As soon as he escaped from it, it floated to the surface, spreading, and Leaper pulled himself cautiously through a tunnel of stilt-roots before snatching a cautious breath on the other side.

Arrows thudded into the empty windturner, only paces away.

Leaper dived again, heading south.

No, wait.

He surfaced again, almost out of sight of the platform where the guests of the banquet swarmed.

First, I'll need that Bag of the Winds. It's the only way to get back to Canopy.

To get revenge on that wife killer Icacis.

Yran will be done for soon enough.

Leaper bobbed in the water, all but naked and gasping, trying to work out where the Bag must be kept. *Where would I keep it, if I were the physician, Unsho?* Curlews screamed in the darkness.

Unbidden, his eyes rose towards the top of the queen's tower of bleached driftwood on its grey coral foundations, where the mated ospreys nested untidily atop the conical, weed-covered roof.

His heart rate slowly settled back to normal.

Leaper crouched in the shadows beneath another bench. This bench was in the physician's study, in an alcove obscured by a hanging in the queen's bedroom.

He'd found an underwater entrance to the palace foundations. Whether by accident or design, he'd been able to crawl into the kitchens. There, he'd been able to not only retrieve his carrysack from the room he'd been given to sleep in, but to help himself to another server's windturner and race up the spiral stair before he could be interrupted. Yanking open the door to the queen's chamber via the fish with the seashell eyes, spotting a silhouette on the balcony, he'd thrown himself under the queen's bed beside the brass-bound chest and curled up there, shivering, cursing himself for not stealing the ship straightaway.

But the silhouette had proved to be the queen's spyglass. It was mounted on a tripod and covered in a waterproof cloth that stirred in the wind.

Then the cross breeze blowing from the balcony into the small space beneath the hanging had revealed Unsho's study to Leaper's floor-level gaze.

The alcove had a small arched window with a lit lantern hanging in it, which allowed the movement of cool air.

Almost as soon as he'd stumbled into it, he'd heard light footsteps on the stair. He'd folded himself into the square space beneath the mangrove-wood bench. It smelled sharply of herbs and sulphur.

The footsteps proved to be neither Mitimiti's nor the queen's.

"Physician!" said Yran's snivelling voice. "Where are you? I need your help. I don't feel well! My Master says—"

Something heavy crashed to the floor with the sounds of metal on wood and glass breaking. Leaper emerged from Unsho's alcove in time to see Yran stumble away from the ruined spyglass, bone sword unsteady in his right hand, left hand cut and bleeding.

Yran's bloodshot eyes locked with Leaper's. They widened.

"You!" he shouted. "I saved you, but you poisoned me! I can't feel my fingers. I can't feel my face. I see the creatures from the Mooring. The winged creatures." He slashed with the sword at the air around him, momentarily distracted. "They're bad luck, those things." Dark eyes sought again the man he'd pulled from the floodwaters at the edge of Canopy. "You're bad luck, too. I should have let the Master's men shoot you. What happened to your oath against killing? We shared the same liver, and you've killed me!"

Leaper tried to manoeuvre around the bed, but Yran leaped over it. Leaper heard the *clunk* as the sword hit the bedpost instead of continuing in its arc towards him.

"You killed Queen Ilik," he shouted back as Yran's momentum carried them both into the alcove. They hit the opposite wall and went down together, hitting the floor hard, boards falling from nowhere on top of Yran, who was on top of Leaper.

I can't waste time with this. Ellin and Estehass could be untying that boat at this moment. He gripped Yran's wrists, one in each hand. It was dark. Yran smelled like vomit.

It made no sense to stay and try to kill a man he'd already killed. Leaper tried to get out from under Yran, but the boards turned out to be shelves rattled loose from the wall and as soon as he let go of Yran's left hand to try and move the boards, Yran grabbed the closest item—a hardwood pestle—and cracked him in the temple with it, so hard that he saw stars.

"I never killed any queens! I made it up, about your woman, Ilik. Yes, I know she was your woman, you talked in your sleep on the raft, all the way while your cursed wind blew us clear of the forest. You told me about the diamonds in her hair. You told me how her throat was cut. I just wanted them to think I was brave. I just wanted them to think I was strong!"

I'm a fool. Of course he was lying. He never had any of the truth-fish. Only death-fish. I've murdered him for nothing.

Leaper moaned at the realisation. *It is like Orin's Servants, after all. It's exactly like them.* His dizziness faded, but the little Crocodile-Rider was already hitting him repeatedly with something else.

Something soft and malleable. Something that didn't hurt.

Something that changed colours to match the bleached driftwood walls whenever Yran raised it above his head. The only clearly resolved part of it was a leather thong at the neck, holding it closed.

He's found it for me.

This innocent man that I've killed has found the Bag of the Winds for me.

Leaper felt tears in his eyes as he seized Bag and sword, heaving both Yran and the boards off himself, finding his feet amid the dust and debris.

"You are brave, Yran," he said hoarsely. "You are strong. I'm so sorry."

Hunching his shoulders, he thrust through the hanging and out of the alcove.

"Wait," Yran called weakly after him. "Come back! We share the same liver!"

Absurdly, as Leaper made his way down the spiral stair, taking them three at a time, holding his stolen treasures high, the minstrel's song about Oniwak repeated over and over in his head. He knew the described event hadn't happened, and yet he pictured it as the words washed over him.

The demon claws were in his back!
No lightning blood, no bow arm black
Could bring it back, could bring it back
The soul that served the god Airak

After he emerged from the palace, he didn't slow down. More than once, he was forced to stop and hide from the Master's beaded men. In reed clumps. Under platforms with his legs braced wide apart to span the space between pilings. Or in the arms of the mangroves.

His skill at impersonation had deserted him. There were no patterns here for him to take up and use. Even the languages the speaking-bone had given him were jumbled in his thoughts; he couldn't be sure which tongue the minstrel had used or which words were the ones he'd been born with.

All that mattered was finding the boat, the twenty-pace boat with its provisions and seagoing sails, and Leaper managed it, somehow.

Somehow, Ellin and Estehass weren't aboard. He freed the sails from their covers along mast and boom, not knowing what else to do with them, letting them hang like heavy, ugly flags.

And he wondered, as he lashed his body, his carrysack, and Aurilon's sword to the south-facing bowsprit shaped like an openmouthed embracer, what else the Rememberer siblings had said to Unsho or Mitimiti in their nakedly truthful moments. He wondered where the Blackpressers might have imprisoned the siblings. Perhaps Ellin and Estehass were tied to the thorny kapok tree in tribute or penitence, even as Leaper secured his much-abused climbing harness to the demon emblem of Cast.

A light wind ruffled the mangrove leaves as Leaper hung there, working at the knots in the neck of the chimera-skin Bag. A single curlew screamed. Bats blundered by. High and faraway lanterns cast dim light on water rippling around platform pilings, trunks, and stilt-roots, the black shapes made twice their true lengths by their reflections. Leaper listened for a few minutes to distant unintelligible shouts, sounds of bodily scuffles, and crying children in houses being hushed by their elders.

Without your magic wind, how will you get the intruders out, Unsho? Then again, after tonight's conflict, they were never going to trust you far enough to drink your tea.

He could just reach the water with his outstretched hand. Cupping some in his palm, he tipped the open mouth of the Bag of the Winds over it, mixing bone powder in with it. Half the water dribbled between his fingers and half the powder blew away in the breeze, but he managed to get some of it to his lips and swallow.

It tasted strongly of salt. *Either the tide is in, or I've stolen a bag of Coin-of-the-Sea.* Leaper licked his palm, gazing hopefully in the direction of the Titan's Forest. The Bag of the Winds would carry him back there, across the flooded plain. If it could carry the whole floating city of Cast, it could certainly carry him, a single man in a single craft, against the current of Ulellin's curse.

Then the manifested hand of the wind punched him in the back, knocking all the air out of him. Sails boomed as they filled and strained behind him.

Too much?

That swift, sudden wind lifted the top layer of water, squeezed it to pellets of white spray, and shot them at him from all directions, hard as fowling blunts. Leaper tried again to howl, but now there didn't seem to be any available air for him to suck in; it parted over the sudden surge of the ship, and there was none left behind. He was choking in empty space.

The boat had no wings, and yet it flew. It was heavy. Wooden. Made to cross water. Winds stronger than any natural wind had flung it into the sky.

The figurehead pressed to his spine, biting like a living serpent instead of a wooden one. A glance back only rewarded Leaper at first with water knives slashing at the cheek he'd turned northwards, but eventually he could make out modest-sized trees bending into the water, the queen's tower listing alarmingly and the Reeds precinct trembling as its foundation poles loosened. The Bag of the Winds violently left his hand.

I've taken too much.

The Master's ship scraped the tops of some mangrove trees as Leaper turned his face back to the front, and he was finally able to take a horrified breath.

Lost. The Bag is lost. The city may be lost, far behind me. An accident. How was I supposed to know how much would be too much?

Within seconds, the ship's underside had cleared a height comparable to that of Erta's tower. Clumsy in shape and dimensions, it had nonetheless taken to the skies like a bird borne before a storm. It rose and plunged, bucked and spun.

Leaper closed his eyes against a wave of nausea.

When he opened them, the black mass of the forest in the distance grew larger as he watched. He tried to glance back a second time, but already the Old Gods' gale had blown him so far, so fast, that Wetwoodknee was out of sight, tower and all, beyond a treeless, wave-ravaged horizon.

PART III

The Winged

TWENTY-FOUR

ON OTHER nights, when Leaper had looked down from great heights, he'd always had the solid safety of something, whether tree trunk or tower, keeping him separated from the ground.

Now he sailed onward in the airborne ship. Through the dark, in a great, slow arc over the Titan's Forest. Clouds kept him company.

Also fear, and shame.

He wanted to forget Yran, the City-by-the-Sea, and all else he'd left behind, but the bowsprit in his spine felt like the blade of the ivory sword, forcing him to remember.

The magical salt wind from the north met and battled the curse of Ulellin, and his vessel rose higher, so high that the blue-on-black starscape of Canopy seemed more distant than the true stars, and in a moment of disorientation, he couldn't be sure that the boat hadn't turned upside down and that the forest wasn't floating above him.

Thirst found him as the hours passed, but he dared not untie himself to find the freshwater the Master had boasted of hiding on board. Light behind and around him seemed an artefact of exhaustion until he realised his thieves' lantern had come to life in his salt-shrunken, ripped-at-the-seams carrysack. It blazed behind him at arm's length, threatening to topple from the bag at any moment, until the boat at last sailed beyond the forest and Airak's light left it once more.

Beyond the forest.

His chance was lost.

Yet he couldn't have stopped. Even with a death wish, he couldn't have jumped, or dropped.

I'm the one who ate the stuff from the Bag of the Winds. If I'd untied myself, the boat might have fallen, but I'd have carried on.

South.

It was too much.

I took far too much.

As the final dregs of night began dribbling away, as Leaper glided over expanses many times the length of the floodplain it'd taken him months to cover in Yran's crocodile-powered raft, the Master's boat began sinking in the sky. The power of both Ulellin's curse and the Bag of the Winds waned with distance and time.

Leaper felt tears in his eyes as the black unknown of the terrain, which he could only assume was as empty of humans as it was of human-made lights or fires, rose up to smash his vessel. He'd failed Ilik, himself, and everyone. Flies would soon drink from his eyes, as he'd drunk from the crocodile's.

Water slapped the boat's underside. It rose up in unseen sheets of spray to either side. At least, Leaper thought it did. He couldn't be sure he hadn't died.

Then the wooden frame of the boat rattled, hard. The last of the north wind drove it aground before falling mercifully away.

All was still.

All was cool and dark and silent. Leaper blinked his grainy, dry eyes and peeled apart his desiccated lips.

I'm not being threatened by the men of Cast anymore, nor have I arrived back in Canopy. What is this place? Where am I now?

The rising sun illuminated a landscape like none he had ever imagined. Between the beached boat and a line of snowcapped peaks standing in the middle distance, there were no real trees at all, nothing even as tall as Wetwoodknee's thorny kapok. Certainly nothing taller than Mitimiti would have been while standing on Leaper's shoulders. The thin, twisty white branches of these shrubs covered crevices in cracked grey stone, their small, green summer leaves halfway to turning yellow and bronze.

Most of the ground was bare and grey. It was a far-flung field scattered with lichen—or moss-covered stones that Leaper supposed were boulders. He'd never seen a *boulder* before, outside of the carved depictions on the Garden Gates.

Thirsty.

I need water.

When he cut himself free from the lashings with his spines, climbed unsteadily down from the tilted, perforated wreck, went involuntarily to his knees, and tried to lean his shoulder against one, he found there was no actual boulder beneath the moss. This closest lime-green egg, spongy to the touch, was some kind of freestanding plant, luminously lovely in its symmetry and speckled with minuscule white blossoms. Other, darker green boulder shapes proved to be bulging masses of telescoping, spiny stems topped with sprays of rust-coloured flowers.

Leaper put his lips in the dew that spangled the closest one. It gave relief, but not enough; he stood up and turned back towards the water that had broken his boat's fall.

It wasn't a single lake, but a string of them. Each was no more than twenty paces across. After he'd slaked his thirst and climbed for a better view onto a boulder that was truly a boulder, he saw the string of petite, mirror-clear lakes continuing in a relatively straight line back the way he'd come.

Back towards the forest. From south to north.

Only, the more he examined them, the more they looked like something he'd seen before. Weathered but still recognisable. Parallel to the string where he'd crashed were more lake-trails. There, the lakes were different shaped, and accompanied by S-shaped troughs, as though a heavy animal had dragged its tail through mulch.

Titan's footprints.

In fact, the rain-filled depressions led from north to south. Straight to the mountains that the Old Gods had partially destroyed in their battle to the death that had produced the Titan's Forest.

The mountains were the same mountains the Old Gods claimed to have given to the winged, the mountains from which a mighty river had once flowed, where pink-skinned sentries had peered through spyglasses no different to the one the queen of Wetwoodknee kept in her tower.

Leaper gazed northwards.

The boat's provisions. Some of them must be intact. I could follow the footprints to Canopy. Or could he? Wouldn't the winds just push him south again? He was tired. So tired, and heart-sick.

Or I could rest here. Fasting. I could die here.

He turned back towards the south. It wasn't only at Dawnsight that he had seen those mountains; he'd seen them at Dusksight as well. He'd seen the relief carving of Ilik, as tall as Airak's emergent, stone gems adorning stone tresses, stone lanterns hanging from stone robes.

Is that my future? My atonement for breaking my oath?

Is that carving my work?

He looked down at his hands. There was blood in his palms from the unsheathing of his spines.

I could follow the footprints to the mountains.

Prophecies had seemed like so many wasted words to him so far, and yet who else remembered the perfect shape and proportions of her? Who else knew and loved her enough to fashion such a tribute to her memory? It had to be him. It would be him.

Whatever revenge he was going to have on the goddesses and gods, however he was going to get back to Canopy, he had to do this first for her, whether it took him a year, ten years, or the rest of his life.

TEN DAYS later, Leaper stood with his back to the setting sun.

His shadow stretched along the empty riverbed. The cave opening, above and beyond him, faced the day's end, seeming to drink its rays.

It was a rough black mouth in the two-hundred-pace-high limestone bluff, the focal point of an enormous amphitheatre that reminded Leaper of the curving trunk wall of the monument tree, where his sister Imeris's name was set for posterity.

It was the long-dry waterfall he'd seen in the Rememberers' visions, he was sure of it. Rocks at the bottom of the cliff, below the cave opening, were worn in patterns consistent with a fall and rapid flow. An arched bridge, twenty paces in span, made of hewn granite blocks, crossed a ledge of dusty, lichen-covered rubble where the west-flowing river had twisted sharply, turning north.

The cave will lead me to the ruined city.

If the curving wall had been wood and not stone, he could have scaled it with his spines. As it was, he had no clue how to get up to that black mouth.

That's where I'll carve the statue of Ilik.

His supplies, all but exhausted over the duration of his trek across the stony plain, had been supplemented with grass seeds ground between rocks, mixed with water into a paste, and cooked over a fire. He'd spotted creatures in the foothills, hairy versions of the rare goats the rich gave as gifts to the Garden, but he had no way of catching or killing one.

I've no weapons but the ivory sword. I've nothing of value but the thieves' lantern, and this far from the forest its only value is in metal and glass.

He'd taken ropes from the ruined rigging of the crashed ship, but the smooth cliff face had few protrusions, and no apparent place to anchor a pick even if he'd had one to throw.

Somehow, I build it. I've seen the completed statue, so the tools must be waiting for me. Help must be waiting for me. It's not my fate to starve here, or fall from that cliff in my attempt to climb it.

I've seen it.

Seeing it was different to finding a means to get there, however.

Leaper sat down, cross-legged, by a heap of more tumbled mossy blocks and columns, the remnants of a dwelling or temple at the edge of the final small, titan's-footprint-shaped lake. He should have been building himself a fire, since each night of his journey had been colder than the last, but he couldn't take his eyes from the limestone cliff.

No bat shapes left the cave mouth with the fading of the light. Leaper supposed this place was too far away from any feeding grounds for them to be able to survive here. No birds flew to roost in the cave's shelter, either.

Leaper frowned.

Wooden watchtowers fell there, too, and pink-skinned sentries crashed to their deaths in the froth at the bottom of the waterfall.

He got up, stretched his aching legs, left his belongings behind in the ruined temple, and picked his way along the dry bed to the place where he'd seen the towers fall in the vision.

It was a thousand years ago, he reminded himself as he lifted granite blocks, ripping the dead root and lichen bridges between them, out of the depression directly beneath the cave mouth. *Any timbers will have rotted away by now.*

Shifting the stones was hard work, and at length it was too dark to see what he was doing. Tracing his steps back to the rubble in blackness by memory and touch, he took a tiny bow drill and some shavings he'd looted from the ship out of his carrysack and kindled a small flame. The fire was too feeble to throw any light on the cliff face, but Leaper imagined he felt the cold breeze of passage of some kind of large flying beast overhead.

It could have been a natural wind, channelled through the high passes, funnelled through the hidden city and out through the cave mouth.

Yet it had been a long time since Leaper had been touched by a natural wind. A spring and a monsoon summer since he'd taken Ilik's broken clock part and promised to replace it.

Ten years since he'd made an oath not to do murder, and ten days since he'd broken that oath.

Has it all been out of my hands?

Heavyhearted, he warmed his hands over the little fire, thinking of the hands of the blackpressers back at Wetwoodknee, of Ilik's hands winding her clocks, and of the hands of whoever had shaped the granite flagstones from sweat and life and time.

Have I been a leaf in a breeze, imagining vainly that I steered my own course through the sky?

In the morning, Leaper continued the work.

Little by little, he uncovered the tumbled timbers of the watchtowers.

Perhaps in the forest they would have decomposed. Here, the cold and the mineral-rich mud from the cave mouth had preserved them. Leaper spent that day and the better part of the next day meticulously excavating the muddy hardwood lengths by hand from the riverbed. Then, stomach grumbling because he hadn't stopped to forage for food, Leaper took the ropes from the ship's rigging and trussed two of the timbers into a rigid ladder.

He measured it with even, weary paces, guessed that it would just be long enough to lean against the cliff face and get him to the cave mouth. Leaper worried that if the wind picked up there was a good chance it would blow the ladder down while he was halfway up.

Yet the surface of the water of the last lake was utterly still, reflecting the clear, orange-to-blue sheet of the star-pricked, early evening sky.

He hesitated, the call for Airak's blessing trapped between lips and teeth. He held the biggest possible broken, burning branch from his fire steady in his left hand.

One no longer walks in the grace of Airak.

As nimbly and swiftly as he was able, carrysack on his back, one-handed, he scaled the ladder and found his footing in the cave mouth, his back once again to the departed sun.

The ground inside the cave was soft beneath his feet. Holding up the firebrand, he could see fifty paces ahead, to where the groove worn by the water narrowed to an arched tunnel some ten paces high and five wide.

To the left of the tunnel, the wall, only a few paces back from the dry riverbank, was covered in relief sculpture from ceiling to floor. Some was purely pictorial, a historical time line of sorts.

Some was writing. Words in something akin to but not quite the same as the physical language of the titans.

THE SOURCE, it said.

Winged creatures, like the one worshipped at Wetwoodknee, were shown as stars falling. Stars became stones. Stones became seeds, which grew into cone-covered conifers shaped like skeletons. Skeletons attracted fallen leaves from the surrounding forest, and took flight on wings that might have been feathered or scaled.

The hair stood up on the back of Leaper's neck. He turned away from the carvings, holding his breath, extending the burning branch towards the other side of the cave. On the other riverbank, to the right-hand side of the arched tunnel, the cavern ballooned into a lair whose ceiling, some hundred and twenty paces high, was covered in limestone teeth.

A slitted pair of orange eyes watched him from near that ceiling.

Leaper's flame danced in the gleam of those eyes, but also in the facets of a million clear jewels that covered the hide of the slender, silvery creature. Diamond scales of various sizes studded the long, sinuous neck and smooth, sharp-nosed head, extending all the way to the flared tip of the long, whiplike tail. In a nest of uprooted bushes and bones, it sat upright on powerful haunches, with folded wings, a proud, forward-thrusting, heart-shaped breast, and no front legs.

"One of them comes on the last day of summer," the creature murmured through flared nostrils in a silent pattern of hot and cold air movements on Leaper's skin. "One of them comes at the time required, on the last day of summer, as was foretold, as was foretold."

TWENTY-FIVE

LEAPER SWALLOWED the urge to answer immediately.

First of all, the shock of it helped him stay silent; he couldn't have been more surprised if the bridge or the ladder had spoken. Which meant that, subconsciously, he'd absorbed more than a little of Canopy's arrogance, having expected that lower peoples—like Mitimiti's, or like the people who had made the carvings in this cave—had, of course, worshipped lower forms of life. He'd expected the winged to be dumb yet powerful animals. Like chimeras.

Recognising that expectation made him deeply ashamed.

Secondly, even if he'd wanted to, he lacked the means to control the winds, to reply in the language of the winged. This was despite the understanding granted him by the stolen speaking-bone. He gripped his burning branch more tightly in an attempt to keep from shaking.

Are you Wept, he wondered, *the largest and most beautiful of the winged? Why were you the only one of your kind spared by the titans? Why did they give you this mountain?*

What was foretold?

Before he could give voice to those questions in an audible blast of Canopian, he took stock of the beast before him a second time. He saw the predatory stillness in the muscle, the intelligent yet resentful gleam in the eyes that went beyond mere instinct or feeble-witted reflection, and the laziness of overconfidence, for what they truly were.

This was a creature that could be flattered and placated. A creature accustomed to homage with an eye for insincerity.

And it had already witnessed his naked surprise.

Holding the image of the firewheel tree in his mind, flowing elegantly from roots to crown, feeding the sense of superiority that had shamed him a moment ago, Leaper embodied at once the boldness of the flaming flowers and a king's calculated necessity of bowing before deities. He went to one knee, eyes lowered, with the burning branch stiffly upright and his empty right palm extended in supplication.

"Most holy salutations," he said, hoping his posture would be understood if not his words, "from one who humbly serves Airak, Lord of Lightning, to one who is deservingly worshipped, body and soul, by the men and women of Wetwoodknee. If one may remark on one's lack of preparedness for such a meeting? One who walks in the grace of Airak was fortunate enough to look upon your likeness, but did not dare dream of laying eyes on your true magnificence. In the world outside, it is not known that you dwell—"

"No, it is not known," the winged one interrupted lazily, the exhalation from its nostrils hot and cold on the back of Leaper's bent neck. "And for good reason. The one they worship was forced to abandon them, in accordance with the bargain."

The bargain? The one you made with the titans in order to secure your safety and this mountain?

"One regrets to receive such ill news—"

"For good reason is this dwelling place not known." The winged one, orange eyes widening, lowered its head from the ceiling to be closer to Leaper. The effect of bringing its flared nostrils closer was to increase the volume—or its equivalence. "It would not do to violate the terms. Yet how can I kill you? It is the last day of summer, and your intrusion was foretold."

Leaper shot a glance at the tunnel opening at the back of the cave.

"One will go at once, if that is your holy desire. Is that the way to the city?"

The winged one drew its lips away from interlocked reddish-brown teeth. They were like myrtle roots stripped of their bark, dripping dark sap.

"There was a city here. A city forming a perfect circle. They called it Time. Time was the name of the circular city here, before thirteen-fourteenths of a titan came. Thirteen-fourteenths of a titan broke the city and broke the source of the spring. All the clocks are quiet."

Thirteen-fourteenths of a titan.

"Which clocks, Holy One?"

Leaper remembered Ilik behind gauzy hangings in the brightness of her daytime chamber, her naked back turned. With complete clarity he saw again the minute tensions and relaxations in the muscles of her shoulders and back, which said she was taking something apart. He'd parted the gauze, laid a finger lightly on her spine and whispered, *What hour is arrived, little clock, little herald of endings? Is it time for hiding, time for lies? Or time to look my lover in the eyes?*

He'd whispered that rhyme to her with growing frequency over the years, and it had always ended in scolding or sending him away.

Until one day, when she'd turned to face him, biting her lip with her crooked tooth. She'd dropped the clock on the floor between them, stepping on it in her haste to embrace him. She'd had her monthly bleed, and he'd had to take the stained bedclothes with him when he went.

"The clocks in the city," snorted the winged one. "She searched for them, the last one to come."

"She?" *Could it be Ilik? If anyone is to make pilgrimage to a city of clocks, it would have been her. But, no. Coming here from Canopy would be a pilgrimage of years, not seasons.*

"She lived in the realm of a wood god. The wood god commanded her, alleged the last one to come. Her trade was to make timekeepers from titan bones." The winged one's smile faded. "But she hungered for something different. Something special, to trap the soul of one-fourteenth of a titan. She needed the bones of Time, and so she'd found her way inside of a clock. A way to the city, Time, but nothing in the city was what she needed. What she hungered for. I am called Hunger. I would have eaten her, but her riddles pleased me. Her riddles pleased me, so I sent her on to the Birdfoot Valley, to find the bones of Time, even though I hungered for her bones."

The skeletal remains littering Hunger's nest seemed suddenly tremendously relevant. Out of the corner of his eye, in the extremely poor light of a single flame, Leaper tried to determine if the bones were human. He failed.

"Do you hunger now, Holy One?" He tried desperately to think up a riddle.

"Of course," was Hunger's reply. "Yet I cannot eat. Not yet."

This time, when the winged one peeled back diamond-crusted lips, the jaw opened as well, twisted root-teeth untangling to reveal a dozen saliva-bathed, white-shelled eggs resting under a forked black tongue. Each egg was large enough to have contained an adult tapir.

Leaper felt the rush as Hunger inhaled through her mouth, closed her jaw gently, and spoke again through the controlled direction and temperature of her exhalation.

"You have seen me, and so the bargain demands that you die. Humans must not see me and I must not tell them what it is that thirteen-fourteenths of a titan does not wish them to know. That is the bargain. My life, for my silence." The creases around her orange eyes deepened with mirth. "Whether my words contaminate the humans or the sight of me does, the bargain is broken. If I contaminate their human minds with truth, so that thirteen-fourteenths of a titan is forced to cast them away, losing the vastness of its power in the process, the bargain is broken."

"The bargain is broken," Leaper echoed, adding Hunger's fondness for repetition to the tiny store of knowledge that might yet see him escape from the cavern with his life.

Is this my labour? Is this my help? Could Hunger be the carver of Ilik's great statue? But she hasn't hands, or even claws. She has wings, a tail, and a mouthful of eggs.

"The bargain is broken," Hunger insisted, "if I go to the forest. The bargain is broken if I do not consume you. Yet you have come on the last day of summer. As was foretold. I cannot consume you. Nor can my children, when they hatch."

"When will they hatch?"

"Soon."

"Do these eggs have a father?"

"I am their mother. I am their father. I am their mother and father."

"Like chimeras," Leaper said, and instantly cursed himself again for thinking of Hunger as an animal. He ducked his head even before the blast of air alternately froze and seared him.

"Like chimeras?" The diamond-scaled tail thrashed. Diamond-covered wings raised and spread, filling the cavern's width, and diamond-studded toes lifted to reveal curved, clear talons. Longer diamond scales covering the chest lifted and stood erect, like ruffled glass feathers. "LIKE CHIMERAS?"

Hunger opened her mouth wide a second time. Either her fury or her dark saliva had turned the white eggs a sickly shade of yellow, and instead of clumping together, they were arranged in single file, their pointy ends facing down her throat.

She swallowed them.

The bargain will be broken if I do not consume you.

The fire in her eyes turned from orange to yellow to searing white. She threw back her head, and the eggs made an obvious bulge as they travelled down her throat and disappeared behind her proud, prominent breastbone. Leaper had lifted his gaze with alarm; it was all he could do not to pivot and sprint for the tunnel.

Yet you have come on the last day of summer.

Her diamond scales turned orange and gold, as veined and opaque as autumn leaves; they lifted like the scales of a pinecone, and the eggs fell out, all twelve at once, as black and shiny as pine nuts.

As was foretold.

Then the cavern filled with light and the heat became all but unendurable as Hunger caught fire and her leaves shrank back into her skin, black and charred and hard, while the eggs in the nest shattered and steamed, the offspring emerging. White-skinned, tapir-sized bird shapes with long tails and beady black eyes floundered in the shards of black shells, nostrils already narrowing as they formed their first words.

What hour is arrived, Leaper thought with dismay, *little clock, little herald of endings? Is it time for hiding, time for lies? Or time to look my demons in the eyes?*

TWENTY-SIX

ONCE SHE had lovingly licked her hatchlings, corralled them between her feet, and eaten their shells, Hunger turned her attention back to Leaper, who was still in his awkward position of obeisance on the other side of the dried riverbed.

"You see now," she said with a cooling wind, "why I could not eat you."

No.

"One sees most clearly, Holy One," Leaper lied. "Whoever foretold for you foretold truly."

Foretelling the future? he wondered. *Is that what humans can do for you, that you can't do for yourself? Because if that's the task expected of me, I really should have run while your attention was on the hatchlings. I'm no Servant of Ulellin.*

But the winged one's next words were indulgently contemptuous.

"I foretold it, wielder of lightning. That one-fourteenth of a titan who commands wind and leaves, does she command them half so well as I? Are the leaves her body and the wind her words, or is she a red-hearted meat-animal? She is a red-hearted meat-animal pulling leaves and winds vainly about herself. My prophecies are better than those of one-fourteenth of a titan."

And besides, he *had* done a little prophecy-making, himself. At least, he'd seen the giant statue in the vision at Dusksight, a statue only he could possibly shape. It was time to be confident. Bold.

Leaper bowed a little deeper.

"No truer words have ever touched my skin, Holy One."

Hunger lavished another lick on one of her offspring; it tilted its narrow, elongated head to watch her with one beady black eye at a time.

"Their skins are soft," she said. "They need hard skins to fly high enough to join their kin. To become the stars. Yet only lightning can harden their skins, and one-fourteenth of a titan is greedy. One-fourteenth of a titan calls lightning only for himself, since the forest was formed. One-fourteenth of a titan, and the humans who serve him."

"One"—*one cannot call lightning, not here*—"would consider it a very great honour to call lightning for the children of mighty Hunger. In—in the—in the forest you mentioned. In the forest, one might be able—"

"The titan is in the forest," Hunger snapped. "We cannot go to the forest. Not I, who must keep to the bargain. Not my children, who have soft skins. They can be harmed. They can be killed. You must harden their skins with lightning while they stand in the cave of Time."

"You *can* go close to the forest," Leaper cajoled. "Under cover of darkness. On a moonless night. The night of the new moon, in fact, the last day of summer. Right now. Tonight."

"I did not foresee any such journey." Her eyes narrowed. "And with my hatchlings learning to fly, it would take a night, and a day, and a night, besides. My children would grow tired. Close to the end of their strength. If they fell, I could not catch them. The ground would catch them. They would die. I may touch the dirt, for my skin is hard, but my children would die, just as lightning dies when it touches the earth. This cave, the cave of Time, is safe for them. The cave belongs rightfully to me and to the sky. But the ground is not mine. The ground is not safe."

"One who walks in the grace of Airak can call lightning to strike them while they're flying. Bring me close enough to the forest." *Airak's teeth, am I to ride this creature now? First the crocodile, then the ship, and now a monster named Hunger?* Leaper had resigned himself to an isolated retirement. A long and gruelling task of hand carving a tribute to his lost love, an atonement. Instead, he was bargaining with yet another master. Others had always wished to use him for his magical abilities. This time, most likely, he'd be eaten afterwards.

Bold. Confident. But who will carve the statue if the winged one eats me?

Hunger lowered her long neck, bridgelike, over the empty riverbed. Her huge, black-scaled head came to rest beside Leaper, so that he crouched at arm's length from her slit-pupilled white eye.

"Very well. As was foretold. It is the last day of summer. You will give my children the gift of hard skins. Climb on my neck. It is time to go. It is time to leave the cave of Time. For a time. I cannot speak while flying.

Nor will you be able to speak to me. But bring the lightning, and I will owe you a debt. Bring the lightning, and we will negotiate a new bargain."

RIDING ON the back of Hunger was no more comfortable than being propelled by the prow of a flying ship that wasn't meant to fly.

Leaper's tongue had shrivelled with thirst within hours. He needed to piss. At dawn, and again at dusk, the winged one landed at the edge of one of the mirror-clear footprint lakes for Leaper to relieve himself and drink his fill. She was a faster flier than her children, but as soon as she glimpsed them catching up to her on the southern horizon, she was impatient to take to the skies again.

"They must not see me on the ground," she insisted in panicked blasts in Leaper's direction. "They must not do as I do. Catch your spines in my scales quickly, wielder of lightning. They must not see me on the ground."

Leaper had spent his childhood in the home of Understorian hunters and learned to work with or bed down on skins of demons. No Canopian demon leather could have withstood the razor-keen slash of his shin or forearm spines. Yet Hunger's scales went unscored. Only his weight on the hooked tips of the spines, catching on the crests of the scales, kept him secured to the arch of her back as she beat her enormous wings.

It was an ungainly takeoff. The winged one extended her striding legs little by little as she covered a thousand human paces of ground, until her sprint finally gave her enough speed to leave the plateau.

Then the great black wings, which had obscured Leaper's view in their frantic beating, snapped level. His steed turned in a slow arc, facing into the wind, settling into a glide.

Leaper's tongue shrivelled again, but he didn't close his eyes. The Titan's Forest was visible once more. Sunset's rose afterglow kissed the great tree trunks at its western edge. Between Hunger and her destination were an inestimable number of paces, yet Leaper was seeing for the first time how the stony plateau with the long line of lakes dropped off into the grassy valley in cliffs just as steep as the ones where Hunger had her lair.

He hadn't noticed before, as the wind-tossed ship had passed over in pitch-darkness. The Bright Plain lay much lower, like the bottom terrace in a garden, filled with grassland and swamp, containing everything from the Titan's Forest to the City-by-the-Sea; all the peoples and their squabbles Leaper had ever known or heard of.

Loneliness caught at him in that moment. He wanted his three mothers, his three fathers, and his two sisters around him. They would berate him. They would interrogate him. They would laugh with him. They would feed him. But that could never happen; they could never all be together again, the way it had been before Unar woke and Leaper went with her to Canopy. Imeris was now searching for her lost leopard-child. Ylly was Audblayin, a goddess, guarded by Nirrin, Imeris's childhood friend.

Oldest-Father had been dead for ten years, sealed into a tree by the sorceress Kirrik.

And Leaper was cursed.

None of us can go back. Not Oldest-Father. And not me.

Leaper twisted in his seat to stare back at the baby winged ones, also rose-tinted, tumbling along behind their mother in the turbulence of her passage. He imagined himself filling with Airak's borrowed power. Smelling charred floodgum, feeling like the sky was his body and white sparks his blood. Calling lightning to the hatchlings, one at a time, until all twelve had turned black as Hunger and were able to safely alight in the grasslands to rest.

I'm not a leaf on the breeze. I'm master of my destiny.

After I've helped her, Hunger will carry me back to the mountains. Soon, we'll be joined by all the Servants of Airak. Somehow I'll get a message to them to leave him, to leave Canopy. They'll make a pilgrimage. Follow the chain of lakes to the cave of Time. They're the ones who will help me, not just to carve the statue but to make the city live again. Together we'll—

His fantasy died as he felt the first magical surge of Ulellin's curse rattling the pinions of Hunger's wings.

She maintained headway for a few moments, but then the wind strengthened again.

I didn't tell her, Leaper told himself calmly, *because she didn't need to know.*

Gliding became out of the question. Hunger's wings began working as hard as they had during takeoff. They lost altitude. Leaper couldn't tell if it was the wind slowing her, or if Hunger slowed voluntarily so that her hatchlings could catch up, in a protective instinct.

She said she was more powerful than Ulellin when it came to commanding the wind. She called Ulellin a red-hearted meat-animal.

The winged one's bellow-breaths expanded her rib cage to dangerous proportions. Leaper spread his limbs wider apart, hooking himself desperately to her spinal protrusions.

She called Ulellin weak, vain, and one-fourteenth of a titan. I didn't break my promise. Hunger broke her promise!

The wind shrieked in his ears. It all but tore him from Hunger's back. His spines skittered free of her scales as she went into a spinning dive. He glimpsed the hatchlings, little brown teeth bared helplessly, being driven towards the ground.

Before he could join them, his shin spines caught at Hunger's shoulder joint. Leaper dangled and screamed, but he didn't fall. Hunger twisted, recovering from the dive, and one of the hatchlings landed across her back, right in front of Leaper. It was about the same length as he was, and sliding. He grabbed it by the legs with both hands, discovering as Hunger tilted again that it was about as heavy as he was, too.

"Tilt the other way!" he shrieked, despite the howl of the wind, despite Hunger having warned him that they wouldn't be able to speak once they took to the sky. He could imagine what she would want to say to him—*You lied to me, wielder of lightning, when you said we could safely approach the forest!*—and he bellowed the words he would have replied with. "Didn't you see me calling lightning to them? You said it was foretold!"

Yet they weren't anywhere near close enough to the forest for him to use Airak's magic. He hugged the yowling, thrashing hatchling to his chest, even as one of its siblings brushed a stand of bamboo with its wing and instantly fell apart, fluttering away in the grass-flattening gale like an emptied bucket of ash.

Another touched the ground, and another. They were tired, and the curse was powerful.

Leaper soon realised with horror that the hatchling he held was the last one left.

I doom you, Ulellin had said—she was good when it came to doom, the goddess of wind and leaves.

by my power

Apparently one-fourteenth of a titan was still stronger than a winged one.

to wander far from home.

And Ulellin didn't care who else was harmed by the deadly winds sent Leaper's way. Not Floorians. Not Yran. Not the hatchlings of the last winged one left alive.

Hunger reacted with rage as she worked her way higher into the sky. Her huge head arched back, and her jaws would have closed over Leaper's head if he hadn't held the hatchling like a shield.

In her terrible, white-hot eye, he saw frustration but also resolve.

I can't kill you now, the eye seemed to say, *but as soon as my last hatchling is deposited safely in the cave of Time, you will die.*

TWENTY-SEVEN

WITH ELEVEN of the twelve hatchlings dead, they made better time.

Or perhaps every journey goes faster when it's your last.

Hunger crossed both valley and stony plateau with the speed and cold precision of a javelin. The day dawned and the cave of Time waited on the southern horizon. Leaper and his living shield dangled over Hunger's neck. Soon enough, the writhing, white-scaled offspring grew quiet in his arms, beady eyes closed, thin wings limp. It was exhausted. He could throw it down in a final act of petty revenge, but why, when this failed expedition was his own fault, his own doomed miscalculation?

There must be a way out. There must be something I can say to save myself.

It wasn't as if he'd ever pictured himself dying an old man. He'd even dared to imagine something heroic in his final moments. Helping Imeris slay a monster. Snatching a magic sword from under the nose of angry Crocodile-Riders. Even being crushed under a winged one's clawed foot would have satisfied the eager, impatient child-self who'd successfully begged his spines from his mothers so early, seeking a place in the sun.

But now that the day of his death had arrived, he could see clearly what it was he'd hoped to achieve in life—and it hadn't been heroics. He'd slain the monster so that Imeris would love him. So that he might belong with his sisters, even though he was the smallest child, the child lacking in extraordinary gifts. He'd needed Aurilon's sword to fulfil the promises made by Aforis, who had vouched for him before the Lord of Lightning.

He'd broken every oath he'd ever taken, to win Ilik's love.

All he'd wanted was to feel that—with all his flaws—he'd finally earned his place among the kings and gods that surrounded him; instead, he'd stolen secrets for a master who burned him to the bone before drowning thousands to keep hold of the reins of absolute power.

It wasn't over yet. He could redeem himself, he could do something worthwhile—*I know it!*—if only he could talk Hunger out of killing him.

I've always been able to think of the right thing to say.

Nothing came to him.

I should have stayed home. All those boring speeches Aforis gave me, all Ousos's frustrated blows, all the disciplinary drainings of my magic—if only they'd worked. If only they'd actually made an impression on me. Too late to listen to them now.

He started to laugh helplessly as Hunger banked towards the cave opening, wings folded. She would barely fit through it. Leaper tried to predict how she'd catch the stone floor with her talons and turn, shoulders hunched, to tuck her tail and huge haunches into the depths of the cavern. Perhaps he could—

No. There was no bark for him to catch. No vines for him to climb.

But what if he landed on something soft—

No. There was nothing but stone, and sticks, and bones.

Well, I've died before. I'll die again.

It was rare for anyone who wasn't a goddess or god to know who they had been, before. Leaper knew. He'd known even before Unar, the Sleeping Girl in their home, had emerged one day, stared at him with yearning and horror, and whispered, *Frog's soul.* He'd known since he stood on a long limb, looking upwards, searching for the sun, and told Oldest-Mother that he wanted go up, that he belonged up.

It's very strange, Oldest-Mother had said, smiling her sweet-sad smile, *but I think you share a soul with somebody I knew. Somebody who made mistakes, who died young, and very close by, but who couldn't bear to leave her sister's side, even in death.*

Little Leaper had felt his closed eyes; he'd always imagined his soul to be trapped between them, in the place where two pictures turned into one picture.

Do you mean I have a bad soul?

Oldest-Mother had kissed him.

You have a good soul. Don't stare at the sun. I've heard of people going blind from staring at the sun in Canopy.

At that time, Leaper had never seen the sun in its unscreened glory. The day they'd climbed and seen not only the sun but the Garden Gates, he'd expected to be moved to joy, and yet in that first moment his spine went rigid with mixed fear and hatred: a flash of something that Frog had felt, before him.

When he'd touched magic for the first time, he'd revelled in the new dimension of his connection to his sister Ylly—who'd always smelled like quince blossom and wood fern but now overwhelmed him with the bitterness of germinating quince seed, blocked his nose with a powder coating of spore—but also had the strange pang that said, *Wasn't I supposed to hate her?*

And then having Aforis gently sever his connection to her and stitch it onto Airak. Blossom and fern curled away like dying vines burned back by the new lightning and obsidian blaze of his heart. He'd been excited to be serving someone he saw as a more powerful deity, but also at the thought that he was leaving the last whispers about Frog behind, starting out on his own path.

How could he have dreamed that Airak was nothing but a mortal thief of one-fourteenth of a soul? *With a spyglass made from a great tree, keeping one eye out for the winged!*

Whoever Leaper was going to be next, he hoped it wouldn't be a lovesick fool struggling to impress people who he thought were his betters but weren't. *I hope I'm born a historian or a hunter. I hope I never serve another god! How would that be, for starting on another path?*

And then the cave mouth closed around him, cutting off the beautiful sunlight he had craved. His heart sank; his head all but brushed the ceiling. The hatchling in his lap came awake, squirming as Hunger's great weight struck the stone shelf, and dust rattled from hanging stone fangs silhouetted against the shrinking sky.

Leaper shoved the hatchling away from him. Unhooked his shin spines. Took a deep breath and held it. Tried to crouch in place, ready for a spring, but Hunger's jaws were already open and swinging towards him.

He threw himself sideways and upside down.

Black-scaled neck thrashing.

Ceiling receding.

Hands catching on the sharp, obsidian feathers covering the wings as they curled.

One wing edge knocked him towards the tunnel that led to Time. Leaper looked up in the split second before striking the wall. There was no time to get his hands up in front of his face.

Then, though he must have been falling, head down, everything seemed suspended and slow. He hadn't felt himself hit the wall, and now he couldn't feel anything but a burning sensation inside the whole of his body and a trickle of liquid running down his cheek.

Maybe tears. Maybe blood.

Leaper blinked and found himself lying on his back at the base of the rock wall, his limbs across the entrance to the tunnel. His gaze was on the dim, distant cavern ceiling. Hunger's slavering jaws appeared there. Her white-hot eyes shone like the sun he'd craved.

Turn away, he screamed at himself, more terrified than he'd ever been, but his neck refused to turn. Something was moving beneath him, raising him abruptly closer to the ceiling, closer to his death; or maybe he was hallucinating. His body wasn't obeying him. If not for the burning sensation, he might have thought his body wasn't there. He couldn't speak to save himself.

Couldn't swallow.

Could hardly breathe.

All he could do was close his eyes, so he did.

TWENTY-EIGHT

LEAPER HAD hoped death would be dreamless.

Instead, Unar stood before him, cradling a baby before the Gate of the Garden. She was sixteen or so, the same age she'd been while she hibernated in the hunters' home.

She wore the torn remnants of a skirt and long-sleeved shirt. Black rags bound her bleeding feet. Her hair was in its customary twin braids. An expression of pain twisted her face almost beyond recognition

"I love you, Isin," she said, and Leaper felt her power flowing through him, healing his wounds. He tried to look down at his body, to feel his hands and feet again, to brush away the injuries the winged one, Hunger, had dealt him and laugh in the monster's rage-filled, fanged face.

But the cave wasn't there.

Nothing was there besides Unar and the baby.

His body ripped itself apart in a shower of blood.

LEAPER'S OLDER sister, Ylly, who'd turned out to be the goddess Audblayin, stared down at him from the wooden sides of a bed. They were in the cave. It was enormous.

No, this is our home.

There were no limestone teeth hanging from the ceiling. It was polished tallowwood. Leaper was home. He was safe.

I still can't feel my body, though.

Panic began to rise in him before he wriggled his fingers, with difficulty, and realised he could feel his body; it was just wrapped tightly in something, arms trapped at his sides.

A blanket. It was difficult for him to focus on it, but he saw the crest of the House of Epatut. He wasn't in a bed, but a cradle. Candles burned on the edge of a shelf that was one with the tallowwood wall. How had his sister brought him home safely to Understorey? Of course, she was a goddess. She must have powers that nobody suspected.

And yet Ylly was a little girl, no more than eight or nine years old. Her long, straight hair had been brushed until it gleamed, and her round cheeks were rosy enough for the pink to show through the blackbean-brown. She smiled. It was the smile of a goddess, even if she didn't know it yet.

"Hush, baby," Ylly cooed. "Baby, you're safe. I made you safe. You were scared and floating and waiting and hating, so I brought you here." She frowned, as though that was something she didn't want to dwell on too closely. "Listen. You can share my mamas. They are the best mamas, they'll cheer you up, you'll love them. You'll see." Her returning smile smoothed out her brow, and she put one finger to Leaper's nose.

He smelled wood fern and quince as he sank into a peaceful sleep.

The godfinder's ti chest was small.

Still, Leaper had found a way to fold himself into it, with his nostrils near the keyhole so that he could still breathe.

Though he'd wished she'd taken up farming tapirs or salamanders instead of flowerfowl, on account of them being so stupid and noisy, this morning a scare by some hungry bird of prey had distracted his guardian for long enough that he'd been able to position himself perfectly to eavesdrop on whatever it was she wanted to speak to Airak's Skywatcher about.

Unar's sharply indrawn breath sounded by the door.

"You look d-different." She sounded terrified. "Aforis."

"You look the same, Godfinder," came a strange man's husky, grave voice. "Though you've been gone a while. Did it really take sixteen years for you to find Audblayin in Understorey? Everyone guessed that you'd died. The goddess Ehkis was slain a second time, and you were not here in Canopy to find her."

"I was sleeping," Unar said in a strangled voice. "You remember. The sleepers."

"I remember everything."

There was no trace of anger in his tone, yet Unar began weeping noisily. It was a distressing, ugly sound that Leaper had never heard before, and it terrified him in turn. What had his guardian done to offend this man? *What does she owe him?* Was she going to hand Leaper over to him as some kind of payment, and if so, how could Leaper have been so foolish as to gift wrap himself inside a ti chest?

She stopped crying presently.

"Hate me," she said raggedly, "but don't hate the boy. He's innocent. He's done nothing."

Leaper's terror increased. Was he going to be sacrificed? Perhaps it would be worth throwing open the lid of the chest and running for it, even though he'd have to make it past both of them. And both of them wielders of magic.

No. Stay still. Stay quiet, he urged himself, heart racing.

"One who walks in the grace of Airak will not turn him away from taking the test at the Temple, when the time comes. One may even consent to tutor him until then."

"He's an adept, Aforis. Couldn't you feel it?"

Aforis sighed.

"The boy is bonded to Audblayin. I suppose he grew up in Understorey below Audblayinland. Should the Temple teach him to call lightning no thicker than a pond reed, and all because the source he draws on lies in the furthest part of Canopy from this point? That seems cruel. One who walks in the grace of Airak is surprised to hear you ask it."

Audblayin sent us here, Leaper recalled. *Because Unar was a Gardener, but Unar disgraced herself, somehow.*

"Audblayin rules new life," Unar argued. "New shoots can be cut and grafted. They thrive where grown trees die from being transplanted."

Aforis sighed again. His voice came closer.

"Why don't you tell me more about the boy. Where he came from. How he ended up in your care. Why there is something familiar about his soul."

He was so loud now that he could only be standing over the table beneath which the ti chest was kept.

Only then did it occur to Leaper that Unar would offer her guest a cup of ti.

The lid of the chest flew open.

Leaper's body disintegrated.

LEAPER SAW again the battle of the titans, as he had seen it in the Rememberer temple of Dawnsight.

He saw how Audblayin's guts like blood-rubbed ropes had spilled from her lurid, green-scaled skin. How, despite one undersized forelimb being ripped from its socket by Ulellin's teeth, Audblayin snapped and clawed at the cliff edge, struggling to climb, shrinking all the time.

How her body, launched by her powerful hind limbs, had gone up head-first into the hole.

And then come down again, her feeble remaining forelimb unable to draw her completely into the cavern.

Or was Hunger in there? Did Hunger drive her back?

That broken claw. It was left behind, while the thing that became Leaper's sister splashed into the base of the falls, crushing already-fallen watchtowers and snapping what remained of her unbroken bones.

RUMBLINGS ECHOED around the cavern.

The rocky ground was shaking.

At least, Leaper thought it might have been shaking; his body still wasn't there. It was dark, and the air tasted of dust, yet repetitive concussions rattled through his skull and he was either dizzy or his face was moving up and down.

Then all was still.

"Too great an impact," Aforis's voice speculated in a whisper, somewhere near his left ear. "In her rage, she's brought the ceiling down and blocked the tunnel entrance. The breeze is still flowing through. We can breathe, but we can't escape. Or can we? If you could wake, you might suggest how to activate the return passage. You always were full of suggestions."

I'm dead, Leaper thought, *and so is Aforis. At least I'll have company until we all get reincarnated. That's if there are any bodies for us to be born into out here. Besides Hunger's hatchlings.*

He started to laugh at that thought, but when he moved his tongue to swallow, a fierce prickling and stinging erupted in his lips, the lower half of his face, and the parts of the back of his head that still had sensation.

All of a sudden, it seemed the rearrangement of his throat had blocked his breath. Leaper had to stop focussing on the whispering and dust taste and bend all his concentration to the problem of how to open his lungs. *Is this what it's like to be born? Maybe this is the new me. That's how I'll build a great statue, even with a broken neck.*

Maybe I'm Aforis's child.

That was funny, too. He choked, feeling tears well in his eyes, even though he was dead. He thrashed his head. Managed to jerk his jaw until the dusty air entered his body again.

Hunger's voice boomed about him, strangely flat and loud.

"YOU HAVE ONLY BOUGHT YOURSELF A SLOW DEATH."

So she can speak the language of Canopy.

Leaper imagined her striking the walls of the cave, breaking the stone teeth with blows while sliding her wings and body over it, letting the sound echo down through the tunnel. It was nowhere near as good as having lips and a tongue. Most of the consonants were difficult to make out and those words had to be guessed by context.

Aforis sighed with all his habitual forbearance, and Leaper was shocked to realise he was really there. The old Skywatcher wasn't left over from the dreams, he was kneeling there, in the tunnel, beside his injured and immobile pupil, sighing at the enemy.

Death god take me.

Aforis is really here, and I have no purpose anymore. I'm ready to leave this cave, this body, and all my failures. It must be Aforis who builds the statue of the queen. I'm a fool who read the vision wrong.

Aforis is the one who lives.

"One who walks in the grace of Airak can't die," Aforis shouted at the winged one in a high-pitched, fairly good impersonation of Leaper's voice. *He's always had a much deeper voice than me.* "Don't you know anything about Canopy? At this distance from the death god, Atwith has no power over me."

"I WILL FETCH ONE-FOURTEENTH OF A TITAN," Hunger answered. "YOU WILL DIE."

"You can't fetch anybody without violating your agreement." *How does Aforis know about the agreement?* "I can't die, but you can. Even if you try to fetch him, he'll kill you with a touch. His Servants will kill you."

"ONE-FOURTEENTH OF A TITAN IS NOT MY GOD. HE IS NOT MY EQUAL. I WILL FETCH HIM, AND YOU WILL DIE."

More rumblings.

More dust.

More floating up and down.

Leaper struggled to focus on breathing. On keeping his throat open, all his cartilages arranged. He didn't dare try to speak again, or to swallow.

His mouth was so dry, there was hardly anything to swallow, anyway. The blood on his face was dried, and a cold wind gusted down the tunnel.

"Well," Aforis mused, "that worked. What should we do now?"

It was too dark for Leaper's eyes being open or closed to make much of a difference, so he let his lids slide shut to keep the dust out. The winged one was right. Even with Aforis beside him, all he *had* done was buy himself a slow death.

He tried to make himself see the Dusksight vision again.

The one with the huge statue of Ilik.

If only he had that broken ring of bone with him. If only he hadn't stuffed it all through the thieves' lantern.

I really did steal it so that I could see her again, even as a poor substitute in stone.

The impulse to laugh this time was easily quashed.

Maybe I'll dream of her. Of the things we did. Or could have done.

DESPERATE THIRST woke him. Brightness on the back of his eyelids turned his vision red, but he had no energy to open them.

"What is that?" Unar asked. Her voice hovered above him, imagined or real. Did it matter? *I didn't dream of Ilik. I didn't dream of anything.*

"A broken aqueduct," answered a male voice. *Not Aforis.* The voice seemed familiar to Leaper, but he couldn't quite place it. "Look. It used to run straight, carrying water from the spring at the centre of the city. The water then flowed into the channel that ran through the winged one's lair."

"You think that's the remnant of the span, down there?" Unar sounded doubtful.

"I'm almost certain of it. I think that strata is continuous with the plateau of the thousand lakes. The plateau I flew over. The whole city's sunk down to that level." The voice firmed even as it grew more distant, as though the crouched owner of it had straightened. "That's the way we should go. We can hardly circle around to the plateau. It's too exposed. The monster would pluck us like spiny plums."

Real, Leaper thought drowsily. At least, he was either drowsy or at the edge of death. *They are real, just like Aforis was real. But where is he? Where am I?*

"What makes you think there's water down there?"

"The snowmelt has to go somewhere," the stranger answered. "Besides, plugging a spring just makes it spring up somewhere else. That's why it's called a spring. Just because it doesn't run through the cave anymore doesn't mean it doesn't run."

"What would you know about springs? Forgive me, but you said that the part of your soul holding the death god's awareness fell silent when you were snatched from the forest."

The death god. Was Hunger truly able to kidnap the death god? Is that how much she truly hates me?

Lizards lay so many eggs and sometimes eat the hatchlings themselves.

And yet. I knew it was a mistake to confuse the winged one with an animal. A human mother might go to such lengths for revenge against her children's killer. And Wept cried a whole ocean of tears on account of her hatchlings, so Mitimiti said.

"The death god's voice has gone silent." The man sounded cool. Sober. Reflective. "Other memories grow stronger. Before I died, before my drowned body became available to Atwith, I lived in Ehkisland. While I lived there, there was something between the rain goddess and me. I think I had the potential to be an adept. I think I should have gone to the Lake the moment I felt the water under the ground and in the sky."

Leaper tried to imagine what a connection to water would be like. He wondered if Aforis's magical surgery was capable of severing him from the lightning god as he'd been severed from the birth goddess, or whether the reduction in powers every time that he changed would leave him with no magic at all.

"You had an affinity for water," Unar muttered. "That was the sign you were sent by Ehkis."

"She wouldn't have drowned me if I'd served her. Then the death god would have chosen a different corpse to inhabit."

"If you'd served her, you would have had to watch Kirrik kill her twice. I'm the Godfinder. If I never have to find Ehkis again, it'll be too soon."

Better to ask why Ehkis didn't serve you, Leaper thought, surprised to still be able to summon anger so strongly in his desperate state. *Why she drowned you in the first place.*

"Well," Unar went on after a significant pause. "How are we going to get Leaper down there without breaking his neck worse than it's already broken?"

"We need something to strap him to, to keep him straight," Atwith said. "A cloth and poles, or a stiff board."

The masts of my broken ship. The sails. The ladder I made from the ancient watchtowers.

"You're very quiet, Aforis," Unar said. "You look like a stiff board."

There was another, longer silence.

"One of us will have to descend into the crevice," Aforis said slowly, finally. "In advance of the others. To scout the way. That individual will need to explore the conduit of the aqueduct, if indeed it remains open, and find something in the ruined city suitable for transporting the patient. If not, water must be brought back here."

"I'll go," Atwith said with a laugh. "I've already died once. I'm sure I can find water, and what's the worst that can happen? I'll drown a second time? When we get back to the forest and I'm host to the death god's stronger soul, my small soul will drown again anyway."

TWENTY-NINE

LEAPER THOUGHT he'd only faded out of consciousness for a moment.

Yet the sunlight on his eyelids was gone. Cool water dribbled over his parched lips, and when he opened his eyes, all around him had changed.

Aforis.

The dark brown hands tilting a gourd over his slack mouth were the same hands that had helped him out of Unar's ti chest. The hands which, years later, had caught him the first time he'd forced himself through the thieves' lantern.

Those hands had shaved Leaper's head when he'd dyed his hair against the rules of the Temple. The first time Leaper had tried to call lightning to a stone bowl of black sand, lost concentration and called the white fire to himself instead, Aforis's hands had pressed on his chest to get his heart started again.

Why did you take me into the Temple? You're not my father. You never owed me anything.

He'd escaped the winged one's lair. Somehow. Aforis was with him. He was alive. That was all he knew.

To Leaper's left and right were a pair of high, parallel limestone ledges. Between them shone a jagged slash of pale blue sky. Their edges were softened by the silhouettes of tufty grasses.

Aforis is with me . . . at the bottom of a hole.

Leaper guessed that the grasses were a hundred paces above him. More cold wind howled down through the gash, but Leaper was snug in his windturner and Aforis was bundled in his black robes and bearskin.

Aforis's head, which had been shaved since he'd started going bald and grey, with white hair being reserved for Airak's Servants, showed short, very black growth beneath the dust. Leaper peered at it in confusion. He tried to see the triangle-shaped scar that Aforis had earned from walking into that sharp branch right before Leaper left Canopy, but it didn't seem to be there. The dust must be covering it, or Leaper wasn't able to focus properly.

Yet the ruined city behind Aforis leaped into perfect focus.

Houses of four and five storeys covered the sheer, pale walls of the crevice. Dark grey slate crowned the houses. They had inward-sloping walls, thinner at the top than at ground level. White paint peeled away from dressed stone, and small ferns grew in the cracks. Their brittle little balconies, with railings of wood carved in interlocking patterns of rectangles and squares, held rows of cracked white clay pots long emptied of their dead plantings and soil by the swirling wind.

Leaper looked at Aforis again.

A jolt like lightning went through him. For an instant, it seemed he looked down on a younger, kneeling, bare-chested Aforis. A leash better suited to an animal connected Leaper's wrist to Aforis's throat.

He wondered how he could be seeing this, a memory that wasn't his, before he remembered the way Frog's memories had seized him twice in the past.

I'm seeing the day Frog tried to use Aforis, her captive, to destroy the Garden.

Wood rested beneath Aforis's bloodied knees. Not stone. The enhanced smell of magic use surrounded them—tallowwood, fresh blood, sap on spines—and a pure and righteous hatred allowed Leaper—Frog—to act as a conduit for Aforis's magic, somehow. It was as if he held Tyran's Talon in his hand.

Wrathfully, he brought lightning down on a baby in a woman's arms.

Not a baby. A goddess. A goddess of Canopy. I hate 'er! I hate 'er!

The instant passed.

Leaper lay on his back, looking up at old Aforis again. *Why that memory? Why here and now?* He tried to raise a hand to press his temples, to rub his eyes, but his hand was a stranger. His hand was useless.

It was Aforis's hand tilting the water gourd again into his mouth. He mustn't gasp. He mustn't breathe it in. He had to concentrate, or he'd drown the way Atwith said he had drowned, except in a mouthful of water instead of a flood.

Atwith. Where is he?

A man stood behind Aforis, much taller and thinner, with a heavy brow, a long, black-bearded jaw, and inscrutable, deep-set brown eyes. He wore nothing but a skirt of stems from a bone tree, which resembled tree bear rib bones, over a loincloth, and he shivered in the frigid wind.

Leaper, mouth wet, encouraged by the success of his swallow, ventured a single word.

"Aoun?" Pressing his tongue to the roof of his mouth felt like a hot knife had been stuck there. He wanted to cry, but he thought that might be painful, too, so he distracted himself by calling to mind the first time he'd seen Aoun.

Leaper remembered panting with exhaustion from the climb up to Canopy. He remembered peering past his older sister in her scale armour. He'd seen the Gatekeeper of the Garden embracing Unar, in the house they'd freshly built for Middle-Father. Unar and Aoun had been friends. Served the goddess Audblayin together. Only, Unar had perhaps clung to Aoun a little too tightly for just friends.

The jolt like lightning passed through Leaper again, showing him one of Frog's memories. He glimpsed the Gatekeeper in the heat of battle, white-robed. At Aoun's side stood an old Servant, who reached for the baby that Leaper had been trying to kill.

The glimpse faded. Leaper lay at the bottom of the limestone crevice with Aforis again. He smelled meat cooking over a peat fire.

Two of Frog's memories in as many minutes, when I've only ever experienced them twice before. What's going on?

"I'm his dead brother," the man who looked like a weirdly young Aoun said calmly with Atwith's voice. "I didn't go to the Lake when I should have, because I didn't want to leave him, but in the end the Lake rose up and came to me. Mere moments after I died, before my human soul even knew it was supposed to go into the ether, my lungs were emptied of water by a god's soul eager to possess me, and my legs carried me to my new niche without a single backward glance. Now I'm—"

"Atwith," Leaper croaked.

"Yes." His smile was modest. Reticent. Distinctly ungodly. "The last winged one, made mad and stupid by grief, brought me here between her teeth in the hopes my mere presence would end you."

"Didn't."

The smile faded.

"I tried to end her, but she wouldn't die. Her death, it seems, isn't Atwith's to bestow." Atwith shrugged. "It's been a long time since I needed weapons to kill, but my Bodyguard carried one, for skinning game. When she found she couldn't pierce Hunger's hardened hide, she wrapped her arms around Hunger's ankle and stayed clinging on until we reached the cave." He shook his head ruefully. "She distracted Hunger with an attack on the hatchling, whose hide is still soft; I think she managed to stick the knife in its underbelly right before Hunger killed her."

"Sorry."

"Her sacrifice wasn't wasted. I found the escape tunnel that Aforis had started digging through the rubble."

Unar's frowning face appeared beside Aforis's. She was really there. Somehow. Unlike the others, she still looked the same. Unlike the others, she hadn't mysteriously grown younger. She grouched as if they all still stood in the boughs of Canopy.

"Maybe the death god here," she said, rolling her eyes at Atwith, "hasn't been able to rid us of the winged one, but he managed to snare a goat. I've taken the risk of putting it on a fire to cook, even though I still can't believe we're eating it. Even kings don't eat goats in Canopy. Can you eat, Leaper?"

"Maybe."

"Speaking pains you?" She shouldered closer to him, drawing a sidelong, irked look from Aforis.

"Yes."

"If you can keep him alive for now with nonmagical doctoring," Aforis murmured, "you can heal him when we get back to the forest."

Unar's abrupt laughter was full of more derision than Leaper had ever thought the Godfinder would direct at Aforis. She was normally unfailingly polite to him.

"Oh, yes? Once we reach the forest? How do you propose we do that? Atwith estimated that he covered a thousand times a thousand paces. Even if we were all fit to travel—and don't tell me you can carry another grown man on a stretcher all that way—it would take us fifty days or more, and the winged one would spot us in a heartbeat. There's nowhere to hide on that plateau, besides in the lakes themselves, and we can't breathe water."

"Then we must find a way back through the lantern."

Through the lantern. That must be the way they came. But how, when its light is out?

Aforis responded wryly to Leaper's quirked eyebrow. "I emerged through your linked lantern while it remained in your carrysack. While you were lying on top of it, in fact. Luckily the seams of the sack came apart instead of strangling me. Unar arrived subsequently. She showed up a day or so after Atwith and his Bodyguard were deposited unceremoniously into the cavern by the winged."

"I've never seen so many birds bearing messages," Unar said wryly. "Canopy was in an uproar. The death god, missing in the middle of a cloud-dark night! They came for me at once. Who better to find Atwith than the Godfinder? What with Aforis missing, too, and a broken lantern that he seemed to have repaired sitting in the middle of my table, even Leaper would have had the brains to open a pane and poke around inside it. Can't say I was impressed to land on my backside in a pitch-black tunnel with an angry monster at the other end."

There was no magic to activate the lantern at my end, but the other lantern stayed behind, bathed in Airak's power.

But it was in Eshland.

No. Aforis must have brought it from Eshland to the Godfinder's table. To Airakland.

The lantern had allowed his friends from Canopy to come to him, but even if they managed to activate this dead and battered twin, it wouldn't let them back through with Leaper accompanying them. No more than Leaper had been allowed in close proximity to Canopy when travelling in the company of the winged.

Gathering his courage, he tried to tell them.

"The curse," he said thickly. His teeth clicked together like hammer and chisel on the "s," sending shooting pains through his head. "It won't work. Ulellin's curse."

"It's not the curse," Unar said sharply. "Listen. Five months ago, Ousos came back from Floor without you, saying Airakland was under threat. Airak bought an early monsoon from the child Ehkis with every tribute in his Temple plus all the sand and glass in Airakland. And Aforis tried to find out from his master, despite all these distractions, whether you'd survived."

"Airak would say only that you were bent on disobeying him again," Aforis said. "So I took some of Unar's flowerfowl and went to see Atwith."

"A Skywatcher in the death god's Temple!" Atwith interrupted, grinning.

"I remember that. I told—Atwith told a Skywatcher that Airak's Servant Leapael was still alive."

"I looked for clues about where you might have gone," Aforis told Leaper. "I found your clandestine abode in Eshland. Your lantern was there, one of the pair you'd made for filching purposes. The lantern rested, malfunctioning, shooting lightning out everywhere, inside the broken halves of a ring of bone more massive than any Old God's bone I'd ever seen. I wondered who you'd stolen the bone from and how you could possibly have known where to find it. When I touched it, I saw terrible things. Visions of the forest's end."

"You should have left it alone," Unar said.

"I loaded the bone pieces and the lantern into a barrow and set off for Airakland. As when inside the house, the lantern was badly affected by the bones' proximity. I thought all the lightning might set the barrow on fire." Aforis sighed. "The Shining One should have been my best option, in the face of my god's recalcitrance, yet I was suspicious of the circumstances of Ousos's return."

"Did she leave you there to die?" Unar demanded of Leaper. "Blink once for—"

Leaper blinked once, emphatically.

"As I conveyed the lantern in the direction of the Godfinder's residence," Aforis said, "it blazed up so brightly that I stopped to lift it out of the barrow, to try and temper it with the god's power. Another, even larger Old God's bone erupted out of it, but before it could flatten me, the other bones rose up to meet it and they annihilated one another in a shower of crimson sparks. The sparks settled into my skin wherever it was exposed. My hands and face. My neck and feet. Within minutes, their red glow faded, but I could still feel them, like bee stings."

God's bones. Annihilated. Who knew they could cancel one another out?

The Rememberers did. Dusksight and Dawnsight. No wonder they kept the two temples far away from one another.

"I feel them now," Aforis went on. He dry-washed his face with his hands, and when he lowered them, Leaper saw the strangeness of the missing scar and black regrowth all over again. "They're doing this to me. Making me age backwards."

Two sclerotic ring bones. One seeing forwards in time and one seeing back, but the backwards-seeing one was the larger. The stronger. The more complete. That's the one holding sway over Aforis now, taking him back.

"You can't be sure that's what's happening," Unar argued. She waved a hand at Atwith. "It could be something more similar to *his* situation. *He* ages according to the work he does, or so he said. That's why he looks younger than Aoun. Plagues, starvation, and battle give him grey hairs. But in the ten years since Imeris made peace with Understorey, there have been far fewer premature deaths for him to preside over."

"I'm sure," Aforis said quietly. "My memories are being affected. I'm growing younger, slowly but surely. Approximately ninety days before I found the lantern, I received a wound that led to a scar on my face. Approximately ninety days after I found it, I woke up and the scar was gone. One day younger for every day that I should be growing older. That much is evident."

"Cheer up, then, old fellow," Atwith said lightly. "If it's true, you've got more monsoons left in you than any other mortal you know."

"With a good many of them as an infant," Aforis answered, turning to fix Atwith with a glare. "From the sounds of it, that's not an experience you've ever dealt with."

"I remember this body's childhood very clearly." Atwith licked his teeth. "Right now I do, anyway. As soon as I go back, I'll probably lose it again. You're right, Skywatcher. Atwith takes only adult bodies, freshly dead. He has no period of vulnerability, as the other deities do. He has no use"—his gaze flicked to Unar—"for a Godfinder."

Looks like he'll be needing a new Bodyguard, though, Leaper didn't quip.

"You give the impression that you've no true desire to attempt a return," Aforis said.

"I don't desire it," Atwith said, shrugging again. "Not at all. Yet my conscience insists that I try. All human lives that begin in the shade of the forest, whether on a boat floating beneath it or up high in its wooden arms, are bound together in one brilliant, tangled ball. When you told the winged one that I was the only one who could cut Leaper's life thread, you weren't far from the truth. Nobody in Canopy is dying right now, in my absence. Though I imagine some are in considerable pain. And some babies are being born soulless. I imagine Audblayin is cursing me for that shortage. If she aged the way that I do, she'd be tearing out handfuls of white hair."

"If she aged the way that I do," Aforis echoed sadly, "she'd have an eternal youth. Will I go to her, instead of to you, once my last hours are spent, I wonder?"

Leaper had briefly contemplated Aforis's death before, and yet dying an old man was different to dying of a strange and inexplicable reverse-aging magic curse.

Well, Leaper knew what it was like to be cursed.

Would Aforis, too, rage against the gods before the end?

Airak is not kind, Aforis had murmured to Leaper, the day that the over-eager boy had failed his first test at the Temple, *but his reach is high and far and wide. And simple. Lightning is there, or it isn't. Things are connected, or they aren't. Nothing complicated like new life, or the wild, or children.*

Nothing like love.

All the students had been given broken obsidian blades to mend. Glassmaking and glassworking were the primary industries of the Temple. Even the most feebly gifted of the freshly recruited adepts had made their black blades whole, but Leaper had failed, that day and on many subsequent days.

Before Unar and Aforis had gotten together to decide his future, in Audblayinland Leaper had felt the birth goddess's presence, light as spidersilk around him. The strands were invisible, but he could smell them, like seeds and sun-warmed leaves. He'd sensed that they could be touched, tugged, and tangled in dormant lives to draw them into the light.

In contrast, Airak had felt like ice in his teeth and black sand in his eyes. Like invincible, unbending metal bars reaching high into the sky, only not quite there, requiring a ferocity of thought to make them real. And then the first time he'd tried, the bars had resisted being placed where he wanted them, throwing him backwards across the room. He'd returned to life with his head bruised from the impact and his floating ribs bruised by Aforis's efforts at revival, his hair standing on end and the other students smirking.

It wasn't until he'd contrived to get his hands on Tyran's Talon that the smirks had faded. In the meantime, Leaper had needed to impress his master with other, more manipulative and insidious talents. He turned his hand to mimicry and deceit in order to be allowed to stay.

If I'd hidden myself in the ti chest a second time, might I have overheard Aforis and Unar regretting what they did to me? Experimenting on me? Grafting me to a different deity?

But I begged for it. Leaper remembered that much. *I begged to be allowed to learn the magic that called lightning. Baby magic? Bean magic? I never wanted that.*

"I'm sorry," Leaper said clumsily to Aforis. "My bones. My lantern. I killed you. Just like I killed Ilik."

Aforis and Unar glanced at one another.

"Like you killed Ilik?" Aforis repeated. "Ilik isn't dead, Leaper. She didn't want you told, because she feared you'd do something rash, but she's alive. Safe. At least, she was when I left her."

THIRTY

LEAPER'S HEART rate tripled.

Wind roared in his ears. He was trying to breathe in and out at the same time; he was choking; bile rose in the back of his throat despite the thought that vomiting would be the end of him, and so much worse than drowning in water.

Alive? Safe? He didn't dare believe them, for fear of being crushed again.

"The scar on Aforis's cheek came from forcing his way through to the farm," Unar said, frowning, putting a hand under Leaper's neck to support it. "Aforis was so preoccupied with the danger Ilik was in that he forgot I'd made those branches my armed sentries. It was his idea to bring her to me. Leaper, you need to relax. Ilik is at my flowerfowl farm." Her tone turned wry. "Let's hope she doesn't touch the lantern, or she could end up stuck here with the rest of us." Then her attention snapped back to Leaper. "I also left her safe, but bloodied and exhausted. I still had the cradle Anahah and Imeris used for their child, and now it's full again. Queen Ilik gave birth to a son on the last day of summer."

The last day of summer?

Leaper stared at the slanted, slate-roofed houses, seeing through their rickety balconies and broken pots. While he'd clung to Hunger's black scales with his climbing spines, Ilik had been giving birth. To their son.

Leaper recalled the king's words on the day they'd both thought Ilik had fallen.

I've always known that Ilik and I would have no children, Icacis had said. *The wind goddess prophesied that when I died without direct descendants, blood of a slave would take my throne.*

The words of Ulellin's curse, on the day Leaper had called lightning to slay Orin's beast in the leafy Temple, came back to him with a jolt of double vision and terrible clarity.

The wind spoke to me of your path, Ulellin had said. *I doom you, by my power, to wander far from home until your mate, your true love, your heart's desire, grows to love another more than you. Only then will you be permitted to return.*

Leaper blinked and was back with his friends in the mountain crevice.

He thought, *The blood of a slave that will take King Icacis's throne is my blood.*

The one that Ilik loved more than Leaper was her newborn son.

"The curse is broken," Leaper said, feeling as numb in mind as he was in body.

One day too late for Hunger to have carried me right back to Canopy.

Unar's expression was sympathetic.

"I'm no Servant of Oxor," she said, "but if Ilik didn't fall instantly in love with that ugly looking baby, I'll eat that weird blanket-shirt you're wearing."

A shadow fell over them.

Immediately, Leaper's companions went into a flurry of motion.

Leaper's instinct was to hunch his shoulders and crane his neck towards the slice of visible sky. Yet again his body failed to obey him. He had to wait for the swooping shape of the black-scaled winged one to appear in the place where his face was already aimed.

Hunger's eyes, as she carved through the blue, were slitted. Her nostrils were wide, drawing in the scent of . . . what? Leaper himself? Then her wings beat down, and she rose, turning back on herself, head and neck vanishing behind the sinuously doubled-back body.

Aforis's abrupt assault on their cooking fire with sandals and beating bearskin answered Leaper's fleeting mental query: *Was she drawn by the smell of the smoke?* Within moments Leaper smelled only singed hair and leather, which in turn was quickly dispersed. Then Atwith popped up beside Unar holding a seared, spitted goat that oozed blood and clear juices, and those smells made Leaper's mouth water so uncontrollably that he almost forgot about the fact they were being hunted by a vengeful immortal—or at least, an intelligent creature that was extremely long-lived.

While he was daydreaming of charred meat, Unar and Aforis were rolling Leaper in some kind of carpet, kicking dust up around him, fumbling with straps. He couldn't really see the straps. Nor could he feel them tighten around his arms and legs. He could glimpse patterns, once colourful, now faded, in the weave.

Not a carpet. A tapestry. A hanging.

Unar and Aforis seized wooden poles he hadn't realised were threaded through the rolled-up tapestry with him. They lifted, carrying him closer to one of the crevice walls, and his field of vision changed. He realised that the deep, house-lined crack in the rock was only one street of the abandoned city, and that the other end of the street finished in tumbled boulders with ice in their cracks, the timbers of more smashed watchtowers protruding from beneath them.

"We can't stay here," Aforis whispered from the foot end of the stretcher. "Hunger's coming back around. Follow me."

"Where are we going?" Atwith whispered back, still awkwardly wielding the steaming, half-cooked goat.

"Back the way we came, down the deep fork in the tunnel. To a structure I believe is a place of worship in the heart of the city."

"Where you found the tapestry."

"Indeed. There aren't any goats to snare, but there's water. The flow from the original spring has ceased, as we feared, but the river resumes from a crack in the gates of a graveyard. You were right about the spring, after all. It simply sprang up again somewhere else."

Leaper was looking at the sky one moment, the cracked plastered ceiling of one of the slate-roofed houses the next. Aforis, taking the lead, was taller than Unar, so that Leaper's feet were raised higher than his head, his neck tilted back at an angle.

He saw a painted frieze of starry skies over snowy peaks, in the place where building met wide, arched tunnel through unornamented rock. Then the party was plunged into blackness, and his mind had time to go over all he had learned.

First, and most important, things first.

Ilik is alive.

Hope flooded him.

The curse is broken. I can go back.

He commenced a mental assessment of his body. Breathing was slightly easier than it had been. The punishing fire that followed any attempt at speech was less agonising.

I have a reason to go back.

"Why are we slowing down?" Unar asked, her voice booming in the close confines of the tunnel.

"There's loose stone underfoot here," Aforis answered. "Go carefully."

Atwith said nothing, but the smell of supper indicated he hadn't fallen far behind.

I have a son. I can go back. She feared I'd do something rash? Like declare my love for her in front of her husband? Like reveal that I'm the father and get myself killed? Well, now Icacis thinks she's dead, the same as I did!

He wasn't angry with her for lying to him. She must have been so afraid, recognising the signs of pregnancy in light of the prophecy that Ulellin had made about Icacis fathering no children. If she had confided in Leaper, what would he have done? *Urged her to go into hiding with me. Shown her our home in Eshland. She could still have faked her death. I could have faked my grief. My whole life was fake. I spied for Airak, I lied to everybody.*

But Ilik hadn't known about all that.

Leaper moved his lips. Flared his nostrils. Opened and closed his eyelids. He tried to judge how much feeling he had in his face, his neck, his ears. Tried to tell the difference between the parts of his head that were touching the tapestry and the parts that weren't.

So, Ilik is free of her jailer, but what about me? A second time, I swore to Airak that I'd serve. That was before he tried to drown me. Before he did drown thousands of Rememberers. I won't serve him again, but he knows I'm still alive.

If he returned to Canopy, the lightning god would certainly sense it.

Unar and Aforis. They sliced me and my gifts cleanly away from Audblayin. They can do the same again. I don't care if I have to give up my magical abilities forever.

From his arms and legs, there was still no information at all.

Unar has to heal me. Her magic won't work outside of Canopy.

Not the faintest tingling. Not a welcome whisker of pain.

I have to get back to my—my family. My body has to be healed. Think, Leaper!

He pushed aside previous reconciliation to uselessness and helplessness. He had to use his mind. His mind was what he had sold to Airak, before his magical abilities had come to the fore. Quick wits were what had saved him, in the forest and outside of it.

He had loved Ilik's mind. How she would watch clock workings and take them apart, and how her face would light up with pleasure when she understood them.

"Unar," he said, "eat the bones. Eating bones makes magic work outside of Canopy."

"What was that?" Unar answered sharply. "Aforis, wait."

They came to an awkward halt.

"What is it?" Aforis asked.

"He said that—"

"I heard what he said. We're not safe here. Hunger could shake down the mountain again in another fit of rage. The parts of the city strong enough to survive squabbling titans are strong enough to—"

"Leaper," Unar interrupted. "Do you mean the bones of the Old Gods?"

"Yes," Leaper said.

"That's a relief," Atwith said blithely, bone skirt clacking.

"Eat Tyran's bone to call lightning," Leaper said, naming Airak in the language of the titans' original human worshippers. "Aulla's bone to call rain."

"You're saying that if it's to work, we've got to match the Old God's bone to our intended action. If I'm to heal you, I need a bone of Audblayin, who was called Bria, is that what you mean?" Her tone turned reflective. "Just like in Understorey. Like how Frog and I were taught magic by—" Unar's face twisted with revulsion.

"Kirrik." Leaper finished her sentence, shying away from a lightning jolt of Frog's memory. A glimpse of the sorceress's beautiful, imperious face. "Yes."

"None of us died here," Atwith said. "No Old Gods, I mean. None of us died in the mountains. We all died on the plain, where the forest sprang up, growing over our remains. Except for Time." His voice turned to a barely audible mutter. "Just as wood and the wild must be separated by justice, birth and death must be separated by time. With time missing, we can't be united. We've been fighting each other since we left him behind."

"What did you just say?" Unar demanded, but Atwith's face was already screwed up in confusion.

"I don't know," he admitted.

"We must go on," Aforis insisted. Leaper couldn't spare a thought for Atwith and his personality lapses. Unar had to heal him. Now. Soon.

"Bria's bone is in Hunger's cave." Leaper didn't know how much more he could bear to say to them, but they had to know this much; they had to know what he'd seen. "Her claw broke off in the cliff edge. A small claw. No bigger than Tyran's Talon. You remember, Aforis."

Aforis was quiet for a moment.

"I remember Tyran's Talon," he said eventually. *Aforis is growing younger. Losing his recent memories because of the reverse ageing.* Aforis nodded, as if his lost memories were firming. "The opportune time to reclaim this claw belonging to Bria is now, while the winged one is out of her lair, searching for the source of the smoke from the fire." He nodded again. "I'll go. The fork lies not far ahead of us. You two, take Leaper to the buried city."

"I must recover my Bodyguard's remains, I'll go with—" Atwith started to say.

"I can't carry Leaper by my—" Unar protested.

"If you're killed, Unar," Aforis said loudly over them, "nobody can be healed and the claw is useless. If Atwith is killed, untold suffering could continue in Canopy. Right now, there are those in agony, unable to die. If his soul stays here, or dissipates, what will happen to the hapless mortals in his care? Besides that, who knows if he can bear to lay a hand on the bone of his opposite number? What if Audblayin and Atwith annihilate one another, like the paired bones that came through the thieves' lantern?"

"So you were listening," Unar murmured, "to what he said about birth and death needing to stay separated."

"Did Audblayin herself not intimate so, at Nirrin's restoration?"

"We'll take Leaper to the buried city," Atwith said meekly. Leaper felt the poles jostle slightly as Atwith balanced the spitted goat on Leaper's knees and took over Aforis's end of the stretcher.

"If I'm successful in locating the claw," Aforis said, "I'll look for you in the place where I found this tapestry hanging. The building which seemed a place of worship. All paths in the city led to it. Surely it was the dwelling place of a deity or a king."

"Or of death," Atwith said.

"You'll see the graveyard. It lies at the bottom of a shaft narrow enough to prevent our escape, yet straight enough to admit sunlight. As I said, the spring flows from the gate. When you see the monuments, you'll see the temple behind them."

Leaper, still tilted back at an angle, saw the soft glow of filtered light on the roof of the tunnel long before Atwith and Unar brought him into the comparatively open space of the ruined city.

He saw a vast wedge of stone. It had probably once protected the city from snow and wind. Now it was sheared off the base of the neighbouring mountain and slammed over the rooftops, cutting them off from the sky, like a door off its hinges leaning over a once-bright room.

Daylight and a trickle of melting snow leaked in at the edges. Where the sun penetrated, moss grew over broken stone and the cracked walls of more multistoreyed, wall-clinging houses with tapering walls. White, horned skulls and white tufts of desiccated skin and fur showed where goats had entered—or fallen into—the ruin but been unable to leave and starved to death.

Black and white feathers, too, blown by the wind, were caught against flagstones in the street or the remaining railings of the wooden balconies. Crickets called in corners, were silenced when the human party of three passed, then started up again in their wake.

Leaper smelled lichen, dust, and old, old wood fires.

Atwith kicked at a goat skull.

"How long do you think that's been here?" he murmured, turning his head to the side.

"I think the cold has slowed down decomposition," Unar answered. "You're the death god. You tell me."

"Do you see the graveyard? The temple that Aforis talked about?"

"He said all roads would lead there. Let's keep following this one."

The temple, when they reached it, was a circular building, also made of limestone blocks. It was difficult to tell whether it had once tapered at the top, like the cliff-hugging houses, since the sliding strata of the collapsed mountainside interrupted what might have been a white-painted plaster dome.

"Let's put Leaper down inside," Unar suggested. "I can make a trip to the graveyard gate for water. You can find wood for a fire and get that goat cooked all the way through. We don't know what parasites it could be carrying."

"The building looks completely dark inside," Atwith replied, craning his neck to peer through the wide, arched entrance. "You want to leave him in the dark?"

"I said to get a fire going, didn't I?"

Leaper said nothing as they lowered him, the top of his head touching cold slate tiles. There was an impression of open, airy space which reminded him uncomfortably of the winged one's lair. He hoped Aforis was keeping out of sight in his search for the claw.

He didn't pray to anyone. *What would Unsho, Mitimiti, and her beloved Guiding Tide of Wetwoodknee make of the great goddess Hunger, I wonder?*

After a while, surrounded by the far-off sound of dripping water and ubiquitous smells of lichen, snow, and long-dead fires, Leaper closed his eyes, drowsing.

Footsteps and the low conversation of a returning Atwith and Unar brought him back into focus.

"I don't know," Unar was saying softly. "I supposed I expected the death god to be . . . sad? Death isn't exactly fun, is it?"

"You'll find as many sad lives as happy ones. Each kind of life only exists relative to others. For every happy, longed-for death that follows an unhappy life, there's a feared death that follows a happy life. Then again, for each soul going to a worse life, there's a soul headed for a better one. So even if I *were* still Atwith at this time, in this place, I'd have no reason to be sad, and if I *were* sad, the birth goddess should be as sad as me, since every life she begins that is destined to experience joy is balanced by one destined for misery." Atwith drew a deep breath. "Is she sad?"

"I don't know." Unar sounded wistful. "Maybe. She banished me so long ago. Sometimes I can't remember what she looks like. I feel her, though, whenever I use her power. If this bizarre plan to eat bones and work Floorian magic turns out as Leaper hopes, I guess I'll be feeling her soon enough."

A jolt heralded another flash of strange memory for Leaper: Adolescent Unar stood on the horizontal trunk of a yellowrain tree in the monsoon. Her hair and red leaf-shirt were sodden. She squinted in confusion at something over Leaper's shoulder. Inexplicable disappointment filled him: *Is that my sister? It cannot be. She looks slow. She looks stupid!*

Leaper took a measured breath in and a measured breath out, and found himself back in the ruined city of Time, wrapped in a tapestry, lying on the cold floor.

There was the sound of sloshing. Then, of dry, hollow timbers dropping onto slate. A sharp warning from Unar was followed by a flare of light as Atwith lifted Leaper's thieves' lantern.

For an instant Leaper was thunderstruck—*how can the lantern be working, so far from Airakland, and after so long?*—but then he realised the light from it was orange, not blue-white. The source of the glow was a pile of coals that had been shoved inside it; the still-hot remnant of some other fire.

"How did you do that so quickly without magic?" Unar asked.

Atwith tapped at one of the unbroken panes of the lantern.

"Curved glass. Sunlight. Dried grass for tinder. Just don't ask me to do it in the middle of the night."

As Atwith built up a fire, somewhere out of Leaper's line of sight, leaping flames revealed the interior of the huge round room. Every part of the curved, plaster-covered, continuous interior wall was covered in intricate, colourful paintings.

They were faded, but the story they told remained clear. Much of it was the same story Leaper had seen in the entry cave in the cliff, where reliefs had shown winged ones falling from the stars, planting themselves in the earth, and growing into leaf-covered creatures that then took to the skies.

But here, in consecutive panels, some of what Leaper had seen in the Dawnsight vision was also depicted. Recurring frequently was a black, man-shaped giant with blazing orange eyes and no other facial features. The giant came out of a burning hole in a black mountain island surrounded by sea. Walking through the water made him turn brown and green, and when he reached a yellow sandy beach, he broke into fourteen pieces. Leaper recognised some of the pieces; Tyran, Aulla, and Bria, who would one day become Airak, Ehkis, and Audblayin.

Others he didn't recognise. Including a wrinkled, two-legged brown piece of titan without a head at all, yet with prominent genitals, who lagged behind the others. They deserted the headless one in a faded, bluish, three-toed impression that might have been a valley or might have been one of the lakes on the plateau. Apparently unable to see, hear, eat, or speak, the headless one nonetheless held a red fruit or large bauble in the palm of his wizened, fingerless paw.

Near the apex of the ceiling, the titans and the winged ones all meshed into a detailed, complex painting that seemed to have been lost when the roof was ruined. Leaper tried to care that the once-thriving culture had been destroyed, but found only scorn.

I've had enough of worshipping monsters. These people should have painted doves and flowers, not violence and death.

Fat sizzled. The spitted goat threw its shadow over the walls. Smoke escaped the room through round holes near the ceiling's circumference. Glass shards dangled from hanging dried straw whose ends were still stuck in the plaster. Atwith walked over to one of the shards, tapping it, setting it to swinging and glittering like a cradle decoration.

"I think mirrors were used to bring light into this room," he said, "before the shafts were driven out of alignment. There's writing here, but I can't read it."

Leaper could read it. It was the same language as in the cave, where the carvings had spelled the words: THE SOURCE.

Here in the house of worship, they were less ambiguous.

BENEVOLENCE WATCH OVER ME.

Benevolence must have been the name of their local winged one.

BENEVOLENCE GUIDE MY STYLUS.

Back when there were more than one.

BENEVOLENCE GUARD TIME AND THE CHILDREN OF TIME.

More than just Hunger and her soft-skinned hatchling.

Unar brought him torn, charred goat flesh, steaming hot and juggled between her hands.

"Leaper. Are you awake? Do you think you can eat this without dying?"

"Yes," Leaper said.

"Be careful."

Chewing felt like driving an adze into his own head, but he was so hungry he took one careful bite, followed by another.

"I can chew it for you," Unar suggested.

"No," Leaper said vehemently after he'd swallowed.

He couldn't feel whether his belly was full, but he judged he was somewhere close to sated when saliva stopped filling his mouth in a kind of ravenous slavering. Aforis hadn't returned, and Leaper tried to sleep again, rather than worry about what might be happening in the cave above, or who was fetching food for Ilik and the baby with Unar mysteriously disappeared from the flowerfowl farm, or whether he should smash the lantern even more than it was already smashed to keep her from accidentally coming through and finding herself in worse peril, trapped in the ruins of Time beside her badly injured ex-lover.

At some point, Unar and Atwith's conversation reached him again. Leaper couldn't help but listen with his eyes closed.

"You're a pretty thing, Godfinder," Atwith murmured, "but once we reach the forest, Atwith would forget you. Only the dead and dying hold his attention."

"What about his Bodyguard?" Unar whispered angrily. "The one who died. The one whose body you wanted to take from the monster, fearing its desecration. The goddesses and gods are hypocrites. You loved that body, or I'm an eyeless salamander."

"You answered your own question, didn't you? She was dying. Now she's dead. You don't understand. I wanted to make a memory for him to look back on, so that he would know what happened to her. So he'd see her sacred remains. Atwith is most tender at the very end."

"That's Atwith, the hypocrite." A pause. "What about you?"

"I could enjoy physical release with you, Godfinder, but it's love that you want, isn't it?"

"Am I unlovable?"

"I can't answer that, but can you answer this? Could Atwith, an immortal, fall in love with a soul he'd known for only one human lifetime, which is less than a day for him? He has affection for the dying, it's true. But it took fifty years of approaching death for him to fall in love with his Bodyguard, and he'll still forget her."

"I thought you couldn't access his memories anymore."

"They are faint. Faded." Atwith sighed. "If I try to focus on them, they vanish altogether, but they seem to still occasionally slip into my mind sideways when I'm not paying attention."

"So you can't remember how he did it." Unar sounded strangely hungry. It wasn't a tone of voice Leaper had heard her use before. Or had he? "You can't recall whatever dark rite he used. How he bound Atwith's perishable knowledge and memories to that freshly captured, imperishable, one-fourteenth of a titan."

"No. If we ever get home, you could ask him."

"If we ever get home." Unar laughed darkly. "I could ask him. I'm asking you. Let me know if it comes to you. If it slips into your mind sideways. I could ask you to do the same thing to my soul. To make me immortal, too. Then we'd have time. To know one another, and love."

THIRTY-ONE

AFORIS'S ARRIVAL came well after nightfall.

He breathed hard, like forge fire bellows, but held a curved, yellowed bone the length of his forearm out in front of his body.

"I discovered it," he panted, "not in the streambed but in Hunger's nest. With furs. Human bones. Golden statues of herself. The armour of the slain Bodyguard. The decaying body of the hatchling."

"You saw her?" Atwith wanted to know, standing cautiously back from the bone. "You saw my Bodyguard?"

"I saw her armour," Aforis said again, stiffly. "One who walks in the grace of Airak is regretful to report that he believes the winged one may have consumed her flesh."

"Oh."

"So the hatchling is definitely dead?" Unar took the bone from Aforis. "And this is definitely the bone of the Old God that we need?"

"The wounds inflicted on the hatchling by the Bodyguard were indeed mortal. As for my identification of the claw, I assume it is correct. I've received no sensations from this remnant as a Skywatcher would expect to do within the sphere of the gods' influence, yet the crusting of crystallised stone around this end suggests the watercourse—"

Leaper tried to laugh loudly and triumphantly, but only managed to squawk and set his throat cartilages in disarray.

Unar knelt by him, placing the bone carefully down beside her. She helpfully straightened out Leaper's neck while he tried to ignore the feeling of blunt knives scraping up and down his skin.

"Eat that," he told her, in between slow, determined breaths.

"It's a big old bone," Unar said, scowling. "How am I supposed to eat it?"

"There was a stone mortar and pestle," Atwith said. "In the graveyard, do you remember? Aforis said it was a kind called granite. He said the woman who died and was buried there had to be an alchemist or a healer."

"I never said that," Aforis said tiredly. "Night has fallen. I came through the graveyard by touch."

"Not to worry. I'll fetch it."

Time stretched out as Leaper waited for Atwith to bring back the mortar and pestle, half excited and hopeful, half filled with dread that the bone wasn't Bria's after all. It seemed to take an eternity for Aforis to cut slivers off the bone with Atwith's little bronze belt knife, and for Aforis and Unar to take turns grinding it under the granite pestle.

Finally, they had a greyish paste for Unar to swallow. Aforis supported Leaper's neck, while Unar stood over him.

"You'd better be right about this, Leaper," Unar said, grimacing as she forced it down, lump by lump, swallow by swallow.

Her hands, fingers spread wide, hovered over him. Her face relaxed; became impassive.

Leaper smelled quince and wood fern. His spirits soared.

It is Bria's bone. They have saved me!

I wandered far from home, as you prophesied, Ulellin, but now my friends have found me and saved me.

Feeling in his body returned in oddly disconnected, nonvital places; there was tingling in the back of his left knee, under his floating ribs on the right side, between the bones of a wrist, inside the arch of one foot.

Tingling turned to pressure. Numbness to pain. For a terrible moment, his body felt like a loosely knotted series of overinflated bladders about to burst. He closed his eyes, because he didn't want to see his bloody insides splattered all over Unar's and Aforis's watching, anxious faces.

It's not working Something's gone wrong. Audblayin's bone has turned rotten so far from her soul!

Then a familiar jolt of lightning heralded another invasion of memory.

Leaper stood outside the Gates of the Garden, trying to protect something important to him, and Unar was trying to kill him with love.

He didn't know how he knew it, but he knew.

How is she doing this? he wondered with fear and fury. *She doesn't love me. If she loved me, she wouldn't be striking down my mother, my sorceress, my ladder back into the sun! She's just like all of them. They don't believe in One Forest. They only want to keep everything for themselves!*

Leaper opened his eyes in the city of Time, locked gazes with Unar, and the pain drained away, starting at his scalp, ending at his tapestry-wrapped toes.

His first words should have been words of gratitude, but other words erupted from his dry mouth.

"You freed Hasbabsah," he gasped. "You knew her treatment was wrong; you took one step on a godless path, but then you stopped and you went back to serving them at their most vulnerable and helpless. Instead of taking them to their Temples, you should have put a knife in every one of them. So slow. So stupid. Why did you stop?"

Unar's expression, in the firelight, looked as though he'd stabbed her through the heart.

"Got comfortable, I suppose," she said hoarsely. "I had to hate myself to get away from you. That's a wound that takes some time to heal. Meanwhile, very little was asked of me. I had my birds, I had you, and they left me to myself. It was peaceful. The pain went away. Or I got better at ignoring and forgetting."

Whatever wellspring of agony had spoken through Leaper fast faded. The things he'd said abruptly made no sense to him. Only searing resentment of the goddesses and gods of Canopy remained.

"Audblayin sent us both away to guard her own power," he said. "You were banished so that Aoun, her Gatekeeper, couldn't be poisoned by notions of inequity. I was banished so that her Bodyguard, my middle-father, would belong to her alone. Airak scarred me and betrayed me. He hoarded lightning so that the winged ones would stay weak."

"Leapael—" Aforis tried to interrupt, but Leaper talked over him.

"Airak and Ehkis together drowned thousands of Rememberers. They swept the consort of the queen of Wetwoodknee, along with half the fishing fleet, out to their deaths at sea. Ehkis keeps all the rain for the forest. Just look how barren that plateau is outside. Its herds must once have supported the people of Time. The white-skinned people of Time, who became the Bird-Riders of Floor, who became the villagers of Understorey, who became the slaves of Canopy. Our gods and goddesses allowed it all."

"Atwith would have killed every one of those humans," Unar whispered, wide-eyed. "He would have killed everyone who knew anything about the coming of the Old Gods or the existence of the winged. Audblayin opposed him. She told me so. She saved what she could save."

Leaper wanted to sit up, but he was still rolled in the tapestry. He glared at the dark brown faces of the three Canopians instead. Atwith said nothing to defend himself; perhaps he couldn't currently remember.

"Maybe she did save what she could save," Leaper said. "Maybe she even had help. Odel was on her side." He only knew it because of his stolen vision. "But maybe before the forest and the barrier were raised, we all had long memories. Maybe we all had access to our previous lives, as the gods and goddesses do. Is that the bargain Odel and Audblayin made with Atwith? To make us forget, so we'd never know that the deities we worshipped were nothing special! They were sorcerers and sorceresses who just happened to come upon unguarded power!"

"I don't know, Leaper." Unar rubbed at the crease between her brows.

"*He* does."

Atwith raised his palms in a defensive gesture.

"I don't know either. Not while I'm here. I'd never be him again, if it were up to me, but you heard what the Servant of Airak said before, that people are suffering. Atwith is needed to put them out of their misery. Don't you think I noticed how much of that bone is still unused?"

Unar jerked back from him, patting something beneath her Godfinder's cloak which must have been the remnant of Bria's claw.

"This bone is of no use to you," she said.

"No? If your healing powers are so legendary, Unar, don't you think you could heal this hole in my soul where Atwith is waiting to enter and take control again?"

"No! That is, even if I could, even if Audblayin's power could come into contact with Atwith's without causing destruction, who knows how much you'd need for that? In case you hadn't noticed, if we want to get you back to Canopy, we have to battle our way past a winged one. You think that little bronze knife you've got is going to get you past her unscathed? Forget the hole in your soul. You might end up with holes in your body that you'll want healed!"

Leaper squirmed, compressed tightly inside the rolled weaving.

"Help me out of here, Aforis," he said.

"Calm down," Aforis replied, hands at the knots beneath Leaper's chin. "You've been at the brink of death. You've seen things that only your previous incarnations could have seen. Breathe in slowly through the nose. Breathe out slowly through your mouth."

Leaper did as he was told. The tapestry's stifling embrace began to loosen.

"I saw visions at Dusksight and Dawnsight, too, Aforis. I saw the creation of the forest. I saw it end."

"Did you, now?"

"Aforis, you saw those things, too," Unar said. "You told me so. When those bones destroyed each other. You said you saw the Old Gods killing one another, soaking the ground with their blood and souls, and the great trees growing up. You said you saw the night-yew."

"If I knew it then, I don't know it now." Aforis grunted as he loosened the final binding. "Perhaps I'll keep the memory of this conversation, God-finder. Perhaps not. In this state, the intensity of events seems to have no bearing on whether I keep them in my mental cabinet or not."

Aforis and Unar both stepped back as Leaper unrolled himself and sat up, working his muscles and joints one by one.

It was then that he saw the climbing spines in his forearms had been healed out.

He remembered begging Imeris to help him convince their parents to put them in. It wasn't fair, he had argued. All of them had spines except for him. He wasn't a baby anymore. What if enemies came, and he was the only one of the children who couldn't climb, and was left behind?

The final argument had been the one that worked. But the implantation had been much worse, and taken much longer to heal, than he'd expected. Once he'd climbed into Canopy, to live out his dream life in the sunlight, his spines had sometimes come in useful. Other times, all they'd done was mark him out as different.

He'd taken the medicine of justice, instead of the medicine of the birth goddess.

Now his warrior's spines lay on the ragged tapestry, completely separate to him. He saw them for what they were: sad trophies taken from slaughtered snakes to make him fit for a life his ancestors would have baulked at.

"I'm so sorry," Unar said, amplifying the distress she assumed he was feeling. "It was my first try at being a bone woman, Leaper. I didn't mean to."

"I don't care. I don't need them," Leaper said, startling himself with the truth.

It felt amazing simply to be higher than ankle level above the ground. Moisture seeped into his eyes.

When he lifted his chin to look at her, he couldn't stop beaming.

"Thank you, Unar," he cried. He looked past her, to the others. "Thank you, Aforis, for finding the claw. Thank you, Atwith. You carried me. You found the mortar and pestle. I thought it was all over. I thought I was done."

"I'll take that tapestry for a blanket," Aforis said, smiling. "I'm exhausted. I need to rest. By all means resume your squabbling, but elsewhere. When I wake, we'll pool our resources and knowledge. We'll find a way to take Atwith back to his worshippers and Leapael back to his newborn babe."

THIRTY-TWO

AFORIS TOOK the tapestry with him and all but collapsed in a heap by the fire.

Leaper leaned against Unar's offered arm, getting completely to his feet.

"Are you well?" she fussed. "Is everything in working order?"

"Yes, I think—"

His gut made a sound like rusty hinges. Organs shifted, gases collected, and he realised the goat which had gone in salty and hard as rock was ready to come out the same way. All the muscles in his belly clenched.

"What's wrong?" Unar demanded.

"Ah. Would you perhaps help me to a more . . . private . . . part of the temple?"

The tears of joy and relief were drying on his cheeks as Unar led him to an antechamber. During the subsequent hourlong evacuation of his bowels, he cried like a woman giving birth, and streaks of fresh blood decorated what he'd produced, but he decided it was too humiliating to ask Unar to heal him again just for that.

"You were a long time," she said, when he returned.

"I think I need to walk," he said, pretending a stiffness in his joints that he didn't feel. "Walking will put everything back in order."

"We can hope so."

Unar took a long, burning timber from the fire, so that he could light his way. It was heavy, but his arms felt fresh.

Leaper made his way to the graveyard. Heard the sound of running water and found the spring beneath a fallen gatepost of pitted limestone. He washed his face, drank from the spring, and touched the smooth skin of his shins and forearms.

This is how I was born. This is how my mother made me.

The scars left by Atwith were gone. His nose was straight, as if it had never been broken.

My baby, he thought with wonder. *My new child. I can't wait to see you as your mother made you. And if Aforis had discovered the thieves' lantern only a few minutes later than he did, I never would have known you existed.*

More tears threatened. He turned back to the graveyard.

It was a field of overlapping circles. Upheavals in the ground had disturbed some of the skeletons, but the plan of the graveyard was clear, even where the bones didn't protrude through the fine grey limestone silt.

Each circular plot, perhaps a family plot, contained at its centre a knee-high, finely chiselled mountaintop of green soapstone capped by paler marble suggesting snow. The feet of all the corpses were arranged so that they touched this central stone.

It was as though the dead were standing on these small stone mountains.

Leaper stared at them for some time.

Our graves are so different. Just look at the Crocodile-Riders, avoiding their dead. Hasbabsah, her body hidden in a sealed room in our tallowwood tree. Oldest-Father, trapped in Ulellin's emergent by Kirrik. My previous body, when I was Unar's sister, Frog, fallen to pieces and also fallen to Floor in the careless, Canopian way.

My sister Ylly will have her bones ground to powder and scattered in the moat around her Temple.

Ilik, who I thought had fallen, is still alive, but now Aforis will age backwards. Will his bones dwindle to nothing at the end, after sixty-two more monsoons? I'll be lucky to live that long.

Leaper's guts groaned, and he moved on along a randomly chosen road. Despite the world's worst and longest squat, he was wide awake and full of energy; he suddenly felt like he could walk for fifty days straight, all the way back across the plateau to Canopy. He wanted to plan their escape now—*now!*—but he had to let the old man sleep.

Old man. Aforis. Becoming younger by the day.

Leaper strode over the arch of a stone bridge that crossed the old water course, to explore one of the wall-hugging houses with tapering walls. This one was somewhat larger than the others. Although the upper storeys were crushed, Leaper passed through a series of rooms, each with a stone basin, each with a stone peacock sitting on the rim. The blue gems set into their grey stone feathers shone in the light of his torch.

I could pry those loose. I could use them for Ilik's giant statue.

The final room held a white marble throne on a dais. Cast golden falcons perched on the arms and back of the chair, while big golden cats stretched out at the foot. The sight of it depressed him.

Some things stay the same, wherever humans are.

Some want to be knelt to. Others kneel.

In the centre of the audience chamber, on the floor, there was a miniature stone replica of the city, crafted in metal and stone. It was part gravestone, part freestanding sculpture, part relief.

Time was a circular city, or had been, with a circular wall, protected by its ring of unassailable mountain peaks. The city wall was interrupted by gates at the four points of the compass. Miniature devices like bronze pinwheels made the miniature bronze falcons over the miniature stone gates flap their wings when Leaper blew into the pinwheels to make them turn.

Ilik would love this. If only I could pry it loose and take it with me. His carrysack was still strapped to his back, badly damaged from its travels and having Aforis erupt out of it; it would never bear the weight of anything made of stone. *Maybe it wouldn't be a bad thing if Ilik were to come through the lantern.*

Only, there's still the problem of Hunger.

Their reunion could wait.

In another house, on another throne, he found the odd remnant of a seated, artificial woman or man. It was a ruin of degraded leather, lacquer, wood, and old glue. Paint and possibly plaster on the face had peeled away from straw stuffing, but visible in the metal chest cage, behind rotted silk robes, were brightly painted wooden lungs, a heart, and kidneys.

Leaper risked putting his burning timber down on the slate tiles, so that he could pull the mannequin's heart out and examine it. Eerily, the disturbance made the whole artificial person collapse forward onto the floor.

He put the heart on the back of the split leather head and left that throne room, brand in hand, with a backwards glance to make sure that the creepy life-sized doll wasn't coming after him.

Probably would have made as effective a king as Icacis.

Funny. When he'd thought Ilik was dead, he'd stopped caring whether or not she loved that fool of a king of Airakland. Now, though, he hurried along a different road to distract himself from wondering how Ilik felt about Icacis now. Obviously she feared him, or she wouldn't have fled to Unar's farm. But what if she was contemplating reconciliation? Icacis had said to Leaper that his throne would go to the blood of a slave.

No. I'll be back in Airakland to convince her otherwise before it even occurs to her to take our son back to that palace. That palace, where they wrecked her childhood creative building projects and trapped her in service to an imbecile.

Surely she'd never voluntarily go back.

He went down the natural, glittering, crystalline staircase of a waterfall turned to stone.

But what if she's found? She'll have to leave the flowerfowl farm to find food. No, don't think about that.

He climbed a series of hewn terraces where old roots and stumps suggested light had freely penetrated and crops had once been cultivated. It was some hours since he'd left the temple, and he wasn't the slightest bit footsore.

Then the whole mountain shivered. Cracks opened under his feet.

Leaper froze midstride on a wide boulevard.

Hunger, he thought nervously. *She has stamina. She flew back here from Canopy, a fifty-day journey for us, without touching the ground. But she never displayed the kind of strength that could crumble mountains.*

The flagstones jittered again.

Water from the new spring runs along a different course. Perhaps parts of the mountain have been eroded. Weakened. Re-formed by the flow. Atwith— that is, the Ehkislander whose drowned corpse was pilfered by Atwith—might know.

Leaper waited to see if the cave ceiling would crash down on his head, but when all returned to stillness, he climbed through what he thought was a low doorway. It proved to be an outlet into the bottom of a cistern.

There, he set his torch aside again, this time to examine what had once been a four-pace-long wooden boat. It must once have floated on the water's surface. Chains running through holes in the hull, hopelessly tangled now, connected levers, hollow glass spheres, pans, pins, the paws of carved cats, and the jaws of wooden goats, in something too complex for even Leaper's mind to follow.

Eventually, on hunting further through the snarl, he found another small model of the city, as wide as his chest. This model had two spring-loaded arms attached to it, one bearing the golden ball of the sun, the other a scattering of greenish, tarnished silver stars.

The rim of the city had twelve rings of triangular markings along its circumference. On some rings, the markings were regular. On others, the markings bunched together at the near edge but were wide apart at the far edge, or vice versa.

Leaper huffed out a perplexed breath, saw fog in front of him, and realised his fingers on the metal rings were growing numb. He set the little city gingerly back down on the frigid stone floor of the cistern and retrieved his torch from its crevice, grateful for the warmth, alert now to the fact that he was inadequately clothed and must keep moving or return to the main fire.

Hunger, in her grief, rattled the mountain a third time, harder than ever. *She's angry. Perhaps when she left the lair, her hatchling was only wounded, and now she's discovered that it's dead.*

Leaper fought to keep his balance on the tilting floor. The pieces of the unknown mechanism rattled against one another.

The hollow glass spheres rolled to the ends of their chains, clashed, and cracked open.

I suppose I will return to the main fire. Even Aforis can't have slept through that one.

But again, he gave the contents of the cistern a backwards, lingering glance.

Ilik, you should be here with me. Seeing this. If not for the winged one, we could live here. You could restore all these lost marvels. I know you could! Forget the secret house I made for us in Eshland. You could do what you love.

The obvious hit him between the eyes, stopping him in his tracks as brusquely as the tremors in the stone had stopped him.

All this time I've been wanting to take her from one cage to another. All I thought about was what I loved. What I needed. How I compared to her husband.

This is what she loves.

Leaper retraced his steps through the now daylit graveyard. He found Aforis awake, kneeling beside one of the exposed skulls, digging carefully to excavate a piece of silver-backed, clear glass mirror.

"Aforis," he blurted out, "tell me again what Ilik looked like when you last saw her. Did she talk about the king? Did she suggest that she might go back to him? How did the two of you plan her escape to Unar's flower-fowl farm?"

Aforis glanced up, his expression wry.

"One who walks in the grace of Airak regrets to say, Leapael, that he cannot remember."

Before Aforis could look back down at the digging, Leaper stepped forward quickly and touched his mentor's face where the scar had been.

"Maybe I can force the memory. You never forgot things in Canopy, before all this happened. You were like a human diary. Your scar. It was right there. Unar said it was from her guard vine."

"Did she?" Aforis sighed. "If you say there was a scar, there must have been. I suppose that when it vanished, so did all my memories of its making."

"But she said so only yesterday. You must have heard her say so. Right before you went to find Bria's claw."

"Bria's claw?"

"Yes. The bone of the Old Gods. You risked your life smuggling it out from under the winged one."

"Did I? I can't remember that either."

Leaper gave up.

He watched in distressed silence as Aforis finished unearthing the glass shard.

"It's clearer than any glass I've seen," the old man mused. "Made from a different sand to any of the sands we had available to us as Servants."

"Scandalous," Leaper said lightly. "I saw some glass spheres, each the size of my head, in a cistern back there. They were pretty good. But a better quality glass than that available at Airak's Temple? Unheard of!"

"It's not unheard of," Aforis grumbled, polishing the piece with his thumb and holding it up to the light. "When I was young, my mother was employed as an arithmetic tutor in the House of Glass."

Leaper wanted to go back inside the temple. He wanted to find Unar and Atwith, to make plans for their escape. To get out before all exits were blocked by rock slides, and before Aforis forgot who Leaper was and the four of them starved to death in the dark.

But he made himself ask,

"What's the House of Glass?"

Aforis favoured him with the second smile of the day.

"It was a guild of merchant glassmakers from Airakland. The three prominent founding families were the Estenanens, Estorinens, and Estedidens."

How prominent could they have been? I read the king of Airakland's correspondence, and I'm sure they were never mentioned.

"But I've never heard of them." Leaper stanched his fast-faltering brand in the dirt at his feet. The length of timber had burned through the night but now was down to a small, smouldering stub. Daylight was getting stronger, and the loss of the orange glow was no real loss.

"They were destroyed for producing finer glassware than the Temple of Airak," Aforis said. "Without permission, the House completely hollowed one of the family floodgums so they could travel down to Floor to trade without risking attack by demons. The barrier kept out any Floorians who might have sought to follow them up the spiral stair to Canopy, but they were betrayed by their own growing reputation. Airak called lightning to the House of Glass and burned it to a black hollow. This glass reminds me of theirs. Formed, ground, and polished by human hands, not magic. Despite their impressive works, the people of Time have ended exactly the same way as the transgressors of the House of Glass."

"There are palaces back there," Leaper said, indicating the direction he'd come from. "Channels. Moving toys. Machines. Clocks. Did you see them?"

"I don't know."

"Such clever people can't all have been killed in the battle between the Old Gods. Of those that survived, they can't all have abandoned it for the forest. Some must have stayed."

Something flickered in Aforis's eyes.

"The winged one. I would suggest our resident demon, Hunger, has raised many litters here. She's self-fertile and able to keep to the letter of her bargain with the Old Gods by sending all of her offspring back to the stars."

"How do you know that about her, Aforis?" *You must have known it well before you left Canopy, or you would have forgotten.*

"Airak has the skies watched, as you recall. Likely he's not the only Canopian deity suspicious of the stars. The memories of our goddesses and gods are imperfect, but they remember many things of importance."

"So you're becoming godlike, not forgetful," Leaper quipped, earning a third smile from Aforis.

"Before I was called to Airak's service, I studied to be a teacher of history." Aforis stood up. He dusted off his knees. "Some historians spoke of documents that our deities had searched out and destroyed. Some of these slates, scrolls, and woodcarvings dealt with chimeras or the origins of Canopy's peoples. Others were detailed accounts of the life cycles of the winged. I don't think Airak himself knew that the winged could reproduce in a similar manner to chimeras. Servants assigned to the watchtrees—"

"Why was I never assigned to the watchtrees?"

"Were told to beware male flying lizards clothed in leaves, perhaps disguised as balls of flame, coming down in the direction of the mountains in the south. If we saw any hatchlings near Airakland, we were to exert all of the god's power to prevent or divert any lightning. As for you. You, in a watchtree. I can picture you, cooking your supper in the focus of the lens."

Ha!

Maybe.

"It's a wonder," Leaper said, "the lightning god didn't change his mind about the agreement with Hunger and send armies to exterminate her. He had more say over Icacis's soldiers than Icacis ever did."

"Canopians have found their way here before. I know of at least one for certain—the clockmaker from Eshland. She made the soul trap that Imeris and Anahah used on Kirrik."

"Hunger sees Canopians coming," Leaper said slowly, remembering. "She makes prophecies about herself, and they come true. That's how she knows when to start brooding her eggs."

"If she prophesied that you would save her—"

"She prophesied that I'd come. She only hoped that I'd save her hatchlings. Aforis, how could any Servant of Airak do as Hunger wanted and call lightning to her hatchlings, unless they carried a piece of Old God's bone about with them? My sister bestowed protective amulets on our family for a while, but she hated every moment of it. Airak would never have allowed it. I found bones of the life and death gods in the clockmaker's home, but if they'd known the bones were there—"

And then Leaper recalled that he had another piece of Old God's bone. It was in his carrysack. It had been there since he fled the City-by-the-Sea.

"Aforis," he said, awed at his own realisation. "Let's go find the others. I think I know a way to get us all safely back to Canopy."

THIRTY-THREE

THE SWORD.

The sword is made from a bone of one-fourteenth of a titan who now calls herself Orin.

Leaper led the way through the upward-sloping tunnel, holding the broken lantern full of live coals ahead of him to light the way. Aurilon's ivory sword, which Yran had used to control his crocodile on their voyage across the floodplain, had been ground into powder by Atwith and mixed into a paste in the stone mortar.

They'd shaped half into a pellet the size of Leaper's fist. His intention was to dose the winged one with it.

Leaper himself had eaten the other half, a deliberate overdose, but after his experience with the Bag of Winds, he was prepared to contain it. The potential to perform magic swirled around him, an invisible caged beast. Somehow, he could smell goats cropping moss on the mountainsides high above his head. He could taste the clouds and dried blood on the talons of distant birds of prey.

But he was saving that potential for the moment he seized control of Hunger.

You weren't born in a crocodile's nest, Yran had warned him on the raft as they rode out the monsoon. *You weren't taught to separate her thoughts from yours. You try to take her from me, and you'll get stuck in her body forever. Your human self will stop eating or drinking, waste away and die. And then you'll die, Canopian, because your soul can't survive in a crocodile's body.*

Leaper would have to learn quickly to separate Hunger's thoughts from his own, or die in the attempt to control her.

You can control her with hate, Frog's childish voice whispered to him, and

he stopped so suddenly, so surprised and appalled, that Unar crashed into
him from behind.

"Oof," she said. "What is it?"

"Did you hear that?"

"Hear what?"

Are you still there? Leaper asked his former self guardedly, in silence, inside his head.

We are all still here, Frog answered, laughing slyly. *You can tell us to go.
You can even make us go. Orin has the power to build barriers, and her power
is in you. But don't you want to know the secret to overriding another's will?*

"Leaper?" Aforis asked. "Is something wrong?"

Leaper took a little of Orin's power and built a barrier inside himself,
sealing Frog's voice away.

No, he told her, knowing she was gone and couldn't reply. *I am me. I don't
want to be you. True, you were never tricked into serving gods, but you never left
the forest, either. I don't want to be cursed like Aforis, trading all that he's learned
for something as commonplace as youth. I've washed my face in the spring water
of Time and the salt of the sea. I've lain with somebody I love.*

I am a father.

How can I be a good father, filled with hate?

"Nothing's wrong," he said, starting forwards again.

He held the lantern in his left hand. In his right hand was a face mask
he'd made from the tapestry and the goat's skull. The pellet of bone paste
rolled about loosely in the shallow bowl of the mask.

When they reached the wall of collapsed stone between the tunnel and
Hunger's lair, the excavated hole where Atwith had crawled was filled in
by loose rock and dust again.

Atwith snorted at the sight of it.

"Stand back, everyone," he said. "I'll move the rubble. I've got the longest arms."

"I'll help," Unar said. "Two people can fit side by side, and I'm not the
one about to run across a cavern and try dosing an angry monster. Sit there
and save your strength, Leaper."

Leaper moved back from the rock pile, put his lantern down and sat
cross-legged on the dirty floor with Aforis. Distracted by the smoothness
of his shins beneath the windturner, he patted them and wondered if Ilik
would find him more or less attractive without his spines.

"At times like this," Aforis murmured, "I think that if I have to grow younger, I'd have it over and done with in a hurry. A single leap of thirty years might be nice."

"What about the memories you'd lose all at once?" *I'd lose my whole life in a leap of thirty years. Everything I've seen. Everyone I've loved.* It dawned on him, then. "You're going to forget him. You're going to lose the memory of him dying, and then the memory of being with him, and then eventually you'll lose the memory of meeting him. You wish that all *that* would be over at once."

"Meeting who?"

Can he have forgotten already?

"Edax," Leaper said. "Your one true love."

At the rock pile, Unar dropped a rock on her hand and swore loudly. Atwith hushed her.

"Edax." Aforis sighed. "Age smoothed the edges of those memories a long time ago. The last time I thought of him, I was watching your head get forcibly shaved, thinking how much like him you were, irreverent and careless, almost as if we'd miraculously procreated and his death had left me behind with you. No. What I'd really miss are my memories of trying to teach one particular very bright, very disobedient pupil. You remember when we met?"

"I remember your arms were like steel bars, hoisting me by the harness out of that ti chest. I'd never felt smaller or more helpless!"

"You wanted to see the sun, to stay in it, all day, every day." Aforis quirked the brow over his white-irised eye. "The first time I informed you that you were free to visit your family in Understorey, you shrieked at me that you would not go back down, that you were never going back down. Naturally, no sooner had Ulellin cursed you, forbidding your descent, it was all you ever talked about."

"No, it wasn't."

"Yes. It was."

"No, it was not."

"So," Atwith said, coming to stand beside them and take a swig of water from a gourd. "Edax, did you say? The Edax that was Ehkis's Bodyguard, appointed not long before I was drowned?"

Aforis sighed.

"There's nothing wrong with my *early* memories," he said. "I was a teacher well before I was a Skywatcher. My mother taught arithmetic. She loved the curiosity of children. My father taught philosophy. He thought every child deserved somebody who believed in their capacity for good. It was natural for me to want to follow them. The king of Airakland employed me to teach the children of the citizens of his niche."

"You were like me." Atwith dusted his hands off. "Trying to ignore the call. I ignored the Lake. You ignored the lightning. I'm told it never works."

"I came late," Aforis said, inclining his head, "to the Temple. I was a grown man, with a man's desires. The strictures didn't settle on me lightly, and I loved Edax, against Airak's wishes. Edax was killed, though not by the gods. The punishment for my small rebellion, which escalated out of my control, was to be reduced from Servant to Skywatcher."

"Master back to apprentice," Atwith said wryly. "I'm sorry you lost somebody you loved." He turned back to the work. It was Unar's turn to stop for a swallow of water and short rest.

"I wasn't the only one," Aforis said softly, eyeing her.

She choked on the water. Spat it out against the tunnel wall.

"Those events lie far behind us, Aforis," she gasped, "like you said."

Aforis turned his regard to Atwith's naked, muscular, sweaty back.

"Not as far for some."

Leaper, who had overheard her advances being rejected by Atwith, decided gallantly to extricate her from the conversation, or at least to share the discomfort all around.

"What I don't understand is," he said brashly, "if Aoun grew up in Ehkisland, what adept severed him from Ehkis so that he could serve Audblayin? You know, like the pair of you severed me?"

Both Aforis and Unar stared at him for several silent seconds.

"I think I know how," Unar said. "I think Aoun's hatred for Ehkis, who drowned his twin brother, was powerful enough that he was able to sever himself from the rain goddess."

Without warning, Atwith stood beside Unar. His stare joined the stares of the others.

"Aoun? My brother, Aoun? Did you say that my brother, Aoun, serves Audblayin?"

Unar took Atwith briskly by the shoulder and turned him.

"Come on. We can't stop. We have to get into that cavern before the bone Leaper ate wears off."

When they resumed shifting the rubble, Leaper thought some of the rocks were thrown with unnecessary force.

At last, the way was cleared, and sunlight from the cavern showed through. The wintry wind entered keenly and immediately, as if reuniting with a friend.

"Can you see her?" Unar hissed at Atwith's feet.

Atwith wriggled backwards until he was able to stand up, his body grey with all the silt stuck to him.

"I see her," he whispered back. "In the nest. Maybe sleeping."

Leaper took a deep breath. Instead of the cave surrounds, he smelled the burrow of some small, subterranean animal with mint and lichen on its breath.

"Let's swap clothes," he said to Atwith, securing the tapestry-padded, goat-skull mask over his face, peering through eyeholes in the musty, torn tapestry and the sockets of the skull. Atwith took off his bronze knife in its belt and his skirt of clacking bone-tree stems. In exchange, Leaper handed him the windturner. He put his various straps and harnesses inside the carrysack, which he also relinquished. The bronze knife seemed a poor substitute for Leaper's lost spines, but if all went well, the winged one's scaly back wouldn't be his place, anyway.

It has to go well. Everybody's counting on me.

Canopy's nearly dead are counting on me.

Ilik doesn't even know I'm coming back to her, but I am. Even though she pretended she was dead.

Unar was watching Atwith while he dressed, trying to seem like she wasn't watching him.

"Better choke down the rest of Bria's claw," Leaper told her brightly, knotting the skirt into place. His voice was muffled through the mask. "I won't want to be kept waiting for healing long after she spills my liver on the floor."

Without the windturner on, his exposed midriff felt cold and vulnerable.

"Just don't let her bite your head off," Unar said. "I don't think I can heal that."

She forced the lump of bone paste down her throat, gagging but keeping it down. Leaper hefted his own, much larger lump in one hand. Atwith deliberately cut his arm on a sharp piece of glass and used the brief well of blood to paint patterns on Leaper's chest and face. At last, he gave a satisfied nod.

Here we go.

Leaper shimmied through the tight channel Atwith and Unar had re-opened. The bone skirt gently clacked about his thighs as he straightened and took his first few strides. He was halfway across the cavern to the winged one's nest before she stirred. The long snake of her neck arched and her folded wings shifted.

He waited to be sure her eyes were focused on him before leaping in the air and twisting as he advanced. His fingers were hooked like claws. He was carving the skin of imaginary enemies. Speaking the silent language he had seen in the visions.

Speaking the language of the titans.

THERE YOU ARE, he danced. *DID YOU THINK THAT BY SHAK-ING DOWN THE WALLS YOU COULD DEFEND YOURSELF FROM MY RETRIBUTION?*

Hunger's nostrils flared.

"What retribution?" She answered in her own language of hot and cold breezes, the language of the winged. "I took you when you were alone, where nobody could see besides your Bodyguard, and she is dead, as the bargain requires. You are no mortal, one-fourteenth of a titan, and so it's of no importance what you see. Retribution. The bargain. It's by your own law that the mortal had to die. Retribution!" Her neck arched higher, and her mouth opened, revealing the oozing, reddish-brown teeth. "Your soul proper has stayed behind in the forest. I don't sense death. Only an angry wild-ness. Perhaps you could not quench the life of that other one. Perhaps it was his fire I smelled. But you can still be a meal for me."

Leaper raised his arms as if they were wings. He ran at Hunger, bound-ing over the empty riverbed, feet pounding the floor of the cave, contort-ing his body as he closed in on the nest.

SEE IF YOU CAN SWALLOW ME, OATHBREAKER! He kicked aside the hatchling's pathetically outstretched paw. *I SEE THE CORPSE OF YOUR CHILD AT YOUR FEET. YOU HAVE BROKEN THE AGREE-MENT, AND YOU WILL CARRY ME TO CANOPY. THERE YOU WILL BE JUDGED!*

He ran straight up the side of the bowl of old bones and other refuse, ready to keep running up the scaly skin of her chest and the curve of her neck. If she was to prevent him from scaling her person as if she were a fallen tree, she had no choice but to swallow him head first.

Her head plunged. Her jaws snapped shut. Leaper was pierced, front and back, by her wooden fangs, and he screamed.

Hunger opened her jaws again as she curled her snout towards the ceiling. Leaper's feet pointed to the sky. He felt the wave of her tongue carrying him down, the bright burn of Unar's healing, and the emptiness of his dangling fingers where the bolus of bone paste had gone ahead of him into Hunger's gullet.

Their minds were abruptly connected.

Like cloud and Canopy joined by lightning.

Leaper felt the crushing mountain of her grief, all but snuffing out the white-hot star that smouldered at the heart of her. Her yearning for the darkest part of the heavens and the loss of her hatchlings, each one a stain of darker darkness in a world already utterly dark.

Those inky silhouettes wavered. Resolved into a human child in a cradle. *Unar's old cradle. The one she kept at the farm.* The brown-faced, bawling child Leaper saw was his own child, summoning him across a terrible emptiness. Yet the bargain chained him in the cave. He couldn't go to the forest. Must not go to the forest. *If I go to the forest, thirteen-fourteenths of a titan will kill us both.*

Leaper wrestled, in his mind, to keep their awarenesses apart, but all of a sudden he couldn't see any difference between the hatchlings and the human child. The same confusion which had sometimes rendered the speaking-bone impotent paralysed him. He was a parent, he would do anything for his child, he would tear apart any who harmed his offspring, he would make them suffer, he would—*Ilik.* Her face blossomed in his thoughts. *The other parent of my child.*

Two parents.

Two hearts beating.

Leaper found himself, smeared with blood and sap, standing on the floor of Hunger's lair, his human body healed again by Unar, the winged one's huge head bowed before him in apparent submission.

That's it. That's how I can tell the difference between her thoughts and mine. One parent or two.

While he was savouring his victory, Hunger struck with her mind, taking back control. Quick as a viper, she seized his throat, as he had seized her moments ago, turning him to face the three Canopian companions who stood not far behind him.

She appealed to them in the language they understood.

The language of Canopy.

"Unar," Hunger said with Leaper's voice. Unar's eyes were as wide as they would go. "Unar, it is Hunger who speaks to you through this mortal boy. Hunger is my name, and I know what you hunger for. You want *him,* the one-fourteenth of a titan who stands beside you."

The glance Unar gave the real Atwith was not in the least hungry. It was terrified. She looked back at Leaper.

"No," she said.

"Help me," Hunger entreated. "Kill the boy, and I will tell you how to become immortal. How to live with him in your forest, forever, as equals. I will tell you how to find the Birdfoot Valley, where the bones of the lost one-fourteenth of a titan lie. You will take his soul for your own and become the fourteenth deity of the forest! All you have to do is slay this one, by whose ignorance my hatchlings were slain!"

Unar trembled uncontrollably.

"I don't think so," she said. "I've killed him one too many times already."

Before her sentence was finished, Hunger had already turned to Atwith.

"You kill him," she babbled through Leaper's lips. "Kill us both! Bringing death is your only task, and here you have failed! Kill, death god! Here! Now!"

"No," Atwith said grimly. "Not here. Not yet."

"Then you," Hunger shouted, using Leaper's hands to seize both of Aforis's forearms, "must make a new bargain with me. You need the bones of Time even more than the others. They are the only cure for your curse. The only stepping-stones for you to reenter the forward flow. Save me, and I will take you to the valley myself."

Aforis pulled his arms free and took a step to the side.

"You're not going to any valley," he said. "You're going home."

"To your son," Atwith said.

"To Ilik," Unar added.

To Ilik, Leaper thought, and raised his hands to the goat skull mask as if he could hold himself together; his vision showed him both Unar's brown eyes and his own stick-legged self as seen from behind, and the two halves felt as if they were sliding apart.

But it was only Hunger's mind sliding back into her body. Into a little ball in her belly. There, the bone pellet rested against the slowly digesting carcass which had once been Atwith's Bodyguard. It was heavy in his stomach, but he knew that he could still fly.

Leaper unfolded his wings, and they brushed the corners of the cavern.

"Climb into my mouth," he told the frightened Godfinder. "It's a long way, and I can only control this body until my human body falls asleep."

THIRTY-FOUR

They flew all morning; all day; all evening without stopping.

Leaper's human body was so fatigued he could hardly sit upright in the winged one's maw. He slouched against his friends, relying on them to keep him upright.

"Water?" Unar shouted in his human ear. One of her arms gripped him tightly about his human waist, while the other held the near-empty gourd. They rode amongst the rootlike tangles of Hunger's teeth.

"In my mouth," Leaper shouted back at her with his human mouth, rigidly holding his jaw open as he spoke even though it made him hard to understand. He had to keep it open, just as Hunger's mouth hung open. Dried to leather by the wind, as Hunger's mouth was, he dared not close it. Not and get the two mouths confused, and end up killing himself and his companions. "Hold on to her teeth while I swallow!"

The forest bulked black and deep on the horizon, smudged orange by the sunset in the west. It looked misleadingly smooth on top, where every locked-together leaf and branch strained for light, except where interrupted by emergents, which strained higher.

It looked deceptively open at the sides, where the first trunks of great trees seemed planted so far apart that wind and the winged alike could avoid them without even trying, so vast were the spaces between. Yet the sunlight directed horizontally through, as keenly as the beam of a lens-focused lantern, torched the sides of a mere two dozen layers before being swallowed by the forest's dark heart.

They passed the point over the plain where the curse had turned Leaper, Hunger, and the hatchlings back the last time.

This time, there was no resistance from Ulellin's winds. Only the wind of their passage. The beat of Hunger's wings.

The curse really did end when my son was born.

My son.

"We have to go to Audblayinland," Unar shouted after she'd sloshed the last of the water into his mouth. "To the Garden."

"Why?" Atwith hollered into Leaper's other ear. "Atwith can't go there. The death god and the birth goddess can't meet."

"Even though I was banished," Unar shouted, "I was never severed from Audblayin. When Leaper falls asleep, the winged one will try to kill him again. She still wants revenge. My powers are strongest in Audblayinland. I can turn the trees against Hunger. Try to cage her. It's the only chance we have. It's where we have to go."

"What about Aforis?" Atwith demanded. "He's strongest in Airakland. Why not go there?"

"He's asleep. When he wakes, he'll have forgotten where we are and what we're doing. Besides, he was never stronger than I was."

"And Leaper?"

"Nor Leaper. Two of them together couldn't do what I could do. Their strength was in lightning, besides. We've seen that lightning only makes the winged ones stronger. We can set you back down in Atwithland but our final destination has to be Audblayinland!"

Through his exhaustion, Leaper knew she was right.

Audblayin is my sister.

I've never asked her for anything, but she'll help us this one time. She'll know what to do. She'll lend her full power to Unar if that's what it takes to drive Hunger back.

Atwith went rigid beside Leaper, who risked a sideways glance with his human eyes.

Cloud-arrows were shooting into Atwith's chest.

"Ahhh!" Leaper cried. He tried to twist away from Atwith, but Unar was there, leaning forward with fascination.

"It's the souls of the dead," she yelled. "They're passing through him!"

Each translucent, fast-coalescing cloud now looked to Leaper like a naked human body stretched long and rope-thin, slightly thicker in the middle and tapering at the ends, spearing into Atwith but not reappearing behind him. The souls were white in the instant they first appeared; they spent a second absorbing the mango glow of the sinking sun, and each one left an amber remnant on the front of Atwith's windturner.

The forest was beneath them. Impenetrable. Speckled with blue-white lanterns like the net of diamonds in Ilik's hair. This was the dense tangle of Eshland. Home of the wood god.

Leaper veered Hunger's body to the east. *Atwithland is the next niche over. We have to find a bone tree. Atwith's Temple is in the crown of a bone tree.*

"Hey! Are you all right?" Unar shouted at Atwith, who, instead of answering, turned his head in a slower, more dignified manner than Leaper had seen from him before. One hand rose to finger the fringes of the wind-turner with distaste. Atwith's gaze locked onto the bone skirt around Leaper's waist, and his expression became incensed.

"You! How dare you?" The death god paid no attention to the misty wraiths spiralling hands first, like sideways divers, into the approximate location of his beating heart.

"I said—" Unar started to repeat herself.

"I heard what you said, Godfinder," Atwith thundered. "You will address me as Holy One, or King of the Dead!"

"Holy One! There's something I'm curious about!" Unar shouted. "You said you can't go into Audblayinland, which makes sense enough, but is there any conflict between yourself and Esh? Any reason you can't go to Eshland?"

"No. Why would—?"

Unar leaned back against Hunger's teeth and kicked Atwith with both feet. All the strength of her thighs was behind the kick. The death god fell backwards, over the edge of Hunger's mouth.

"Ahhh!" Leaper cried again. Hunger lurched, attempting to hover. She was too big, and they started to lose height. Atwith's fall could be tracked by the stream of souls shooting into him. Hunger plummeted not far behind.

"Fly on to Audblayinland," Unar remonstrated, her head sticking out over the edge of Hunger's jaw. Leaper smelled the sweet sharpness of passionfruit pulp and hookvine sap—*Unar's magic*—as fresh green foliage reached up from Canopy to cushion and cradle the falling god.

She's the Godfinder, Leaper reminded himself, cursing his instinct to recover Atwith. *She doesn't kill gods. She saves them.*

The winged one struggled to climb again. Leaper heard faint screams of terror from the people of Eshland. His human pectorals ached, though they were not the muscles straining. His human nostrils flared, though they weren't the ones sucking at the air, calling on the wind and stars to aid him.

They cleared the tops of the trees, swinging north towards Audblayinland.

"Whatever agreement Hunger had with the Old Gods to conceal herself and stay secret is well and truly over now!" Unar hooked her legs around Hunger's teeth again, resteadied Leaper with her right arm, and reached for Aforis with her left. All the wild careening and commotion must have woken him, but Leaper couldn't spare a thought for his mentor.

Audblayinland.

Part of him dreaded taking the unpredictable winged one directly to his childhood home, to the tree where his mothers and fathers had raised him. His old family was there. They could be hurt. Anything could happen.

Another part of him whispered, *Ilik and our son are your true family now. And they're safe in Airakland.*

I'm so tired.

"There!" Unar pointed to the tallowwood emergent, standing high above the other great trees of the canopy. At the heart of the Garden, surrounded by still water, Audblayin's inner sanctum, smooth as an egg, gleamed in the fading light.

The winged one dived towards the platform in front of the Garden's great Gates. Her approach frightened worshippers who had been heading home, including two heavily pregnant women, one noble and one out-of-nicher, and a girl carrying empty baskets on her head. They scrambled back towards the safety of the Temple.

Leaper watched the ornate monuments to Canopian power grow nearer, and remembered his excitement on first arriving at the Garden as a nine-year-old boy. He'd been far too enthused to really grasp the fact that his sister Ylly would be going through that battle-scene-covered Gate and emerging rarely, if at all. On his first night in Airakland, he'd bawled with homesickness and loneliness, muffling the sound with both fists on account of Unar snoring at his back. Imeris and Ylly had been annoying, yet devoted to him.

Help me, Ylly. Tell me what to do. You were always the quiet one. Gentler than Imeris. Trustworthy and kind.

It was still too far for his human eyes to see, but through Hunger's eyes, he saw the goddess and all her Servants and Gardeners standing just inside the open Gate. There, they were protected by wards well known to keep out humans, but could those wards stand strong against the winged?

The lanterns on the platform were lit, and the Gatekeeper carried a larger lantern, held out from white robes that fluttered in the breeze. *Aoun, who was a friend to Unar and to my youngest-mother, Oos.*

Audblayin's Bodyguard stood in a ready stance beside the goddess, white tunic and long split skirt stained by bark at bosom and knee. Her big pale feet, shod in studded sandals, were braced wide. Blue Understorian eyes blazed above a pair of bared steel blades. *Nirrin. You were our neighbour in Understorey. Imeris's friend.*

Ylly looked beautiful and brave, tall and slender, draped in pale green and purple silk. Her hands relaxed at her sides. Living, purple-flowering pea plants twined lovingly up her wrists, and the wind tugged at her long, loose hair.

It's me, Ylly, he ached to tell her. *It's your little brother, Leaper.*

But then he remembered how the man who hosted Atwith had begged Unar to heal the wound in his soul so that Atwith could never control him again, and he felt nauseated at the thought of quiet, gentle Ylly being used by what Hunger had derisively called one-fourteenth of a titan.

They landed in a cloud of splinters made by Hunger's hind claws against the tallowwood platform. Servants and Gardeners gasped and stepped back, but neither the goddess Audblayin, nor Gatekeeper Aoun, nor Bodyguard Nirrin, flinched from the threat.

Leaper laid the winged one's sinuous neck down flat. He half clambered, half fell from Hunger's mouth. Dimly, he was aware of Unar and Aforis helping each other down onto the platform. As soon as they were clear, he closed his mouths, both monstrous and human, and tried to find some moisture with which to speak.

My teeth are wrong.

Hunger's teeth.

The lines were blurring again. His tongue was long and forked. No, short and round. He tried to hold Ilik's face in his mind but couldn't seem to find it.

Ylly recognised him and ran forwards through the invisible wards, arms outstretched.

Almost as soon as she did, the will of the eternal goddess within seemed to clamp down on her, as Leaper's will had clamped down on Hunger. It brought her to a standstill, arms tightly crossed. Nirrin and Aoun promptly moved forward to flank her protectively, leaving the others behind and inside the wards.

Leaper went to meet her in his human body, his own pair of protectors to either side.

"Holy One," Unar and Aforis chorused tiredly, swaying as they bowed.

"Leaper," Audblayin said, ignoring them, eyes on Leaper's face. Impossibly, the single word contained love, hatred, fear, and longing. "What have you done?"

Nirrin's eyes stayed on the winged one.

"Holy One," the Bodyguard said tightly, "it would take all of your power, and more, to destroy that monster. We could do it, but the wards around the Garden would fail. The barrier, also. Chimeras and other demons would come, and a hundred Hunts would not be enough to vanquish them. Many would die. Their faith in the Temple would be lost, and who would worship you then? Without worship, the barrier could never be raised again. It would be the end of Canopy."

One Forest, Frog whispered with glee; she had gotten loose in Leaper's head again, and he had nothing left with which to resist her. *Just look at that stinking, slinking slave, mauled by a demon but still eager to leave her people down in the dark with them to die. Yes. Release Hunger. Make them fight. Make them do it. Destroy the barrier!*

"I've come home," Leaper said, and Hunger's lips moved fruitlessly behind him, for she hadn't the voice box or syrinx for sounding out words. "That's all I've done, Ylly. Ulellin cursed me, but the curse is broken, and I've come home. Aren't you glad to see me? You loved me once."

"Leaper!" Audblayin said again, but this time it was Ylly who embraced him, hard, against all laws forbidding contact between mortal and godly flesh, and this time it seemed the goddess inside could do nothing to prevent the transgression. "I love you. Please tell me what is happening."

"I've stolen Orin's magic and used it to temporarily tame the last of the winged. But the magic only lasts until I fall asleep. Then she'll be herself again. She'll want to murder me." He looked past Ylly, despairingly, at Nirrin. "You can't protect me, after all. Can you?"

Nirrin's head twitched sharply in the negative.

The Bodyguard's fierce dedication filled Leaper with sorrow; it was perhaps the saddest he'd ever felt. Even worse than when he'd thought Ilik was dead, because that had been a sadness mixed up with wrath and self-recrimination, and this was simply a repeating pattern that he saw no way to break. *It was never me being not good enough for the gods. It was always them not being good enough for all of us.* For every Floorian or Understorian who railed against the unfairness of the structure of the forest, there would be a hundred like Nirrin, who accepted that they were born less, that they deserved less; who had taken that lie and made it such a part of themselves that they'd defend to the death not only the people who snapped off their spines and tossed them off tree branches, but the very barrier that kept the downtrodden from climbing to safety.

"Can't you order the winged one away, Leaper," Aoun asked, "the same way that you ordered her to come here? Could Orin not order her away, if it was Orin's power that you used?"

"Orin alone is no more powerful than Audblayin," Unar answered grimly, "and Orin's influence wanes with distance from Canopy. Hunger *would* go. She'd come straight back. Her children are dead, all of Canopy has seen her, and she's no reason to keep to her bargain anymore. Killing her is the only answer." She spread both arms wide, appealing to Ylly. "Holy One, please. Reach out to the neighbouring niches along the barrier. I can help you draw on their power. There wasn't a goddess or god I hadn't found besides Atwith, and I found him in Hunger's lair, in the end. Use me as a conduit and destroy her. If the barrier falls, so be it."

"No," Leaper said. Both his hands rested on Ylly's shoulders. He stood at arm's length from her. "Killing her isn't the answer."

His attention turned inward. He ignored the slavering of Hunger, who anticipated his imminent descent into unwilling slumber. He ignored Frog's raving at him to tear down the barrier forever. In his mind, he saw again Yran's desperation in the palace at Wetwoodknee.

What happened to your oath against killing? Yran had cried as he hit Leaper, over and over, with the Bag of the Winds. *We shared the same liver, and you've killed me!*

The oath against killing. How Leaper's skin had crawled as he'd ended those hideously transformed Servants of Orin, and how natural and easy had come his vow never to kill again. Although, looking back years later, he hadn't been able to think of any other way besides blasting the beast with Airak's power. What would he do, given a second chance, if he were standing eye to eye with Orin's monster again?

"What is the answer, Leaper?" Ylly asked.

"Slap him," Unar said sharply. "He's falling asleep. He mustn't fall asleep!"

I mustn't fall asleep. To one side of the Garden Gate, the potbellied cottage with the arched entrance where his middle-father, Bernreb, had lived, stood cold and empty. Unar had created that home. She'd grown it from the tallowwood tree, moulded its rooms, and filled it with comfortable beds, though Bernreb hadn't needed them, because Bodyguards didn't need to sleep.

Ylly slapped him.

Bodyguards don't need to sleep.

"Make me your Bodyguard," Leaper said, staring into his sister's eyes. Ylly gaped at him. Nirrin reacted by raising her weapons higher and taking a step back.

"I will die if my goddess commands me," she said.

"There's no need for you to die," Aforis said.

"The position can't be rescinded from an adept," Aoun said. "Ten years ago, Orin was helpless to withdraw the gifts she'd bestowed on her Bodyguard, Anahah, when he betrayed her. Our goddess was able to replace Bernreb with Nirrin, but only because Bernreb had no magical talent. Nirrin has no choice but to serve until death."

"Or until the goddess dies," Ylly said, not looking away from Leaper's face.

"There's another way," Aforis insisted. "Leaper is the proof and precedent."

"Aforis and I," Unar said, "can cut Nirrin off from your power, Holy One. We can graft her onto the god of lightning. We've done it before with Leaper. Nirrin will become Airak's adept. She'll wield his power. Then Leaper will be free to become your Bodyguard, though you'll need to bring a branch of the night-yew to him, since he can't pass through the Garden's wards any more than I can."

Silence.

Leaper swayed. His grip on Ylly's shoulders was suddenly the only thing holding him up. The fate of Canopy, of Hunger, of the barrier, seemed to matter less with every second that passed by.

So tired.

He locked his knees desperately to keep from collapsing. The Garden Gate was turning grey.

"Go ahead, Godfinder," Nirrin said. "I've prepared myself. Do it!"

Ylly's eyes roved over Leaper's face.

"Is it what you want, Leaper?" she whispered. "To be Audblayin's Bodyguard for the rest of your life?"

She was talking about the goddess as if about another person, the same way that Aoun's brother had talked about Atwith.

"I tried Kirrik's way," he whispered back, "and it got me killed. I tried Audblayin's way, and lived in the dark. Airak's way, and I was a slave who thought he was free. Killing is not the way, but neither is meekly waiting for death. I'm finding us a new way, Ylly. If any part of you is still my real sister, please help me to find a new way."

Grey Gates, skies, and goddesses turned to black.

A new way.

Leaper smelled tallowwood sap melded with scorched black sand. It was Unar and Aforis, working together. Ylly's shoulders turned to an insubstantial mist of wood fern and quince blossom and his hands went through them; Leaper felt himself falling. Heard the crisp clank of Aoun setting his bronze lantern down on the wood and the pounding of the Gatekeeper's feet as he raced back into the Garden.

There was no fear. Only relief.

Leaper sighed and closed his eyes.

THIRTY-FIVE

WHEN LEAPER opened his eyes, the tableau had hardly changed.

Ylly stood in front of him, her wrists clutching his forearms, the living vines she wore as bracelets tangled around his body, holding him up and on his feet. Nirrin stood beside her, tear tracks down her cheeks but weapons still at the ready.

Aoun held a yew branch in one hand, green-needled and bearing both tiny white flowers and tiny red fruit.

Leaper realised he could taste sweetness and a turpentine tang. Concurrently, with his other tongue, sweaty clothing and filthy sandals overlaid the metallic salt savour of Atwith's Bodyguard, his most recent meal. Forcing focus to his human form, Leaper straightened.

All his tiredness had washed away.

Leaper gratefully kissed his sister, the goddess, on both cheeks. He kissed Nirrin, who had allowed him to usurp her place. She grimaced, but allowed it. Then Leaper turned his back to them, now facing Aforis, Unar, and the winged one.

In place of her burned and blackened pinecone-like scales, Hunger now wore a new coat of waxy, gleaming, dark green tallowwood leaves. Each long leaf curved in its characteristic tallowwood shape, ending in the type of drooping, slender tip that would channel monsoon rain away. Hunger's claws were the grey-brown of tallowwood bark, her teeth the colour of its pale heartwood, and her eyes the colour of its amber.

"Now, that," Unar said, "is a fine new Bodyguard you have there, Holy One."

"Even I," Nirrin murmured, "could not guard you so well as one of the winged."

All the scents of the rainforest that Leaper had missed since being separated from his magic by the floodwaters carrying him away from Floor assaulted him now.

The normal gift of enhanced senses given to an adept, on top of Orin's magic, alerted him to wild animals both near and far. He smelled wet monkey fur, the damp powder of moths feeding in night-blooming flowers, fruit bat stink, rotting mulch disturbed by the toe pads of frogs, ulmo perfume, honey kiss fruit, and the caramel of scented satinwood in Unar's farm, where the flowerfowl were still *just* wild enough for his yearning for Ilik to reach them.

Ilik. I'll come to you.

Tears stung his eyes.

I can't come to you. I'm the Bodyguard of Audblayin. How I swore I'd leave them, and take all of good-hearted humankind along with me, and now I'm serving them again. There's no escape.

He scrubbed at the tears with the back of his arm, which shocked him again with its smoothness, since the spines were gone.

There is a way. A new way. Things can't go back to the way they were.

"Ylly," he said. "Unar. Can I speak to you in private, please?"

And before the astonished, half-protesting faces and voices of Aforis and the Servants, he dragged both women into Middle-Father's cottage, dodging the trickle of water that divided the opening, and slammed the door behind them.

"It's pitch-black in here," Unar observed. "Already homesick for the tunnels near Time?"

"Be quiet, Unar!" Leaper all but shouted. "We solved the immediate problem, the problem of me falling asleep, but our problems aren't over, and thinking about the tunnels near Time is the opposite of helpful. The only thing that's stopping Hunger from taking me over is thinking of Ilik."

"Queen Ilik of Airakland?" Ylly asked quietly. "But she's dead."

"She's not dead, Ylly. I need her. I have to go to her. Not only that, but I have to leave the forest. I have to take Ilik, and as many of her subjects and your Servants as will agree to come, far away, to some place where you and the other goddesses and gods can't hunt them or drown them or trap them in the dark anymore."

"That could be an even bigger problem."

"Because I'm your Bodyguard, I know. And because you need human worshippers to maintain your power, but you've ruled for a thousand years. Isn't that long enough?"

"No. I mean, yes, it is long enough." Her voice trembled. "I mean, those are not the reasons why you cannot go. It is because the only thing stopping Audblayin from taking me over is being with you, Leaper. Near this home, which is a copy of the home we left in Understorey. Where our three mothers and three fathers raised us. If she does get control again, she will never let you leave."

Airak's teeth, Ylly. You are still your old self inside. It never occurred to me that you needed rescuing. After all this time.

More tears threatened. Leaper blinked rapidly. It was instinct for him to try to peer at her face, and after a moment he realised there was a blue-white light coming from somewhere. It was the ripped carrysack on his back. The broken thieves' lantern.

Smashed glass panes or no, the light had returned to life at the heart of it. Leaper drew it free of the leather by its bronze handle, being careful not to put his hand into the light, lest he be transported through it to Unar's farm.

"Sturdily constructed, that frame," Unar said. "So let me get this straight. If we're to keep that winged one from tearing down the forest, Leaper has to stay with Ilik. If we're to keep the immortal soul of Audblayin from resuming control of our Ylly, and killing Leaper for his intent to betray her, Ylly has to stay with Leaper. I could try to convince Ilik to come and live here in this house with you, Leaper, but you should know that she doesn't much like being a prisoner indoors, and also you're planning on fleeing the forest with what sounds to me like quite a crowd of people."

Leaper and Ylly stared hopelessly, silently at each other.

"Even if Audblayin didn't hunt you down, Leaper," Unar went on, "as soon as you left the forest, you'd lose the gifts bestowed on you as a Bodyguard, which includes the ability to stay awake forever, and once you went to sleep, Hunger would have control of herself again, and we'd be straight back where we started."

More silence.

"I'll die," Ylly said.

"What? No!" Leaper exclaimed.

"If I die, Audblayin will have to start again as a newborn baby. You'll have something like twelve or sixteen years to build your new city, Leaper.

Between twelve and sixteen years before she becomes self-aware and chooses a new Bodyguard."

"Less than that," Leaper said, glancing at Unar. "Canopy has a God-finder."

"Not if I go with you," Unar said.

"I wish we could all go," Ylly cried.

"No new children would be able to be born," Unar said, "if you left Canopy, if the law that governed Atwith holds true for you, too." Then her eyes widened.

"What is it?" Ylly asked.

"The law that governed Atwith," Unar repeated, chewing her lip in speculation. "He asked me to heal the hole where Atwith's soul had been. That poor boy. When I ate that nasty bone, I perceived the hole, the place that he meant, but I thought it would take too much magic, and there was a limited amount available to me. This time, if Ylly is willing, there will be enough. The barrier would be weakened, but only for a while, and we have a winged one here to defend against demons. Yes. Yes!"

"Are you saying what we think you're saying?" Leaper demanded.

Unar's expression was terrible and joyful.

"Yes! The fact of the dead boy's personality and soul remaining inside the shared body wasn't the only thing we learned from Atwith. I think I can cut Audblayin's soul away from Ylly's without harming Ylly. It would be as if Audblayin's body had died. Only, Ylly would get to keep the body, going back to her old self while Audblayin's soul drifted off into the ether to find another newborn to be reincarnated into."

It was Leaper's turn to repeat Unar's words, more slowly and with emphasis.

"You think," he said.

"I'm almost sure." Unar said. "Now listen, Leaper, you must promise me one thing before I do this."

"A payment now?" His brow furrowed with confusion. "After everything else you've done for nothing?"

"You must promise to take that winged one and her soul far away from Canopy. Hunger's bargain, to stay out of sight, is about more than just keeping Canopians safe from her habit of snacking on humans and her physical propensity to destruction. She'd be an irresistible temptation to any with sorcerous knowledge."

"You mean the kind of knowledge Kirrik had."

"Yes. Listen. Kirrik's power came from merging her soul with a chimera's. Our gods' and goddesses' immortality, their ability to pin memories—knowledge—to their souls instead of their bodies—comes from merging their souls with pieces of the soul of that titan. Hunger is smaller than a titan. But she's greater than a chimera. And the barrier is to keep chimeras out. The other demons are mundane and don't matter. Promise me you'll fly her away from here, as soon as you can."

"I promise," Leaper said, and with a jolt of Frog's memory saw Unar as a laughing child, holding his baby self up out of a shabby crib, her bright-eyed face full of love and grand intentions.

The old Unar, standing in the cottage with him, sighed.

"Then I'll do it. If you're agreed, Ylly?"

"Go ahead, Godfinder. I've prepared myself," Ylly said, using Nirrin's words but with more excitement than trepidation. "I can help you, Unar. I remember when Audblayin brought Nirrin's soul back into her body, after Kirrik had used it for so long. I know something about moving souls in and out of bodies. All of Audblayin's power will flow to you, everything but the maintenance of the wards around the Garden and the power that keeps Leaper from sleeping. All of it, I swear, only let me guide you."

They seized each other's hands and gripped tightly. Leaper wanted to talk more. Things were moving too fast. He didn't think they'd properly considered the consequences of failure.

But since when have I ever properly considered the consequences of failure?

Magic roared up around them, ripping through Leaper from the inside of his nostrils, out. The smell of crushed tallowwood leaves, which he'd thought was a single smell, separated into a hundred smells like a blinding rainbow of a hundred inconceivable colours. The worms in the earth under the roots of the great tree, the fish eggs gestating in the pools formed by its boughs, and the embryos inside sleepy possums digesting its leaves all smashed into his awareness and then peeled away again, leaving him lonelier than he'd thought it was possible to feel, even though he wasn't alone, because Hunger's awareness was still there, waiting.

"Ilik," Leaper said. Like the word of a spell, it severed him immediately from the danger.

"Leaper," Ylly breathed, letting go of Unar's hands and throwing her arms around her little brother. "Leaper, it worked. I'm free. I'm free!"

He hugged her back, marvelling at how much he'd missed her without even knowing.

"Don't leave, Ylly," Unar said tiredly. When Ylly had let go of her hands, she'd staggered, and now she leaned heavily against the wall. "Don't let them see you, or they won't believe you're not a goddess anymore. I want you to go, right now, and crouch down in the fireplace, behind the screen. Leaper and I will go out to face the Servants of the Garden."

Ylly obeyed, one-fourteenth of a titan suddenly reverted to her uncertain, Understorian, mortal self.

"What exactly are you going to tell them?" Leaper asked at Unar's back, but she was already opening the door.

She'd taken two steps before Audblayin's Gatekeeper confronted her. Leaper had never seen Aoun so discomposed. His stance was wide and unsteady. His nostrils were flared. He showed his teeth. His fingers crushed the lantern's handle as though it were the only thing holding him connected to the world.

"You killed her?" he roared in Unar's face, bending over so that they were eye to eye. Behind Aoun, Nirrin gasped. *Of course. Nirrin isn't connected to Audblayin anymore. Only the Gatekeeper, still her Servant, could sense his deity's death.*

"Isn't that why you said nothing when she sent me to Airakland, Aoun?" Unar replied in a low, weary voice. "She knew that I was dangerous. Didn't you? Didn't you know that I'd kill her one day?"

Aoun roared again, wordlessly, and swung the heavy Gatekeeper's lantern. It connected with Unar's temple, glass breaking, metal and skull crunching. The blow swung both of them around, so that Unar's back was to the edge of the platform.

Her eyes glazed. Blood running down her face, she reached blindly for Aoun's face and didn't find it in the moment before her body spasmed, then went rigid.

Unar tipped backwards, away from Aoun.

She fell, dead, from the Gate of the Garden, down to the depths of Floor.

THIRTY-SIX

Leaper hurled himself recklessly toward the edge.

It was too late. Unar was gone. Aforis seized him beneath the arms from behind. Dragged him back.

"Be careful," he bellowed in Leaper's ear. "Leapael, your spines are gone!"

"My mother is gone," Leaper babbled before he knew what he was saying; Unar hadn't been his mother; he'd had three perfectly good mothers; but they had been the mothers of his Understorian self. The Godfinder had been his mother in the sun. He wanted to throw Aoun after her. Aoun, who had been her friend and who had now murdered her for no good reason.

But Aoun breathed like a man on the brink of drowning who had resurfaced. He stared into the space where Unar had been, and Leaper relived the careless moment in which Unar had admitted to killing the goddess of new life.

"A regrettable action," Aforis said, holding Leaper tightly, regarding the Gatekeeper critically. "Now not only have you deprived yourself of a Godfinder for locating Audblayin's new incarnation, but you've committed murder and can no longer enter the Garden."

Aoun sat, drew his knees to his chest, and buried his face in his hands.

Leaper, abruptly crushed by guilt at how distantly he'd always treated Aforis, and how ungratefully, clutched at his mentor and buried his face in layers of bearskin.

"She saved my life, Aforis," he gasped. "She took care of Ilik while the curse kept me from returning. She came to find me. You both did."

"Come along," Aforis said gruffly. "Leave your oversized domesticated demon here for now. The goddess you serve has perished, but is your bond with her still strong? Are you still Bodyguard?"

Leaper tested the connection. Nodded.

"Then we'll take Nirrin to her new master, her new family, in Airakland. You have family waiting in Airakland, too."

Family.

Unar had been part of his family. But how could he blame Aoun for assuming Unar had attacked Audblayin, when Leaper himself had so recently assumed she would attack Atwith? Unar had always been unpredictable. Dangerous. Old stories whispered by Leaper's mothers when they thought he was asleep, of dark deeds in Unar's past, had given her an aura she'd never been able to shake.

"I have to change my clothes," Leaper said. "I can't go to Airakland wearing a skirt of bones taken from the death god." He let go of Aforis, still shaking.

Nirrin shook, too.

"Audblayin trusted her," the ex-Bodyguard said hollowly. "I trusted her. We all did. Her second-to-last act was to sever me from my goddess, so that I couldn't even feel it when she died. How can I go with you? How can I trust you?"

"Can't you feel it?" Leaper whispered. "Can't you see the metal bars in the sky? Airak's calling you. You have to go to him."

"Airak will have seen the winged one," Aforis said. "But he can't turn his great spyglass towards Audblayinland. He can only watch the sky. We'll tell him the truth. That the traitor Unar, once called the Godfinder, tricked Nirrin into changing her allegiance, the better to strike the goddess down undefended. The Gatekeeper has meted out justice. It's finished."

Leaper had once counted himself a fine liar, yet he couldn't imagine naming Unar a traitor in the Temple of Airak.

Nirrin sheathed her weapons. She shook her head.

"Bernreb's clothes," she said to Leaper. "I think he left some behind in the cottage. All is as he left it. Besides the glider droppings."

Leaper went back inside the door and closed it behind him. Only moments ago, he'd performed the almost identical action with Ylly and Unar beside him. The lantern still rested on the floor.

He went to the fireplace, where Ylly crouched in the gloom.

"Aoun killed Unar," he said huskily.

"Oh, no. No, Leaper!"

"The plan worked. They all thought Unar killed you. We're going to Airakland. Aforis, Nirrin, and I. You're going to Airakland, too, but not with

us, and not to the Temple. They're all in shock right now, but soon enough
they'll come in here looking for Audblayin's body. You have to go through
my thieves' lantern to Unar's farm. It works both ways now that both lanterns are in Canopy. A bit of a squeeze, but it might as well be an open
door."

"Leaper, I'm so sorry, I didn't mean for that to happen. I didn't think—"

"Unar did." Leaper smiled despite himself. "Mother knew what would
happen. She did it anyway."

"You called her your mother." It was said half questioningly, half in
wonder.

"She's your mother too now. Dead in childbirth, freeing you from Audblayin, delivering you to a new life." Leaper shook his head. "Ylly, when
you get to the farm, Ilik and her newborn son will be there. She's in hiding
from the king. If she sees you, she'll think you're Audblayin. She'll be terrified. Please tell her that she's safe. Please tell her I'll be there in about five
days."

"I will. I promise."

Ylly knelt by the lantern and reached for the light. On her first try, she
cut herself on the broken glass and snatched her hand back. Sucking on
her bleeding finger, knocking the offending shard away with the wadded-
up hem of her robe, she tried again, and on the second attempt the magic
grasped her.

It sucked her into the blue-white light the same way that the souls of
Canopy had been sucked into Atwith's chest.

Leaper's instinct was to immediately pack it away into his carrysack, but
he needed the light if he was to find Middle-Father's old clothes. Nirrin
had been Bodyguard for ten years, and so anything left behind by Bernreb
had been at the mercy of moths and monkeys since then. Leaper hadn't
seen his middle-father in all that time, but from memory the father who
shared his blood had gone as scantily clad as possible at all times, objecting
to the heavy, formal tunic and long split skirt that denoted a deity's Bodyguard.

One of the white tunics, with the sleeves hacked off, was folded in
a musty drawer. It was Bernreb's size, made for broader shoulders than
Leaper's. Beneath it was a green split skirt, which had once been lengthy
before it, too, had fallen victim to a sharp pair of cloth shears.

Leaper dressed slowly. All the energy of his revival seemed to have drained

away. It could have been grief. It could have been apprehension at the
thought of having to face Airak, having to conceal his connection to a
winged one from one-fourteenth of a titan. While also dealing with Aforis's
inevitable confusion once the man fell asleep again, aged backwards another day, and forgot everything that had happened at the Gate.

Or it could have been Audblayin's death. She was his source of power
now. The source of his eternal alertness.

A shadow blocking the lantern and a soft sound behind him made him
turn from the chest of drawers. He found himself gazing at a baby, cradled
at chest height in a woman's arms, yawning with a toothless mouth as small
and brown as a split, ripe fig. The baby's closed eyes were curved darker
lines in a soft dark face. The brows were no more than guessed shadows.
Curled brown fingers poking out from peach and pink wrappings were
smaller than any fingers had a right to be.

Leaper lifted his gaze. His eyes found Ilik's eyes.

"The cloth," he said stupidly. "It's got Odel's mark around the edge.
Odel's colours."

"Your sister Imeris left it behind," Ilik said. "The Godfinder told me it
was a gift to Imeris from Odel himself. Before that, it was a tribute from
Imeris's birth mother, a silk weaver of the House of Epatut."

"That cloth has lived as many strange and separate lives as we have."

"I haven't been to Odelland myself yet. I haven't paid tribute to the Pro-
tector of Children, but I will go. Perhaps even to pay him back with his
own cloth."

Leaper swallowed, with difficulty, around a lump in his throat.

"Ilik, is this our baby?"

"Yes." Her brown eyes were deep and wide. They held him firmly in his
human body, even though he could feel the curious hands of Servants and
Gardeners touching Hunger's crouching, statue-like mound, tugging at her
leaf-scales, exclaiming at their inability to pluck them.

"What have you called him?" *Tadpole?* Middle-Mother had laughingly
suggested. *Snake Egg. Millipede. Fishy.*

"His name is Builder."

Builder. First the trouble swallowing. Now he couldn't breathe. It was
as if his neck were broken all over again. *Builder, son of Leaper.* He cleared
his throat with care. Looked at Ilik properly, noting the thinness of her
cheeks and the hollowness under her eyes, the fullness of her bosom, the

amorphous blob of her short, unstyled hair, and her cracked, unlacquered fingernails. He couldn't reproach her for faking her death, even though it could have gotten him killed. Builder's life was more important. Builder was everything.

Builder.

"What kind of name is that, Ilik? It's not a Canopian name. It's not an Understorian name. It's not even a name used among Crocodile-Riders."

"Neither is—"

"Airak's teeth, I wish you had—"

"Forgive me, Leaper, I couldn't risk—"

They kissed, carefully and with only their lips touching, their chins forming a vaulted Temple ceiling over the sacred altar of their child.

"Don't wake him," Ilik whispered into Leaper's mouth, her eyes still closed. Leaper pulled back, grinning.

"*You* don't wake him." Then his smile faded. "And don't pay any tribute to Odel, either. We're not staying long. Where he's going, he won't need that kind of protection."

Ilik's smile faded, too, mirroring his, and she drew the sleeping baby back a step.

"What do you mean, we're not staying long? I knew you'd come up with some mad plan—"

"It's not mad, Ilik, please, let me put it to you! Short of threatening the woman I love best in the world with the pitiful thread of lightning I'd only humiliate myself trying to call unassisted in Audblayinland, there's nothing I can do to force you to do anything you don't want to do. And I promise not to try. There isn't time for me to tell you everything that's happened to me or to describe every place I've been, but there is one place I'd very much like to describe to you."

She relaxed from the balls of her feet back down, flat-footed, to the wooden floor.

"Tell me," she said guardedly.

"There's the ruin of a circular city, made of stone, in the mountains. On foot from Canopy, the journey is something like fifty days. There was a talking demon there, who devoured the city's people, but now I hold the demon's leash. I saw clock gears bigger than houses, Ilik. Water-powered machines. Incredible things made by people, by hand, without magic. If we took enough forest folk with us, we could bring that city back to life again. You could get the water flowing. The machines working. You could restart the clocks."

She pressed her lips tightly together. Stared through him, he supposed, at the city of Time. Builder began grunting and stretching. Small noises quickly turned to outraged, tiny screeches.

Aforis will wonder what I'm doing. What's taking so long.

"I need time to think about it," Ilik said finally, shifting Builder's weight from one arm to the other.

"Good idea," Leaper said. "Go back though the lantern. I'll be in Airakland in five days." He kissed her good-bye. Tried to kiss Builder, too, but the boy twisted and Leaper's lips missed.

By the time Ilik had squeezed herself and the shrieking baby back through in a blaze of blue-white light, Aforis had thrown the cottage door open. *I need to hide the light!*

All the older man found in the bedroom was Leaper tightening the laces of his carrysack. The bedsheet-covered lantern was stuffed in the fireplace where Ylly had hidden. If Leaper took the lantern with him to confront Airak, there was a good chance it would be repossessed by the Temple, and he'd be needing it later.

"Are you ready?" Aforis asked, squinting into the gloom.

"As ready as I'll ever be." Leaper hurried to join him.

Outside, Nirrin and Aoun were as he'd left them. The bone skirt clacked in Leaper's hands.

"My new master," Nirrin asked Leaper, staring at the skirt. "Is he kind?"

"No," Leaper answered, feeling sick. Unar had died to free Ylly, but at the added cost of trapping Nirrin, who had spent years in the ether while her body was Kirrik's helpless puppet. "If not for Unar's healing, I'd show you the terrible scars my master inflicted on me."

If you return, Airak had said, *when you return, you, or another with gifts equal to yours, will serve me with your whole heart. You, or that other, will swear your oaths a second time and be more deeply and tightly bound by them than any of my Servants has ever been bound before.*

It was as if Airak had known Nirrin would be the one returning to serve him, not Leaper. But how could that be?

As they departed the platform before the Gate, Aforis took the bone skirt from Leaper and turned back to the deflated Gatekeeper, Aoun. Aoun, who was now denied the Garden. The very same Servant who, less than an hour before, had been the staunchest Gatekeeper the Garden had ever known.

"Gatekeeper," Aforis said, and Aoun lifted his crumpled, tortured face from his hands in response.

"Yes?"

"Have you ever travelled to Atwith's Temple?"

"No."

"Ever received any communication from Atwithland?"

"No." A spark flared in Aoun's deep-set eyes. "I serve the goddess of new life."

Aforis crouched beside him, laying a bracing hand on the other man's back.

"And it's imperative that you continue serving her. But before you resume the custom of wandering naked and taking alms, there's something in Atwith's Temple you must see. Someone you must meet. I beg you, take this skirt of bones and put it in the hands of its owner. Atwith himself."

"Impossible. Atwith and Audblayin can never—"

"You yourself are neither." Aforis was gentle but relentless. "And it's not true that they can't meet. She has gone to him now. She must go to him before she can be born again. I promise, if you meet with Atwith, you won't regret it."

"How can you promise that? What do you know?"

Aforis hesitated.

"I don't know anything. There is a curse on me, and what fleeting thoughts I have are quickly lost. Yet this resolution remains."

Aoun took the skirt of bones.

"The first time I laid eyes on you," he told Aforis, "a sorceress held your leash. She used you to set the skies on fire with lightning. You threw yourself off the edge of this platform at the first opportunity, rather than allow her to keep using you."

"The goddess Ehkis saved me. She sent me back to Airakland. Where my Temple was destroyed. I, too, catastrophically failed my master that day."

"I'll take this to Atwithland. I'll meet with Atwith. And if I sense Audblayin in his halls, I'll beg for her forgiveness."

Aforis rejoined Nirrin and Leaper. They tried to leave a second time, but before they could take more than twenty steps away from the crowd of Servants and Gardeners surrounding the immobile winged one, they were accosted by an older Servant with a shaved head.

"Tarry another moment, Skywatcher Aforis, I beg you!" the woman called. Aforis waited for her to catch up to him. "Do you mean to leave this demon here?"

"It's not my demon," Aforis said, smiling.

"She won't move," Leaper told the Servant. "She won't harm you. You were all there when Audblayin made me her Bodyguard. So long as I don't fall asleep, the forest is safe."

"That's where you're wrong, short-lived Bodyguard to my dead mistress." The shaven-headed Servant folded her arms and narrowed her eyes. "The barrier is weak. Permeable. The very thing your promotion was supposed to prevent has come to pass. Can't you feel it?"

Leaper took a deep breath in through his nostrils, drawing in with the scent of mushed fungus, moulted owl feathers, and tapir dung the magical information he'd been too distracted to dwell on.

The barrier *was* weak. All the invisible threads of life that had pulsed so strongly around him were muted. Only the wards around the Garden and the thread connecting Leaper himself to the Temple remained robust.

"You're right," he said, shamefaced. Distantly, he could sense the edges of vigorous, thick, impenetrable barrier separating Canopy from Understorey, along the border of the long, curling, eastern niche of Oxorland, where the sun goddess held sway, and in the south at the falling fig, where Audblayinland, Ehkisland, Ukakland, Irofland, and Oxorland all met. "Our part of the barrier is barely there," he admitted. "My sister Imeris made peace between the niches and Understorey, so we don't have attacks from Gannak or, gods forbid, from the Loftfol fighting school, to worry about. But what Nirrin said, about demons entering, and about frightened people failing to pay tribute, starting a cycle of vulnerability, could still come true."

"What should we do?" the Servant demanded, looking to Nirrin, who was still dressed and armed as Audblayin's Bodyguard should be, even though her allegiance had changed.

"You must send Gardeners and Servants from house to house, Iririn," Nirrin answered, seeming stricken that she wouldn't be the one to lead them. "Warn them of the danger of demons. Offer to bring pregnant women, the elderly, and parents with small children behind the wards of the Garden. All others must be evacuated to the palace. The king must send his soldiers, along with every fuel finder and woodworker, with axe and saw and as many cutting tools as you can gather together, to cut the branch roads behind us as we leave Audblayinland. The entire niche must be separated from the rest of Canopy, for the protection of the other kingdoms, and to keep the panic, fear, and failure of other barrier sections from spreading. When Audblayin's power returns to full strength, we can regrow the roads."

Iririn nodded, unfolding her arms, looking ready to begin chopping at branch roads herself.

"We don't know how long the barrier will be weak," Nirrin went on. "We don't know how long it will take for Audblayin to be reborn, or where she will be. The people may need to stay behind wards or walls for successive monsoons, for a season, or for less than half a moon."

"The Garden and Palace can feed them through several monsoons, if need be," Iririn said. "But Nirrin, won't you come with me to the king to explain all of this? The flying monster, the change in Bodyguard, the death of the goddess?"

Nirrin glanced at Leaper and sighed.

"It may be best if the king isn't told about the change in Bodyguard," she said. She looked to Aforis. "But we will be passing by the palace on the way to Airakland. If the Skywatcher will permit a short delay."

"The pressure drawing those who serve Airak to the south is in both of us," Aforis told her. "If you can tolerate delay, so can I."

"There's something else you haven't thought of," Leaper told Nirrin. "If you want the roads severed as quickly as possible, there are others you can call on. Understorians. My mothers don't have spines, but they all once lived in the Garden. My fathers have sworn not to kill chimeras, but other demons have often been their prey. Send a bird to them. They'll come. Understorians will help you."

Iririn looked repulsed, but Nirrin nodded briskly.

"Of course. Iririn, fetch writing materials and one of the messenger birds from a cage in my high study marked 'Our Mistress's Mother.' Obviously I no longer have any right to give you orders, but quickly, please."

The Servant dashed to obey.

"Your fathers," Aforis said while they waited. "They're hunters?"

"They taught Imeris everything she knew," Leaper answered, grinning. It wasn't strictly true; Imeris had gone to Loftfol and duelled Odel's Bodyguard Aurilon every year for five years. But it was Bernreb who'd presented her with her first blade, and Marram who'd taught her how to fly.

He almost pitied any dayhunters that tried to get by them.

THIRTY-SEVEN

Leaper, Nirrin, and Aforis gazed up at the palace of the king of Audblayinland.

They stood on a smooth, white floodgum path. It connected their tree to the belly of the king's gobletfruit tree-trunk dwelling, which was fancifully shaped like the figure of a man standing. Its two largest windows and main balcony formed the eyes and mouth of the figure. They glowed orange with braziers, which exuded insect-repelling smoke and smouldered in the dark.

"It's creepy-looking," Leaper said. The rooms of the palace were hollowed from the broad chest and square-jawed head of the figure. Both branch-arms were raised high, so that the leafy tips of the spread, reaching fingers formed a green gobletfruit canopy interlocking with the foliage erupting from the head.

No other tree's foliage touched that of the palace. It was a figure standing alone.

Which means chimeras won't be able to come near it. Once this road under our feet is cut away.

"It definitely looks friendlier in the daytime," Nirrin said. "Attention! King's soldiers! Show yourselves, if there are sentries at their posts. I have an urgent message for His Royal Highness from the Garden."

As they waited for the ponderous, bronze-studded gate to be unlocked and two soldiers, armed with spears, to march along the floodgum path to meet them, the entirety of the gobletfruit tree that hosted the palace shivered, shedding a thumb-thickness of its smooth brown skin all at once in great rolls and curls.

"What was that?" Leaper asked Nirrin. *Weak as Audblayin is right now, I felt the magic. I smelled the gobletfruit sap.* The approaching soldiers ignored the peeling bark, even as a big sheet of it hit the path ahead of them. "Audblayin's bones!"

"We don't swear by her bones here," the closest soldier said, grinning, kicking the bark aside with one sandalled foot as he closed. He wore a short brown skirt and tunic, with leather armour over the top.

"We swear by Audblayin's pelvis," added the other soldier. She pointed with her spear at the head section of the palace. Leaper squinted at something grey which crowned the forehead of pale reddish-brown new bark. "That's the source of the magic that makes our palace grow new skin so quickly and shed it all the time. So's nothing can get purchase, see? Not demons, and not Understorians."

"That's exactly why we've come to see you," Aforis said.

It occurred to Leaper that he didn't need to be there while they discussed the failure of the barrier and set about preparing Audblayinland for what was to follow. Just as the soldiers began nodding and agreeing to take Aforis and Nirrin to their king, Leaper excused himself, promised to return quickly, and ran lightly along the branch roads towards another gobletfruit tree.

I've seen enough of palaces.

He came to a halt in front of the oval-shaped door of the House of Epatut. There, a different kind of guard waited to accost him.

"Not so fast, stranger," a little girl said, threatening him, shockingly, with the bared spines of an Understorian warrior.

Leaper peered at her in the light of the single Airak's lantern fixed to the high road along which he'd come. Her face was black as onyx, and as beautiful, yet she had Understorian spines. Maybe she'd fallen from Canopy as a babe and been raised again later, but that wasn't possible; her accent was entirely Canopian. Leaper drew himself indignantly up, letting his own speech fall into the pattern of the firewheel tree.

"One who walks in the grace of Audblayin," he said, barely catching himself before saying Airak, "would have words with Wife-of-Epatut, if it please her to receive me."

"It doesn't please her," the girl said. "The silk markets are closed, and this house is not a market. You're too shabbily dressed to be a very good merchant, anyway. When will you fools learn? She isn't interested in marrying again."

"Where did you get those spines?" Leaper demanded, distracted by them, hardly listening. "From Loftfol? I can't believe it. They're just selling them to anyone, these days, are they? When I was granted mine—"

Before he could blink, the extended spines were at his throat.

"When you were granted yours?" the girl inquired. "I see neither spines nor empty creases."

Leaper swallowed carefully.

"I lost them not long ago, in service of my life, thanks to the Godfinder. My name is Leaper. I've a proposition for your mistress, not a marriage proposal but a chance to leave the past that haunts her behind. I've got nothing to hide. Imeris was my adopted sister. But we haven't got long. Audblayin is dead, and the barrier has fallen. If Wife-of-Epatut won't pack up her House and come with me to Time, she'll have no choice but to take refuge with the other citizens, either at the palace or behind the wards of the Garden."

The girl withdrew her spines, stepped back, and gaped at Leaper.

"Audblayin dead! How?"

"Betrayed by the Godfinder," Leaper lied. It came more easily than he'd dreaded. "Servants and soldiers alike will be looking more closely at anyone with ties to Understorey in the wake of this terrible crime."

She took a while to consider this, and Leaper realised she was older than he'd first assumed; maybe fourteen or fifteen monsoons.

"My name is Oken," she said eventually. Grudgingly. "I suppose Aunty Igish will have to see you. Go inside. Ahead of me." Without taking her eyes from him or presenting a front-on target, she opened the oval-shaped door.

Leaper walked down a hallway filled with smoke. The insect-repelling fires here had only recently been extinguished and the door closed for the night. He stopped when he reached a room that reminded him of the storage sections of the palace of Airakland, where slaves stacked the festive makings of yearly celebrations while they weren't wanted. It was crowded with merchandise. Including a stack of stitched, leather-bound books. Leaper flipped through one. Its paperbark pages were empty.

At the far end, a portrait of Ylly smiled gently down at him from above a long supper table. The table was covered in roasted flowerfowl and steaming mounds of jackfruit mashed with macadamia, which hadn't been touched, but which made his mouth water.

A busty, pop-eyed woman with colourful silk scraps woven through her hair stood beneath the portrait staring up at it, talking to it.

"I did everything you told me to do, but you knew. You knew I was unworthy."

Oken prodded Leaper's back, silently steering him to a wooden chair with high arms and back—*a prison chair!*—and glaring at him until he sat down.

"Epi?" Wife-of-Epatut turned hopefully, eyes shining, fixed on nothing. "I've made you a new tunic." Slowly, in the silence, her eagerness faded. She looked at Oken. "He's not here, is he? I've imagined him."

"Yes, Aunty."

Igish put her hand to her heart when she saw Leaper sitting in the chair. "Who is this?"

"It's Leaper. Foster brother to Imeris, Aunty."

"Oh." Igish took a deep breath in and out, and then another one, apparently seeking to calm herself, but one hot tear escaped her eye, her hands fluttered, and she erupted into weeping. Oken patted her arm and tried to hush her. When the tears dried up, Igish lifted her lashes and asked her niece huskily, "I'm sorry, was I crying again?"

"Yes, Aunty."

"What does he want? What do you want, boy? Hopper? Jumper? Whatever you're called?"

Leaper controlled the urge to get to his feet.

"Igish," he said earnestly. "Birth mother of Imeris. Wife-of-Epatut. Whatever *you* are called. You lost Imeris as a baby, when she fell. Later on, you lost your nephew—"

"Son," Oken hissed.

"Your son, Epi, when he fell. It was in the middle of a footrace, wasn't it? Imeris told me. Anyway, I've just become a father myself, and I'm leaving Canopy. In light of all that's happened to you, I wondered if you might like to come with me, to the place my son's mother and I are taking him—that is, to a place where there is sunlight and relative safety, but where the children don't fall."

"The children don't fall," Igish echoed faintly, her bulging eyes getting wetter by the second. "What place is that?"

"It's far to the south. A ruined city in the mountains—" Igish began crying harder than she had before, tearing at her hair, howling. Oken seized Leaper by the elbow and began removing him from his chair. "What are you doing?"

"You've distressed her enough for one evening," Oken said. "I think we'll wait around for that messenger from the palace before we start packing our supplies for the siege. If demons come, I'll deal with it."

"Really?" Leaper said contemptuously, staying put in the chair. "How much gold did you fling at the Haakim to get those spines? Exactly how many demons did you kill while you were down there?"

"I never trained under the Haakim. My teacher was the Huntingim. There was a dayhunter in the training temple one time, but he told us to leave it alone, that it would leave when it couldn't climb higher or find any food."

"Oh, your teacher told you not to kill it. I see!" He wrenched his elbow out of her grip, but she began twisting her fingers in his hair, next, in an attempt to remove him.

"You remind me of a boy from Gannak who was there. He tried to feed me to that dayhunter. Tried to stuff me in the window of the training temple, and when it didn't work, he just let me fall. But I floated. Even though I'm only a girl and my mother had never been to the Temple of Odel, nor sent anybody on my behalf! I'm no—"

"Oken!" Igish's voice interrupted loudly. "Oken, wait! Leave him. I do want to go with him! I want to go with him to the place where children don't fall!"

"Yes, Aunty!" Oken chimed, standing back from Leaper at once. He rubbed at his scalp, scowling.

"Tell me again," Igish commanded gruffly. "A ruined city in the mountains, you said. Far away to the south."

"Very far," Leaper said. "You couldn't continue your work here. You might never be able to come back."

"The children don't fall, you say." Igish was unblinking.

"Nobody falls. That is, they might trip over and fall, but not very far. They wouldn't fall to their deaths in the dark. They wouldn't fall to the demons."

They could fall to their deaths in empty cisterns, the small voice of Leaper's conscience pointed out perversely. *And how do you know what demons might emerge, in Hunger's absence?*

Yet Leaper would be there, in one form or another, to defend the people of the new city.

"And you are the only one who knows the way?"

Leaper shook his head.

"Anyone can find it. All they need do is travel south. But they'd have to travel in secrecy, or the god or goddess of their niche might try to prevent them leaving. And I'm the only one who knows the short way. A way to cross the distance in less than a day. You'd have to be sure of your decision. My short way is one way only. The magic won't work in the opposite direction. There isn't any magic in the mountains, not like there is here."

"No Audblayin. No Odel," Igish mused.

"No Odel, but also no need for him."

"I'll come with you. All my household will." She met Oken's eye, and the girl answered with,

"Yes, Aunty!"

Leaper couldn't help but smile. These two were his first recruits to Ilik's cause. One a fighter. The other a skilled merchant and weaver.

"We depart from Airakland," he said, "as soon as we can. If you ask for the Godfinder's flowerfowl farm, you'll be shown the way. You really should leave Audblayinland tonight. We can travel together, if you want protection, company—"

"We'll travel on our own," Igish said. "There will be no shortage of company."

"Aunty has six workshops and thirteen significant-sized warehouses," Oken told him reluctantly. "When she says all her household will come, she means all three hundred and thirteen workers, along with their families."

"Nobody should be forced to leave Canopy," Leaper insisted. "And the goddesses and gods mustn't be forewarned."

"I'm starting a new flowerfowl venture," Igish said dreamily. "My workers need retraining in Airakland. The silk, looms, breeding boxes, and other materials they take with them are as payment for their training. Any who wish to remain in the silk trade may take over the warehouses I plan to abandon."

Leaper smiled and gave her a courtly bow.

"So long as you understand there'll be no nobility to buy your silk in the mountains. You may need it for bedding, for moon bleeding or for babies' napkins." He turned to Oken. "There will be nothing out there except what you bring and what you make. No poetry, blades, books, or wine. Your spines won't work. They won't stay sharp. They won't stay clean. It's the wild."

Oken shrugged irritably. "The wild doesn't have nothing; it has every-thing. This forest is wild. You and I come from the wild."

Behind her, Igish had ducked into a side room and reemerged clutching a potted mulberry tree to her chest with both hands.

"Why do you linger in my hallway, foster brother of Imeris? Didn't you say we were short of time?"

Leaper licked his lips.

"We are, Wife-of-Epatut. Perilously short. Although I wonder if I might have those books. Somebody I know is going to need them. And are you going to leave all that food back there, sitting on the table?"

It took longer than five days for Leaper, Aforis, and Nirrin to reach Airakland.

Along the way, everyone who recognised Nirrin's clothes stopped her to ask what had happened at the Garden.

Yes, Audblayin was dead. Yes, Audblayinland was infested with demons and the roads had been cut, but they would be healed as soon as possible. No, there was no flying master demon living in the Garden and gobbling up children by the dozen.

Not unless Airak strikes me down with lightning, Leaper thought. *There could be some subsequent gobbling.*

The last time Leaper had looked up at the Temple of Airak, the wooden structure had hummed with the lightning god's magic. To a Servant's senses, bright strings of light or the smell of their potential paths had connected the blackened limbs to all of Canopy.

On this morning, as Audblayin's adept, he saw it for what it was: a corpse. Inside the lifeless tree skeleton waited a small, petty piece of something that had once been a titan. Carefully sequestered in its own realm. Suspicious of the rest of itself.

Yet still capable of striking Leaper down. *I have to be careful.*
Obsequious. Self-effacing.

He summoned the speech pattern of an out-of-nicher by recalling the shape and growth patterns of a windgrass plant. Windgrass was quick grow-ing and common, yet sweet smelling and useful for almost everything.

"I am nervous," Nirrin said, following his gaze. "Airak might not want me. Because I am weak. Because I am white."

"No weaker than me," Leaper said. "Only slightly whiter."

"You had the famous Godfinder to vouch for you."

"I had Aforis. So will you. They should be the nervous ones. You mightn't want them."

Nirrin smiled. It might have been the first time Leaper had made her smile; he couldn't remember seeing it before.

"If they turn me away, I do not know where I will go. My father will want me back to take over his forge, but how can I go back to hammering and climbing when I once flew?"

Leaper frowned, distracted. He held his arms out and flapped them a little.

"Hey. Why can't I fly? Audblayin's Bodyguard flies."

"Audblayin's Bodyguard flies within the boundary of the wards of the Garden."

"Oh." He let his arms fall back to his sides. "Well, I'm never getting in there, am I?"

"The Bodyguard before Bernreb found a way," Nirrin said, "to magically alter his mind so that he had no memory of the murders he'd done. You could try it."

"No. I'm afraid I need the memories of all my murders. That's what keeps me from murdering again."

Ousos emerged from the reflective obsidian gate of the Temple. Stroking her axes, she smirked greenly with one side of her mouth as if she hadn't left Leaper to die at the edge of Floor.

"Warmed One," she said to him, strangely polite. To Aforis: "Skywatcher."

While they hadn't yet been to Unar's farm, Aforis had enjoyed a comfortable night's sleep in an Ilanland lodge. He'd travelled another day back in time as he dreamed. Yet he clearly hadn't travelled so far back that he'd forgotten Ousos. Leaper, sleepless, had watched over him through each night. It felt like an odd reversal of the burden of care between them. Hardly any time had passed since Leaper had needed Aforis to save him.

"Shining One," Aforis said to Ousos by way of greeting. "Has our master sent you in anticipation of our reception?"

"M'Lord Airak will receive you," Ousos answered, nodding. "Ulellin, visiting goddess of wind and leaves, will receive you, too." While Leaper and Aforis shared a startled glance at this information, Ousos thrust her face into Nirrin's. "Who's this, then?"

"One who would serve the lightning god," Nirrin said, bravely swimming in Ousos's breath without pulling away, though several rows of the small spines implanted along her ribs by Kirrik erupted nervously through her shirt.

"Another Understorian," Ousos complained. "We'll have a hard time chaining those!"

She referred to the metal mechanisms that had locked Leaper's spines into his long bones before the lightning god had come to trust him. He'd forgotten to warn Nirrin about that possibility.

Leaper *had* warned Nirrin about having to repair shattered obsidian. She'd given it a few practice tries on a discarded hand mirror after they'd crossed the border, and to Leaper's relief, the bond Aforis and Unar had forged between Nirrin and Airak functioned as it should.

Not that Aforis could remember doing it. The old man had been taken aback when they'd told him, for the sixth morning in a row, that Audblayin's Bodyguard was accompanying him to Airakland to be a Skywatcher. Leaper hated seeing him unable to remember.

But at least he accepts that he's cursed. At least he trusts me.

"Why don't you walk ahead of us some, Skywatcher?" Ousos suggested. "Lecture your new applicant all about the layout of the Temple." She gave Nirrin a little shove towards Aforis. "Always did like lecturing, the hoary bore."

When they were a few paces ahead in the entry hallway, Ousos linked arms with Leaper, strolling leisurely with him as though they were the best of friends.

"Surprised to see me?" Leaper asked her when they'd lagged enough to be out of earshot. "Thought you'd drowned me with that early monsoon? Is this where you drag me into a cupboard and take my head off with an axe?"

"I'm hurt, Leaper," Ousos snarled softly. "No, really, my feelings are trod into dirt. It's hardly my fault you were left behind. I know your spines weren't working and you couldn't see straight what we had to do. I'd have helped you climb back into Canopy, if you hadn't been all bent on heading to Gui at a rather vital time. Those squeezing dick-fleas were stealing M'Lord's skull, weren't they?"

"They were."

"Then you understand why I had to get back in such a hurry. We both served Airak as best we could. Worked well together, even. Turned the tables on that brother and sister tried to kill us, didn't we? It's ridiculous for us to be enemies, just because of some mix-up with the monsoon." Ousos leaned in companionably closely, and ventured, even more quietly than before, "I don't have to worry you'll mention, in front of the Holy Ones, me squeezing that dirt-kissing bone man, right?"

THIRTY-EIGHT

AFORIS LED the party into Airak's open-roofed audience chamber.

Not through the main tribute hall with its crowd of would-be worshippers, but through the smaller spymaster's entrance so familiar to Leaper from his former life.

Airak sat on a throne of snowflake obsidian, on a dais of blackened floodgum. The black-and-white-haired head, crowned with sprouting arm-length branches of polished silver, was bowed. He was robed in silver. His bared face, arms, and legs were half black and half white. Airak ate fried mushrooms and eggs with a leaf-spoon from a bowl made of tree squash. A silver goblet rested at his elbow.

Eliligras, his Bodyguard, was a tall, thin shadow behind the throne.

Ulellin, whom Leaper had last seen outside her Temple ten years before, was all dark brown, clad in green. She wafted with her Bodyguard about the margins of the room, where heaped black, pink, and white sands waited for the lightning god or his Servants to transform them into glass.

"Holy Ones," Aforis said, bowing deeply. Leaper, Ousos, and Nirrin quickly followed suit.

The wind goddess wore windowleaves, front and back, which covered her from chest to knees. They were stitched together with vines at the edges. Ulellin's hair moved as if underwater, in currents of wind nobody else could feel or see. As she drifted, she trailed her slender hand over stone crucibles, brass braziers, and long-handled glass-grasping tools. Her feet disturbed nothing around her; when she walked over the edge of a pile of white sand, she left no footprints behind.

"Here he is," she said so softly that Leaper could barely understand her. "The boy that I cursed, come back to Canopy. In this time, to this place. As I knew he would."

"You sound like the winged one," Leaper replied swiftly, so loudly and boldly that he shocked Nirrin and Aforis into stepping back, but it was Airak that he needed to show deference to, not the wretched waif. "Hunger, too, was confident that I'd dance like a puppet on strings to her own ends."

Airak said that Ilik and I were being watched. I assumed he meant by spies. Maybe even Ulellinland spies; it was Ilik's niche, after all. But of course, he meant Ulellin herself, being whispered to by the wind.

Ulellin laughed, neither surprised nor angered by Leaper's response.

"Instead," she said, "you destroyed the last nest full of eggs that she'll ever hatch. No child of Hunger can come to Canopy, now. No flock of wind-stealing upstarts will reach Airak's glass gate. No leaf-clad star-spawn will be lightning-speared by inexperienced Skywatchers, ignorant of the danger that they would have made those hatchlings invulnerable at a stroke. The rebellion of Hunger and her kin is over before she could begin it. That was why I had to let you live, Leaper."

She had prophecies about both of us. And she told Airak what she saw.

"That's why I let you live, Leaper," Airak said grimly, wiping his chin, lifting his head, "though you disobeyed me a thousand times."

They knew. Both of them.

"I see. Holy One. Thank you for your mercy."

But how much did Ulellin see? She knew I would journey to the mountains, but does she know Ilik is alive? Has she seen the second founding of Time? Is she toying with us?

"The prophecy I spoke concerning your true love was true enough," Ulellin elaborated smugly, "yet it masked a deeper one which concerned you. Which promised that you would eliminate the threat of Hunger and snuff out the products of her last hatching. Both portions of that prophecy have come to pass, and here is Audblayin's discarded Bodyguard, to fulfil the final portion of it." She graced Nirrin with a tight, malicious smile.

They can't know about Unar cutting Audblayin's soul away from Ylly. If they did, they'd never risk having powerful adepts in their presence. They can probably sense the weakness of the barrier in Audblayinland. But what about the fact that Hunger is my puppet now?

Airak stood up, setting his empty bowl beside the goblet on the arm of the snowflake obsidian throne. He stepped down from the dais and came to stand in front of Nirrin, who respectfully lowered her eyes but didn't cringe.

"This is the one, Ulellin?" Airak asked.

"Yes," the wind goddess said. "I saw that face in the final moments of the vision. The wind whispered that she would serve you in his place. That she would serve you well."

Nirrin bowed again, shallowly, and beyond her Leaper caught a glimpse of Aforis, who gazed back at Leaper with puzzlement—*he doesn't remember Hunger at all*—and gratification. Aforis was proud to hear of Leaper's reported accomplishments. Leaper was so pained by Aforis's pride that he almost missed Ulellin's next remark.

"You had to let him live before, My Lord of Lightning," she said, "yet here is his replacement. There's no need for him to live any longer."

"I am Bodyguard to Audblayin," Leaper exclaimed.

"You were. Now she's died and been reborn a male child. You're of no more use to the birth god than you are to your former master, and you've learned dangerous things."

She can't touch me. Not in Airak's Temple. It's Airak I have to convince; it's always been Airak.

Leaper threw himself to the floor in supplication.

"Holy One," he begged, pressing his forehead to the floodgum. "You've always trusted me to keep your secrets. Nothing's changed."

"Holy One," Aforis said with stiff dignity, "Audblayin, woman or man, will expect you to keep to the consensus between deities prohibiting attacks on one another's Servants. You have an honourable record on this matter, though the wind goddess speaks openly of having desired to destroy Leapael even when he was your Servant."

"M'Lord Airak," Ousos blurted, no doubt prompted by the potential for Leaper to start spilling secrets there and then, "I saw Leaper's loyalty to you with my own eyes. In the muck of Floor, with enemies all around. He even threatened to kill me if I failed you! I swear it by your holy bones. You can trust him."

"I'm leaving Airakland," Leaper told the floor. "I'm going back to Audblayinland. It wants defending from demons. You wanted oaths sworn to you by somebody my equal in skill, and Nirrin's here. Nirrin is sure to surpass me. I'm no threat to you, Holy One. You'll never hear my voice or feel my magic. You'll never see my face again."

"Stand up, Leaper," Airak said. Leaper did as he was told.

Audblayin's bones. He's going to execute me. Hunger will have her body back again. She'll tear Canopy apart trying to find me. Even though I'll be dead and gone.

"They plead so prettily for their lives, in Airakland," Ulellin said sulkily.

"For the first time, my disgraced Skywatcher and my Shining One are in agreement," Airak observed. "Four mortals in alignment, like a rare configuration of stars. Go to Audblayinland, Leaper. Nirrin will replace you in more ways than one, do you understand? See that you stay in Audblayinland. If you make any moves against me, she will know."

I'm going to live. The forest, too.

Leaper released the breath he'd been holding. He shouldn't have been so worried. After all, he'd seen a vision of the end of the forest. Hunger hadn't been in it. Yet by letting him go, Airak and Ulellin confirmed for him the fallibility of future-seeing.

"Thank you, Holy One."

"Go. Aforis will escort you to the glass gate."

Leaper obeyed his old master, the lightning god, one final time.

By the time they passed out of sight of the sentries at the gate, Aforis seemed so confounded by what he'd heard in the Temple that he kept on walking with Leaper along the high road, muttering to himself about winged ones and hatchlings, all the way to Unar's flowerfowl farm.

Leaper stood with him at the arch covered with brown vines; the sole portal admitting visitors to the branch road that led to the farm. He could hear the roosting birds stirring, reluctant to fly down to Floor just yet, squabbling for spaces in the sun.

"What is it?" Aforis asked.

"Will it still work, now that Unar is dead?"

Aforis's face tightened. His eyes turned wet.

"What do you mean? Why didn't you tell me that Unar had died?"

"The curse is getting worse, Aforis. You can't go on like this. You can't stay and help me. You have to go and find the lost fourteenth god."

The words *curse* and *fourteenth god* had an effect on Aforis, seeming to restore a little of what he'd lost.

"No, no. I'm fine, Leapael. I remember now. She killed Audblayin and was struck down by Aoun in turn. You see? It's just Nirrin I'm worried about. She came from a niche where there was a concerted effort to emancipate slaves. Other free Understorians surrounded her. Who will protect her here?"

Leaper squeezed Aforis's arm.

"She was a Bodyguard, Aforis. A Hunter, too, I heard. Which means, since she survived, whatever demon it was was slain. She can survive a bit of Ousos's bullying."

Inside the farmhouse, Unar's absence hit him all at once. In the sitting room, he stared at the ti chest and tiny potted plants. Her own miniature version of the Garden. Leaper spotted the thieves' lantern on a preparation surface in the kitchen corner. Above it, hanging from a hook, swung the faulty lantern Leaper had given Unar, his first illicit attempt at making lanterns, which the Godfinder had used for starting fires in her little iron stove.

He stared at it until a baby's scream snapped his attention back to who it was he'd come home to.

"Ilik?" he called, following the long tunnel through the hollowed bough to the nursery. There, familiar hands thrust a bundle capped with a puckered, bawling face between him and the bright portals admitting the morning sun.

"Take him," the once-queen decreed, and Leaper lifted his son into the crook of his elbow.

If he'd expected some spark of recognition from Builder, he was disappointed. The baby screamed louder.

"What does he want?" he called after his lover's retreating back.

"Maybe my milk!" came the ever more distant reply. "Maybe he's wet. He could need to burp. Or fart. Maybe he's hot. Maybe he's cold. Or bored. I *need* to relieve myself, Leaper!"

"Right," Leaper said, fixing the list she'd just given him in his head. He couldn't feed Builder, but he methodically went through the other possibilities, patting the tiny back for burping and rubbing the tiny tummy in case of gas trapped at the other end. He changed the old swaddling for new, checked the tiny chest for sweat and the tiny limbs for cold. "Are you bored, little one? Is my little Builder bored? Father will sing you a song."

It was what you did with babies. Sing songs. He knew that much. No appropriate songs popped into his head.

"O Oniwak of Airakland," he warbled foolishly, "the crossbow steady in his hand—"

Ilik returned before he could reach the song's ridiculous chorus. Her posture was straighter, her expression bemused. Builder had not stopped crying.

"He's hungry, after all," she said, unlacing her sash and opening her robe.

Leaper held the bundled baby out to her, and time seemed to stop. It was perfect. Everything was perfect. Builder's hands, reaching for his mother. Ilik's hands, reaching for the child. Builder's warm weight in Leaper's hands. The sunlight slanting through the room and the smell of satinwood.

They are going to the city, he thought, *and Hunger will go with them, but my human body has to stay here.*

Without Audblayin's gifts, everything is undone.

Ilik lifted Builder away from him, and Leaper thought he might weep, as loudly and bitterly as Wife-of-Epatut had ever done.

"Tell me more about the city," Ilik said, attaching Builder by the mouth to one of her swollen breasts, but as she finished the sentence, her gaze rose. Leaper turned to find Aforis, Oken, and Wife-of-Epatut crowded behind him.

"We'll see the city soon enough," said Oken. Her spines were wrapped, her fists on her hips. "Aunty can't be swayed from her decision to go. Tell us more about this secret, quicker way you have of getting there."

Leaper lifted his chin.

"It's in the kitchen," he said.

Leaper moved the thieves' lantern to the top of the ti chest. The five of them stood around it, gazes fixed on it. It was more impressive than the smashed one he'd left in Bernreb's cottage, Leaper supposed, but he couldn't blame Oken for looking so sceptical.

"That's going to take us to the mountains in the south?"

"Not yet," Leaper said. "Not until I've taken its twin to the ruins of Time."

"In a place of many people," Ilik muttered to herself, "the work of survival is accomplished quickly."

"These ruins," Oken said. "They have running water."

"Yes," Leaper said.

"Where there are few people," Ilik said, "each one must carry the rough knowledge of all, for survival."

"The mountains have game to hunt," Oken said, "and herbs to gather."

"Yes," Leaper said. *At least, I assume some of the plants are edible.*

"But no inhabitants?" Aforis asked ingenuously. "It's counterintuitive that the Bird-Riders and Fig-Eaters of Floor would not have returned there, if it's as well provisioned as you say. The new gods needed slaves, for construction and for worship. Clearly, they acquired an excess. They found themselves with too many of the pale mountain people for them to protect with the limited magic they had, and so some were released into Understorey." His expression clouded. Then his eyebrows rose. "But of course. The winged one, who had flown freely over mountains and river, forest and sea, going by a different name in every human place where she was worshipped, was forced by the new gods' arrival to restrict herself to the lair, where before she had only been seen once in a generation."

"What is a winged one?" Oken asked.

Aforis did not seem to hear her.

"That winged one," he said, "could hunt chimeras and duck-beaked water lizards no longer. She hungered for them, even as she ate her way through the remnant of the city of Time. Wept was no longer her name. Benevolence was no longer her name. Her new name was Hunger."

"Aforis," Leaper said, "why didn't you tell me all that before? In the cave, when she broke my neck, when we were trying to find a way to escape from her?"

"I don't know." Aforis smiled and met Leaper's eyes. He clutched his parchments, but there was nothing inked there about Hunger or Time. "You defeated her, Leapael, that's something I do know. I don't know how, but I know you defeated her." *Because you remember,* Leaper wondered, his heart aching again, *or because you heard Ulellin say so?* "The ruins of the city are safe for people now. These silk makers will build it. It will be beautiful, and it will last a long time, even longer than before. Ilik and her son will raise palaces from the stone." He turned to the once-queen, beaming. "For every one your mother-in-law took from you, you'll make it again on a grander scale."

But Ilik had realised something was wrong.

"Are you well, Aforis?" she asked, brow furrowed. "You'd vanished, leaving behind the strange lantern. I stayed away from it. Kept Builder away, until Ylly came."

"He's not well," Leaper said abruptly. "It's my fault. I brought the curse down on him. For every day that goes by, Aforis, instead of ageing, grows a day younger. It's why he's having trouble remembering things."

"I'm fine—"

"You're not fine! Hunger wouldn't tell us where the valley is, but she gave us a clue. She said she sent the clockmaker there, the one from Eshland whose riddles pleased her. She said the Birdfoot Valley contained the bones of Time, the one-fourteenth of a titan whose soul never came to Canopy with the thirteen other Old Gods. At best, the bones of Time will cure you. At worst, being so distant from Canopy will break the hold that the curse has over you."

"No," Aforis said, lifting the thieves' lantern resolutely by the handle. "I'll do that after I've helped you to build your city."

"Others will build the city, Aforis. You're a Skywatcher, an adept, but not outside the forest. Out there, your labour is an ordinary man's labour, no more."

"I was a teacher first," Aforis said sternly. "I have logic, mathematics, scholarship, and history in my head that remain valuable, no matter where I am. I learned them forty years ago, and so they're safe from the curse. Leapael, I have defied the lightning god two times in my life. First for love of Edax, and second for love of you. Shall I abandon you now? You need me."

Leaper took Ilik's hand and drew her close.

"Ilik has logic, mathematics, scholarship, and history in her head, too. You've been a father to me, you helped save me from Hunger, but now I've got Ilik, promised by the wind goddess to build palaces with her own two hands. I'm all grown up, Skywatcher. Your duty is discharged."

Aforis's expression softened.

"As you say."

Leaper rummaged among Wife-of-Epatut's things for the bound books of empty pages she'd brought for him. He pressed them, with a roll of pigment sticks, into Aforis's hands.

"Start by keeping notes for yourself. Every night before you fall asleep. Write down what's happening to you, and that the Birdfoot Valley is where to go looking for the cure. Promise me you'll find the bones of Time."

Aforis clutched the books to his chest.

"I promise presently to search out this valley, Leapael, but before I do, I'll find for you, and for Ilik, and for Wife-of-Epatut, the citizens of Time. While I am here, an adept I remain. I will find your people, buy their freedom, lift sigils from their tongues, and send them through this lantern to the mountain. Unar would have done it, had she survived."

Craggy-faced, with red-rimmed eyes, he looked like a beggar. He looked like a king.

"How will you buy their freedom?" Oken asked, with interest.

"With the valuable goods that Leaper gathered in Eshland," Ilik suggested.

Leaper gave Ilik a look that was partly ashamed, partly approving.

"When Audblayin takes his place in the Garden and appoints a new Bodyguard," Leaper told Aforis, "you'll know it's time to go. If I can find more clues in the meantime, or find the valley itself, I'll make a map. I'll send it back to you. The slow way. I imagine I'll sense it, when another Bodyguard is appointed. When my sleeplessness is taken away. On that day, promise me you'll travel through the lantern yourself. On that day, if Hunger doesn't get hold of me, I'll leave Canopy, too. We'll meet again in Time. I'll help you."

Aforis was already taking notes.

"When Audblayin takes his place in the Garden," the Skywatcher murmured as he wrote, "and appoints a new Bodyguard, it will be time for me to travel through the lantern. Leapael, father of Builder, is all grown up. I'm to meet him in the ruins of Time."

THIRTY-NINE

LEAPER SAT in front of the blazing fire.

It was the evening of the day in which he'd confronted Airak. He, Ilik, and Builder had travelled instantly through the thieves' lantern. They had gone from Unar's farm to Bernreb's cottage outside the Garden.

On the chairs and benches beside Leaper sat Ilik, Leaper's sister Ylly, his fathers Bernreb and Marram, and his youngest- and middle-mothers, Oos and Sawas. Builder snuffled sleepily in Sawas's arms.

Leaper's oldest-mother, also called Ylly, had claimed to be too frail to climb, and stayed behind in their home further down the tallowwood tree, in Understorey. They had reactivated all of Oldest-Father's old traps and believed the tallowwood tree to be safe from demons for now.

An advantage to the weakness in the barrier. It was the first time that Oos and Sawas had been to Canopy since before Leaper was born. Marram had never seen the Gates of the Garden before.

Bernreb, who hadn't made the journey since vacating his post as Bodyguard ten years prior, had laughed uncontrollably at the sight of Leaper wearing his old clothes.

He and Sawas are besotted with their grandson. After listening to Leaper's long and weary tale, they'd both swiftly declared their intent to travel with Ilik to Time.

Oos wished to stay behind in Understorey with Oldest-Mother, old Ylly, her beloved. Only Marram had yet to make a decision. It was sunset, and Leaper had a final task to carry out after dark.

Ilik's hand lay comfortably enfolded in his own. He'd felt the impulse, earlier, to leave his Understorian family behind for an hour or two. To leave Builder with his grandmother while Leaper went with Ilik to some abandoned house, to renew his intimacy with her in what might have been their final opportunity.

But the roads to the tallowwood were cut. Already, there were dayhunter and spotted swarm droppings all over the neighbouring trees. And besides, as Sawas had taken him aside to inform him, apparently no mother was fit for lovemaking less than a month after giving birth.

"I miss Oldest-Father's fish," young Ylly said, smacking her lips, getting up to throw her leaf-plate of fish bones into the fire. She looked impishly over her shoulder at Middle-Father, who had both brought and prepared the meal, but his mouth was full, and he couldn't answer.

"Is the pain fresh for you?" Youngest-Father asked Ylly. "Were you able to mourn him before, or could you not feel wholly yourself?"

"Sometimes it was like a dream," Ylly said. She stayed by the hearth, staring into the flames. "Sometimes I was myself. Usually in the presence of one of you. Or Imeris."

"They should have sung songs about Imeris in Wetwoodknee," Leaper grumbled. "Instead, they sang about that fool, Oniwak."

"I think," Marram announced, "Instead of going to Time, I shall go to Wetwoodknee."

Everybody looked at him.

"What?" Middle-Father exclaimed, spraying fish.

"I thought the problem with Time," Leaper said, unable to suppress a smile, "was that there weren't any great trees. You said your wings would be useless there. You could still sing, you said, but not fly."

"If you will make me a map," Marram said, "or many maps, Leaper, using the bird's-eye view you gleaned from your experience with the winged, I shall take maps to all the villages of Understorey. I shall take them to the Bird-Riders and the Fig-Eaters of Floor. Aforis supposed that our ancestors were the original inhabitants of Time. It would be nice to give those who dwell in darkness the opportunity to return, even if slowly and by foot over the plain and plateau."

"I'll make maps for you, Youngest-Father. After dark." Leaper shared a meaningful glance with Youngest-Mother. They had agreed she'd go into the Garden to search out several amulets of Bria's bone that Ylly thought she could remember, as Audblayin, hiding in her study. Those pieces of bone might be used by adepts for healing, in the future, in the new city. Later, some other person could fetch the treasure trove left behind by the clock-maker of Eshland. "There'll be mapmaking materials in the Garden. Youngest-Mother will bring them, and bring the finished maps to you before Ilik and the others go through the lantern to the mountains."

Ilik stirred at his side.

"Before we go through, you mean."

"No. Not me."

She sat up straighter beside him.

"Why not you?"

Leaper's grip on Ilik's hand tightened. He couldn't put off telling her any longer.

"My human body stays here. If I leave, the connection to Audblayin that keeps me from needing sleep will be broken. That giant, leaf-covered beast outside, that flying, human-eating demon, Hunger, would be released from my control. She'd seek revenge, on me ahead of anyone else. I'll be with you in the new city, but not in this body, Ilik. Until Audblayin returns to the Garden, I'll be the mind behind the monster. I'll be the hand behind the terrible power of the last of the winged."

Ilik was silent for a while. Everybody was, until Bernreb started choking on a fish bone, and Marram had to pound him on the back to help dislodge it.

"But it was going to be amazing," Ilik managed to whisper at last. "After all this time. No more hiding. No more lying. You were going to be my king. I was going to be your queen."

"The new city won't have any kings or queens." *For as long as I can help it. Humans being humans. Thrones being made to be sat on and be grovelled before.* "Only areas of expertise. Areas of responsibility. Like a guild. Like Loftfol. Nobody higher or lower. Everyone helping one another."

Even as he said it, he knew it was a futile dream. Humans helped one another, sometimes. Other times, they stole from each other, enslaved one another, or threw each other from high places to die.

But it's a new way, and I will try it. And Builder won't be a slave, and he won't be eaten by demons, or grow up pining for the sun.

"I never liked being a queen," Ilik admitted. "Will your human body stay in this cottage? Or in Airakland?"

"Here. In hiding. Youngest-Mother will seal me in behind a wall, as the Godfinder was once sealed in our home."

"Sealed behind a wall? How will you eat? How will you live?"

"When the Godfinder was with us," Marram told Ilik, "she was asleep. In hibernation. She didn't need to eat or drink. Audblayin's power nourished her. All she did was dream."

"We should say some words for Unar," Bernreb said gruffly. "I had not seen her for many a monsoon, but she brought Ylly the elder and Oos to our home. She brought Ylly the younger. She brought my Sawas to me and made our son's life possible. She followed him to a monster's lair, healed him, and brought him safely home."

The faces around the fire grew long and sad.

"Esse," Marram countered wryly, "would have pointed out that Unar also brought Frog into our lives. She brought Kirrik."

"She loved Aoun," Oos whispered. "I can't believe that he killed her."

"Have a happier reincarnation, Unar," Sawas murmured to the flickering hearth. "You couldn't sing to save your life, but if you hadn't asked to learn to swim, I'd still be a slave in the Garden, or worse."

"May this sleep be dreamless, Unar," Bernreb said. "Unlike your hibernation. May you not disturb the peace of the new child that you become."

"Leaper's sleep will be slightly different." Oos said to Ilik, and the others shook themselves slightly, as if coming out of a trance. "He'll dream, but it'll be a waking, true dream, of living with you, beside you, in Hunger's body. I daren't put him in as deep a sleep as Unar's, or Hunger will break free. But he'll be in Canopy, not Understorey. Audblayin's power will strengthen, and as it does, it will surround him. It will keep him alive, though I suspect he'll age at the normal rate."

"Oh." Ilik hugged herself.

Leaper hugged her, his arms over her folded ones, smelling snow cherry, stale whale oil, and baby sick, feeling her chest moving as she breathed, reluctant to let her go.

"If there's anything you're afraid of. Any detail I've forgotten to tell you that you'd like to know. Now is the time to ask. We won't be able to speak once Youngest-Mother puts me into hibernation. Hunger can't speak the language of Canopy." *Not without smashing at cave walls.* "Nor the language of the Crocodile-Riders. Nor any audible language, really."

"Whatever language she speaks," Ilik said stubbornly, "I can learn it. And you'll speak to your son even if you have to carve glyphs into the cliff side with your hind claws."

She kissed him.

Maybe there will be a way to speak, but there won't be a way to make love. Or to give Builder brothers and sisters. Not until the city is transformed, Hunger's role in its rebuilding and defence is done, and Audblayin appoints another to be Bodyguard in the Garden.

When that day comes, if I escape Audblayin and Hunger both, I'll be the luckiest man alive. But you'll be too old for children, my love.

Leaper retrieved the thieves' lantern. He handed it to her.

"You know what to do. Hang it from one of Hunger's teeth. Go through the light, with Builder, Ylly, Bernreb, and Sawas. You'll come out at Unar's farm in Airakland. Aforis is in charge of the lantern there. Wait seven days before you go back through. By then I'll have delivered this lantern to the mountains."

"Seven days? I thought you said you flew between Canopy and Time in less than a day and a night."

"I did. We did. But there's something else I need to do first. In Wetwood-knee." He kissed her again. *One last time.* "There's much to prepare. Do what you want with Unar's things. Butcher the flowerfowl or set them free. Take plant cuttings. Take fruit." He gestured towards the leaf-plate she'd abandoned on her chair and guffawed. "Eat the rest of your fish. There might not be any in those cold-water lakes. I hope you like goat."

Ilik laughed through her tears.

"I bought a goat once. Perhaps you remember. I bought it in secret, from a trader from Gui. It was expensive. Not as expensive as the crocodile-jaw knife I used to cut its throat. That poor goat. The knife was nowhere near as sharp as obsidian. I know, because one who walks in the grace of Airak had to use the bloody thing to saw through her hair."

"After a week, she'll walk in the grace of Airak no longer," Leaper said softly, tracing her hairline with his fingertip. "She'll walk the halls of Time, and make her own grace."

Moonlight bathed the great Gates of the Garden.

Leaper had lost his spines, but the carvings, depicting Hunts and battles between niches that stretched from the founding of the Garden to mere centuries from the present, gave him purchase. Tiny lightning bolts were inlaid silver. Tiny spear points were real steel. Polished gems were the eyes of chimeras. Emeralds, deeply embedded, formed the tiny leaves of vines wreathing the sacred head of the depicted birth god or goddess. Leaper's bare toes found every sharp edge and keen point.

Swearing under his breath, he climbed. One hand clutched Oos's climbing harness. It was the same one she'd used in her ascent to Canopy.

Youngest-Mother was twenty-odd years older than him, after all. Even if Leaper himself, Bodyguard of Audblayin, couldn't pass through the wards, he could help her to the top and steady her as she swung a leg over.

The platform lanterns were lit, adding to the inconvenient brightness. On an ordinary day, the adventurers might quickly have been spotted. Yet the Garden was noisy with newcomers, and the new Gatekeeper was unaccustomed to the natural sounds of her ward-securing rounds—much less the shouts and rustlings of children in bushes who should have been sleeping in the hammocks strung up for them everywhere, their supervising parents setting the bridges creaking and swaying, low conversation between elders with aching bones, the Servants in shifts trying to grow food for the refugees but frustrated by the slippery unavailability of their power, and the weary new mothers slapping soiled cloth napkins against rocks, washing their waste away in the many tinkling waterfalls and streams that fell from the Garden to Floor.

Leaper and Oos had both dressed in dark colours. Their clothes had been altered to resemble a fuel finder's rags and a merchant daughter's finery respectively, delivered via rope and pulley by Ylly the older. If Oos could successfully slip down to the ground on the other side of the wall, hidden by tree ferns, she'd assured Leaper she could find bone amulets, ink and parchments and return with them, disguised by the chaos.

They heard the hoots and splashes of delinquents swimming in the moat around the inner sanctum. Soon after, the wind carried the Gatekeeper's bellowed threats to them.

"Now," Oos whispered to Leaper. He hauled her up the final arm's length of the way. Helped take her weight while she cleared the points on top of the wall. Lowered her gently over.

Accidentally, his arm brushed against the wards.

Have you stolen food? Aoun's voice asked strongly in his head. *Stolen the sovereignty of another's body, or stolen human life?*

Yes, Leaper replied to the wards, waiting for his arm to be thrown violently back. *I stole food from the City-by-the-Sea. I stole the sovereignty of Hunger's body. I stole from Orin's beastly, transformed Servants when I struck them with the lightning god's power, ending their lives.*

The wards rifled through his memories. Leaper saw himself in Unar's arms. Opening his eyes after her healing. Drinking water and eating roasted goat. Feasting at Wife-of-Epatut's table.

Insisting to Ylly in a determined whisper that killing was not the way.

The wards didn't throw him back, but parted under his hand. Without thinking, he followed Oos into the Garden, dropping to rich, dark soil beneath tree ferns that reminded him of how he'd trapped Ellin.

"Impossible," Oos said, goggling at him. "How—?"

"Dying, I think," Leaper guessed, holding his hands up in front of his face and gazing at them. "The wards only looked back as far as when my neck was broken. I should have died, then. My soul was free, for a while, I think. I heard Frog's voice. Being at the brink of death must have erased my crime of slaying Orin's creature. Or else . . ." He felt self-consciously at his neck. "Or else the creature was never considered human by Audblayin, despite its origins. And maybe since Hunger was never part of Canopy, stealing her body doesn't count." *But what about Yran? I poisoned him. Even after he said we shared the same liver.*

"This is extremely fortuitous, Leaper. Instead of Bernreb's cottage, we can hide you in the Garden itself. Your connection to Audblayin will be even stronger."

"But where?"

"Shhh! I think I know. Follow me. You'll need to make the maps first."

They crawled through a grotto of moss and myrtle trees. Tangled black branches were leafless in winter, and the moss was dry and cold under Leaper's knees and the heels of his hands. When they came out by a small stand of persimmons, the late, sweet-smelling, dew-covered fruit dropping as Leaper and Oos brushed the laden branches, they slipped, smiling, through a gathering of older women who surrounded a grunting younger woman giving birth, and ran across one of the swinging bridges.

Another crossing took them to a hedged garden of grasses, where old men had abandoned their hammocks for the rustling tufts. From there, the pair of conspirators passed a cluster of cooking pots where bulrush roots were being boiled over carefully tended twig flames. *She hasn't lived here in my lifetime, but she still knows the way.* At last they came to the edge of the moat. Leaper stabbed himself on the thorns of a pomegranate tree.

"Wait here," Youngest-Mother whispered, shucking her tunic and layered skirts. Leaper looked politely away, but out of the corner of his eye he saw her, wearing loincloth and breast-wrap, diving smoothly between the water-lilies.

She didn't surface until she was halfway across the moat. Middle-Mother was the best swimmer among them, but Youngest-Mother wasn't bad. She climbed up, dripping, below a circular window in the egg-shaped inner sanctum, and didn't hesitate to throw herself headfirst through the opening.

Leaper counted the stars while he waited, holding her discarded clothes.

Are they all winged ones, I wonder? Are any of them truly stolen lanterns, Airak's creations, as we were taught?

The splash of a thrown oilcloth-wrapped bundle alerted him to Oos's return. Feeling very exposed, he crouched in the moon shadow of the pomegranate, urging her with his eyes to swim faster.

Nobody stumbled across them. Her grin as she tugged her resisting clothes on over wet limbs told him exactly what was in the bundle.

"You'll make the maps under the eaves of the Gardener's Gathering pavilion. Somebody's hung lanterns there. I can see them."

She led him to the delicate, flowerlike, open-sided tower, with pointed roofs as layered as her altered skirts. The lanterns were there so that children with nets could catch fat moths for frying. They ignored Leaper, who sat with his back to a pillar, while Oos held the pilfered inks.

The landscape between Canopy and Time came alive in his mind. Hours passed before he looked up from the thirteenth map.

"There," he said, stoppering the ink gourd. "One map for each Understorian village."

"Marram will no doubt make copies," Oos said. She secured the rolls inside her waterproof bundle before drawing Leaper to his feet. His hips and back were stiff from sitting under the lanterns for so long. They were alone. The moth-catching children had succumbed to sleep. "Come this way. To the loquat grove."

Moonlight glinted from serrated dark green leaves. Snoring rose from hammocks. Sleepy lorikeets complained. Oos stopped to dig for something under a certain tree. A small, delighted whine escaped her upon unearthing some greenish tarnished object whose segments barely held together.

"Your jewellery?" Leaper asked. He knew she'd come from a high-ranking family. Her father had been a king's vizier.

"My bells," Oos murmured, taking his hand again, leading him on.

They came to a pair of squat, fat-bellied, leafless trees, painted with lichens whose colours in the moonlight were indeterminate. From the loquat grove, the bulging trees looked like useless, fruitless, tradition-honoured sentinels standing to either side of the path. Yet when Oos circled to the side of one, he saw there was a door of sorts in the hollow trunk.

"Here's where I'll sleep?" he predicted.

"The prison trees," Oos agreed softly. "Once the nightmare of disobedient slaves. The fallen leaves inside stay dry. They'll make a perfect bed for you."

Leaper pointed at her bundle.

"How will you smuggle stolen goods out of the garden? Won't the wards stop you?"

"The wards," she said, following him inside the hollow, rolling up a layer of her skirts for his pillow, "are weakest in one direction, and that direction is down. Just the direction in which I was planning to go."

There was room for him to lie down, fully stretched out, though his feet touched the inside of the trunk of the tree.

Youngest-Mother kissed him on the forehead, as she'd done when he was a child.

"Enjoy the wind under your wings, little one," she said. "Enjoy the sun."

Leaper closed his eyes. He felt himself floating somewhere lightless.

Then the stars burst into being above him

Below, he saw the platform in front of the Garden. A winged one was coiled there. The thieves' lantern, glowing blue, dangled from the wooden cage of her teeth.

Let me stay with you, Hunger entreated, an abrupt presence beside him. *We can share my solid form. Let me speak; let me help you. Since my fall, I have seen it all.*

Leaper fought to wall her away in his wake with the weak magic of Audblayinland and the distant, still active, magic of Orin. Tallowwood smell surrounded them.

The trees grew tall, Hunger said, *watered by their blood. Germinated in iron-rich rivers, mighty and strong grew the great trees, but one-fourteenth was missing. Let me stay with you, Leaper, and I shall show you where he lies. I will take you to the Birdfoot Valley. You will not need my body, when you have his bones. His spirit. In my body, you are still mortal, but you can become immortal if you devour him. If one fourteenth is not enough for you, there are other, whole titans upon the earth! I can deliver you to the places where they walk. Or, we could merge our souls, right here and now, as the dead woman suggested.*

That wasn't a suggestion, it was a warning! Leaper pushed at her with a brusquely formed image of both hands. Like a boy trying to push a bear out of his kitchen. She was bigger. She was stronger. Any offer to merge souls was a lie; his smaller self would be consumed by her.

I can take you into the sky. So high that we need never touch the ground again. Don't you want to find out what is up there, to live forever in the sun?

No, Leaper insisted. *I want to be with Ilik.*

As before, calling up the image of Ilik's face banished the winged one's resistance. She became smaller. Angrier, but smaller. Not a bear anymore. A hornet.

And then she was gone.

He opened Hunger's eyes—his eyes—and saw the top of the Garden Gate level with the low point of his shoulder. When he arched his neck, so that his head was higher than the wall, he found he could see the whole Garden at once. His vision and smell were more acute, but his hearing seemed more muffled than it had been when he had human ears. Oos stood by the sealed, seamless prison tree, tying bark rope to her climbing harness.

Leaper lashed his long tail. Exquisite sensation thrilled through the leaf-scales that covered him. He lifted his wings, and made a breeze that set the prison tree's branches clattering together.

Oos didn't look up.

FORTY

Leaper soared.

The wetlands north of the forest, now that the floodwaters had receded, were covered in vast flocks of nesting or resting swamp birds whose alarm cries filled the skies when Leaper's moon shadow passed over them.

He couldn't see them taking flight, but he felt them in the minute movements of his leaf-scales, as if he were running human hands over the surface of water and land, touching every reed and bamboo island with his fingertips.

Wetwoodknee looked like a toy, seen from the heights. Something rickety, built by children from twigs and twine and then abandoned to the monsoon, toy boats and barges bunched up against it by the growing flow.

Yet presumably with her spyglass, from her tower, the queen of the City-by-the-Sea had seen him coming. With Mitimiti at her side, the one-eyed maid copying her movements clumsily as if learning the dance for the first time, Erta spun before the kapok tree. She'd lit a fire on the dais and was not chanting this time, but waving the fanlike fronds of the cabbage palm tree.

Paying homage in the language of the winged. Leaper felt the hot and cold breezes of her words, even at a distance.

"Under the eyes of the stars," she cried, "protect your own true people."

The Master of Cast and his dishevelled men, beads glittering coldly in the moonlight, wavelets lapping at the underside of their mobile invading city, watched Leaper wheel above them with fear and indecision. They called their own back to the slave-powered ships, presuming their fortifications somehow defensible.

Erta whirled on, jarring the boards, her words smelling of exhilarated sweat and the killifish on her ragged breath.

"By the salt tears you shed, for the sake of the name we remember you by!"

Emerging from their homes, the people of Wetwoodknee pointed and gasped. Mothers fell to their knees, clutching terrified children, until their parents in turn could clasp their trembling hands and turn them to clapping, in a rhythm of four swift beats and two slow ones. Leaper quickly realised it was the rhythm of his heart.

Absurdly, it pleased him to hear it.

Then he was distracted by the sight of one of the blackpressers. Clad in a windturner. Carrying buckets of water, sniffing for the smoke of a fire. It was Yran. *Impossible*; Leaper dived dangerously closer, needing a better look. A different angle. There they were. The black bun. The horrified grimace showing perfect, gleaming white teeth. *Unsho's work.*

"Wept," the queen danced. Her layered pearl necklaces jangled against her crocodile-leather windturner. The bells on the wooden carving vibrated each time she landed. "Throw back our enemies!"

Obligingly, Leaper threw her enemies back.

Catching the air in great scoops of clean flow, which obeyed his will, he broke Cast free of the Mooring precinct. He sent the city spinning up the coast, away from the river mouth.

Seeking altitude, prepared to go after the drifting buildings and buffet them a second time, he was startled by the wind whispering through his leaves in yet another language he was easily able to understand.

They will drift to a pair of islands connected by a sand bridge, the wind promised. *Islands with no trees, and the ships with their masts broken. Hungry, they will dive for oysters, and be dived on in turn by duck-beaked water lizards. The slaves will take one island, and their keepers will take another, and the sand will be washed away for fifty years, until a storm reunites them.*

He couldn't whisper back to the wind. It had no mind. Only hands to feel the currents of the future, as Leaper had felt the water and the land.

Satisfied, he turned away from Wetwoodknee. Towards the mountains.

And now the wind sang a different song.

It sang to him while he stayed over the horizon, away from Canopy, so that he couldn't be seen by the pieces of titan who thought the last of the winged was gone for good. It sang as the sun rose and his real shadow skimmed across scattered grey boulders, glowing green moss-cushions and the mirror lakes with three toes that were the footprints of Old Gods.

By the time the cave that had served as Hunger's lair came within the range of his sharpened sight, he knew a hundred things he hadn't known before.

He knew that Imeris and Anahah would find the Birdfoot Valley and restore their leopard-child.

He knew that the queen's statue wouldn't be built in the mountains because she was a queen, arbitrary child of an arbitrary line, but because she would become the famed clockmaker of Time, restoring the flow of the spring and the waterfall, harnessing that flow for the grinding of grain, and feeding those who had fled the forest.

He knew that far behind him in Airakland, Kirrik's enslaved son Irdis, fathered by Icacis's older brother, Sikakis, would assume the throne left vacant when Icacis died of loneliness and grief. An artefact of Old God's bone, sensitive to finding so-called fruit of the same tree, would proclaim Irdis the new king.

Icacis needs me more than you, Ilik had said, and she'd spoken the truth, but now Builder needed her even more, and Time waited for them both.

A gentle snow began falling as Leaper entered his domain. His mountains.

The thieves' lantern was deceptively dark between his teeth.